BY RICHARD K. MORGAN

TAKESHI KOVACS NOVELS

Altered Carbon

Broken Angels

Woken Furies

Market Forces

Thirteen

The Steel Remains

THE STEEL
REMAINS

THE STEEL
REMAINS

RICHARD K. MORGAN

BALLANTINE BOOKS · DEL REY · NEW YORK

Copyright © 2009 by Richard Morgan

All rights reserved.

Published in the United States by Del Rey, an imprint of
The Random House Publishing Group, a division of Random House, Inc., New York.

Del Rey is a registered trademark and the Del Rey colophon is a trademark of
Random House, Inc.

Originally published in hardcover in Great Britain by Gollancz,
a division of The Orion Publishing Group, in 2008.

ISBN 978-0-345-49303-3

Printed in the United States of America on acid-free paper

www.delreybooks.com

9 8 7 6 5 4 3 2 1

First U.S. Edition

Text design by Karin Batten

This book is for my father,

John Morgan,

for carrying me past the seaweed.

"I think you look on death as your friend," she murmured. "That is a strange friend for a young man to have."

"The only faithful friend in this world," he said bitterly. "Death is always sure to be at your side."

—Poul Anderson,
The Broken Sword

THE STEEL
REMAINS

CHAPTER 1

When a man you know to be of sound mind tells you his recently deceased mother has just tried to climb in his bedroom window and eat him, you only have two basic options. You can smell his breath, take his pulse, and check his pupils to see if he's ingested anything nasty, or you can believe him. Ringil had already tried the first course of action with Bashka the Schoolmaster and to no avail, so he put down his pint with an elaborate sigh and went to get his broadsword.

"Not this again," he was heard to mutter as he pushed through into the residents' bar.

A yard and a half of tempered Kiriath steel, Ringil's broadsword hung above the fireplace in a scabbard woven from alloys that men had no names for, though any Kiriath child could have identified them from age five upward. The sword itself also had a name in the Kiriath tongue, as did all Kiriath-forged weapons, but it was an ornate title that lost a lot in translation. "Welcomed in the Home of Ravens and Other Scavengers in the Wake of Warriors" was about as close as Archeth had been able to render it, so Ringil had settled on calling it the Ravensfriend. He didn't *like* the name especially, but it had the sort of ring people expected of a famous sword—and his landlord, a shrewd man with money and the potential for making it, had renamed the inn the same way, setting an eternal seal on the thing. A local artist had painted a passable image of Ringil wielding the Ravensfriend at Gallows Gap and now it hung outside for all the passing world to see. In return, Ringil got bed and board and the opportunity to sell tales of his exploits to tourists in the residents' bar for whatever was dropped into his cap.

All that, Ringil once remarked ironically in a letter to Archeth, *and a blind eye turned to certain bedroom practices that would doubtless earn Yours Truly a slow death by impaling in Trelayne or Yhelteth. Heroic status in Gallows Water, it seems, includes a special dispensation not available to the average citizen in these righteous times.* Plus, he supposed, you don't go queer baiting when your quarry has a reputation for rendering trained swordsmen into dogmeat at the drop of a gauntlet. *Fame,* Ringil scribbled, *has its uses after all.*

Mounting the sword over the fireplace had been a nice touch, and also the landlord's idea. The man was now trying to persuade his resident celebrity to offer dueling lessons out back in the stable yards. *Cross blades with the hero of Gallows Gap for three Empire-minted elementals the half hour.* Ringil didn't know if he felt that hard up yet. He'd seen what teaching had done to Bashka.

Anyway, he dragged the Ravensfriend from the scabbard with a single grating clang, slung it casually over his shoulder, and walked out into the street, ignoring the stares from the audience he had been regaling with tales of valor about an hour ago. He guessed they'd follow him at least part of the way to the schoolmaster's house. It couldn't do any harm, if his suspicions about what was going on were correct, but they'd probably all cut and run at the first sign of trouble. You couldn't blame them really. They were peasants and merchants, and they had no bond with him. About a third of them he'd never even seen before tonight.

Introductory comment from the treatise on skirmish warfare that the Trelayne Military Academy had politely declined to publish under his name: *If you don't know the men at your back by name, don't be surprised if they won't follow you into battle. On the other hand, don't be surprised if they will, either, because there are countless other factors you must take into account. Leadership is a slippery commodity, not easily manufactured or understood.* It was simple truth, as gleaned in the bloody forefront of some of the nastiest fighting the free cities had seen in living memory. It was, however, the Lieutenant Editor in Trelayne had written kindly, *just too vague for the Academy to consider as viable training material. It is this ambivalence as much as any other that leads us to decline your submission.* Ringil looked at that last sentence on the parchment and suspected a kindred spirit.

It was cold out in the street. Above the waist he wore only a leather jerkin with loose half-length sailcloth sleeves, and there was an un-seasonal early chill sloping down the spine of the country from the Majak uplands. The peaks of the mountains that the town nestled under were already capped with snow, and it was reckoned that Gallows Gap would be impassable before Padrow's Eve. People were talking again about an Aldrain winter. There had been stories circulating for weeks now, of high-pasture livestock taken by wolves and other, less natural predators, of chilling encounters and sightings in the mountain passes. Not all of them could be put down to fanciful talk. This, Ringil suspected, was going to be the source of the problem. Bashka the Schoolmaster's cottage was at the end of one of the town's cross streets and backed onto the local graveyard. As by far the most educated man in the tiny township of Gallows Water—its resident hero excluded—Bashka had been handed the role of temple officiator by default, and the house went with the priest's robes. And in bad weather, graveyards were a fine source of meat for scavengers.

You will be a great hero, a Yhelteth fortune-teller had once read in Ringil's spittle. *You will carry many battles and best many foes.*

Nothing about being a municipal exterminator in a border-town settlement not much bigger than one of Trelayne's estuary slums.

There were torches fixed in brackets along the main streets and river frontage of Gallows Water but the rest of the town must make do with bandlight, of which there wasn't much on a night this clouded. True to Ringil's expectations, the crowd thinned out as soon as he stepped onto an unlit thoroughfare. When it became apparent where he was headed specifically, his escort dropped by more than half. He reached the corner of Bashka's street still trailing a loose group of about six or eight, but by the time he drew level with the schoolmaster's cottage—the door still gaping open, the way its owner had left it when he fled in his nightshirt— he was alone. He cocked his head back to where the rubberneckers hovered at the far end of the street. A wry grin twitched his lips.

"Stand well back now," he called.

From among the graves, something uttered a low droning cry. Ringil's skin goosefleshed with the sound of it. He unshipped the Ravensfriend from his shoulder and, holding it warily before him, stepped around the corner of the little house.

The rows of graves marched up the hill where the town petered out against outcroppings of mountain granite. Most of the markers were simple slabs hewn from the self-same stone as the mountain, reflecting the locals' phlegmatic attitude to the business of dying. But here and there could be seen the more ornately carved structure of a Yhelteth tomb, or one of the cairns the northerners buried their dead under, hung with shamanistic iron talismans and daubed in the colors of the deceased's clan ancestry. As a rule, Ringil tried not to come out here too often; he remembered too many of the names on the stones, could put faces to too many of the foreign-sounding dead. It was a mixed bag that had died under his command at Gallows Gap that sweltering summer afternoon nine years ago, and few of the outlanders had family with the money to bring their sons home for burial. The cemeteries up and down this stretch of the mountains were littered with their lonely testimony.

Ringil advanced into the graveyard, one bent-kneed step at a time. Clouds broke apart overhead, and the Kiriath blade glinted in the sudden smear of bandlight. The cry was not repeated, but now he could make out smaller, more furtive sounds. The sounds, he reckoned unenthusiastically, of someone digging.

You will be a great hero.

Yeah, right.

He found Bashka's mother, as it seemed, grubbing around in the dirt at the base of a recent headstone. Her burial shroud was torn and soiled, revealing rotted flesh that he could smell from a dozen paces upwind even in the cold. Her deathgrown nails made an unpleasant raking sound as they struggled with the casket she had partially unearthed.

Ringil grimaced.

In life, this woman had never liked him. As temple officiator and priest, her son was supposed to despise Ringil for a worthless degenerate and a corruptor of youth. Instead, as a schoolmaster and man of some education himself, Bashka turned out to be far too enlightened for his own good. His easygoing attitude to Ringil and the late-night philosophical debates they occasionally got into at the tavern earned him vitriolic reprimands from visiting senior priests. Worse still, his lack of condemnatory zeal gave him a reputation in the religious hierarchy that ensured he would always remain a humble teacher in a backwater town. The mother, naturally enough, blamed the degenerate Ringil and his evil influence for her son's lack of advancement, and he was not welcome in the schoolmaster's house while she drew breath. This latter activity had come to an abrupt halt the previous month, following a swift and unquenchable fever, sent presumably by some preoccupied god who had overlooked her great righteousness in religious matters.

Trying not to breathe through his nose, Ringil tapped the flat of the Ravensfriend on a convenient grave to get her attention. At first she didn't seem to hear the noise it made, but then the body twisted wrenchingly around and he found himself looking into a face whose eyes had long ago been eaten by whichever small creatures took care of that sort of thing. The jaw hung slack, most of the nose was gone, and the flesh of the cheeks was mottled and holed. It was remarkable that Bashka had even recognized her.

"Come on out of there," said Ringil, readying his sword.

It did.

It came through the dead woman's rib cage with a cracking, sucking sound, a corpsemite fully a yard long not counting the tendril appendages it had used to puppet the corpse's limbs. It was gray in hue, not unlike some species of smooth-skinned maggot, which its body in many ways resembled. The blunt snout of the thing ended in chomping jaws set with horny ridges that could shatter bone, and Ringil knew that the tail end looked much the same. Corpsemites didn't excrete their waste, they oozed it from pores along the slug-like body, a substance that, like their saliva, was lethally corrosive.

No one knew where they came from. Folklore had it that they were originally lumps of witch's snot, hawked up and animated to voracious life by their evil owners for reasons most of the tales were rather vague on. Authorized religion insisted variously that they were either ordinary slugs or maggots, possessed by the souls of the evil dead, or demonic visitations from some cemetery hell where the spiritually unworthy rotted, fully conscious, in their graves. Archeth had had a slightly saner theory: that the mites were a mutation produced by the Kiriath's experiments with lower life-forms centuries before, a creature designed to dispose of the dead more efficiently than conventional scavengers would.

Whatever the truth, no one was quite sure what level of intelligence the corpsemites had. But somewhere in their evolution, natural or otherwise, they'd learned to use the carcases they fed upon for a whole host of other purposes. A body could serve them as a hiding place or an incubation bed for their eggs; if not too badly decayed, it might become a means of rapid motion or disguise; and, in the case of humans or wolves, it could be a digging tool. It was the use of human corpses that triggered the spate of zombie sightings throughout the northwest whenever the winters were hard.

Ringil had occasionally wondered whether the corpsemites didn't also manipulate carcasses as a form of play. It was entirely his own macabre idea, conjured up when he first read about the creatures in accounts by travelers to the Kiriath wastes. After all, he reasoned to his father's librarian, a corpsemite's own secretions would eat through a wooden casket nearly as fast as a corpse's decaying hands could open it, so why else would they bother? The opinion of the librarian, and later of his father, was that Ringil was a very sick young man who ought to concern himself, as his elder brothers already did, with more natural pursuits like riding, hunting, and bedding the local wenches. His mother, who no doubt already had her suspicions, said nothing.

From his one or two previous encounters with these creatures, Ringil also knew that they could be very—

The corpsemite flexed its body free of the encaging ribs, leapt straight at him.

—*fast.*

He hacked sideways, rather inelegantly, and succeeded in batting the thing away to the left. It hit a headstone and dropped to the ground writhing, sliced almost in half by the stroke. Ringil brought the sword down again and finished the job, mouth pursed with distaste. The two severed halves of the creature twisted and trembled and then lay still. Demons and the souls of the evil dead were not, it seemed, up to repairing that kind of damage.

Ringil also knew that corpsemites moved in groups. As the slimy filigree of a tendril appendage touched his cheek, he was already spinning around to face the next one. The drops of secretion burned. No time to wipe it off. He spotted the creature, coiled on top of a Yhelteth tomb, skewered it on reflex. The tendrils recoiled and the thing made angry chittering noises as it died. Ringil heard a clatter of response from the other side of the tomb and saw movement. He stepped wide around the worked stone slab, saw the two smaller mites hauling themselves up out of the wreckage of a rotted coffin and its equally far-gone contents. A single downward blow sliced them both irreparably open, body fluids gushing like pale oil from the wounds. He did it again, just to be sure.

The fifth mite landed on his back.

He didn't think at all. In retrospect, he guessed it must have been pure revulsion that drove him. He dropped the sword with a yell, reached down to the fastenings of his jerkin, and tore them open with both hands. In the same motion he shrugged himself halfway out of the garment while the corpsemite was still finding out that the leather was not his real skin. The jerkin sagged under the creature's weight, helped him to pull clear. The tendrils around his waist and over his shoulders were still creeping toward each other and they didn't have time to tighten against the movement. His left arm came free and he whirled like a discus thrower, hurling the bundle of jerkin and mite off his right sleeve and away among the headstones. He heard it hit something solid.

Tendrils had touched him on the chest and back—later he would find the weals. Now he snatched up the Ravensfriend and stalked after his jerkin, eyes and ears open for any remaining members of the group. He found the garment, partially dissolved, at the base of an ancient moss-grown slab near the back of the cemetery. *Not a bad throw, that, from a standing start.* The corpsemite was still trying to disentangle itself from the leather and flapped confusedly at him as he approached. Its jaws were bared and it was hissing like a new sword in the cooling trough.

"Yeah, yeah," he muttered and plunged the Ravensfriend down point-first, impaling the mite on the earth. He watched with somber satisfaction as it died. "That was clean on today, you little shit."

He stayed among the graves long enough to start feeling the cold again, and to take a brooding interest in the slight but unmistakable paunch that was beginning to threaten the aesthetics of his narrow-hipped waist. No further corpsemites showed themselves. He took an uncontaminated shred of his jerkin as a rag and cleaned the body fluids off the Ravensfriend's bluish surfaces with fastidious care. Archeth had insisted the Kiriath blade was proof against all and any corrosive substances, but she had been wrong about things before.

The final outcome of the war, to name but one.

Then, finally, Ringil remembered that the creatures had touched him and, as if on cue, the blisters they'd left began to burn. He rubbed at the one on his cheek until it burst, deriving a certain brutal amusement from the thin pain he got out of it. Not what you'd call a heroic wound, but it was all he'd have to show for the evening's exertions. No one would be coming out here to check on the carnage until it got safely light.

Oh well, maybe you can narrate it into a couple of pints and a fowl platter. Maybe Bashka'll buy you a replacement jerkin out of sheer gratitude, if he can afford it after he's paid to rebury his mother. Maybe that towheaded lad from the stables will listen in and be impressed enough to overlook this gut you're so intent on developing.

Yeah, and maybe your father's written you back into his testament. Maybe the Yhelteth Emperor is a queer.

That last was worth a grin. Ringil Angeleyes, scarred hero of Gallows Gap, chuckled to himself a little in the chill of the graveyard, and glanced around at the silent markers as if his long-fallen comrades might share the joke. The quiet and the cold gave him nothing back. The dead stayed stonily unmoved, just the way they'd been now for nine years, and slowly Ringil's smile faded away. A shiver clung at his back.

He shook it off.

Then he slung the Ravensfriend back across his shoulder and went in search of a clean shirt, some food, and a sympathetic audience.

CHAPTER 2

The sun lay dying amid torn cloud the color of bruises, at the bottom of a sky that never seemed to end. Night drew in across the grasslands from the east, turned the persistent breeze chilly as it came. *There's an ache to the evenings up here,* Ringil had said once, shortly before he left. *It feels like losing something every time the sun goes down.*

Egar the Dragonbane, never very sure what his faggot friend was on about when he got into that kind of mood, still couldn't make sense of the words now, best part of a decade on.

Couldn't think why he'd remembered them right now, either.

He snorted, shifted idly in his saddle, and turned up the collar on his sheepskin coat. It was a reflexive thing; the breeze didn't really bother him. He was long past feeling the cold on the steppes at this time of year—*yeah, wait till winter really gets here and it's time to grease up*—but the mannered huddling gesture was part of a whole wardrobe of idiosyncrasies he'd brought home with him from Yhelteth and never bothered to unlearn. Just a hangover, just like the southern memories that stubbornly refused to fade, and the vague sense of detachment Lara had cited in council when she left him and went back to her family's yurt.

Damn I miss you, wench.

He did his best to put some genuine melancholy behind the thought, but his heart wasn't in it. He didn't really miss her at all. In the last six or seven years he must have sired close on a dozen squalling bundles from the gates of Ishlin-ichan to the Voronak tundra outposts in the northeast, and at least half the mothers had as close a place in his affections as Lara. The marriage had just never worked at the same level as the initial roll-in-the-summer-grass passion it was based on. At the council hearing for the separation, truth be told, what he'd felt mostly was relief. He'd offered only token objection, and that more so Lara wouldn't get more pissed off than she already was. He'd paid the settlement and he'd been plowing another Skaranak milkmaid within a week. They were practically throwing themselves at him, anyway, with the news that he was single again.

Still. A little short of decorous, that one.

He grimaced. *Decorous* wasn't a word he used, wasn't *his* fucking word at all, but there it was, embedded in his head along with everything else. Lara was right, he should never have made the vows. Probably never would have done but for those eyes as she lay in the dusk-lit grass and opened herself to him, the startling jade-edged pupils that stabbed him through with memories of Imrana and her muslin-hung bedchamber.

Yeah, those eyes, and those tits, my son. Tits she had on her, old Urann himself would have sold his soul for.

That was more like it. That was a thought for a Majak horseman's head.

Fuck's sake stop brooding, will you. Count your Sky-given blessings.

He scratched beneath his buffalo-hide cap with one hard-nailed finger and watched the twilit figures of Runi and Klarn as they prodded the herd back toward the encampment. Every buffalo he could see was his, not to mention the shares he held in the Ishlinak herds farther to the west. The red-and-gray clan pennants he and the other two flew at the necks of their staff lances bore his name in Majak script. He was known throughout the steppes; every encampment he went to, women fell at his feet with open legs. About the only thing he really missed these days were hot-water baths and a decent shave, neither of which the Majak had a lot of use for.

Couple of fucking decades ago, my son, you didn't have much use for them, either. Remember that?

True enough. Twenty years ago, Egar's outlook, near as he could recall, wasn't much different from that of his clan fellows. Nothing wrong with cold water, a stoked communal sweat bath every few days, and a good beard. Not like these effete fucking southerners with their perfumed manners and woman-soft skins.

Yeah. But twenty years ago you were an ignorant fuck. Twenty years ago you didn't know your dick from a sword hilt. Twenty fucking years ago—

Twenty fucking years ago, Egar was no different from the next wispy-chinned Majak buffalo herdboy. He'd seen nothing of the lands beyond the steppes, believed himself sophisticated because his elder brothers had taken him to Ishlin-ichan to lose his virginity, and could not have grown a beard to save his life. He believed implicitly in what his father and brothers told him, and what they told him was, basically, that the Majak were the roughest toughest drinkers and fighters on earth, that of all the Majak clans, the Skaranak were the hardiest, and that the northern grasslands were the only place any real man would even consider living.

It was a philosophy that Egar disproved for himself, at least in part, one night in a tavern in Ishlin-ichan a few years later. Attempting to drink away his father's untimely death in a stampede, he got into a childish fight with a swarthy, serious-eyed imperial, a visiting Yhelteth merchant's bodyguard, it later turned out. The fight was largely Egar's fault, *childish* was the adjective applied to it—and him—by the imperial, who then went on to trounce him with an unfamiliar empty-hand fighting technique and without drawing his sword. Youth and anger and the anesthetic power of the drink kept Egar on his feet for a while, but he was up against a professional soldier for the first time in his life and the result was a foregone conclusion. The third time he got knocked to the floor, he stayed there.

Effete fucking southerners. Egar grinned in his beard, remembering. *Right.*

The tavern owner's sons had thrown him out. Sobering up in the street outside, Egar was smart enough to know that the dark, serious warrior had chosen to spare his life when he could with all justification have killed him outright. He went back in, bowed his head, and offered an apology. It was the first time he'd thought something through like that in his life.

The Yhelteth soldier accepted his contrition with a gracious foreign elegance, and then, with the peculiar camaraderie of fighting men who've just avoided having to kill each other, the two of them proceeded to get drunk together. On learning of Egar's loss, the man offered slightly slurred condolences and then, perhaps shrewdly, a suggestion.

I have got, he enunciated carefully, *an uncle in Yhelteth, a recruiter for the imperial levy. And the imperial levy, my friend, is pretty fucking desperate for manpower these days, 's the truth. Lot of work down there for a young man like you, doesn't mind getting in a scrap. Pay's good, the whores are fucking unbelievable. I mean that, they're famous. Yhelteth women are the most skilled at pleasing a man in the known world. You could have a good life down there, my friend. Fighting, fucking, getting paid.*

The words were among the last things Egar clearly remembered from that end of the night. He woke up seven hours later alone on the tavern floor with a screaming head, a vile taste in his mouth, and his father still dead.

A few days after that, the family herd got divided up—as his foreign drinking companion had probably known it would be. As the second youngest—and thus second to last in line—of five sons, Egar found himself the proud owner of about a dozen mangy beasts from the trailing end of the herd. The Yhelteth bodyguard's words floated back through his mind with sudden appeal. *Fighting, fucking, getting paid.* Work for men who didn't mind getting in a scrap, famously skilled whores. Versus a dozen mangy buffalo and getting pushed around by his brothers. It didn't feel like making a decision at all. Egar stayed with tradition as far as selling out his share in the herd to an elder sibling went, but then, instead of hiring on as a paid herdsman, he gathered his purse, his lance, and a few clothes, bought a new horse, and rode south for Yhelteth, alone.

Yhelteth!

Far from being a haunt of degenerates and women wrapped head-to-foot in sheets, the imperial city turned out to be paradise on earth. Egar's drinking companion had been right on the money. The Empire was arming for one of its habitual forays into the trading territory of the Trelayne League, and blades for hire were in high demand. Better yet, Egar's broad frame, fair hair, and pale blue eyes apparently made him all but irresistible to the women of this dark, fine-boned race. And the steppe nomads—for so he came to think of himself in time—had a reputation in Yhelteth that wasn't much inferior to their own opinion of themselves back home. They were thought pretty much by everyone to be ferocious warriors, phenomenal carousers, and potent, if unsubtle, lovers. In six months, Egar earned more coin, drank and ate more rich food, and woke up in more strange, perfumed beds than he would have believed possible even in his wildest adolescent fantasies. And he hadn't even *seen* a battle up to this point, let alone taken part in one. The bloodshed didn't start until—

Snuffling sounds and a shout yanked him from his memories. He blinked and looked around. Out on the eastern point of the herd, it looked like the animals were proving fractious and Runi was having problems. Egar put his mood away, cupped callused hands to his mouth.

"The bull," he bellowed in exasperation. How many times did he have to tell the lad, the herd followed its leaders. Dominate the bulls and you had the rest. "Leave the fucking cows alone and get that bu—"

"'*Ware runners!*"

Klarn's shout was shrill, the age-old terror of the steppe herdsman named in a panic-stricken cry from the other flank. Egar's head jerked around and he saw Klarn's arm outflung to the east. Sighting along the pointer, eyes narrowed, he spotted what had spooked Runi's side of the herd. Tall, pale figures, half a dozen or more of them, skimming as it seemed through the chest-high steppe grass.

Long runners.

Runi saw them, too, and drew himself up crossways to cover the herd. But by now his mount had snuffed the runners, too, and would not hold. It skittered back and forth, fighting the rein, terrified whinnies clearly audible on the wind.

No, not like that.

The warning yelped in Egar's mind, closely followed by the knowledge that there was no time to shout it, and just as much point. Runi was barely sixteen, and the steppe ghouls hadn't troubled the Skaranak seriously for over a decade. The closest the lad had ever been to a living runner were the stories old Poltar told around the campfire, and maybe the odd carcass dragged into camp to impress. He had no knowledge of what Egar had learned in blood before Runi was born. *You can't fight the steppe ghouls standing still.*

Klarn, older and wiser, had seen Runi's error and was spurring his own far from willing mount around the dark mass of buffalo, shouting. He had his bow off his back, was reaching for shafts.

He'd be there too late.

Egar knew that much, the same way he knew when steppe brush was dry enough to burn. The runners were less than five hundred paces out from the herd, ground they could cover in less time than it takes a man to piss. Klarn would be late, the horses would not hold, Runi would come off and die there in the grass.

The Dragonbane cursed, unshipped his staff lance, and kicked his Yhelteth-bred warhorse into a charge.

He was almost there when the first of the runners reached Runi, so he saw what was done. The lead ghoul passed Runi's shrieking horse, pivoted on one powerful backward-hinging leg, lashed out with the other. Runi tried to spin with the horse panicking beneath him, made one hopeless thrust with his lance—and then talons like scythe blades clouted him backward out of the saddle. Egar saw him reel to his feet, stumbling, and two more of the runners fell on him. A long, wrenching scream floated up from the grass.

Already at full gallop, Egar played his only remaining card. He hooked back his head and howled, the Majak berserker ululation that had turned blood to ice in the veins of men on a thousand battlefields across the known world. The awful, no-way-back call for death, and company in the dying.

The steppe ghouls heard and their long, pointed heads lifted, bloody-snouted, questing for the threat. For the scant seconds it took, they gaped emptily at the mounted figure that came thundering across the grassland, and then the Dragonbane was upon them.

The first runner took the lance full in the chest and fell back, punched along with the velocity of the horse's charge, scrabbling and spitting blood. Egar reined in hard, twisted and withdrew the lance, quadrupled the size of the wound. Wet, rope-like organs came out on the serrated edges of the blade, tugged and tore and spilled pale fluids as he ripped the weapon clear. The second ghoul reached for him, but the Dragonbane had already turned about, and his warhorse reared to the attack, flailing out with massive steel-shod hooves. The ghoul yelped as one snaking arm got smashed aside, and then the horse danced forward a step as only the Yhelteth trainers could make them, and one hoof sank a terminal dent into the runner's skull. Egar yelled, clung on with his thighs, and reversed his lance in both hands. Blood sprinkled across the air.

Six and a half feet long, known and feared by every soldier who had ever had to face one, the Majak staff lance was traditionally crafted from the long rib of a bull buffalo and fastened at either end with a foot-long double-edged sawtooth blade a handbreadth wide at its base. In earlier years, the iron for these weapons was unreliable, full of impurities and poorly worked in small, mobile forges. Later, hired as mercenaries by the Trelayne League, the Majak learned the technology for a steel that would match their own ferocious instincts in battle, and the lance shafts came to be made of Naom forest wood, specifically shaped and hardened for the purpose. When the Yhelteth armies finally swept north and west against the cities of the League for the first time, they smashed apart like a wave on the waiting steppe nomad line and their lances. It was a military reversal the Empire had not seen in more than a century. In the aftermath, it was said, even Yhelteth's most seasoned warriors quailed at the damage the Majak weapons had done to their comrades. At the battle of Mayne's Moor, when leave was given to retrieve the bodies of the slain, fully a quarter of the imperial conscript force deserted amid stories that the Majak berserkers had eaten pieces of the corpses. A Yhelteth historian later said of the carnage on the moor that *such scavenging animals that came fed in an agitated state, fearing that some mightier predator had already fallen on the carpet of meat and might yet fall on them.* It was fanciful writing, but it made its point. The Yhelteth soldiers called the lance *ashlan mher thelan,* the twice-fanged demon.

The runners came at him on both sides.

Egar struck quarterstaff-style, high left and low right, while his horse was still dropping back to all fours. The low blade gutted the right-hand runner, the high blocked a downward-lashing arm from the left and smashed it. The injured ghoul shrilled and Egar paddled the staff. He got an eye and some scrapings of skull on the left blade, nothing from the other side where the gutted runner was down in the grass and screaming as it bled out. The ghoul whose eye and arm he had taken commenced staggering and pawing at the air like a drunk caught in a clothesline. The rest—

Sudden, familiar hissing, a solid *thunk,* and the injured creature shrilled again as one of Klarn's steel-headed arrows jutted abruptly out of its chest. It reached down with its remaining functional hand, plucked puzzledly at the protruding thing, and a second arrow took it through the skull. For a moment it clawed up at the new injury and then its brain caught up with the damage, and the long pale body crashed into the grass beside its gutted companion.

Egar counted three more ghouls, hunkered down and hesitating on the other side of Runi's body. They seemed unsure what to do. With Klarn nudging his horse in from the side, a fresh arrow nocked and at his eye, the odds had tipped. No one Egar had met, not even Ringil or Archeth, knew if the long runners were a race with the reasoning powers of men or not. But they had been harrying the Majak and their herds for centuries, and the two sides had each other's measure.

Egar dismounted into sudden quiet.

"If they move," he told Klarn.

Hefting his lance in both hands, he stalked through the grass toward Runi and the creatures that wanted him. Behind his unmoving features, in the pit of his stomach, he felt the inevitable worm of fear. If they rushed him now, Klarn might have time to put two shafts in the air at most, and the runners stood close to three yards tall when they cared to.

He'd just given away his advantage.

But Runi was down, bleeding into the cold steppe earth, and every second he lay there meant the difference between reaching the healers in time and not.

The ghouls shifted in the sea of grass, hunched white backs like the whales he had once seen sounding off the Trelayne coast. Their narrow, fanged faces hovered at the end of long skulls and muscular necks, watching him slyly. There might be another one crouched prone somewhere, as he had seen them do when stalking. He could not remember now how many he'd counted in that first glimpse.

It seemed suddenly colder.

He reached Runi, and the chill gripped him tighter. The boy was dead, chest and belly laid open, eyes staring up at the sky from his grimy face. It had at least been quick; the ground around him was drenched with the sudden emptying of blood from his body. In the fading light, it seemed black.

Egar felt the pounding come up through the soles of his feet like drums. His teeth clenched and his nostrils flared with it. It swelled and washed out the chill, exploded through the small spaces in his throat and behind his eyes. For a moment he stood in silence, and it felt as if something was rooting him to the ground.

His eyes snapped up to the three steppe ghouls in the gloom ahead of him. He lifted his lance in one trembling hand and threw back his head and *howled,* howled as if it might crack the sky, might reach Runi's soul on its path along the Sky Road, sunder the band he walked on, and tumble him back to earth again.

Time ceased. Now there was only death.

He barely heard the hiss of Klarn's first arrow past his flank as he stormed toward the remaining runners, still howling.

CHAPTER 3

The window shattered with a clear, high tinkling and whatever had come through it thumped hard on the threadbare carpet in the center of the room.

Ringil shifted in the disarray of bed linen and forced one eye open. The edges of the broken glass glinted down at him in sunlight far too bright to look at directly in his present condition. He rolled over on his back, one arm pawing about on the bed for his companion of the night before. His hand encountered only an expanse of patchily damp sheet. The boy was gone, as they usually were well before the sun came up. His mouth tasted like the inside of a dueling gauntlet and his head, it dawned on him slowly, was thumping like a Majak war drum.

Padrow's Day. Hurrah.

He rolled back over and groped around on the floor beside the bed until his fingers brushed a heavy, irregularly shaped object. Further exploration proved it to be a stone, wrapped in what felt like expensive parchment. He dredged it up to his face, confirmed what his fingers had told him, and unraveled the paper. It was a carelessly torn piece of a larger sheet, scented and scrawled with words in Trelayne script.

Get Up.

The writing was familiar.

Ringil groaned and sat up amid the sheets. Wrapping himself in one of them, he clambered off the bed and stumbled to the newly broken window. Down in the snow-sprinkled courtyard, men sat on horses, all dressed in steel cuirasses and helmets that winked mercilessly in the sun. A carriage stood in their midst, curved lines in the snow marking where it had turned to a halt. A woman in fur-lined hood and Trelayne robes of rank stood by the carriage, shading her eyes as she looked up.

"Good afternoon, Ringil," she called.

"Mother." Ringil suppressed another groan. "What do you want?"

"Well, I'd say breakfast, but the hour is long gone. Did you enjoy your Padrow's Eve?"

Ringil put a hand to one side of his head where the throbbing seemed to be worse. The mention of breakfast had thrown an unexpected flip into his stomach.

"Look, just stay there," he said faintly. "I'll be down in a moment. And don't throw any more stones. I'll have to pay for that."

Back inside the room, he sank his head into the bowl of water beside the bed, rubbed his hair and face with it, scrubbed the inside of his mouth with a scented dental twig from the jar on the table, and went about locating his discarded clothes. It took longer than you would have expected for a room that small.

When he was dressed, he raked his long fine black hair back from his face, bound it with a piece of dour gray cloth, and let himself out onto the landing of the inn. The other doors were all securely closed; there was no one about. Most of his fellow guests were doing the civilized thing and sleeping off the Padrow's Day festivities. He clattered down the stairs, still tucking his shirt into his breeches, quick before the Lady Ishil of Eskiath Fields got bored and ordered her guard to start breaking down the inn's front door.

Slipping the bolt on the courtyard entrance, he stepped outside and stood blinking in the sunlight. The mounted guard didn't seem to have moved at all since he left the window, but Ishil was already at the door. As soon as he appeared, she put down her hood and draped her arms around him. The kiss she placed on his cheek was courtly and formal, but there was a tighter need in the way she hugged him. He reciprocated with as much enthusiasm as his pounding head and queasy stomach could manage. As soon as she got that from him, she stepped back from the embrace, held him at arm's length like a gown she thought she might put on.

"Well met, my beautiful son, well met."

"How did you know which window to break?" he countered sourly.

The Lady Ishil gestured. "Oh, we asked. It wasn't difficult. Everyone in this pigsty of a town seems to know where you sleep." A delicately curled lip. She let him go. "And who with."

Ringil ignored that one. "I'm a hero, Mother. What do you expect?"

"Yes, are they still calling you Angeleyes in these parts?" Peering into his face. "I think Demoneyes suits you better today. There's more red in there than the crater at An-Monal."

"It's Padrow's Day," he said shortly. "Eyes this color are traditional. And anyway, since when did you know what An-Monal looks like? You've never been there."

She snorted. "How would you know that? I could have been there anytime in the last three years, which is how long it's been since you last chose to visit your poor aged mother."

"Mother, please." He shook his head and looked at her. *Aged* was, he supposed, an accurate enough statement of his mother's forty-something years, but it hardly showed. Ishil had been a bride at thirteen, a mother of four before she was twenty. She'd had the following two and a half decades to work on her feminine charms and ensure that whatever Gingren Eskiath's indiscretions with the other, younger females who came within his grabbing radius, he would always come back to the marriage bed in the end. She wore kohl in the Yhelteth style, on eyes and to etch her lips; her hair was bound back from a delicate, barely lined forehead and cheekbones that screamed her family's southern ancestry. And when she moved, her robes caught on curves more appropriate to a woman half her age. In Trelayne high society, it was whispered that this was sorcery, that Ishil had sold her soul for her youthful aspect. Ringil, who'd watched her dress enough times, thought it more likely cosmetics, though on the soul selling he had to agree. Ishil's aspirational merchant-class parents might have secured for their daughter a lifetime of luxury by marrying her into the house of Eskiath, but like all commerce it came at a price, and that price was life with Gingren.

"Well, it's true, isn't it?" she insisted. "When were you last in Trelayne?"

"How is Father?" he asked obliquely.

Their eyes met. She sighed and shrugged. "Oh, you know. Your father's . . . your father. No easier to live with now he's gray. He asks after you."

Ringil arched an eyebrow. "Really?"

"No, really. Sometimes, when he's tired in the evenings. I think maybe he's beginning to . . . regret. Some of the things he said, anyway."

"Is he dying, then?" He could not keep the bitterness from his voice. "Is that why you're here?"

She looked at him again, and this time he thought he saw the momentary brilliance of tear sheen in her eyes. "No, that's not why I'm here. I wouldn't have come for that, and you know it. It's something else." She clapped her hands suddenly, pasted on a smile. "But what are we doing out here, Ringil? Where is everyone? This place has about as much life to it as an Aldrain stone circle. I have hungry men and maids, horses that need feeding and watering. I could do with a little food myself, come to that. Doesn't your landlord want to earn himself some League coin?"

Ringil shrugged. "I'll go and ask him. Then maybe you can tell me what's going on."

THE LANDLORD, BY HIS FACE AS HUNGOVER AS RINGIL, DID BRIGHTEN somewhat at the mention of Trelayne currency. He opened the dining chamber at the back of the residents' bar, ordered bleary-eyed stable hands to take care of the horses, and wandered off into the kitchen to see what was salvageable from the previous night's feast. Ringil went with him, made himself an herbal infusion, and carried it back to one of the dining chamber's oak trestle tables, where he slumped and stared at the steam rising from the cup as if it were a summoned sprite. In due course Ishil came in, followed by her men and three ladies-in-waiting who'd presumably been hiding in the carriage. They bustled about, making far too much noise.

"Traveling light, I see."

"Oh, Ringil, be quiet." Ishil settled herself on the other side of the table. "It's not my fault you drank too much last night."

"No, but it's your fault I'm awake this early dealing with it." One of the ladies-in-waiting tittered, then flushed into silence as Ishil cut her an icy glance. Ringil sipped at his tea and grimaced. "So you want to tell me what this is about?"

"Could we not have some coffee first?"

"It's coming. I don't have a lot of small talk, Mother."

Ishil made an elegant gesture of resignation. "Oh, very well. Do you remember your cousin Sherin?"

"Vaguely." He fitted a childhood face to the name, a wan little girl with downward-falling sheaves of dark hair, too young for him to want to play with in the gardens. He associated her with summers at Ishil's villa down the coast at Lanatray. "One of Nerla's kids?"

"Dersin's. Nerla was her paternal aunt."

"Right."

The silence pooled. Someone came in and started building a fire in the hearth.

"Sherin has been sold," Ishil said quietly.

Ringil looked at the cup in his hand. "Really. How did that happen?"

"How does it always happen these days?" Ishil shrugged. "Debt. She married, oh, some finished-goods merchant, you don't know him. Name of Bilgrest. This was a few years ago. I sent you an invitation to the wedding, but you never replied. Anyway, it seems this Bilgrest had a gambling problem. He'd been speculating on the crop markets for a while, too, and getting it mostly wrong. That, plus maintaining appearances in Trelayne, wiped out the bulk of his accumulated capital, and then like the idiot he was, he stopped paying into the sureties fund to cut costs, and then a ship carrying his merchandise got wrecked off the Gergis cape, and then, well." Another shrug. "You know how it goes after that."

"I can imagine. But Dersin's got money. Why didn't she bail them out?"

"She doesn't have *much* money, Ringil. You always assume—"

"We're talking about her fucking *daughter,* for Hoiran's sake. And Garat's got well-heeled friends, hasn't he? They could have raised the finance somehow. Come to that, why didn't they just buy Sherin back?"

"They didn't know. Bilgrest wouldn't tell anybody the way things were going, and Sherin went along with the charade. She was always so proud, and she knows Garat never really approved of the marriage. Apparently, he'd already loaned them money a couple of times and never got it back. I think Garat and Bilgrest had words. After that, Sherin just stopped asking. Stopped visiting. Dersin hadn't seen either of them for months. We were both down at Lanatray when we heard, and by the time the news got to us and we got back to the city—it must have been at least a week by then. We had to break into the house." She shuddered delicately. "It was like walking into a tomb. All the furniture gone, the bailiffs took everything, even the drapes and carpets, and Bilgrest just sat there with the shutters closed, muttering to himself in the dark."

"Didn't they have any kids?"

"No, Sherin couldn't. I think that's why she clung to Bilgrest so hard, because he didn't seem to care about it."

"Oh great. You know what that means, don't you?"

Another little pool of quiet. The coffee came, with yesterday's bread toasted to cover its stiffness, an assortment of jams and oils and some reheated broth. The men-at-arms and the ladies-in-waiting fell on it all with an enthusiasm that made Ringil slightly queasy all over again. Ishil took a little coffee and looked somberly back at her son.

"I told Dersin you'd look for her," she said.

Ringil raised an eyebrow. "Did you? That was rash."

"Please don't be like this, Gil. You'd be paid."

"I don't need the money." Ringil closed his eyes briefly. "Why can't Father do it? It's not like he doesn't have the manpower."

Ishil looked away. "You know your father's opinion of my family.

And Dersin's side are practically full-blood marsh dwellers if you go back a couple of generations. Hardly worthy of his favors. Anyway, Gingren won't go against the edicts. You know how things are since the war. It's legal. Sherin was sold legally."

"You could still appeal it. There's provision in the charter. Get Bilgrest to go on his knees to the Chancellery, offer public apology and restitution, you act as guarantor if Dersin can't come up with the cash and Father doesn't want to get his hands dirty."

"Don't you think we tried that?"

"So what happened?"

Sudden, imperious flare of anger, a side of Ishil he'd nearly forgotten. "What happened, Ringil, is that Bilgrest *hanged himself* rather than apologize. That's what happened."

"Ooops."

"It isn't funny."

"No, I suppose not." He swallowed some more tea. "Very noble, though. Death before dishonor and all that. And from a finished-goods merchant, too. Remarkable. Father must have been impressed despite himself."

"This is not about you and your father, Ringil."

The ladies-in-waiting froze. Ishil's shout bounced off the low roof of the dining chamber, brought curious faces gawping at the doorway to the kitchen and the window out into the yard. The men-at-arms exchanged glances, wondering almost visibly if they were expected to throw some weight around and drive these peasants back to minding their own business. Ringil caught the eye of one of them, shook his head slightly. Ishil compressed her lips, drew a long deep breath.

"This doesn't concern your father," she said quietly. "I know better than to rely on him. It's a favor I'm asking of you."

"My days of fighting for the cause of justice, truth, and light are done, Mother."

She drew herself up on her seat. "I'm not interested in justice or truth. This is family."

Ringil closed his eyes again, massaged them with finger and thumb at the bridge of his nose. "Why me?"

"Because you know these people, Gil." She reached across the table and touched his free hand with the back of hers. His eyes jerked open at the contact. "You used to rub our faces in the fact enough when you lived at home. You can go places in Trelayne that I can't, that your father *won't* go. You can—"

She bit her lip.

"Break the edicts," he finished for her drearily.

"I promised Dersin."

"Mother." Abruptly, something seemed to dislodge a chunk of his hangover. Anger and a tight sense of the unfairness of it all came welling up and fed him an obscure strength. "Do you know what you're asking me to do? You know what the profit margins are on slaving. Have you got any idea what kind of incentives that generates, what kind of behavior? These people don't fuck about, you know."

"I know."

"No, you *don't* fucking know. You said yourself, it's weeks since this went down. If Sherin's certifiably barren—and these people have warlocks who can find that out in pretty short order—then she's a sure shot for the professional concubine end of the market, which means she's probably *already* been shipped out of Trelayne to a Parashal training stable. It could take me weeks to find out where that is, and by then she'll more than likely be on her way to the auction block again, anywhere in the League or maybe even south to the Empire. I'm not a one-man army."

"At Gallows Gap, they say you were."

"Oh, *please.*"

He stared morosely into the depths of his tea. *You know these people, Ringil.* With less of a headache, he might have laughed. Yes, he knew these people. He'd known them when slavery was still technically illegal in the city-states and they made an easier living from other illicit trades. In fact, *known* didn't really cut it—like a lot of Trelayne's moneyed youth, he'd been an avid customer of *these people.* Proscribed substances, prohibited sexual practices, the things that would always generate a market with ludicrous profit margins and shadowy social leverage. Oh, he *knew* these people. Slab Findrich, for example, the drilled-hole eyes and the spit he always left on the pipes they shared.

Grace-of-Heaven Milacar, murdering turncoat minions with excessive chemical kindness—seen through the neurasthenic fog of a flandrijn hit, it hadn't seemed so bad, had in fact quite appealed to a louche adolescent irony Ringil was cultivating at the time. Poppy Snarl, harsh painted beauty and weary, look-you-can't-seriously-expect-me-to-put-up-with-this counterfeit patience before she inflicted one of the brutal punishments for which she was famed, and which invariably crippled for life. He'd gone down on her once, Hoiran alone knew why, but it seemed like a good idea at the time, and he went home after with the unaccustomed scent of woman on his mouth and fingers, and a satisfyingly complete sense of self-soiling. Snarl and Findrich had both dabbled in the slave trade even when it was frowned upon, and both had rhapsodized about what could be achieved in that sector if the lawmakers would just loosen up a little and open the debt market once and for all.

By now they'd be up to their eyes in it.

Suddenly he was wondering how Grace-of-Heaven looked these days. If he still had the goatee, if he'd shaved his skull ahead of incipient baldness, the way he always said he would.

Uh-oh.

With a mother's eye, Ishil saw the moment pivot in him. Perhaps she knew it before he did himself. Something changed in her face, a barely perceptible softening of the kohl-defined features, like an artist's thumb rubbing along sketch lines he'd drawn too harshly. Ringil glanced up and caught it happening. He rolled his eyes, made a long-suffering face. Ishil's lips parted.

"No, don't." He held up an advisory hand. "Just. Don't."

His mother said nothing, but she smiled.

IT DIDN'T TAKE LONG TO PACK. HE WENT UP TO HIS ROOM, TORE through it like an irritable whirlwind, and flung a dozen items into a knapsack. Mostly, it was books.

Back down in the residents' bar, he retrieved the Ravensfriend and the Kiriath scabbard from their place above the fireplace. By now there were people about, tavern staff and guests both, and the ones who knew him gaped as he took the sword down. The scabbard felt strange as he hefted it; it was the first occasion in a long time that he'd unpinned it from the mountings. He'd forgotten how light it was. He pulled about a handbreadth of blade free, held it up to the light, and squinted along the edge for a moment before he realized there was no real purpose to the action and he was just posturing. His mood shifted minutely. A tiny smile leaked from the corner of his mouth, and with it came a gathering sense of motion he hadn't expected to feel.

He parked scabbard and sword over one shoulder, held his knapsack dangling in the other hand, and wandered back to the dining chamber, where they were clearing away the remains of Ishil's entourage's food. The landlord stopped with a tray in each meaty hand and added his gape to the collection.

"What are you doing?" he asked plaintively.

"Change of scenery, Jhesh." Ringil shifted the knapsack up onto his other shoulder and clapped the man briskly on one apron-swathed flank. It was like patting a side of ham. "I'm taking a couple of months off. Going to winter in Trelayne. Should be back well before the spring."

"But, but, but . . ." Jhesh scrabbled for purchase and a measure of politeness. "I mean, what about your room?"

"Oh. Rent it. If you can."

The politeness started to evaporate. "And your tab?"

"Ah yes." Ringil lifted a finger for a moment's indulgence and went to the door into the courtyard. "Mother?"

They left Jhesh at the door, counting the money with less enthusiasm than the amount involved should have warranted. Ringil followed Ishil's regal trail to the carriage and swung himself up into the unaccustomed luxury of the interior. Woven silk paneling on the inside of walls and door, glass in the windows, a small ornate lantern slung from the roof. A profusion of cushions scattered across two facing bench seats broad and long enough to serve as beds, padded footrests tucked underneath. A hamper on the floor in one corner along with flasks and goblets. Ishil leaned herself into one corner and sighed with relief as the last lady-in-waiting scrambled aboard.

"At last! What you see in this place, Ringil, I'll never understand. I'll swear none of those people has bathed properly in a week."

He shrugged. She wasn't far out. Heated baths were an out-and-out luxury in places like Gallows Water. And this time of year, bathing down at the river was fast becoming an unattractive proposition.

"Well, Mother, it's the common herd, you know. Since the League implemented the bathhouse tax, they've just lost all interest in personal hygiene."

"Ringil, I'm just *saying*."

"Yeah, well, don't. These people are my friends." A thought struck him, the meager grain of truth at the center of the lie. He stopped the lady-in-waiting as she tried to close the door. He hooked a hold on the top edge of the door, leaned out and forward, and just managed to prod the coachman's booted calf. The man jumped and raised a fist clenched around a whip butt as he looked around for the source of the affront. When he saw who'd touched him, the arm dropped as if severed, and he went white.

"Oh, gods, your worthiness, I'm so sorry." The words choked out of him. "I didn't mean—that is, I thought—please, I'm *so* sorry."

Your worthiness?

That was going to take some getting used to again.

"Right, right. Don't let it happen again." Ringil gestured, vague directions with his free hand. "Look, I want you to swing by the graveyard on the way out of town. There's a blue house there, on the corner. Stop outside."

"Yes, your worthiness." The man couldn't get himself back around to face the horses fast enough. "Right away, sir. Right away."

Ringil hinged back into the carriage and pulled the door closed. He ignored his mother's inquiring look. Finally, when they'd clattered out of the courtyard and picked up the street, she had to ask.

"And why are we going to the graveyard exactly?"

"I want to say good-bye to a friend."

She did one of her little wearied-inhalation tricks, and he was shocked at how completely it translated him back over a decade to his teens. Caught once more creeping into the house through the servants' quarters at dawn, mingling with the maids. Ishil standing at the top of the kitchen stair in her dressing gown, arms folded, face scrubbed pale and clean of makeup, severe as an angered witch queen.

"Gil, must we be so *painfully* melodramatic?"

"Not a dead friend, Mother. He lives next to the graveyard."

She arched one immaculately groomed eyebrow. "Really? How absolutely delightful for him."

The carriage trundled through the barely waking town.

When they reached Bashka's house, the storm door was pulled closed across the front entrance, which usually meant the schoolmaster was still in bed. Ringil jumped down and went around the back, through the graveyard. Frost crunched underfoot in the grass and glistened on the stone markers. A solitary mourner stood amid the graves, wrapped in a patched leather cloak, wearing a brimmed hat that shadowed his face. He looked up as Ringil came through from the street, met the swordsman's eye with bleak lack of care and what might have been a gleam of unforgiving recognition. Ringil ignored him with hungover aplomb. He picked his way between the graves and went to peer in the nearest window of the cottage. On the other side of the grimy glass, the schoolmaster was pottering inefficiently around with pans and kitchen fire and, by the look of his face, dealing with his own modest hangover. Ringil grinned and rapped at the window pane. He had to do it twice before Bashka's directional sense kicked in and he realized where the noise was coming from. Then the schoolmaster gestured eagerly at him to come around to the front door. He went back to the carriage and leaned in the open door.

"I'm going in for a moment. Want to come?"

His mother stirred restlessly. "Who is this friend of yours?"

"The local schoolmaster."

"A teacher?" Ishil rolled her eyes. "No, I don't think so, Ringil. Please be as quick as you can."

Bashka let him in and led him past the bedroom toward the kitchen. Ringil caught a brief glimpse through the open bedroom door, a sprawled, curved form amid the sheets, long red hair. He vaguely remembered his last sight of the schoolmaster the night before, stumbling down the street between two local whores, bawling at the stars some mangled priestly creed with obscene body parts inserted in place of gods' names. It had gone pretty much unremarked in the general merriment.

"You got Red Erli in there?" he asked. "She really go home with you?"

Bashka was grinning from ear to ear. "They *both*, Gil, they *both* came home with me. Erli *and* Mara. Best Padrow's Eve ever."

"Yeah? So where's Mara?"

"Ran off after. Stole my purse." Even this admission didn't seem enough to knock the grin off Bashka's earnest face. He shook his head mellowly. "Best Padrow's *ever*."

Ringil frowned. "You want me to go around and get it back for you?"

"No, forget it. Didn't have a great deal left in there anyway." He shook his head like a dog shaking off water, made shivering noises. "And I think it's fair to say the maid earned every minted piece."

Ringil grimaced at the epithet *maid* attached to Mara.

"You're too soft, Bash. Mara never would have pulled something like that with any of her regulars. Not in a town this small. She wouldn't dare."

"It doesn't matter, Gil, really." Bashka sobered briefly. "I don't want you to do anything about it. Leave Mara alone."

"You know, it was probably that little shit Feg put her up to it. I could—"

"Gil." Bashka looked at him reproachfully. "You're spoiling my hangover."

Ringil stopped. Shrugged. "Okay, your call. So, uhm, d'you need some quick cash then. To get you through till the holiday's over?"

"Yeah." Bashka snorted. "Like *you* can really afford to lend it to me, Gil. Come on, I'm fine. Always set a bit aside for Padrow's, you know that."

"I've got money, Bash. Someone just hired me. Blade contract. Paying gig, you know? I've got the cash, if you want it."

"Well, I *don't* want it."

"All right. I was just asking."

"Well, stop asking then. I told you, I'm fine." Bashka hesitated, seemed to sense the real reason for Ringil's visit. "So, uh, you going away? With this blade contract, I mean?"

"Yeah, couple of months. Be back before you know it. Look, really, if you need the money, it's not like you haven't bailed me out in the past and—"

"I told you, I'm fine, Gil. Where you going?"

"Trelayne. Points south, maybe." Suddenly he didn't feel like explaining it all. "Like I said, be back in a few months. It's no big thing."

"Going to miss you, midweek nights." Bashka mimed moving a chess piece. "I'll probably have to go play Brunt up at the forge. Can just imagine what *those* conversations are going to be like."

"Yeah, I'll miss—" He stumbled on it, old shards of caution, even here. "Our conversations, too."

No you won't.

The realization lit up like a crumpled paper tossed into the fire. Bright lick of flame and a twisting, sparkling away that ached briefly, then was gone. *You're not going to miss your nights of chess and chat with Bashka here, Gil, and you know it.* And he did know it, knew that in the upriver districts of Trelayne, company twice as sophisticated as the schoolmaster's could be had at pretty much any coffeehouse you cared to step into. Knew also that, despite Bashka's kindness and the few topics of common interest they had, the man was not and never really had been his friend, not in any sense that mattered.

It hit him then, for the first time really, through the stubborn ache in his head, that he really was going back. And not just back to bladework—that was an old quickening, already touched, like checking coin in your purse, and then tamped away again in the pulse of his blood. That wasn't it. More than that, he was going back to the brawling, bargaining human sprawl of Trelayne and all it meant. Back into the heated womb of his youth, back to the hothouse dilettante climate that had bred and then sickened him. Back to a part of himself he'd thought long rooted out and burned in the charnel days of the war.

Guess not, Gil.

He made his farewells to the schoolmaster, clowned his way out with a wink at the bedroom door, got away as fast as he decently could.

He hauled himself into the carriage, sank into a corner in silence. The eager coachman cracked his horses into motion. They pulled away, through the quiet streets, past the town limits and low wooden watchtowers, up the high road along the foothills below the mountains and Gallows Gap, westward toward the forests and the Naom plain and the sea beyond. Westward to where Trelayne waited for him in shimmering splendor on the shore, sucking at him, now the image was planted in his mind, even from here.

Ringil stared out of the window at the passing scenery.

"So how was he?" Ishil asked at last. "Your teacher friend?"

"Hungover and broke from whoring, why do you ask?"

Ishil sighed with elaborate disdain and turned her face pointedly to stare out of the other side of the carriage. The coach bumped and rattled along. The ladies-in-waiting smirked and glanced and talked among themselves about clothes.

The new knowledge sat beside him like a corpse no one else could see.

He was going back to what he used to be, and the worst of it was that he couldn't make himself regret it at all.

In fact, now the whole thing was in motion, he could hardly wait.

CHAPTER 4

ring me Archeth.

The summons went out from the throne room like a circular ripple from the flung stone of the Emperor's command. Courtiers heard and, each competing for favor, gave hurried orders to their attendants, who sped in turn through the labyrinthine palace in search of the Lady *kir*-Archeth. The word passed from attendants to servants, and from servants to slaves, as the entire pyramid of authority turned its attention to this sudden diversion from the day-to-day drudgery of palace life. Serpent rumor coiled outward alongside the bare instruction, placing the tone in the Emperor's voice somewhere between irritation and anger, a vocal spectrum that everyone at court, including even quite senior invigilators, had learned in recent years to treat with acute alarm. Best for all concerned, then, that Archeth present herself at speed.

Unfortunately, as was so often the case these days, the Lady Archeth was nowhere to be found. Since the Shaktur expedition, it was whispered, she had grown moody and taciturn and ever more unpredictable in situations where considered diplomacy really should have been the order of the day. She was given to prowling the corridors of the palace and the streets of the city at odd hours, or disappearing into the eastern desert alone for weeks on end, equipped, they muttered, with rations of food and water that verged on the suicidal. In the daily round at the palace, she was equally insensitive to lethal risk; she neglected her duties and heard rebukes with an impassivity that verged on insolence. Her days at court, it was said, were numbered.

Bring me Archeth.

The unfulfilled command echoed and lapped at the palace walls where they surrounded the outermost of the imperial gardens. Several among the courtiers began to panic. They cast the summons outward from the walls and down into the city itself, this time in the hands of imperial messengers, the so-called King's Reach, famously skilled at finding and retrieving people anywhere within the far-flung borders of the Empire. Liveried in black and silver, these men spread out through the streets in groups, threading beneath the painted cupolas and domes of the city's heart—the architecture that Ringil had once rather unkindly described as looking like a party of prostitute snails—knocking on the doors of likely pipe houses and taverns, slapping known associates about with casual brutality. It was a stupendous misuse of resources, a battleax to chop onions, but it was the Emperor's command and no one wanted to be found lacking in response. There'd been too many examples made since the accession.

It took those of the Reach with the best luck about an hour to find out from tradesmen on the Boulevard of the Ineffable Divine that Archeth had last been seen strolling down toward the imperial shipyards, a long-hafted engineer's hammer gripped purposefully in one hand and a krinzanz pipe in the other. From there it was a simple matter for these half a dozen messengers to trace the route, enter the yards, and pick a way among the skeletal keels of vessels under construction, asking after Archeth at every turn. It was an even simpler matter for the yard workers to turn and eloquently point.

At one end of the shipyard, a battered and stained Kiriath fireship stood isolated from its more conventional wooden neighbors on dry-dock props that appeared over time to have rusted solid with the hull. It was one of the last to be brought in from the desert while Akal the Great still sat on the throne and would countenance the expense, and an aura hung about it, of abandonment and black iron malice. The Reachmen, handpicked and known for their great courage in straitened circumstance, eyed the vessel without enthusiasm. Kiriath works were everywhere in the city, had been for centuries, but these contraptions set a shiver at the spine; bulge-bodied and looming, like some freak sea creature hauled up from the depths in an unlucky trawler's nets; set about with unfamiliar gills, feelers, and eyes, all suited more to a living entity than any built device, skin scarred and blistered from repeated entry into a realm where human flesh and bone would melt to nothing in a single searing instant, where only demons might dwell, and carrying who knew what enduring underworldly taint from the places it had been.

And from within the closed iron cylinder, more precisely from the mouth of one downthrown open hatch in a row of five that were set into the underside of the hull, came the furious, repeated clang of metal pounding on metal. The sound, it seemed, of something trying to escape.

Glances went back and forth; hands dropped to the hilts of well-worn weapons. The Emperor's messengers drew closer at a pace that declined with every step they took into the shadow of the fireship's propped bulk. Finally, they piled to a halt just inside the circumference of the dry-dock framework that supported the vessel, and a good dozen paces back from the hatch, all of them careful not to step on any of the drooping feelers that trailed from the hull and lay flopped in the shipyard dust like so many discarded carriage whips. No telling when something like *that*, no matter the intervening years of disuse, might twist and snap to sudden, murderous life, coil about an unwary limb, and jerk its owner off his feet and screaming into the air, to be lashed back and forth or slammed to pulp against the grimy iron flank of the ship.

"*Syphilitic son of an uncleansed, camel-fucking CUNT!*"

A massive metallic crash fringed the final word, but could not drown it out. The messengers flinched. In places, blades came a few inches clear of their sheaths. Hard on the echoes of the impact, before anyone could move, the voice started up again, no cleaner of expression, no less rabidly furious, no less punctuated by the clangor of whatever arcane conflict was raging in the confines of the hull. The messengers stood frozen, faces sweat-beaded from the fierce heat of a near-noon sun, while recollected witch rumors crept coldly up and down their bones.

"Is it an exorcism?"

"It's krinzanz," reckoned a more pragmatic member of the party. "She's off her fucking head."

Another of the messengers cleared his throat.

"Ah, Mistress Archeth . . ."

". . . motherfucking closemouth me, will you, you fucking . . ."

"Mistress Archeth!" The Reachman went up to a full-scale shout. "The Emperor wills your presence!"

The cursing stopped abruptly. The metallic cacophony died. For a long moment, the open hatch yawned and oozed a silence no less unnerving than the noise that had gone before. Then Archeth's voice emerged, a little hoarse.

"Who's that?"

"From the palace. The Emperor summons you."

Indistinct muttering. A clank, as the engineer's hammer was apparently dropped, and then an impatient scrambling sound. Moments later, Archeth's ebony head emerged upside down from the hatch, thickly braided hair in stiff disarray around her features. She grinned down at the messengers, a little too widely.

"All right," she said. "I've done enough reading for one day."

BY THE TIME THEY GOT BACK TO THE PALACE, THE KRIN COMEDOWN HAD hit and the Emperor was waiting in the Chamber of Confidences, a fact whose significance was not lost on the ushering courtiers Archeth encountered en route. She saw the glances they exchanged as she passed them. The Chamber of Confidences was a tented raft of rare woods and silks anchored in the center of an enclosed pool fifty yards across and windowed only from above. Water cataracted down the cunningly sculpted marble walls at the circumference of the chamber, rendering eavesdropping an impossibility, and the waters of the pool were stocked with a species of highly intelligent octopi who were fed regularly on condemned criminals. What was said in the Chamber of Confidences was for the ears of either those utterly trusted by the Emperor or those who would not be leaving. And in these uncertain times, it was not always easy to tell which of those two groups someone might fall into.

Archeth watched with drugged disinterest as the two senior courtiers who had taken it upon themselves to deliver her this far cast furtive glances down into the pool. Beneath the ripples of the water, it was impossible to see anything clearly. A wobbling patch of color might be an uncoiling octopus or simply a rock, a stripe through the water a tentacle or a frond of seaweed. The courtiers' expressions reflected every uncertainty as if they were in the grip of a bowel disorder, and the rippling, pallid light of the chamber conspired further to enhance the impression of illness on their faces.

The face of the slave who poled their coracle across the pool was by contrast as emotive as a stone. He knew he was needed to bring his Emperor back, and he was in any case a deaf mute, carefully chosen, maybe even specifically mutilated for the duty. He would neither hear nor give away any secrets.

They reached the raft and bumped gently against its intricately carved edge. The slave reached up for one of the canopy supports and steadied the coracle while the courtiers climbed out with evident relief. Archeth went last, nodding her thanks as she passed. It was automatic— Kiriath habits, hard to break even now. Like any piece of furniture, the slave ignored her. She grimaced and followed the courtiers through the maze of hanging veils within the canopy, into candlelit opulence and the imperial presence. She dropped to one knee.

"My lord."

His radiance Jhiral Khimran II, first son of Akal Khimran, called the Great, and now by royal succession Keepmaster of Yhelteth, Monitor of the Seven Holy Tribes, Prophet Advocate General, Commander-in-Chief of the Imperial Armed Services, Lord Protector of the High Seas, and Rightful Emperor of All Lands, did not immediately look up from the sprawled body of the young woman with whom he was toying.

"Archeth," he murmured, frowning at the swollen nipple he was rolling between his thumb and forefinger. "I've been waiting nearly two hours."

"Yes, my lord." She would not apologize.

"That's a long time for the most powerful man in the world, Archeth." Jhiral's voice was quiet and unreadable. He slid his free hand across the soft plain of the woman's stomach and into the shadow between her cocked thighs. "Too long, some of my advisers have been telling me. They feel you"—his hand moved deeper and the woman stiffened—"lack respect. Could that be true, I wonder?"

Most of Archeth's attention was on the woman. Like a lot of the harem, this one was a northerner, long-limbed and pale-skinned. Large, well-shaped breasts, not yet marked by motherhood. It was impossible to make out hair color or facial features—the black muslin wrappings of the harem veil covered her from the neck up—but Archeth was betting she was from the rather erroneously titled free mercantile states. The Yhelteth markets had seen a lot of this type recently, as the northern economies tottered and whole families were sold into slavery to pay their debts. From what Archeth heard on the trade-route grapevine, the free cities were fast becoming home to a whole new class of slavers; canny entrepreneurs who made their rapid fortunes acquiring the local flesh at knockdown prices and then selling it on southward to the Empire, where the centuries-old tradition of servitude made for a massive established market and a never-slaked hunger for exotic product. A woman like this one might easily increase her initial sale value by a factor of fifty on the long march south into imperial lands. With profit margins like these, and war debt in most cities still largely unpaid, it was hardly a surprise that the League had rediscovered its enthusiasm for the trade. Had neatly and cheerily rolled back nearly two centuries of abolition in order to facilitate the new flow of wealth.

The Emperor looked up from what he was doing.

"I require an answer, Archeth," he said mildly.

Archeth wondered briefly if Jhiral planned to hurt the woman while she watched, to punish the alleged lack of respect by proxy. A calmly rational rebuke for the intensely black woman before him, while the milk-white woman in his lap suffered the physical cruelty like some kind of inverted avatar. Archeth had seen it done before, a male slave lashed bloody for some trumped-up infraction and, against the backdrop of tortured cries and the wet slap of the lash, Jhiral remonstrating gently with one of his chiefs of staff. He was not and never would be the warrior his father had been, but Jhiral had inherited the same shrewd intelligence and with it a depth of court-bred sophistication that Akal Khimran, always in the saddle at one end of his empire or the other, had never troubled to develop.

Or maybe the woman was simply there to tantalize. Not much was secret in the imperial palace, and Archeth's preferences were widely whispered of, if not actually proven or known.

She cleared her throat and lowered her eyes deferentially.

"I was working, my lord. In the shipyards, in hope of some progress that might benefit the realm."

"Oh. That."

Something seemed to shift behind the emperor's eyes. He withdrew his hand from between the pale woman's thighs, sniffed delicately at his fingers like a gourmet chef, and then clapped her on the rump. She coiled out of his lap with what looked like schooled decorum, and crept out of the imperial presence on her knees.

"You may rise, Archeth. Sit near me. You two." He nodded at the courtiers, who might have been made of wood for all the life they showed. "Get out. Go back to . . . whatever valuable tasks it is you usually fill your time with. Oh, and—" Upturned hand, a regal gesture of magnanimity. "Well done. There'll be a little something in the new season's list for you, no doubt."

The courtiers bowed out. Archeth seated herself on a cushion at Jhiral's left hand and watched them go, torn between envy and scorn. As soon as the veils had fallen behind them, Jhiral leaned across and gripped Archeth's jaw tightly in his hand. His fingers were still damp, still scented with the white woman's cunt. He pulled Archeth to him and stared at her as if her skull were a curio picked up from some bazaar stall.

"Archeth. You really must get it through your head, the Kiriath have *gone.* They left you behind. You do accept that, don't you?"

So here was the punishment after all. Archeth stared away over Jhiral's shoulder and said nothing. The Emperor shook her jaw impatiently.

"Don't you, Archeth?"

"Yes." The word dropped out of her mouth like rotten meat.

"Grashgal refused to take you with him, and he said they wouldn't be coming back. *The veins of the earth will take us from here as once they brought us. Our time and tasks are done.*" Jhiral's voice was kindly, avuncular. "Wasn't that it, the An-Monal valediction? Something like that?"

Her throat lumped. "Yes, my lord."

"The Kiriath age is over, Archeth. This is the human age. You'd do well to remember that, and stick to your new allegiances. Eh?"

She swallowed hard. "Majesty."

"Good." He let go of her jaw and sat back. "What did you think of her?"

"My lord?"

"The girl. She's new. What do you think? Would you like me to send her to your bedchamber when I'm finished with her?"

Archeth forced down the scalding behind her eyes and managed a dry, self-possessed voice.

"My lord, I fail to see why I would want such a favor."

"Oh come, come, Archeth. Do you see an invigilator in here? We are alone—and worldly, you and I, soaked through with the storm of education and experience this world has given us." The Emperor gestured with his scented hand. "Let us at least enjoy the pleasures that derive. Laws graven in stone are all well and good for the common herd, but are we not above such paltry considerations?"

"It is not given to me to question the Revelation, my lord."

A swift borrowing of the Prophet's words, weighty with the echo, and solid coin as a result. Jhiral looked miffed.

"Clearly not, Archeth. *To none in the material realm is it given.* But consider, as even the Ashnal interpretations do, that there must surely be compensation for the burden of leadership, a loosening of ties intended for governance of those less able to govern themselves. Come, I shall send the girl to you as soon as you return."

"Return, my lord?"

"Oh yes. I'm sending you to Khangset. It seems there's been some disturbance there. Some kind of reavers. The reports are rather incoherent."

Archeth blinked. "Khangset is a garrisoned port, my lord."

"Just so. Which makes it all the more strange that anyone would be stupid enough to launch an attack on it. Ordinarily, I'd simply send a detachment of the Throne Eternal my father was so fond of, and then forget about it. However, the messenger who brought the news seemed to think there was some kind of sorcery at work." Jhiral saw the look Archeth gave him and shrugged. "Science or sorcery, the man's a peasant and he's not clear on these distinctions. I can't say I am myself, come to that. Anyway, you're my resident expert on these things. I've had a horse saddled for you, and you can have that detachment of the Throne Eternal I mentioned. With their very own and most holy invigilator attached, of course. Since you're feeling so pious these days, that should suit you down to the ground. They're all waiting in the west wing courtyard. Quite impatiently, by now, I should imagine."

"You wish me to leave immediately, my lord?"

"Yes, I would be immensely grateful if you would do that." Jhiral's voice dripped irony. "At a hard ride, I'd imagine you could reach Khangset by tomorrow afternoon, wouldn't you?"

"I am wholly yours to command, my lord." The ritual words tasted ashen in her mouth. With Akal, it had been different, the same words but never the same taste. "My body and my soul."

"Don't tempt me," said Jhiral drily. "Now, do you have any requirements above and beyond the men I've allocated?"

"The messenger. I'd like to question him before I leave."

"He's going back with you. Anything else?"

Archeth thought about it for as long as she dared. "If this was an attack by sea, I'd like to have Mahmal Shanta's opinion on any wreckage we find."

Jhiral grunted. "Well, he'll be delighted, I'm sure. I don't think he's been off that housebarge of his since the Ynval regatta, and even that was only to inspect the new navy launches. He certainly hasn't been on a horse this year."

"He is the foremost naval engineering authority in the Empire, my lord."

"Don't lecture your Emperor, Archeth. It's not good for your health." The tone of the veiled threat was playful, but Archeth knew she'd struck a nerve. "I'm well aware of the court appointments my dear father made, and why he made them. Very well, I'll send to the cantankerous old bastard, and he can meet you at the city gates. You'll be good company for each other, I imagine."

"Thank you, my lord."

"Yes." Jhiral rubbed at his chin and caught the scent of the slave girl on his fingers again. His nostrils flared slightly, and he made a dismissive gesture with the hand. "Well, you'd better go then, hadn't you?"

Archeth got to her feet, rituals at the ready.

"I speed to do your will."

"Oh, please, Archeth. Just get out of my sight, will you."

On the way out, she passed the pale-skinned slave girl where she sat between the inner and outer curtains, awaiting the imperial summons. She'd lifted her veil, and Archeth saw that she was, perhaps unsurprisingly, quite beautiful. Their eyes met for a brief moment, and then the girl looked quickly away. A scarlet flush spread down over her face and breasts.

From within came the sound of Jhiral clearing his throat.

The girl scrambled back to her hands and knees and crawled toward the gap in the curtains. Her breasts swung heavily with the motion. Archeth placed one hand on her shoulder, felt a flinch go through the smooth flesh where she touched. The girl looked up.

"Your veil," Archeth mouthed, in Naomic.

Parted lips, a soft, panicked sound. The girl began to tremble visibly.

Archeth gestured calm with both hands, crouched beside her and settled the veil carefully in place, reached up inside the muslin to tuck away a loose fall of candlewax-colored hair.

On the other side of the inner curtains, Jhiral cleared his throat again, louder. The girl lowered her head and began once more to crawl, under the curtain and into his imperial radiance's presence. Archeth watched her go, lips pressed tight to cover for the gritted teeth beneath. Her nostrils flared, and the breath that came through them was audible. For a single insane moment, she stood there and strained toward the inner curtain.

Get the fuck out of here, Archidi. Right now.

Just another slave, that's all. It flitted through her head, faster than she could catch at it. She wasn't sure whom the thought was referring to.

She turned and left.

Went obediently about her Emperor's business.

CHAPTER 5

Where the broad westward flow of the River Trel split and spread in tributaries, and wore itself into the soft cushioned loam of the Naom coastal plain like the lines etched across a man's palm, where the sea spent its force across acres of mudflat and marsh and could not easily threaten man-made structure, one of Grace-of-Heaven Milacar's distant ancestors had once spotted a less-than-obvious strategic truth— to wit, that a city surrounded by such a maze of mingled land and water would in effect be a kind of fortress. Well, being by nature a modest as well as an inventive man, this root patriarch of the Milacar line not only went ahead and founded an ingenious settlement you could only reach with local guides through the marsh; he also renounced the right to name the city after himself and called it instead Trel-a-lahayn, from the old Myrlic *lahaynir*—blessed refuge. Out of this vision, and the eventual laziness of men's tongues, Trelayne was born. And over time, as stone re-

placed wood, and cobbles covered mud streets, as blocks and then towers rose gracefully over the plain to become the city we all know and
love, as the lights, the very lights of that subtle fortress came to be visible to caravanserai and ship captains a full day and night before they
reached it, so the origins of the city were lost, and the clan name *Milacar,* sadly, came to be valued no more than any other . . .

At least, that was Grace-of-Heaven's end of the tale, backed up now
as always with consistent narrative passion if not actual evidence. There
weren't many who would have had the nerve to call him a liar to his face,
far less interrupt him with the accusation at his own dinner table.

Ringil stood in the brocade-hung entryway and grinned.

"Not this horseshit again," he drawled loudly. "Haven't you got any
new stories, Grace?"

Conversation drained out of the candlelit dining chamber like the
last of the sand from an hourglass. Bandlight seeped coldly into the
quiet from window drapes along the far wall. Gazes flickered about, on
and off the newcomer, in among the gathered company. Some at the
broad oval table looked around, arms in richly tailored cloth braced on
chair backs—squeak of shifting chair legs and the soft brush of heavy
robes in motion across the floor. Well-fed and contented faces turned,
some of them still chewing their last mouthful, momentarily robbed of
their self-assurance. Mouths open, eyes wide. The machete boy
crouched at Milacar's right hip blinked, and his hand tightened on the
hilt of the ugly eighteen-inch chopping blade at his belt.

Ringil caught the boy's eye. Held it a moment, no longer grinning.

Milacar made a tiny clucking sound, tongue behind his top teeth. It
sounded like a kiss. The boy let go of the machete hilt.

"Hello, Gil. I heard you were back."

"You heard right, then." Ringil switched his gaze from boy to master.
"Seems you're as well informed as ever."

Milacar—always rather less svelte than he would probably have liked,
rather less tall than his claim to ancestral Naom blood suggested he
should be. But if these elements had not changed, then neither had the
stocky, muscular energy that smoked off him even when he sat, the sense
that it wouldn't take much to have him come up out of the chair, big

cabled arms falling to a street fighter's guard, fists rolled up and ready to beat the unceremonious shit out of anyone who was asking for it.

For now, he settled for a pained frown, and rubbed at his chin with the pads of his index and middle fingers. His eyes creased and crinkled with a smile that stayed just off his lips. Deep, gorgeous blue, like the sunstruck ocean off the headland at Lanatray, dancing alive in the light from the candles. He held Ringil's look and his mouth moved, something inaudible, something for Ringil alone.

The moment broke.

Milacar's doorman, whom Ringil had left encumbered and struggling to hang his cloak and the Ravensfriend, arrived red-faced and cringing in his wake. He wasn't a young man and he was puffed from sprinting up the stairs and down the corridor after his escaped charge.

"Uhm, his worthiness Master Ringil of Eskiath Fields, licensed knight graduate of Trelayne and—"

"Yes, yes, Quon, thank you," Milacar said acidly. "Master Ringil has already announced himself. You may go."

"Yes, your honor." The doorman darted a poisonous glance at Ringil. "Thank you, your honor."

"Oh, and Quon. Try to keep up with the uninvited arrivals, if you could. You never know, the next one might be an assassin."

"Yes, your honor. I'm truly sorry, your honor. It won't happen agai—"

Milacar waved him out. Quon shut up and withdrew, bowing and wringing his hands. Ringil crushed out a quiver of sympathy for the man, stepped on it like a spilled pipe ember. No time for that now. He advanced into the room. The machete boy watched him with glittering eyes.

"You're not an assassin, are you, Gil?"

"Not tonight."

"Good. Because you seem to have left that big sword of yours behind somewhere." Milacar paused delicately. "If, of course, you still have it. That big sword of yours."

Ringil reached the table at a point roughly opposite Grace-of-Heaven.

"Yeah, still got it." He grinned, made a leg for his host. "Still as big as ever."

A couple of outraged gasps from the assembled company. He looked around at the faces.

"I'm sorry, I'm forgetting my manners. Good evening, gentlemen. Ladies." Though there were, technically, none of the latter in the room. Every female present had been paid. He surveyed the heaped table, matched gazes with one of the whores at random, spoke specifically to her.

"So what's good, my lady?"

Shocked, gently rocking quiet. The whore opened her purple-painted mouth in disbelief, gaped back at him. Ringil smiled patiently. She looked hopelessly around for guidance from one or another of her outraged clients.

"It's all good, Gil." If the room bristled at Ringil's subtle insult in addressing a prostitute ahead of the gathered worthies, Milacar at least was unmoved. "That's why I pay for it. But why don't you try the cougar heart, there in the yellow bowl. That's especially good. A Yhelteth marinade. I don't imagine you'll have tasted much of that sort of thing in recent years, out there in the sticks."

"No, that's right. Strictly mutton and wolf, down among the peasants." Ringil leaned in and scooped a chunk of meat from the bowl. His fingers dripped sauce back across the table in a line. He bit in, chewed for a while, and nodded. "That's pretty good for a bordello spread."

More gasps. At his elbow, someone shot to his feet. Bearded face, not much older than forty, and not as overfed as others around the table. Burly beneath the purple-and-gold upriver couture, some muscle on that frame by the look of it. A hand clapped to a court rapier that had not been checked at the door. Ringil spotted a signet ring with the marsh daisy emblem.

"This is an outrage! You will not insult this company with impunity, Eskiath. I demand—"

"I'd rather you didn't call me that," Ringil told him, still chewing. "*Master Ringil* will do fine."

"You, sir, need a lesson in—"

"Sit *down*."

Ringil's voice barely rose, but the flicker of his look was a lash. He locked gazes with his challenger, and the other man flinched. It was the same threat he'd offered the machete boy, given voice this time in case the recipient was drunk or just hadn't ever stood close enough to a real fight to read Ringil's look for what it promised.

The burly man sat.

"Perhaps you should sit down, too, Gil," Grace-of-Heaven suggested mildly. "We don't eat standing up in the Glades. It's considered rude."

Ringil licked his fingers clean.

"Yeah, I know." He looked elaborately around the table. "Anyone care to give up their seat?"

Milacar nodded at the whore nearest to him, one seated guest away from where he held court in the big chair. The woman got to her feet with well-schooled alacrity, and without a word. She backed gracefully off to one of the curtained alcove windows and stood there motionless, hands gathered demurely at one hip, posed slightly to display her muslin-shrouded form for the rest of the room.

Ringil moved around the table to the vacated seat, inclined his head in the woman's direction, and lowered himself onto her chair. The velvet plush was warm from her arse, an unwelcome intimacy that seeped up through his breeches. The diners on either side of him looked studiously elsewhere. He held down an urge to shift in his seat.

You lay frozen in your own piss for six hours at Rajal Beach and played dead while the Scaled Folk nosed up and down the breakwaters with their reptile peons looking for survivors. You can sit still in a whore's heat for half an hour. You can make polite Glades conversation here with the great and gracious of Trelayne.

Grace-of-Heaven Milacar cleared his throat, lifted a goblet.

"A toast, then. To one of our city's most heroic sons, returned home and not before time."

There was a pause, then a sort of grumbling tide of response around the table. The faces all buried themselves hurriedly in their drinks. It was, Ringil thought, a little like watching pigs at a trough. They finished the toast and Milacar leaned across his nearest guest to get his face less than a foot from Ringil's. His breath was sweet with the wine.

"So now the theatrics are out of the way," he said urbanely, "perhaps you'd like to tell me what you're doing here, Gil."

The pale eyes were crinkled at the corners, amused despite themselves. Between the trimmed mustache and goatee, the long, mobile lips were downcurved with humor, taut with anticipatory lust, tips of the teeth just showing. Ringil remembered the look with a jolt under his heart.

Milacar had gone bald, or nearly so, just like he'd said would happen. And he'd shaved it all down to a stubble, just like he'd always said he would.

"Came to see you, Grace," he said, and it was almost the whole truth.

"CAME TO SEE ME, HUH?" MILACAR MURMURED IT LATER, AS THEY LAY in the big silk-sheeted bed upstairs, spent and stained and curled together, pillowed on each other's thighs. He raised himself slightly, grabbed Ringil's hair at the back of his neck, and dragged his face, mock-tough, back toward his flaccid crotch. "The fuck you did. You're a lying sack of highborn shit, Gil, same as you ever were." He twisted his fingers, tugging the small hairs, hurtfully. "Same as when you first came to me fifteen fucking years ago, Eskiath youth."

"Sixteen years." Ringil beat the grip on his nape, tangled fingers with Grace, and brought the back of the other man's hand around to his lips. He kissed it. "I was fifteen, remember. Sixteen fucking years ago, and don't call me that."

"What, *youth*?"

"Eskiath. You know I don't like it."

Milacar pulled his hand free and propped himself back a little on his elbows, looking down at the younger man who lay coiled across him. "It's your mother's name as well."

"She married it." Ringil stayed with his face bedded in the damp warmth of Milacar's crotch, staring off into the gloom near the bedchamber door. "Her choice. I didn't get that much."

"I'm not convinced she had much choice herself, Gil. She was, what, twelve when they gave her to Gingren?"

"Thirteen."

Small quiet. The same muffled bandlight from the dining chamber spilled in here unrestrained, an icy flood of it across the carpeted floor from the bedroom's broad river-facing balcony. The casements were back, the drapes stirred like languid ghosts, and a cool autumn breeze blew in past them, not yet the chill and bite there was in the upland air at Gallows Water, but getting that way. Winter would find him here as well. Ringil shifted, skin caressed to goose bumps, small hairs on his arms pulled erect. He breathed in Grace's acrid, smoky scent and it carried him back a decade and a half like a drug. Riotous wine and flandrijn nights at Milacar's house on Replete Cargo Street in the warehouse district; carefully steeping himself in the decadence of it all, thrilling at the subtle compulsion of doing Grace-of-Heaven's will, whether in bed or out. Down to the docks for collections with Milacar's thuggish wharf soldiers, sneaking the streets of the Glades and upriver for deliveries; occasionally chased by the Watch when someone got caught and squealed, the odd scuffle in a darkened alley or a safe house, the odd few moments of forced swordplay or a knifing somewhere, but all of it, the fights included, too highly colored, too much fucking *fun* at the time to really seem like the danger it was.

"So tell me why you're really here," Grace said gently.

Ringil rolled over, rested his head and neck on the other man's belly. The muscle was still there, firm beneath a modest layer of middle-aged spread. It barely quivered when it took the weight of his sweat-soaked head. Ringil gazed up idly at the painted scenes of debauchery on Milacar's ceiling. Two stable lads and a serving wench doing something improbable with a centaur. Ringil blew a dispirited breath up at them in their perfect little pastoral world.

"Got to help out the family," he said drearily. "Got to find someone. Cousin of mine, got herself into some trouble."

"And you think I've started moving in the same circles as the Eskiath clan." The belly Ringil was pillowed on juddered with Milacar's laughter. "Gil, you have seriously overestimated my place in the scheme of things these days. I'm a criminal, remember."

"Yeah, I noticed how you were sticking to your roots. Big fuck-off house in the Glades, dinner with the Marsh Brotherhood and associated worthies."

"I still keep the place over on Replete Cargo, if it makes you feel any better. And in case you've forgotten, I am from a Brotherhood family." There was a slight edge in Grace-of-Heaven's voice now. "My father was a pathfinder captain before the war."

"Yeah, and your great-great, great-great, great-and-so-on grandfather founded the whole fucking city of Trel-a-lahayn. I heard it coming in, Grace. And the truth is still, fifteen years ago you wouldn't have given civil house room to that prick with the dueling cutlery on his hip tonight. And you wouldn't have been living upriver like this, either."

He felt the stomach muscles beneath his head tense a little.

"Do I disappoint you?" Milacar asked him softly.

Ringil went on staring up at the ceiling. He shrugged. "It all turned to shit after '55, we all had to ride it out somehow. Why should you be any different?"

"You're too kind."

"Yeah." Ringil hauled himself up into a sitting position, swiveled a little to face Grace-of-Heaven's sprawl. He got cross-legged, put his hands together in his lap. Shook his hair back off his face. "So. You want to help me find this cousin of mine?"

Milacar made a no-big-deal face. "Sure. What kind of trouble she in?"

"The chained-up kind. She went to the auction blocks at Etterkal about four weeks ago as far as I can work out."

"Etterkal?" The no-big-deal expression slid right off Milacar's face. "Was she sold legally?"

"Yeah, payment for a bad debt. Chancellery clearinghouse auction, the Salt Warren buyers took a shine to her, chain-ganged her out there the same day apparently. But the paperwork's scrambled, or lost, or I just didn't bribe the right officials. Got this charcoal sketch I'm showing around that no one wants to recognize, and I can't get anyone to talk to me about the Etterkal end. And I'm getting tired of being polite."

"Yes, I did notice that." Grace of Heaven shook his head bemusedly. "How the blue fuck did a daughter of clan Eskiath end up getting as far as the Warren anyway?"

"Well, she's not actually an Eskiath. Like I said, she's a cousin. Family name's Herlirig."

"Oho. Marsh blood, then."

"Yeah, and she married in the wrong direction, too, from an Eskiath point of view." Ringil heard the angry disgust trickling into his voice, but he couldn't be bothered to do anything about it. "To a merchant. Clan Eskiath didn't know what was going on at the time, but really, I don't think they'd have lifted a finger to stop it even if they had."

"Hmm." Milacar looked at his hands. "Etterkal."

"That's right. Your old pals Snarl and Findrich, among others."

"Hmm."

Ringil cocked his head. "You got a problem with this all of a sudden?"

More quiet. Somewhere in the lower levels of the house, someone was pouring water into a large vessel. Milacar seemed to be listening to it.

"Grace?"

Grace-of-Heaven met his eye, flexed a suddenly hesitant smile. It wasn't a look Ringil recognized.

"Lot of things have changed since you went away, Gil."

"Yeah, tell me about it."

"That includes Etterkal. Salt Warren's a whole different neighborhood these days, you wouldn't recognize the place since Liberalization. I mean, everyone knew slaving was going to take off, it was obvious. Poppy used to talk about it all the time, Findrich, too, when you could get him to talk at all." The words coming out of Milacar's mouth seemed oddly hurried now, as if he was scared he'd be interrupted. "But you wouldn't believe how big it's grown, Gil. I mean, *really* big money. Bigger than flandrijn or krinzanz ever was."

"You sound jealous."

The smile flickered back to life a moment, then guttered out. "That kind of money buys protection, Gil. You can't just wander into Etterkal and thug it like we used to when it was all whore masters and street."

"Now, there you go, disappointing me all over again." Ringil kept his tone light, mask to a creeping disquiet. "Time was, there wasn't a street anywhere in Trelayne you wouldn't walk down."

"Yes, well, as I said, things have changed."

"That time they tried to keep us out of the Glades balloon regatta. *My people built this fucking city, they aren't going to keep me penned up in the dreg end of it with their fucking silk-slash uniformed bully boys.*" The levity sliding out of his tone now as he echoed the Milacar of then-ago. "Remember that?"

"Look—"

"Of course, now you *live* in the Glades."

"Gil, I told you—"

"Things have changed, yeah. Heard you the first time."

And now he couldn't cloak it any longer, the leaking sense of loss, *more* fucking loss, soaking through into the same old general, swirling sense of betrayal, years upon pissed-away years of it, made bitter and particular on his tongue now, as if Grace-of-Heaven had come wormwood into his mouth in those final clenched, pulsing seconds. Pleasure into loss, lust into regret, and there, suddenly, the same sick spiral of fucked-up guilt they sold down at the temples and all through the po-faced schooling and lineage values and Gingren's lectures and the new-recruit rituals of bullying and sterile manhood at the academy and *every fucking thing* ever lied and pontificated about by men in robes or uniform and—

He climbed off the bed as if there were scorpions in the sheets. Last shreds of afterglow smoking away. He stared down at Milacar, and the other man's scent on him was suddenly just something he wanted to wash off.

"I'm going home," he said drably.

He cast about for his clothes on the floor.

"They've got a dwenda, Gil."

Gathering up breeches, shirt, crumpled hose. "Sure they have."

Milacar watched him for a moment, and then, abruptly, he was off the bed and on him like a Yhelteth war cat. Grappling hands, body weight heaving for a tumble, pressed in, wrestler close. Raging echo of the flesh-to-flesh dance they'd already had on the bed. Grace-of-Heaven's acrid scent and grunting street fighter's strength.

Another time, it might have lasted. But the anger was still hard in Ringil's head, the frustration itching through his muscles, siren whisper of reflexes blackened and edged in the war years. He broke Milacar's hold with a savagery he'd forgotten he owned, threw a Yhelteth empty-hand technique that put the other man on the floor in tangled limbs. He landed on him with all his weight. Milacar's breath whooshed out, his furious grunting collapsed. Ringil fetched up with one thumb hooked into Grace-of-Heaven's mouth and the other poised an inch off his left eyeball.

"Don't you pull that rough-trade shit on me," he hissed. "I'm not one of your fucking machete boys, I'll kill you."

Milacar choked and floundered. "*Fuck* you, I'm trying to help. Listen to me, *they've got a dwenda in Etterkal.*"

Locked gazes. The seconds stretched.

"A dwenda?"

Milacar's eyes said *yes,* said he at least believed it was true.

"A fucking *Aldrain,* you're telling me?" Ringil let Grace-of-Heaven free of the thumb hook. "An honest-to-Hoiran member of the Vanishing Folk, right here in Trelayne?"

"Yes. That's what I'm telling you."

Ringil got off him. "You're full of shit."

"Thank you."

"Well, it's either that or you've been smoking too much of your own supply."

"I know what I've seen, Gil."

"They're called the Vanishing Folk for a *reason,* Grace. They're *gone.* Even the Kiriath don't remember them outside of legends."

"Yes." Milacar picked himself up. "And before the war, no one believed in dragons, either."

"It's not the same thing."

"Well, then you explain it to me." Grace-of-Heaven stomped across the bedchamber to where a row of gorgeous Empire-styled kimonos hung from a rack.

"Explain what? That some albino scam artist with a lot of eye makeup has got you all making wards and running for cover like a bunch of Majak herdsmen when the thunder rolls?"

"No." Milacar shouldered himself brusquely into plum-colored silk, tugged and knotted the sash at his waist. "Explain to me how the Marsh Brotherhood sent three of their best spies into Etterkal, men with a lifetime of experience and faces no one but their lodge master could match with their trade, and all that came back out, a week later, were their heads."

Ringil gestured. "So this albino motherfuck's got better sources than you, and he's handy with a blade."

"You misunderstand me, Gil." Grace-of-Heaven smeared on the uncertain smile again. "I didn't say these men were dead. I said all that came back were their heads. Each one still living, grafted at the neck to a seven-inch tree stump."

Ringil stared at him.

"Yeah, that's right. Explain *that* to me."

"You saw this?"

A taut nod. "At a lodge meeting. They brought one of the heads in. Put the roots in a bowl of water and about two minutes after that the fucking thing opens its eyes and recognizes the lodge master. You could see by the expression on its face. It's opening its mouth, trying to talk, but there's no throat, no vocal cords, so all you can hear is this clicking sound and the lips moving, the tongue coming out, and then it starts fucking weeping, tears rolling down its face." Milacar swallowed visibly. "About five minutes of that, they take the thing out of the water and it stops. The tears stop first, like they're drying up, and then the whole head just stops moving, slows down to nothing like an old man dying in bed. Only it wasn't fucking dead. Soon as you put it back in the water . . ." He made a helpless motion with his hand. "Back again, same thing."

Ringil stood, naked, and the bandlight through the opened balcony windows felt suddenly colder. He turned to look at the night outside, as if something were calling to him from beyond the casements.

"You got any krin?" he asked quietly.

Milacar nodded across the room at his dressing table. "Sure. Top left drawer there, couple of twigs already made up. Help yourself."

Ringil crossed to the dresser and opened the drawer. Three yellowing leaf cylinders rolled about in the bottom of the little wooden compartment. He lifted one out, went to the lamp at the bedside, and bent to light up from the wick. The krinzanz flakes inside the cylinder crackled as the flame caught; the acid odor prickled at his nostrils. He drew hard, pulled the old familiar taste down into his lungs. Scorching bite, chill moving outward. The krin came on like an icy fire in his head. He looked back out to the balcony, sighed and walked out there, still naked, trailing smoke.

After a couple of moments, Grace-of-Heaven went after him.

Outside, it was a rooftop view across the Glades to the water. The lights of sister mansions to Milacar's place glimmered amid the trees in their gardens and the lamp-dotted, twisting streets between, streets that centuries ago had been footpaths through the marsh. The estuary curved in from the west, the old dock buildings on the other bank swept away now to make space for ornamental gardens and expensive thanksgiving shrines to the gods of Naom.

Ringil leaned on the balcony balustrade, held back a sneer, and struggled to be honest with himself about the changes. There'd been money in the Glades from the very beginning. But in the old days it was a little less smug, it was clan homes with views to the wealth that had built them unloading across the river. Now, with the war and the reconstruction, the docks had moved downstream and out of sight, and the only structures that looked back across the water at the Glades mansions were the shrines, ponderous stone echoes of the clans' renewed piety and faith in their own worthiness to rule.

Ringil plumed acrid smoke at it all. Sensed without looking around that Milacar had followed him out onto the balcony.

"That ceiling's going to get you arrested, Grace," he said distantly.

"Not in this part of town it's not." Milacar joined him at the balustrade, breathed in the Glades night air like perfume. "The Committee doesn't do house calls around here. You should know that."

"So some things haven't changed, then."

"No. The salients remain."

"Yeah, saw the cages coming in." A sudden, chilly recollection that he didn't need, one he had in fact thought was safely buried until day before yesterday when his mother's carriage rattled across the causeway bridge at the eastern gate. "Is Kaad still running things up at the Chancellery?"

"That aspect of things, yes. And looking younger on it every day. Have you ever noticed that? How power seems to nourish some men and suck others dry? Well, Murmin Kaad is definitely in the former camp."

In the Hearings Chamber, they uncuff and pinion Jelim, haul him twisting bodily from the chair. He's panting with disbelief, coughing up deep, gabbled screams of denial at the sentence passed, a skein of pleadings that puts gooseflesh on skin among the watchers in the gallery, brings sweat to palms and drives shard-like needles of chill deep under the flesh of warmly clothed arms and legs.

Between Gingren and Ishil, Ringil sits transfixed.

And as the condemned boy's eyes flare and wallow like those of a panicking horse, as his gaze claws along the faces of the assembled worthies above him as if in search of some fairy-tale salvation that might somehow have fought its way in here, suddenly he sees Ringil instead. Their eyes meet and Ringil feels it as if he's been stabbed. Against all probability, Jelim flails an arm free and jabs upward in accusation, and screams: It was him, please, take him, I didn't mean it, it was him, IT WAS HIM, TAKE HIM, IT WAS HIM, HIM, NOT ME . . .

And they drag him out that way, on a dreadful, trailing shriek that everyone assembled knows is only the beginning, the very least of the raptured agonies he'll vent in the cage tomorrow.

Below in the chamber, on the raised dais of the justices, Murmin Kaad, until now watching the proceedings with impassive calm, looks up and meets Ringil's gaze as well.

And smiles.

"Motherfucker." A tremor in the matter-of-fact tone he was trying for. He drew on the twig for sustenance. "Should have had him killed back in '53 when I had the chance."

He glanced sideways, caught the way Grace-of-Heaven was looking at him.

"What?"

"Oh beautiful youth," Milacar said gently. "Do you really think it would have been that easy?"

"Why not? It was chaos that summer, the whole place was packed with soldiery and loose blades. Who would have known?"

"Gil, they just would have replaced him with someone else. Maybe someone worse."

"Worse? Fucking *worse*?"

Ringil thought about the cages, how in the end he'd been unable to look out of the carriage window at them as they passed. The scrutiny in Ishil's face as he turned back to the interior of the carriage, the impossibility of meeting her eyes. The warm flush of gratitude he felt that the rumble and rattle of the carriage's passage drowned out whatever other noises might otherwise have reached his ears. He was wrong, he knew then. His time away from the city, time buried in the shadow of Gallows Gap and its memories, had not kept him hardened as he'd hoped. Instead, it had left him as soft and unready as he'd ever been, as the belly he'd grown.

At his side, Milacar sighed. "The Committee for Public Morals is not dependent on Kaad for its venom, nor was it ever. There's a general hate in the hearts of men. You went to war, Gil, you should know that better than anyone. It's like the heat of the sun. Men like Kaad are just the focal figures, like lenses to gather the sun's rays on kindling. You can smash a lens, but that won't put out the sun."

"No. Makes it a lot harder to start the next fire, though."

"For a little while, yes. Until the next lens, or the next hard summer, and then the fires begin again."

"Getting a bit fucking fatalistic in your old age, aren't you?" Ringil nodded out over the mansion lights. "Or does that just come with the move upriver?"

"No, it comes with living long enough to appreciate the value of the time you've got left. Long enough to recognize the fallacy of a crusade when you're called to one. Hoiran's teeth, Gil, you're the last person I should need to be telling this to. Have you forgotten what they did with your victory?"

Ringil smiled, felt how it leaked across his face like spilled blood. Reflex, tightening up against the old pain.

"This isn't a crusade, Grace. It's just some scum-fuck slavers who've gone off with the wrong girl. All I need is a list of names, likely brokers in Etterkal I can lean on until something gives."

"And the dwenda?" Milacar's voice jabbed angrily. "The sorcery?"

"I've seen sorcery before. It never stopped me killing anything that got in my way."

"You haven't seen this."

"Well, that's what keeps life interesting, isn't it. New experience." Ringil drew hard on the krinzanz twig. Glow from the flaring ember lit the planes of his face and put glitter into his eyes. He let the smoke up, glanced across at Grace-of-Heaven again. "Anyway, have *you* seen this creature?"

Milacar swallowed. "No. I haven't, personally. They say he keeps to himself, even within the Warren. But there are those who have had audience with him, yes."

"Or so they claim."

"These are men whose word I trust."

"And what do these trustworthy men have to say about our Aldrain friend? That his eyes are black pits? That his ears are those of a beast? That he flickers with lightning as he walks?"

"No. What they say is . . ." Another hesitation. Milacar's voice had grown quiet. "He's beautiful, Gil. That's what they say. That he's beautiful beyond words."

For just a second, a tiny chill ran along Ringil's spine. He put it away, shrugged to shake it off. He pitched the stub of his krinzanz twig away into the nighttime garden below and stared after the ember.

"Well, I've seen beauty, too," he said somberly. "And that never stopped me killing anything that got in my way, either."

CHAPTER 6

B y the time they made camp, a clouded darkness held the sky above the steppe.

The news of the runner attack had reached the tents ahead of them; the night herdsmen who came out to relieve them included a cousin of Runi's who rode back at speed to tell his other kin. Egar followed on foot, leading his horse with Runi's body slung over it while Klarn rode at a respectful distance, watchful as a raven. When they reached the Skaranak encampment, there were torches burning everywhere and practically the whole clan gathered with Runi's family at their head. Even Poltar was there, the gaunt, shaven-skulled shaman and his acolytes standing aloof from the throng, the implements of consecration ready in their hands. There had been a subdued muttering back and forth among those waiting, but it died away to nothing when they saw the blood-soaked form of their clanmaster leading the horse into the glow of the torches.

The steppe ghouls had died hard. Their marks were on the Dragonbane from head to foot.

Egar lowered his eyes so he would not have to look at Narma and Jural. Neither Runi's mother nor father had wanted their son to ride herd so early, but in council Egar would not forbid it since the boy was of age. Runi had promise, he was an enthusiastic boy, and he'd had a way with the animals since he could walk.

Added to which, anything was preferable to having him slouch around with the other sons of buffalo-wealthy Skaranak, swilling rice wine and yelling unimaginative abuse at passing women. Right, Clanmaster? Better that young Runi pack that in and start making something of himself.

And now Runi was torn apart and already cooling as Egar lifted his roughly bound body from the horse's back. The Dragonbane shifted his burden, bore it up in both arms, wincing as the weight pressed back against slash wounds on chest and upper arms. He came forward one numb step at a time to present Runi to his parents.

Narma broke down crying and fell on her son's exposed face, so it was hard for Egar to keep the body in his arms. He tried not to stagger. Jural turned his face away, hid his tears in the darkness so he would not be shamed before the clan.

It was at times like this that the Dragonbane wished heartily he'd never fucking returned from the south or assumed the mantle of clanmaster.

"He died a warrior's death."

He intoned the ritual words, cursing inwardly at the idiocy of it all. *A sixteen-year-old boy, for fuck's sake.* If he'd had the time to become a warrior, maybe he'd have lived through the raid. "He will be honored with the name of clan defender forever in our hearts." He hesitated and mumbled, almost inaudibly, "I'm sorry, Narma."

Her wailing went up a notch. It was that moment that Poltar the shaman chose to assert his own formalized role.

"Woman, be still. Will the Dwellers look with favor on a warrior so beset with female noisemaking? Even now he looks down on you from the Sky Road to his forefathers, and is shamed before them by this hubbub. Get away and light candles for him, as a woman should."

What happened next was by no means clear in anybody's mind

afterward, least of all Egar's own. Narma, it seemed, was not going to relinquish her hold on Runi's corpse. Poltar stepped closer and tried to persuade her by main force. There was a brief scuffle, an escalation of weeping, and the flat cracking sound of a palm against a face. Runi tumbled from Egar's arms and hit the earth with a dull thud, headfirst. Narma started screaming at the shaman and Poltar hit her open-handed. She collapsed over her son like a badly tied bundle of firewood. Egar pivoted, guilt and undispelled rage surging for release, and decked the shaman with every ounce of strength left in his right arm. Poltar flew fully five feet backward from the end of the Dragonbane's fist and hit the ground on his back.

There was a breath-choked pause while everyone caught up.

One of the acolytes took a step toward Egar and then thought better of it as he saw the look on the Dragonbane's bloodied face. The other three hurried to Poltar's side and helped him to sit up. The crowd murmured uneasily, a word slithering on the edge of being pronounced. The shaman spat blood and said it for them.

"Sacrilege!"

"Oh, give it a rest." Egar, drawling but a lot less unconcerned than he made out. Because Poltar was about to be a fucking problem.

If there was one force on the steppes that the Majak acknowledged equal to their own general toughness, it was the shifty, lightning-blast power of the Sky Dwellers. The Dwellers were not like the southerners' God in His meticulous, archive-keeping imperialism. They were jealous, fickle, and unpredictably violent, and had no time for such clerkish, inclusive ways—they sent storms or plagues at random to remind the Majak of their place in the scheme of things, set men against each other for amusement, and then played dice with one another to decide who would live or die. In short, they acted not unlike the leisured and powerful among men, and the shaman was their only empowered messenger under the sky. To offend the shaman was to offend the Dwellers, and those who offended, it was understood, would sooner or later pay a heavy price.

Now the oldest acolyte took it up, brandishing his summoning stick at the assembled Skaranak.

"Sacrilege! Sacrilege has been done! Who will atone?"

"You'll fucking atone if you don't shut up." Egar strode toward the speaker, determined to nip this in the bud. The acolyte stood his ground, eyes wide with fear and insane faith.

"Urann the Gray will—"

Egar grabbed him by the throat. "I said *shut up*. Where was Urann the Gray when I needed him out there? Where was Urann when this boy needed his help?" He cast a glance around at the frightened faces in the torchlight, and for the first time in his life he felt an overpowering contempt for his own people. His voice rang louder. 'Where is fucking Urann every time we need him, heh? Where was he, Garath, when the runners took your brother? When the wolves stole your daughter from her cradle, Inmath? Where was he when the coughing fever came and the smoke from the funeral pyres rose on every horizon from here to Ishlin-ichan. *Where was that gray motherfucker when my father died?*"

Then Poltar was back on his feet and facing him.

"You speak as a child," he said in a quiet, deadly voice that nonetheless carried to the whole watching crowd. Consummately staged—it was the man's profession after all. "Your time in the south has corrupted you to our ways, and now you'd bring disaster on the Skaranak with your sacrilege. You are no longer fit to govern as clanmaster. The Grey One speaks it with the death of this boy."

The crowd murmured, but it was a confused sound. There were plenty of them who had little time for Poltar and the leisurely lifestyle his status brought him. Egar wasn't the only cynic on the steppe, nor the only Skaranak warrior to have gone south and come back with a wider picture of how the world worked. Three or four of the associate herd owners had themselves been mercenary captains for Yhelteth, and one of them, Marnak, had fought beside the Dragonbane at Gallows Gap. He was older than Egar by at least a decade, but still whiplash-swift when it was needed, and his loyalty was forged deeper than anything the shaman could call on. Egar spotted his grim, leathered face there in the torchlight, watchful and ready to skin steel. Marnak caught his clanmaster's look and nodded, just once. Egar felt gratitude sting at his eyes.

But there were others.

The weak and the stupid, in their dozens, huddled now in among their fellows, afraid of the cold night beyond the firelight and anything in it. Afraid almost as much of anything new that might unseat a vision hemmed in by vast empty skies and the unchanging steppe horizon. Egar saw their faces, knew them for the ones who looked away as he met their eyes.

And behind these faces, feeding and playing on these fears, stood the greedy and the entrenched, whose hatred of change welled up from the more prosaic concern that it might upset the old order, and so their own privileged position within the clan. Those for whom the Dragonbane's return as a hero had been hailed not with joy but with cool mistrust and a sharp look to herd ownership and hierarchy. Those who—it shamed him to admit the fact—included a couple of his own brothers at least.

For all these people, Poltar the shaman and his stubborn beliefs represented everything that the Majak stood for, and everything that might be lost if the balance shifted. They would not stand with Egar; at best they might only stand by. And others might well do something worse.

Clouds shredded across the band as if frayed by its edge; silver light spilled on the plain to the south. Egar cast a seasoned commander's eye across the simmering uncertainty he saw in his people, and called it.

"If Urann the Gray has something to say to me," he said loudly, "he can come here and say it personally. He doesn't need a broken-down buzzard too idle to earn his meat like a man to speak for him. Here I am, Poltar." He held his arms wide. "Call him. Call on Urann. If I have committed sacrilege, let him open the sky and strike me down here and now. And if he doesn't, well, then I guess we'll know that you do not have his ear, won't we?"

There were gusts of indrawn breath, but it was the sound of spectators at street circus, not outraged faith. And the shaman was glaring poisonously at him, but he didn't open his mouth. Egar masked a savage joy.

Got you, you motherfucker!

Poltar was trapped. He knew as well as Egar that the Dwellers were not given to manifesting themselves much these days. Some said it was because they were elsewhere, others because they had ceased to exist, and still others because they never had existed. The true reasons were, as

Ringil would have put it, *hugely fucking immaterial.* If Poltar called on Urann, nothing would happen and he'd be made out a fool, not to mention powerless. And Egar's borderline flirtation with sacrilege could then be safely construed by the other men of the clan as warrior honor in the face of a mangy old broken-down charlatan.

"Well, Shaman?"

Poltar drew his moth-eaten wolf-skin robe about him and cast a look around at the crowd.

"The south has addled this one's brains," he spat. "Mark me, he will bring the ruin of the Gray One upon you all."

"Get to your yurt, Poltar." The boredom in Egar's voice was layered on but entirely manufactured. "And see if you can't find your misplaced manners there. Because the next time I see you lay hands on a grieving parent like that, I'll slit your fucking throat and hang you out for the buzzards. You." His arm shot out to indicate the oldest acolyte. "You've got something to say?"

The acolyte looked back at him, face rancid with hatred, biting back the words that were so obviously swilling around in his mouth. Then Poltar leaned across, muttered something to him, and he subsided. The shaman threw one more haughty look back at the Dragonbane, then pushed his way rudely into the crowd and left, followed by his four companions. People turned to stare after them.

"Help for the family of this fallen warrior," called Egar, and gazes swiveled back to where Narma still crouched weeping over her dead son. Women went to her, laying on soft hands and words. The Dragonbane nodded at Marnak, and the grizzled captain crossed to his side.

"That was well done," Marnak murmured. "But who's going to officiate at the pyre if the shaman stays sulking in his yurt?"

Egar shrugged. "If needs must, we'll send to the Ishlinak for a spellsinger. They owe me favors in Ishlin-ichan. Meantime, you keep an eye on that particular yurt. If he so much as lights a pipe in there, I want to know about it."

Marnak nodded and slipped away, leaving the Dragonbane to brood on what might be coming. Of one thing he was certain.

This was far from over.

CHAPTER 7

Ringil went home, bad-tempered and grit-eyed with the krin.

The Glades presented an accustomed predawn palette for his mood—low-lying river mist snagged through the tortured black silhouettes of the mangroves, high mansion windows like the lights of ships moored or run aground. The cloud-smudged arching smear of the band, nighttime glimmer gone dull and used with the approach of the day. The pale, unreal gleaming of the paved carriageway beneath his feet, and others like it snaking away through the trees. All the worn old images. He followed the path home with a sleepwalker's assurance, decade-old memories overlaid with the last few days of his return. Nothing much had changed on this side of the river—excepting of course Grace-of-Heaven's polished insinuation into the neighborhood—and this might easily have been any given morning of his misspent youth.

Bar this bloody great sword you've got slung on your back, that is, Gil. And the belly you've grown.

The Ravensfriend wasn't a heavy weapon for its size—part of the joy of Kiriath blades was the light and supple alloys their smiths had preferred to work in—but this morning it hung like the stump of some ship's mast he'd been lashed to in a storm, and was now forced to drag on his back one sodden step at a time up onto a beach of doubtful respite. *Lot of things have changed since you went away, Gil.* He felt washed up with the drug and Grace's caving in. He felt empty. The things he'd once clung to were gone, his shipmates were taken by the storm, and he already knew the natives around here weren't friendly.

Someone behind you.

He drifted to a slow halt, neck prickling with the knowledge.

Someone moving, scuffing softly among the trees, off to the left of the path. Maybe more than one. He grunted and flexed the fingers of his right hand. Called out in the damp, still air, "I'm not in the fucking mood for this."

And knew it for a lie. His blood went shivering along his veins, his heart was abruptly stuffed full with the sharp, joyous quickening of it. He'd love to kill something right now.

Movement again, whoever it was hadn't scared off. Ringil whirled, hand up and reaching past his head for the Ravensfriend's jutting pommel. The sword rasped at his ear as he drew, nine inches of the murderous alloy dragging up from the battle scabbard and over his shoulder before the rest of the clasp-lipped sheath on his back split apart along the side, just as it was made to. The rest of the blade rang clear, widthways. It made a cold, clean sound in the predawn air. His left hand joined his right on the long, worn hilt. The scabbard fell back emptied, swung a little on its ties; Ringil came to rest on the turn.

It was a neat trick, all Kiriath elegance and an unlooked-for turn of speed that had cheated unwary attackers more times than he could easily recall. All part of the Ravensfriend mystique, the package he'd bought into when Grashgal gifted him with the weapon. Better yet, it put him directly into a side-on, overhead guard, the bluish alloy blade up there for all to see and know for what it was. Their move—up to them to decide if they really did want to take on the owner of a Kiriath weapon after all. There'd been more than a handful of backings-down in the last ten years when that blue glinting edge came out. Ringil faced back along the path, hoping wolfishly that this wouldn't be one of them.

Nothing.

Flickered glances to the foliage on either side, a measuring of angles and available space, then he dropped into a more conventional forward guard. The Ravensfriend hushed the air apart as it described the geometric shift, faint swoop of the sound as the blade moved.

"That's right," he called. "Kiriath steel. It'll take your soul."

He thought he heard laughter in return, high and whispering through the trees. Another sensation slipped like a chilled collar about the back of his neck. As if his surroundings had been abruptly lifted clear of any earthly context, as if in some way he was *gone*, taken out of everything familiar. Distance announced itself, cold as the void between stars, and pushed things apart. The trees stood witness. The river mist crawled and coiled like something living.

Irritable rage gusted through him, took the shiver back down.

"I'm *really* not fucking about here. You want to waylay me, let's get to it. Sun's coming up, time for scum like you to be home in bed or in a grave."

Something yelped, off to the right, something crashed suddenly through branches. His vision twitched to the sound; he caught a glimpse of limbs and a low, ape-like gait, but crabbing away, fleeing. Another motion behind it, another similar form. He thought maybe he saw the glint of a short blade, but it was hard to tell—the predawn light painted everything so leaden.

The laughter again.

This time it seemed to swoop down on him, pass by at his ear with a caress. He felt it, and flinched with the near physicality of it, twisted half around, staring . . .

Then it was gone, the whole thing, in a way he felt sink into his bones like sunlight. He waited in the quiet for it to return, the Ravensfriend held motionless before him. But whatever it was, it seemed it was finished with him for now. The two scrambling, maybe human shadows did not return, either. Finally, Ringil gave up an already loosening tension and stance, angled the scabbard carefully off his back, and slid the unused sword back into place. He cast a final look around and resumed walking, stepping lighter now, rinsed out and thrumming lightly inside with the unused fight arousal. He buried the memory of the laughter, put it away where he wouldn't have to look at it again too closely.

Fucking krinzanz nerves.

He came to Eskiath House in rising tones of gray as the sky brightened from upriver. The light pricked at his eyes. He peered in through the massive iron bars of the main gate, felt oddly like some pathetic ghost clinging to the scene of an earthly existence there was no way back to. The gates were secured with chains, and ended in long spikes that he knew—he'd done it when he was younger—there was no easy way to get over. No traffic this early; outside of the servants, no one would even be stirring. For a moment, his hand brushed the thick rope bellpull, then he let his arm fall again and stepped back. The quiet was too solid to contemplate shattering with that much noise.

He summoned an uncertain sneer at this sudden sensitivity and skulked off along the fence, looking for a gap he'd made there in his youth. He squeezed—*just barely!*—through and forced his way out of some uncooperative undergrowth, then strode onto the broad gravel-edged lawns at the rear of the house, careless of the crunching sound he made over the stones at the border.

A watchman came out onto the raised patio at the noise, stood at the sweeping stair with his pike and a fairly superfluous lantern raised in either hand. Ringil could have reached and killed him in the time it took the man to drop the lamp and bring the pike to bear; it was a dull, angry knowledge in his bones and face, a surge with no focus. Instead he raised a hand in greeting, was subjected to a narrowed, peering gaze. Then the watchman recognized Gil, turned wordlessly away, and went inside again.

The door to the lower kitchens was open as usual. He saw the reddish, flickery light it let out into the dawn, like the leak of something vital at the bottom corner of the mansion's stern gray bulk. Ringil went around the edge of the raised patio, fingers trailing idly along the worn, moss-speckled masonry, down three stone steps and into the kitchen. He felt the pores in his face open up as they soaked in the heat coming off the row of fires along the side wall. He smiled into it, breathed it in like homecoming. Which it was, after a fashion, he supposed. *As warm a homecoming as you're ever likely to get around here, anyway.* He looked around for somewhere to sit. Anywhere, really; the long scarred wooden tables were still empty of produce, and no one had yet come down here to start preparing food for the day. A single small serving girl stood tending one of the big hot-water cauldrons; she looked quickly up from her work, seemed to smile at him, then looked away again almost as fast. For all the noise she made, she might as well have been a ghost.

And in the doorway at the far end of the kitchen, someone else was waiting for him.

"Oh well, *what* a surprise."

He sighed. "Good morning, Mother."

The day really was shaping up like his youth revisited. Ishil stood in the raised threshold at the far end of the kitchen, two steps up from the level of the flagged floor and as if poised on a dais. Her face was fully made up and she wore robes that she'd not normally choose to go about the house in, but aside from this she was a perfect copy of the mother he'd had to face all those crawling-in-from-the-night-before mornings so long ago.

He dragged out a stool, sat on it. "Been to a party?"

Ishil descended regally into the kitchen. Her skirts scraped on the flagstones. "I'd have thought that was my line. You're the one who's been out all night."

Ringil gestured. "You're hardly dressed for staying in yourself."

"Your father has had guests from the Chancellery. Matters of state to consider. They are still here, waiting."

"Well, it's good to know I'm not the only one who's been up working late."

"Is that what you've been doing?" Now she stood on the other side of the table from him. "Working?"

"After a fashion, yes."

Ishil gave him an icy smile. "And there was I thinking you'd just been out rutting with your former acquaintances."

"There are various ways to extract information, Mother. If you wanted a more traditional approach, you should have stuck with Father and his thugs."

"Tell me then," she said sweetly. "What have your unorthodox methods brought to light about Sherin's whereabouts?"

"Nothing very much. The Salt Warren's sewn up tighter than a priest's sphincter. It'll take me time to work around that." He grinned. "Lubricate entry, so to speak."

She switched away from him, haughty as an offended cat. "*Augh.* Do you *have* to be so coarse, Ringil?"

"Not in front of the servants, eh?"

"What's that supposed to mean?"

Ringil gestured over his shoulder at the girl by the cauldron, but when he turned to look, he saw she'd slid noiselessly out and left him alone with Ishil. Couldn't really blame her, he supposed. His mother's temper was legendary.

"Never mind," he said tiredly. "Let's just say I'm making slow progress, and leave it at that."

"Well, he wants to see you, anyway."

"Who does?"

"Your father, of course." Ishil's tone sharpened. "Haven't you listened to a word I've been saying? He's up there now with his guest. Waiting for you."

Ringil let his elbows rest on the table. He set one hand diagonally against the other, closed his fingers around, and looked at the clasp they made. He made his voice carefully toneless.

"Is he now?"

"Yes, he is, Gil. And he's not in the best of tempers. So come *on.*"

Prolonged rasp of her skirts along the floor. Abruptly, it set his teeth on edge. She made the length of the table before she realized he hadn't gotten up to follow her. She turned, fixed him with a hard stare that he knew of old and didn't bother to meet.

"Are you coming or not?"

"Take a wild guess."

"Gil, this isn't *helpful.* You promised—"

"If Gingren wants to talk to me, he can come down here and do it." Ringil gestured at the empty space between them. "It's private enough."

"You want him to bring guests into the *kitchens*?" Ishil seemed genuinely aghast.

"No." Now he looked at her. "I want him to leave me the fuck alone. But since that doesn't seem to be an option, let's see how badly he really wants to talk, shall we?"

She stood there for a couple of moments more, then, when he didn't drop his gaze or move more than a stone, she stalked up the steps and out without a word. He watched her go, shifted his position a little, hunched his shoulders, and looked up and down the empty kitchen as if for witnesses to something, as if for an audience. He rubbed his hands together and sighed.

Presently, the girl from the cauldron materialized again, at his shoulder this time and with a silent, pallid immediacy that made him jump. She held a hinge-lidded wooden flagon in her hands, out of which crept wisps of steam.

"An infusion, my lord," she murmured.

"Yeah, uhm." He blinked and shook off a shiver. "Could you not creep up on me like that, please."

"I'm sorry, my lord."

"Right. Leave it there, then."

She did, and then withdrew as silently as she'd appeared. He waited until she was gone before he tipped back the lid on the flagon and hunched over it, breathing in. Bitter green odors steamed out; heat rose off the surface of the water the herbs had been steeped in, soaked around his gritty eyes like a soothing towel. It was far too hot to drink. He stared down instead at the distorted, darkened reflection of his face in the water, cupped the uncertain vision of himself between his palms, as if afraid it might boil off and fade like the steam it was wreathed in. Finally, he slid the flagon carefully aside, slumped forward with his chin to the table, cheek pressed against one outflung arm, and stared blankly down the table and off into the space beyond.

He heard them coming.

Booted footfalls on stone, and suddenly something told him, some whispered hint of witch clarity he'd maybe picked up out there in the early-morning mist, some legacy of the uncanny laughter that had brushed by as if inviting him to turn and follow, still whispering now around the bowl of his skull, *telling him what to expect next.* Then again, it might just have been the sputtering remnants of the krin, a hallucinatory effect that wasn't unknown among its users. One way or another, a coldly sober Ringil would later be unable to shake memory of this feeling that was almost knowledge, as shadows darkened the doorway and the footfalls approached. He came up off the table with that premonition, back straightening, sharp enough now, but the whole motion edged with a druggy weariness that felt somehow like resignation . . .

"How now, Ringil." Gingren boomed it out as he stomped down into the kitchen, but there was a false tone in the heartiness, like a missed step. "Your mother said we'd find you down here."

"Looks like she was right, then."

Father and son looked each other over like reluctant duelists. Gingren cut a big, blocky figure in the low-beamed kitchen space, waist perhaps a little thickened these days, much the same way Grace-of-Heaven's had gone, features maybe a little bloated and blurred with the years and the good living—and now with staying up all night, Ringil supposed—but aside from these things, he was still pretty much the man he'd always been. No give in the flinty stare, no real space for regrets. And his son, well, not much change there, either, no matter how hard Gingren might look for it, and in the few days that Ringil had been back, truth be told, Gingren hadn't done much looking. They'd encountered each other an inevitable number of times in various parts of the house, usually one or the other of them talking to someone else, which served as buffer and barrier and in the end excuse not to offer more than some grunted, grudging acknowledgment as they passed. The hours they kept didn't coincide any better than they had in Ringil's youth, and no one in the house, not even Ishil, saw any merit in trying to bring them closer together than they chose to be.

But now . . .

And finally, the knowledge crashed in on him, like something tearing a seam. Soft-footed and slim despite the years that had grayed his temples, Murmin Kaad stepped down into the room.

"Good day, Master Ringil."

Ringil sat rigid.

"Ha! Cat got his tongue." But Gingren had been—was perhaps still, just about—a warrior, and he knew what the sudden stillness in his son meant. He made a low gesture at Kaad with one hand, a warning to stay back. "Lord Justice Kaad has come here as my invited guest, Ringil. He'd like to talk to you about something."

Ringil stared very carefully straight ahead.

"So let him talk."

Brief hesitation. Gingren nodded, and Kaad stepped across to the far side of the table. He made a show of pulling out one of the crude wooden stools, of settling onto it with ironic magnanimity for the lack of ceremony or plush. He rearranged his cloak about him, pulled up closer to the table edge, rested his hands on the scarred surface in a loose clasp. A silver ring chased with gold inlay and the city's Chancellery crest bulked on one finger.

"It is always good," he began formally, "to see one of the city's honored sons so returned."

Ringil flickered him a glance. "I said talk, not tongue my arse clean. Get on with it, will you."

"Ringil!"

"No, no, Gingren, it's all right." But it clearly wasn't—Ringil saw the quick stain of anger pass across the other man's face, just as rapidly wiped away and replaced with a strained diplomatic smile. "Your son and the Committee have not always seen eye-to-eye. Youth. It is, after all, not a crime."

"It was for Jelim Dasnel." The old anger fizzled in him, blunted a little with the comedown. "As I recall."

Another brief pause. Behind Ringil, Gingren made a knotted-up sound, then evidently thought better of releasing it into speech.

Kaad put on the thin smile again. "As *I* recall, Jelim Dasnel broke the laws of Trelayne and made a mockery of the morality that governs us all.

As did you, Ringil, though it grieves me to recall the fact in your family home. *One* example had to be made."

The anger found its edge, shed the comedown blur and glinted clean and new. Ringil leaned across his half of the table, fixed Kaad with lover's eyes.

"Should I be grateful to you?" he whispered.

Kaad held his gaze. "Yes, I would think you should. It could as easily have been two cages at the eastern gate as one."

"No, not *easily.* Not for a lickspittle little social aspirant like you, Kaad. Not with a big fat chance to get on the Eskiath tit in the offing." Ringil manufactured a smile of his own—it felt like an obscenity as it crawled across his face, it felt like a wound. "Haven't you sucked your fill yet, little man? What do you want now?"

And now he had him. The rage stormed the other man's face again, and this time it held its ground. The smile evaporated, the patrician mask tightened at mouth and eyes, the groomed, half-bearded cheeks darkened with fury past dissembling. Kaad's origins were pure harbor-end, and the disdain with which he'd been viewed by the high families as he rose through the legislature had never been concealed. The ring and the badges of rank had come hard, the stiff smiles and party invitations from Glades society clawed forth like blood; wary respect if not acceptance, never acceptance, mined from the lying aristocratic heart of Trelayne with cunning and cold, inching calculation, one shored-up bargain and veiled power play at a time. In Ringil's sneer, the other man could hear the creak of that shoring, the sudden cold-water chill of knowing how flimsy and man-made it all was, and how at blood-deep levels that had nothing to do with material wealth or rank displayed, nothing had or ever would change. Kaad was still the tolerated but unappreciated guest in the house, the grubby, harbor-end intruder he'd always been.

"How dare you!"

"Oh, I dare." Ringil let one hand slide up to rub casually at his neck, alongside the upjutting spike of the Ravensfriend's pommel. "I dare."

"You owe me your life!"

Ringil slanted a look at his father, calculated more than anything to further infuriate Kaad, to dismiss him as a threat worth keeping his eye on.

"How much more of this do I have to listen to?"

Gingren smouldered to anger. "That's enough, Ringil!"

"Yeah, I'd say so, too."

"You tell." Kaad, getting up now, face still mottled with fury. "Your degenerate, your fucking *ungrateful* degenerate son, you tell him—"

"What did you call me?"

"*Ringil!*"

"You tell him where the lines are drawn, Gingren. Right now. Or I leave, and I take my vote with me."

"His vote?" Ringil stared at his father. "His fucking *vote*?"

"*Shut up!*" It was a roar fit for a battlefield, a great tolling bellow in the confines of the kitchen. "Both of you! Just shut up and start acting like a pair of adults. Kaad, sit down. We're not finished. And Ringil, no matter what you think, you'll keep a courteous tongue in your head while you're under my roof. This is not some roadside tavern for you to brawl in."

Ringil made a small spitting sound. "The roadside taverns of my acquaintance have cleaner clientele. They don't like torturers much in the uplands."

"What about the murderers of small children?" Kaad seated himself again, with the same fastidious attention to the drape of his cloak. He shot Ringil a significant look. "How do they react to that?"

Ringil said nothing. The old memory seeped in his mind, a flow he stanched before it got properly started. He placed his hands around the flagon of steaming tea and stared downward. Still too hot to drink. Gingren saw his chance.

"We're trying to help you, Ringil."

"Are you *really*, Father."

"We know you've been sniffing around the Salt Warren," said Kaad.

Ringil looked up abruptly.

"You're having me followed?"

Kaad shrugged. Made a small, worldly gesture. In Ringil's head, recollection of the walk home slipped into focus. Sounds of soft pursuit. The prickle at his neck. Watchers among the trees, scuttling away.

He let the smile that was a gash split his face again.

"You want to be careful, Kaad. You let your Committee thugs creep up too close on me, you're liable to find yourself fishing them out of the harbor in chunks."

"I'd advise you against threatening Chancellery staff, Master Ringil."

"It wasn't a threat. It's what'll happen."

Gingren made an impatient noise. "Point is, Ringil, we know you're not getting anywhere with Etterkal. That's what we can help you with. What Lord Kaad here can help you with."

Something like a sense of wonder crept up in Ringil. He sensed vaguely the shape of what was before him, felt carefully around its edges.

"You're going to get me into the Salt Warren?"

Kaad cleared his throat. "Not as such, no. But there are, let us say, more profitable avenues of inquiry that you might pursue."

"Might I?" asked Ringil tonelessly. "And what avenues are those?"

"You are looking for Sherin Herlirig Mernas, widow of Bilgrest Mernas, sold under the debt guarantors' charter last month."

"Yeah. You know where she is?"

"Not at this precise moment. But the resources of the Chancellery might very well be opened to you in a way that they have not yet been."

Ringil shook his head. "I'm done with the Chancellery. There's nothing worth knowing up there that I don't already know."

Hesitation. Gingren and Kaad swapped glances.

"There is the issue of manpower," began Kaad. "We could—"

"You could provide me with enough Watch uniforms to turn the Salt Warren upside down. Break some heads and get some answers. How about that?"

Again, the exchange of looks, the grim expressions. Ringil, for all he'd known what the response would be, coughed out a disbelieving laugh.

"Hoiran's fucking balls, what *is* it about Etterkal?" Though, if Milacar was to be believed, he already knew, and was starting to realize it must, after all, be taken seriously. "The place was a fucking *slum* last time I was here. Now everyone's too fucking scared to go knock on the gate?"

"Ringil, there is more to this than you understand. More than your mother understood when she called you back."

"Yeah, that's becoming very clear." Ringil stabbed a finger at his father. "You wouldn't lift a finger to help Sherin when they sold her, but now I'm banging on the Salt Warren gate, it suddenly merits attention. What is it, Dad? You want me to stop? Am I going to upset the wrong people? Am I going to embarrass you again?"

"You take this matter too lightly, Master Ringil. You do not understand what you are about to involve yourself in."

"He just said that, Kaad. What are you, a fucking parrot?"

"Your father is motivated principally by concern for your well-being."

"Candidly, I doubt that. But even if it were true, that leaves you. What's your end of this, you conniving old fuck?"

Fist slammed onto the table, Kaad half risen from his seat.

"You will *not* speak to me in that way," he said thickly.

Then he was reeling backward off the stool, falling, both hands up to his face, mashing in the sound of a high shriek and streaming with the heated tea. Ringil got up and tossed the emptied flagon across the table after him, onto the flagstone floor, where it lay, still steaming slightly from the mouth.

"I'll speak to you exactly how I like, Kaad." He was oddly cold and calm now, tranquil in the understanding that this and all it implied had been unavoidable from the moment he agreed to come home. "You got a problem with my mouth, I'll see you on Brillin Hill Fields about it."

Kaad rocked back and forth on the floor in the puddle of his own cloak. His hands still clutched at his face. He made a mewling sound through the fingers. Gingren stood mute with disbelief, staring from the downed justice to his son. Ringil ignored him.

"*If* you can get someone to show you which end of a sword you're supposed to pick it up by, that is."

"*Hoiran damn your fucking soul to hell!*"

"If you really believe what you preach, he's already done that. Alongside all my carnal sins, I don't think roughing up the local magistrature is going to impress the Dark King all that much. Sorry."

By now Gingren had gone around the end of the table and was kneeling by Kaad's side. The justice slapped away his efforts to help. He climbed to his feet, face already turning pink and raw looking across nose and one cheek where the tea had evidently burned worst. He pointed a trembling finger at Ringil.

"On your own head, Eskiath. This will be on your own head."

"It always is."

Kaad gathered his robes about him. From somewhere, he mustered a sneer. "No, Master Ringil. Like all your kind, the consequences of what you do are borne by others. From Gallows Gap to the cages at the eastern gate, it is others, always others, who pay the carriage for your acts."

Ringil twitched forward a quarter inch. Held himself back.

"Now you'd really better get out," he said quietly.

Kaad went. Perhaps he saw something in Ringil's eyes, perhaps he just didn't see any way to salvage value from the situation. He was, after all, a political animal. Gingren hurried after him, one furious backflung glance at his son in lieu of words. Ringil stood still a couple of moments after they'd gone, then slumped under the gathering weight of the comedown. He leaned flat palms on the table in front of him, gazed at the emptied flagon there.

"Wouldn't have thought it was still that hot," he murmured, and chuckled a little to himself. He looked around for the serving girl, but she hadn't reappeared. He squinted down toward the door out to the garden, where the light was now getting bright enough to hurt his krin-stunned pupils. He thought about going to bed, but in the end, he just sat back down at the table and sank his head in his hands instead. A fading trace of the drug whined about in the back of his head.

Gingren found him there, unmoved, what felt like hours later.

"Well, now you've done it," he growled.

Ringil wiped hands down his face and looked up at his father. "I hope so. I don't want to have to breathe the same air as that fuck again."

"Oh, *Hoiran's teeth!* What is it with you, Ringil? Just for once tell me, *what the fuck is wrong with you?*"

"What's wrong with me?" Suddenly Ringil was off the stool, scant inches out of his father's fighting space. His arm scythed out, pointing eastward. *"He sent Jelim to die on a fucking spike!"*

"That was *fifteen years ago.* And anyway, Jelim Dasnal was a degenerate, he—"

"Then so am I, Dad. So am I."

"—fucking *deserved* the cage."

"Then so did I!"

It screamed up out of him, the dark poison pressure of it, the same nagging ache that had driven him up the pass at Gallows Gap, like biting down on a rotten tooth, the pain and the sweet leak of pus behind it, the taste of his own hate in his mouth, and a trembling that now he found he couldn't stop. Gingren saw it, and wavered in the blast.

"Ringil, it was the *law.*"

"Oh *lizardshit!*" But abruptly the force of his rage was no longer there, the krin drop was crushing it out, falling on him harder now with every waking second, bleaching away his focus. He went back to the stool and seated himself again, voice flung dull and disinterested back over his shoulder at Gingren where he stood. "It was a political deal, and you know it. You think they would have hung Jelim up at the eastern gate if his surname had been Eskiath? Or Alannor, or Wrathrill, or any other name with a Glades punch behind it? You think any of those raping sadists up at the Academy are ever going to see the sharp end of a cage?"

"That," said Gingren stiffly, "is not something we—"

"Oh, *fuck off.* Just forget it." Ringil dumped his chin into one cupped hand, defocusing vision of the grain in the table's wooden surface as the comedown leaned in on him. "I'm not going to do this, Father. I'm not going to argue about the past with you. What's the point? Look, I'm sorry if I fucked up your negotiations with the Chancellery."

"Not just mine. Kaad could have helped you."

"Yeah. Could have, but he wasn't going to. He just wanted—you *both* just want—me to stay away from the Salt Warren. The rest is just distraction. It isn't going to help me find Sherin."

"And you think thugging your way into Etterkal is?"

Ringil shrugged. "Etterkal took her. That's where the useful answers are going to be."

"Hoiran's teeth, Ringil. Is it really worth it?" Gingren came to the table, leaned on it at his son's shoulder, leaned over him. His breath was sour with stress and lack of sleep. "I mean, one fucking merchant's daughter, barren anyway, and too stupid to look to her own welfare in good time? She's not even a full cousin."

"I don't expect you to understand." *Any more than I understand it myself.*

"She'll be soiled goods by now, Ringil. You do know that, don't you? You know how the slave markets work."

"Like I said, I don't expe—"

"Good, because I *don't*." Gingren thumped the table, but with a despairing lack of real force. "I *don't* understand how the same man who helped save this whole fucking city from the lizards can stand there and tell me that getting back one raped and brutalized female is more important to him than protecting the stability of the very same city he fought so hard to save."

Ringil looked up at him. "So it's about stability now, is it?"

"Yeah. It is."

"Want to expand on that?"

Gingren looked away. "This is under seal of council. I can't divulge—"

"Fine."

"Ringil, I promise you. On the honor of the Eskiath name, I swear it. It may not seem like much, you stirring up trouble in Etterkal, but there's a threat at the heart of all this and it's easily the equal of those fucking lizards you threw off the city walls back in '53."

Ringil sighed. He rubbed the heels of his palms in his eyes, trying to dislodge the feeling of grit.

"I had a rather minor part in lifting the siege, Father. And to be honest I would have done the same thing for any other city, including Yhelteth, if we'd had to fight there instead. I know we're not supposed to say that kind of thing these days, seeing as how we're back to being sworn enemies with the Empire. But it's the truth, and truth is something I'm kind of partial to. Call it an affectation."

Gingren drew himself up. "Truth is not an affectation."

"No?" Ringil summoned energy and stood up to leave. He yawned. "Doesn't seem any more popular around here than it was when I left, though. Funny, they always said it was one of the things we were fighting for back then. Light, justice, and *truth*. I distinctly remember being told that."

They stood looking at each other for a couple of long moments. Gingren drew breath, audibly, as if it hurt to do. The expression he wore shifted.

"You're still going, then? Into Etterkal. Despite everything you've just heard."

"Yeah, I am." Ringil tilted his head until his neck gave up its tension with a click. "Tell Kaad not to get in my way, eh."

Gingren held his gaze. Nodded as if just convinced of something.

"You know, I don't like him any more than you do, Ringil. I don't like him any more than the next harbor-end cur. But curs have their uses."

"I suppose they do."

"These are not the most honorable of times we find ourselves in."

Ringil hoisted an eyebrow. "You reckon?"

Another silence, into which Gingren made a noise that might, locked behind closed lips, have been a laugh. Ringil masked his disbelief. His father hadn't laughed in his company for the best part of two decades. Uncertainly, he let the trace of a smile touch his own mouth.

"I've got to go to bed, Dad."

Gingren nodded again, pulled in another breath that seemed to hurt him.

"Ringil, I . . ." He shook his head. Gestured helplessly. "You, you know . . . if you'd just been . . . If only you . . ."

"Didn't like to suck other men's cocks. Yeah, I know." Ringil came to life, heading for the door, walking quickly past Gingren so he wouldn't have to watch his father's face twitch in revulsion. He paused at the other man's shoulder, leaned close and murmured, "But the problem is, Dad, I do."

His father flinched as if he'd struck him. Ringil sighed. Then he raised a hand and clapped Gingren roughly on the chest and shoulder.

"It's okay, Dad," he said quietly. "You've got two other red-blooded sons to make you proud. They both did pretty good at the siege."

Gingren said nothing, did nothing, made no audible noise. He might as well have been a statue. Ringil sighed again, let his hand drop from his father's shoulder and walked away.

Sleep. Sleep would help.

Right.

CHAPTER 8

Khangset was still smoldering.

Archeth sat in the saddle on the ridge above the town, spyglass forgotten in her hands, staring down toward the harbor and the damage. Her mount shifted beneath her, uneasy at the damp acrid stink of ashes that came and went on the buffeting wind. The Throne Eternal detachment spread out along the ridge around her, elaborately impassive and professional, befitting reputation. But Archeth had already heard a couple of bitten-back oaths in the breeze as they saw what lay below. She couldn't really blame them. Despite everything she'd been warned to expect, she was having a hard time believing it herself.

She knew Khangset somewhat, had been there on several occasions with the Kiriath engineering corps during the war. The Scaled Folk had come ashore all along this coast in the early years of the fighting. They killed and burned everything they found with an efficiency that was almost human, and invariably they retreated beneath the waves again before the Empire's legions could respond. Akal, always a realist in tactical matters, swallowed his pride and called for Kiriath help. Grashgal sent the engineers.

Now, along the harbor wall and beach line, the Kiriath fortifications were smashed through in half a dozen places, smooth glassy ramparts showing gouges whose exposed edges were jagged and rainbow-colored in the early-afternoon sun. Whatever had done the damage hadn't stopped there—beyond each breach, the path of destruction tore into what lay behind with a totality Archeth hadn't seen since the war. Stone structures had been reduced to stumped ruins; wooden buildings were simply gone, only charred ash and fragments to signal they had ever existed at all. The harbor waters were spined with truncated, listing masts from vessels that had gone straight to the bottom. Rubble from a toppled lighthouse lay along the wharf. The whole place looked as if it had been swiped by some reptile god's massive clawed hand.

The dead numbered in the hundreds.

She might have guessed that much from what she saw through the glass, but by then guessing was unnecessary. On the landward slopes of the ridge, they'd come upon a tangled exodus of townspeople and beaten soldiery, commanded, if that was the word, by one of the few remaining officers from the Khangset marine garrison. Shaken and wincing, the young lieutenant had given her his tight-lipped account of the raid. Unearthly shrieking from out to sea, balls of living blue fire, and ghost figures stalking the smoke-filled streets, slaughtering all in their path with weapons made of glimmering light. *Nothing worked,* he told her numbly. *I saw our bowmen put shafts into them at fifty feet, full draw. Steel-tipped fletch, at that range, it should go right through a man, full armor, the works. It was like the arrows just fucking dissolved or something. When they got twenty feet off our barricade, I led a charge. It was like fighting in a nightmare. Felt like you were moving underwater, and they were fast, they were so fucking fast . . .*

He stared off into the memory of it like someone three times his age.

What's your name? Archeth asked him gently.

Galt. Still staring emptily away. *Parnan Galt, Peacock Company, Fiftieth Imperial Marines, Seventy-third Levy.*

Seventy-third. Like the messenger who'd brought the news to Yhelteth, he would have been a boy when the war ended. In all probability, he'd never seen combat outside standard anti-piracy policing and the odd bit of riot control. Few regular troops after the Sixty-sixth had. Archeth pressed a hand on his shoulder, rose, and left him sitting there with his memories. She didn't ask him to come on with them to the town.

She detailed a Throne Eternal sergeant and his squad to take charge of the refugee column where it was, then pressed on with the rest of the company, skeptical voices in her head warring with a creeping sense that something really was badly wrong. That the young lieutenant and the original messenger actually had both been witness to something new and not easily explained away. That their terrified accounts were not just the babble of men who'd never seen battle in all its filth-caked finery.

No? The skeptic in ascendancy now. *Remember* your *first battle, do you? Majak berserk-skirmishers tearing through the lines at Baldaran. Howling across the field, panic in the ranks. Grass slicked down like a pimp's hair with the blood. You went down that first time, grabbed at Arashtal's arm and found it severed in your grasp. You screamed but no one heard, you moved like sludge. Didn't* that *feel like a nightmare?*

And ghost figures? Glimmering unknown weapons? Dissolving arrows?

Subjective impression. Night-fight terrors. The archers freaked out like everybody else, shot wide or fucked up on the draw.

Hmm.

And now, whatever the raiders had or hadn't been, Khangset lay below her, gashed and torn and smoking like a freshly disemboweled belly on some chilly northern battleground.

"Sacred fucking Mother of the Revelation." Mahmal Shanta, distracted as he struggled to control his prancing horse at her side. It was unclear if he was cursing the animal or the destruction below. "What the hell happened here?"

"I don't know," Archeth said thoughtfully. "Doesn't look good, does it?"

Shanta glowered and struggled to sit his mount with a modicum of dignity. He was useless in the saddle, always had been. His age-knobbed hands clamped the reins like a rope he was trying to climb.

"Looks like a fucking replay of Demlarashan, is what it looks like," he growled.

Archeth shook her head. "Dragons didn't do this. There's too much left."

"You know anything *other* than dragonfire that would go through Kiriath moldings that way? God *damn* this *fucking* horse."

Archeth reached across and laid a soothing hand on the jittery animal's neck. Murmured and clucked to it the way her father had taught her. The horse settled a little, partway convinced that here at least was someone who knew what was going on and could control it.

Be nice if that were true, she caught herself thinking, perhaps more wryly than current circumstances merited. *Failing that, be nice if humans were as easy to fool as horses.*

Hey, Archidi, last time I checked, they were.

Oh yeah, that old warrior disconnect. It came on in full force now, humor bleak and black *while homes smolder around you and the unarmed afflicted weep for what's lost so you don't have to. Pull on the cold, clinking mail of your professional detachment, Archeth Indamaninarmal, inhabit it until it starts to feel warm and accustomed, and in time you'll forget you're wearing it at all. You'll only notice when it works, when it stops you feeling the steel-edged bite of something that might otherwise have gotten through and done you some damage. And then you'll just grin and shiver and shake off the blow, like warriors do.*

It was a part of herself she'd never quite been able to hate.

Which was perhaps fortunate because lately, that very same amused detachment was proving handy at court.

She glanced back over her shoulder, down the ridge to where Pashla Menkarak, Most Holy and Revered Invigilator first class for the Revelation Divine (Throne Eternal attached), sat wrapped in the black-and-gold cloak of his office and perched in his saddle like a vulture. His head was tipped at an angle to beat the sun's rays, and he was apparently staring directly back up the slope at her.

"Motherfuck," she muttered.

Shanta saw where she was looking. "You'd better watch what you're saying around him," he said softly. "From what I've seen so far, this one's keen."

"Yeah," Archeth sneered. "Well, they all start out that way. Give him a couple of months at court, then we'll see. Be rolling around on a bed of tits and ass getting his dick greased just like all the rest."

Shanta rolled his eyes at the vulgarity. "Yes, or maybe he'll remain as immune to court sophistication as you have, Archeth. Ever think of that?"

"Guy like that? He lacks my moral core."

"Perhaps not. Stories I hear out of the Citadel these days, that's not the way things are moving. They say it's a whole new breed coming through the religious colleges now. Hard-line faith."

"Oh, good."

Movement down the line. She wheeled her horse about, and the ashen wind blew in her face. Faileh Rakan, captain of the Throne Eternal detachment, was trotting his mount down the rank of his riders toward them. She sighed and put on the mask of command. Shanta sat his horse in expectant silence. Rakan reached Archeth and dismounted for respect. He took sword hilt in his right hand, capped it with his left, and bowed.

"Commander, my men are deployed. We await your orders."

Archeth nodded.

"Right then," she said brightly. "I suppose we'd better go down and take a closer look."

ONCE AMONG THE RUINS, THOUGH, THAT COUNTERFEIT ENTHUSIASM stained through into something that was almost the real thing.

From long acquaintance, she recognized it for the same scavenger urge that fed her expeditions into the desert and, in earlier times, the Kiriath wastes; the same thirst that drove her time and again back to the uncooperative Helmsmen in the few remaining fireships. There was meaning to be gleaned out there, a transcendence of the surface of things that glimmered and beckoned like harbor lights seen through the wrap of foul weather at night. You saw an answer, steered by its beacon, and, briefly, the world seemed that much less pointless. You felt, for just that short time, that you might be getting somewhere.

Tangled in with all of that and gaining force came another, less assured sensation. One she supposed Faileh Rakan and his men were all feeling, clean, upfront, and handily fervent behind their stony Throne Eternal demeanor:

Outrage.

Slow building, incandescent, the mighty and majestic insulted pride of Empire. *Rage,* that someone had *dared,* had felt at violent liberty in this time of *agreed peace* to assail a designated imperial port and do harm to men and women under the *Revelation-inspired patronage* of his radiance Jhiral Khimran II.

For Archeth, who'd seen rather more than she'd have liked of how the *agreed peace* had been hammered out, the feeling was fatally tainted. But it hung around anyway, a bit like muscle ache after a long ride or treacle on the edges of a poorly washed baking tray. She knew enough, despite what she'd seen, to rein in her cynicism.

Look:

Yhelteth unites a massive territory in comparison with any of its political competitors, you know. By and large, it treats those living within its borders with a degree of codified respect not popular elsewhere.

I know that.

All right then. It might not be civilized universality the way Grashgal always liked to talk it up, it might not be the future he claimed to see in his dreams. But it's not a bad functional substitute. Yhelteth at least aspires in that direction.

That much was true: A sort of rough-and-ready inclusiveness prevailed among the imperials, something born in about equal measures out of the religious universalism of the Revelation, an ascetic warrior egalitarianism in the original culture of the nine tribes—*now down to seven, yeah, I know, don't ask*—and some shrewdly applied intelligent self-interest. Take up citizenship and the conversion it entailed, send a couple of your sons to the levy when they were of age, pay taxes calculated not to drive you and your family into penury or the mountains and the life of a bandit. Oh, and while you're at it, steer clear of debt and disease. Chances were—*mostly*—if you did all that, you'd never starve, never have your home burned down and your children raped before your eyes, never have to wear a slave collar. With luck you might even live to see your grandchildren grow up.

Is that so bad, Grashgal? Is it?

She'd lived her life trying to believe it was not.

This—drifting smoke, and puffs of ash from footfalls, and a charred child's rib cage crushed under a fallen beam—*is not part of the deal. This, we do not* fucking *permit.*

She stood by the cracked and shiny black charcoal angle of the beam, where it met the last remaining upright timber in the roofless house. The sensation surged up in her throat, took her by surprise. The colder, analytical end of her feelings dropped suddenly away, out of easy reach. The ruin rushed her with its silence. Stench from what was left of the bodies in the wreckage around her, uncomfortably familiar despite the years gone past. Ash and less well-defined muck clogged onto her boots to well above the ankle. Her knives were a pointless weight at boot and belt. Smoke came billowing through the wreckage on a change of wind, and stung her in the eyes.

"So there you are."

Mahmal Shanta stood outside the dwelling, framed in a stone doorway that had somehow escaped the devastation to the wall it was once set in. Off his horse, the engineer seemed to have regained a modicum of good humor. He cocked an eyebrow at the phantom entrance and stepped through, squinted around at the mess and grimaced. She couldn't tell if he'd spotted the corpses yet or not, but he couldn't have missed the stench.

"Seen enough?"

She shook her head. "Not enough to make any sense of it."

"Is that what we're doing here?" Shanta came closer, peering at her face. "You been crying?"

"It's the smoke."

"Right." He cleared his throat. "Well, since you're foolhardy enough to actually want an explanation for all this, I thought you might like to know Rakan's boys have found us a survivor. Maybe we could ask her."

"A survivor? Here?"

"Yes, here. It seems while everyone else was stampeding out into the surrounding countryside, this one was smart enough to find a hiding place and sit tight in it." Shanta gestured back out to the street. "They've got her down by the harbor, they're trying to feed her. Apparently, she's been living off beetles and rainwater for the last four days, hasn't been out of her hidey-hole since the raid. She's not what you'd call calm right now."

"Great." Archeth looked deliberately around the ruined house one more time. The corner of her gaze caught on the child's crushed rib cage again, as if each upjutting, snapped-off rib was a barb made expressly for that purpose. "So let's get the fuck out of here."

"After you, milady."

Out in the street, some of the pressure seemed to come off. Late-afternoon sunlight slanted down across the piles of rubble; birds sweetened the air with song. Down the hill, the sea was a burnished, glinting fleece to the horizon. The heat of the day was beginning to ebb.

But the ruin stood at her back like a reproach. She felt like an ungracious guest, walking out on mortified hosts.

Shanta came past her, woke her from the moment and broke her free.

"You coming?" he asked.

Halfway down the road to the harbor with him, she remembered.

"So what was all that about back there? *Foolhardy enough to actually want an explanation,* what's that supposed to mean?"

Shanta shrugged. "Oh, you know. We're not a people that cares much about ultimate causes, are we? Show the flag, roll out the levy. Punish *someone* so we all feel better, doesn't much matter who. Remember Vanbyr?"

Archeth stopped and stared at him. "I'm not likely to have forgotten it."

"Well, there you go then."

"I'm not here to show the flag and look for scapegoats, Mahmal. This is a fact-finding mission."

"Is that what Jhiral told you?" The naval engineer pulled a face. "You must have caught him on a good day."

They stood locked to a halt on the ash-smeared street stones, listening to the echo of Shanta's words on the breeze, searching each other's faces for the next step. The silence grew rooted between them. The relationship went back, but they didn't know each other well enough for this.

"I think," Archeth said finally, quietly, "that perhaps we'd best both concentrate on doing what we were sent here to do, and let our concerns for our Emperor remain a matter for private thought and prayer."

Shanta's lined, hawkish face creased into a well-worn court smile.

"Indeed, milady. Indeed. Not a day goes by that Jhiral Khimran does not feature pointedly in my prayers." A slight but formal bow from the chest up. "As I am sure is the case for you as well."

He made no mention of what it was he prayed for on his Emperor's behalf. Archeth, who didn't pray at all, made an indeterminate noise of assent in her throat.

And they went on down the ashen thoroughfares together, quiet and a little more hurried now, as if the ambiguity in Shanta's words stalked after them, nose to the ground and a peeled glimpse of teeth revealed.

CHAPTER 9

It was still light when he got up.

Somewhat surprised by the fact, Ringil wandered yawning about the house in search of servants, found some, and ordered a hot bath drawn. Then he went down to the kitchens while he was waiting, scavenged a plate of bread and dried meat, and ate it standing at a window, staring absently through the glass at late-afternoon shadows on the lawn. The kitchen staff bustled about him in steam and shouted commands, carefully ignoring his presence, more or less as if he were some expensive and delicate statue dumped inconveniently in their midst. He looked about for the girl who'd served him tea but didn't see her. When the bath was ready, he went back upstairs and soaked in it until the water started to cool. Then he toweled off without help, dressed with fastidious care from the new wardrobe Ishil had funded for him, put on the Ravensfriend and a feathered cap, and took himself out for a walk.

The Glades were suffused with dappled amber sunlight and thronged with strollers out enjoying the last of the autumn warmth. For a while he contented himself with drifting among them, ignoring the glances the sword on his back attracted, and letting the last dregs of the krin rinse out in the glow from the declining sun. High in the eastern sky, the edge of the band arched just visible against the blue. Ringil caught himself staring blankly up at it, and out of nowhere he had an idea.

Shalak.

He picked his way down to the moss-grown Glades quayside, where there were tables and chairs set up for the view, stalls serving lemonade and cakes at inflated prices, and a steady traffic of small boats picking up and dropping off parties of expensively dressed picnickers from the upriver districts. Eventually, he managed to find a boatman halfway willing to take him downriver to Ekelim, and jumped lightly aboard before the man could change his mind. He stood in the stern as they pulled away from the shore, watching the Glades as it receded, face washed warm with stained-glass sunset light, only faintly aware that he was striking a pose. He sat down, shifted about on the damp wood with due attention to his new clothes and the slant of the Ravensfriend until he was more or less comfortable, and tried to blink the sun out of his eyes.

"Not many days like this left in the year," the boatman commented over his oars. "They say we're in for an Aldrain winter."

"Who does?" Ringil asked absently. They were always predicting an Aldrain winter. It would be what passed for presaging doom among the entrail-readers at Strov market now that the war was over and won.

The boatman was keen to expound. "Everyone thinks it, my lord. The fisher crews down at harbor end all say it's harder to land silverfry this year than they've ever known before. The waters are colder flowing in from the Hironish isles. And there've been signs. Hailstones the size of a man's fist. On the marsh flats at south Klist, they've seen strange lights at dawn and evening, and people hear a black dog barking through the night. My wife's brother stands forward lookout for one of Majak Urdin's whalers, and he says they've had to sail farther north this year to sight spouts. One day at the end of last month they went out beyond the Hironish, and he saw stones of fire falling from the band right into the water. There was a storm that night and . . ."

And so on.

Ringil went ashore at Ekelim with the echoes of it all still in his head. He headed up Dray Street from the harbor, hoping a little belatedly that Shalak hadn't found occasion to move premises anytime in the last decade. It was slow progress through the milling early-evening crowds, but the cut and fabric of his new clothes helped open a path. People didn't want trouble, even at this end of the river. There were members of the Watch paired on street corners, watching the press and toying twitchily with long wooden day-clubs; in resolving any dispute, they were going to see the same things in Ringil's clothing as everyone else. He'd get the rich man's benefit of the doubt, and anyone on the other side of the equation was going to get dragged down a side alley and given a swift, timber-edged lesson in manners.

He reached the corner of Dray and Blubber, and grinned a little. He needn't have worried about the passing of time here. Ten years on, Shalak's place hadn't changed any more than a priest's mind. The frontage was the same scoured stonework and dark, coffee-stain windows lit dimly from within, the same heavy browed eaves drooping so low across the front door you could bash your head if you'd grown up sufficiently well nourished to gain the height. The same cryptic sign swinging outside on its rusted iron bracket:

COME IN AND SEE.

Back in the early years, before the war, there'd been another set of words up on that sign: COME IN AND LOOK AROUND—YOU MIGHT SEE SOMETHING THAT LIKES YOU, surrounded by a ring of arcane—and, Ringil always suspected, fake—Aldrain glyphs. But then came the '50s, the war and the dragonfire and the alien invaders from the sea. What had once been a harmless come-on for the dilettante Vanishing Folk enthusiasts Shalak made his living from was now suddenly a statement of sorcerous intent that verged on treason. Some said it was the west that the Aldrain had vanished into, and it was out of the west that the Scaled Folk were coming now; Shalak had his windows smashed by angry mobs a couple of times, had stones thrown at him in the street on more occasions than he could easily count, was summoned repeatedly to appear before the Committee for Public Morals. He got the message. The sign came down, the glyphs were scrubbed off every surface inside the shop, and any claims of magical powers for the items Shalak sold were replaced with disclaimers stating that nothing was known for certain of Aldrain lore, that no one had seen a dwenda in living memory, and that their whole existence was, in all probability, a bunch of children's fairy stories, nothing more. Ringil always suspected how deeply it hurt Shalak to hand-letter those little notices—whatever the affectations of his clients, the man himself had always been a true believer. But when, with youthful brashness, he broached the subject, Shalak had offered in return only a pained smile and good-citizen platitudes.

We all must make sacrifices, Ringil. It's the war. If this is all I suffer, you will not hear me complain.

Oh, come on! Ringil, plucking a notice from a carving at random, brandishing it. *This shit?* "No one in living memory has seen a dwenda." *Fuck's sake, Shal. No one in living memory's seen Hoiran walk, but I don't notice them closing down the fucking temples. What a bunch of fucking hypocrites.*

People are frightened, Ringil. There was a livid bruise around Shalak's left eye. *It's understandable.*

People are sheep, Ringil raged. *Moronic fucking sheep.*

With that, Shalak had made no sign that he disagreed.

He hadn't changed much, either, in the intervening years. The close-cropped beard was shot through with white now rather than gray, and there was less hair to balance it atop the lined forehead, but otherwise it was the same faintly lugubrious clerk's face that peered up from the leather-bound tome it was bent over, as Ringil opened the door to the little shop and ducked inside.

"Yes, noble sir? How may I be of service?"

"Well, you can knock off the ornate honorifics, for a start." Ringil took off his cap. "Then you might want to have a go at recognizing me."

Shalak blinked. He removed the eyeglasses he'd been using to peruse the book, and stared hard at his new customer. Ringil made a leg.

"Alish? No, wait a minute. *Ringil? Ringil Eskiath? Is that really you?" Shalak hopped off his chair, came forward, and seized Ringil by the arms. "Hoiran's *teeth,* what are *you* doing back here?"

"Came to see you, Shal."

Shalak rolled his eyes and let go. "Oh please. You know Risha's going to claw your eyes out if she sees you batting your lashes at me like that." But you could see, despite it all, he was pleased. "Really, why'd you come back?"

"Long story, not very interesting." Ringil seated himself on the corner of a table laden with odd lumps of stone, semiprecious gems, and obscure metalwork. "Could use some advice, though, Shal."

"Advice from me?"

"Hard to believe, huh?" Ringil picked up a chunk of tangled iron wire with a glyph worked into its center. "Where'd you get this?"

"A source. What do you want advice about?"

Ringil looked elaborately around the shop. "Take a wild guess."

"You want *Aldrain* advice?" Shalak pulled a face, chuckled. "What's the matter with you, Gil? You come into some money you don't need all of a sudden? I'd have thought, you know, a man like you, the Kiriath stuff has got to be more your thing."

"I've got all the Kiriath stuff I need." Ringil gestured with two crooked fingers at the pommel jutting over his shoulder. "Anyway, I'm not buying anything. Just want your opinion on a couple of things."

"Which are?"

"If you had to kill a dwenda, what's the best way to go about it?"

Shalak gaped. "What?"

"Come on, you heard me."

"You want to know how to kill a *dwenda*?"

"Yeah." Ringil shifted irritably, picked at a loose thread on his, yeah, *new* fucking tunic, what kind of fucking workmanship did Ishil think . . . "Yeah, that's right."

"Well, I don't know. First off, you'd need to *find* one to kill. No one's seen the Vanishing Folk in—"

"Living memory. I know, like the sign says. But let's assume, just for the sake of argument, I *have* found one. Let's assume he's in my way. How do I take him down, Shal?" Ringil tipped his head to indicate the pommel of the Ravensfriend. "Could I do it with this?"

Shalak pursed his lips. "It's doubtful. You'd have to be very fast indeed."

"Well, that has been said about me on occasion." He didn't add that those occasions had receded increasingly into the realm of memory over the past few years. There were always the stories, of course, the war legends, but who—other than himself, in Jhesh's tavern, increasingly wearily—still told those?

Shalak took a turn about the cluttered space in the shop. He rubbed at his forehead, dodged a hanging wooden assemblage of wind chimes, grimaced.

"Thing is, Gil, we don't really know much about the dwenda. I mean, this stuff I sell, it's mostly junk—"

"It is?"

The merchant gave him a sour look. "All right, all right. I make a living from hints and half-truths, and what people desperately want to believe. I don't need you to remind me of that. But the core of this, all this, is something even the Kiriath couldn't map. They fought the dwenda for possession of this world once, you know. But if you read their annals, it's pretty clear they didn't really know what they were fighting. There are references to ghosts, shape-shifting, possession, stones and forests and rivers coming to life at Aldrain command—"

"Oh *come* off it, Shal." Ringil shook his head. "Tell me you're not that naïve. I'm looking for a considered opinion here, not something I can get out of any gibbering idiot down at Strov."

"That's what I'm giving you, Gil. A considered opinion. Outside of oral legend and a few runic scribbles on standing stones along the west coast, we don't have anything but the Indirath M'nal chronicle to tell us what the Aldrain were really like. It's the only reputable source. Everything else the Kiriath wrote on the subject draws on it. And the Indirath M'nal says, among other things, that the dwenda could command water and stone and wood to life."

"Yeah, and I knew Majak herders back in the day who thought the Kiriath were all fire-blackened demons." Ringil cranked up an arm, made a jabbering mouth with his hand. "Rejected from the Depths of Hell to walk the Earth in Eternal Damnation. Blab-blab-blab. Kind of shit gets made up every day by people too stupid to look for the realities. You should have heard the boatman who brought me up here from the Glades. Fire in the northern sky, lights in the marshes, a black dog heard barking through the night. Doesn't occur to anyone to wonder how exactly you can tell it's a *black* dog just from the fucking *bark* it makes."

Shalak cocked his head. He frowned. "What is this, Gil? What are you so angry about?"

It brought him up short. He stared at the neatly swept floor of the little shop and raised an eyebrow at the strain in his own just-silenced voice.

"What's wrong, Gil?"

He shook his head. Sighed. "Doesn't matter. It's nothing. Late night, too much carousing, you know me. I'm sorry. Go on, you were saying."

"*You* were saying. That people are too stupid to look for the realities and they hide in superstition instead. And that's true enough, but you're missing the point. You're talking about humans, and ignorant humans at that. The scribes who wrote the Indirath M'nal weren't either. They were the cream of Kiriath culture, highly educated and already well traveled in places most of us have a hard time imagining. And the dwenda *scared* those guys, that's the truth, it's there in the way the texts are written. Clear as the face on a harbor-end whore."

Ringil thought back to the Kiriath he'd known; Grashgal, Naranash, Flaradnam, Kalanak, and all the others, names gone blurred with the years. He thought of the impassive aura of command they'd carried into the war with the Scaled Folk, the methodical savagery with which they fought. It was a mask, Archeth insisted to him once, part of the courtly gravitas that informed Kiriath culture from its roots; but if she was right, it was a mask that never came off, not even when Naranash bled out on the beach at Rajal, grinning and leaking blood through his teeth while Ringil crouched uselessly beside him.

Looks like you'll have to do the rest without me, eh. Are we winning, lad?

Ringil glanced about—the Yhelteth flank, crumpling and tearing like cheap armor under repeated blows as the reptile advance slammed into them, the crisscross panic of fleeing soldiery from the shattered lines and the screams of those broken or burned or ripped apart all along the beach, the landing barges fleeing back across the bight, evacuating those lucky enough to make the shallows . . .

Yeah, he told Naranash. *We're winning: Looks like Flaradnam held the breakwater after all. We're driving them back.*

The Kiriath knight spat up blood. *That's good. He's a good lad, 'Nam, he'll follow through. Shame I'm going to miss that party.* He coughed throatily for a moment. *You keep hold of that sword, you hear? Best friend you'll ever have. Friend to* ravens, *remember that. Make sure—*

And the reptile peon was on Ringil, long shriek and the rasping, scaled impact against his cuirass. He staggered and went over backward in the sand. The long spiked tail lashed around, the claws dug in, and Ringil screamed back in the creature's face at the pain, smashed the pommel of the Ravensfriend into its eye. The peon shrilled and its fangs snapped shut inches from his throat. He got his left forearm in the way, guarding, dropped the Ravensfriend and stabbed two stiffened fingers from his freed right hand into the creature's eye, down past the socket and into the brain behind. The peon thrashed and shrieked and snapped, and he rolled it over in the fountaining storm of sand it was making with its tail. Pinned it there with his body weight while his fingers burrowed and shoved in up to the hilt. The eyelid flapped up and down on his knuckles like a trapped moth's wing scraping in the cup of a boy's closed palms. The tail lashed about, damp sand came up in shovel loads, swiped him across the face, got gritty into his mouth as he sucked breath and snarled and fought and then, finally, *finally,* with a high whining noise in its throat and a shivering convulsion, the fucking thing died.

And by the time he staggered back to his feet, so had Naranash.

He never knew if in those last moments the Kiriath knight had seen the peon attack, understood what was going on and had drawn his own fading conclusions about the state of the battle. If at the end he'd known that Ringil had lied to him.

But Ringil had never seen him afraid.

"You sure you're interpreting the texts right?" he asked Shalak. "I mean, maybe the language—"

"I grew up speaking Tethanne as well as Naomic, Gil. My mother made me learn to read it as well. I've seen copies of the translations they made of the Indirath M'nal in Yhelteth, I've seen the commentaries on it, and I know enough of the High Kir original to follow those commentaries. And I'm telling you, Gil, the day the Kiriath went up against the Vanishing Folk, they were scared."

Shalak clasped his hands at waist height and cast his head back a little. Ringil remembered the pose from summer gatherings of the city's Aldrain enthusiasts that he'd attended in his youth. Everybody huddled together and chattering in early-evening gloom, taking wine in little fake Aldrain goblets in the tiny gardens at the back of the shop. There was a quote coming.

"*How should one fight an enemy that is not wholly of this world?*" Shal declaimed. "*They come to us in ghost form, striking snake-swift out of phantasmal mist, and when we strike back they return to mist and they laugh, low and mocking in the wind. They—*"

But now the rest of it was gone, carried away on the cool breeze out of nowhere that blew up Ringil's neck. He snapped back to the previous night, the krin-skewed walk home from Grace-of-Heaven's place and swooping laughter past his face like a caress. He felt the same shiver creep up his neck again and found he'd raised a hand involuntarily to touch his cheek where the laughter had seemed to touch . . .

"Pretty conclusive, wouldn't you say?"

Shalak, finished now with his quotations, looking at him expectantly. Ringil blinked.

"Uh—yeah." He scrambled to cover for his disconnection. "I guess. Uhm, that bit about *not wholly of this world*. They say the Aldrain came from the band originally, don't they? And that's where they went back to. You think that's possible?"

"With the Aldrain, anything's *possible*. But likely?" Shalak shook his head. "You talk to any decent astronomer, here or in the Empire, they'll tell you the band is made up of a million different moving particles, all catching the sun's rays. That's why it shines, it's like dust motes in a sunbeam. It's just not a solid arch the way it looks. Hard to see how anything could live in the middle of something like that."

Ringil brooded. "The Majak believe that the band is a pathway leading to the Sky Home of the honorable dead. A ghost road."

"Yes, but they're savages."

Ringil remembered Egar's scarred and tattooed features, slightly surprised at the sudden flare of affection it triggered. It was how the steppe nomad would cheerfully have described himself—*I ain't fucking civilized, Gil,* he'd said one campfire night on the march to Hanliahg. *That's not something I'm ever going to need*—but still Shalak's automatic sneer went home like a barb. He held down a spurt of unreasonably defensive anger.

"I don't know," he said carefully. "You spend any time that far north, you get to see some strange shit in the sky. You should get yourself up there sometime. And anyway, here we are talking about the Aldrain as ghost warriors. So you know, maybe there's something in it."

"Ringil, I really don't think you can stack a bunch of shamanistic gibbering up against the gathered writings of the Kiriath's finest minds and expect it to make a pile the same height."

"All right. So you tell me—how did these finest minds among the Kiriath beat the Aldrain?"

Shalak shrugged. "With machinery, it seems. The way the Kiriath did most things. There are a lot of references to—"

Outside in the street, someone started shouting. Something thumped audibly against the wall. Shalak flinched, perhaps with the old memories, and went swiftly to one of the shop's grimy windows. He peered out for a moment, then relaxed.

"It's just Darby," he said. "Another one of his episodes, looks like."

"Darby?" Ringil got up and drifted toward the window, ducking the wind chimes. "What's he, a neighbor of yours?"

"Thankfully not." Shalak shifted slightly to give Ringil space at his side, and nodded at the scene on the other side of the glass. "Look."

In the early-evening sunlight outside, the crowds had parted and drawn back, become a silhouetted whole, a curtain closing in a broad oval of cobbled street. In the center of this impromptu arena, a solitary figure stood isolated. His clothing was obviously ragged beneath a longish, dirty blue coat that looked somehow familiar, and he brandished some kind of crude cudgel in a two-handed ax grip. At his feet, a pair of elegantly attired forms rolled about on the cobbles, clutching at themselves where blows had obviously been delivered.

"Darby," Shalak repeated, as if that were explanation enough.

"And the others?"

The shopkeeper pulled a face. "No idea. Clerks-at-law by their coats, they're probably down from the courts at Lim Cross, sessions'll be turning out about now. Darby doesn't like lawyers much."

That much was evident. Darby loomed over the two men he'd put on the ground, lips peeled back off his teeth, eyes staring. His hair was a tangled gray mess, visibly greasy from lack of washing, and he had a beard down to his chest to match. He was saying something to the men, but you couldn't hear it through the window glass.

For all of that, the weapon in his hands was absolutely steady.

The sinking sun caught on an epaulet buckle, and inside Ringil's krinzanz-tender head, familiarity leapt into recognition. He swore softly to himself.

And then the Watch arrived.

Six men strong, they forced their way through the curtaining crowd of spectators with shoulders and well-judged jolts from the ends of their day-clubs. Darby watched them come. They spilled out into the cleared space in a loose group, saw the cudgel, and maybe recognized the coat the way Ringil just had. They glanced back and forth at one another. The stunned men at Darby's feet lay where they were, still prone, dazed in the flooding sunlight, half aware at best of what was going on. No one said anything. Then the watchmen began to spread out, sliding warily around the edge of the cleared space like coffee in the rim of a tipped saucer, skirting their target, looking to surround and overwhelm.

Darby saw it and grinned in his beard.

Ringil was already on his way out the door.

The first attacker came up on Darby from the rear, just off his left shoulder. It was an obvious move, not hard for him to anticipate. Those in front couldn't, after all, conduct the fight across the living bodies of fallen worthy citizens. Plus, the long shadows cast on the cobbles telegraphed the attack. The watchman came in swinging his club down, and Darby wasn't there anymore. He'd stepped back and aside, an odd, unlooked-for elegance in the move, almost like dance. The watchman was caught, arms up with the club, falling forward into his move. Darby swung hard, with the cudgel held horizontal, into the man's unprotected belly and lower ribs. The impact sounded like an ax in wood. The watchman made a choked shriek.

The others rushed in as best they could.

Darby slid the cudgel clear like it was a sword, but it wasn't. It was rough and blunt and the watchman's weight was folded over it. In the moment the difference cost him, a second club wielder slammed him across the shoulders. It was a mistake—not trying for the head. Darby staggered and snarled, but he didn't go down. The watchman tried to hook his feet out from under him and Darby stabbed backward with the cudgel, got the man in the face. Blood splashed in the sunlit air. Darby whooped at the sight of it, leapt the clerks' bodies, and landed cat-like between two of the other watchmen before they could register what was happening. The cudgel whirled about him in a blur. The crowd swayed back with a fairground chorus of excited yells. The cudgel caught one of the Watch about the head and sent him staggering, but either it missed the other or the man was a cannier fighter than his fellows.

This much Ringil saw as he came through the door, this much he'd more or less assumed—the coat was its own prophecy of how the fight would go. But now the untouched watchman nearest to Darby waded in, club held in a two-handed sword grip, feinting and blocking, bellowing hoarse and low to those of his comrades still on their feet.

"Get in behind him! Bring this fuck *down*, will you!"

He was younger than Darby by a generation, and faster. He blocked Darby's cudgel, looped it away, and got in a savage blow to the older man's elbow. Darby howled obscenities, gave up no *fucking* inch of ground, swung back. Something in Ringil cheered at the sight. The young watchman skipped outside the swing, then rushed in with his club braced baton-style. He pinned Darby's arm to his body, pinned the cudgel, and shoved him back a solid pace. A second watchman saw his chance and jumped in behind. He hooked his day-club over Darby's head, took it back hard at the throat, and dragged his victim backward and down, a couple of yards away from where the two law clerks were finally sitting up and taking notice. Darby choked and thrashed and, finally, went to the ground over his attacker's bent knee. The young watchman stepped up, dodging Darby's flailing feet, and swung a long hard kick into the downed fighter's groin. Darby squawked and convulsed.

The others closed in. The clubs rose and fell.

"That's enough! He's down."

But now the Watch's blood was up. The shout alone was never going to be enough and Ringil, clear in the knowledge, was moving forward even as the words left his lips. He reached up left-handed, grabbed a day-club as it came up, and yanked hard on it. The surprised watchman lost his grip and stumbled. Ringil got a grip on the man's collar with his other hand, manhandled him impatiently out of the way. Then he waded in and used the commandeered club to break up the fun.

Jolt into belly, smash knuckles on an opposing club, tangle legs—*block! shove! hurt!* It was awhile since he'd fought with a stick—some village commons contest Jhesh had inveigled him into a few years back when Ringil's finances were at low ebb and the storytelling wouldn't cut it for his tab—but the dynamics never really went away. He'd trained extensively with mocked-up Majak staff lances in the Academy, before they let him loose on the real thing, and then there were Yhelteth empty-hand techniques that spilled out into a form using a simple bamboo pole . . . The watchmen were trained as well, of course, but not with much care, and this new attack was the last thing they'd looked for. It took Ringil a scant few seconds to drive them off the man on the ground, and then he had them repelled into a wary circle similar to the one they'd approached Darby with in the first place. Difference was, this time two of them were already down on the cobbles and out of it, courtesy of Darby's earlier efforts, and the other four, nursing a host of minor injuries, did not know what to make of this newcomer, I mean, *look,* man: moss-soft cloak of blue that quite visibly would have cost them a year's wages, clothes beneath of equally fine embroidered cloth, a sword on his back, a killing calm in his eyes, and the stolen day-club, held out one-handed and pointing as if it were a bladed weapon.

Ringil turned very slowly, marking each man along the shaft of the leveled club, daring them to come back at him.

"I think you made your arrest," he said evenly. "Let's call it a day, shall we?"

"You're interfering with Watch business," blustered the young, fast one who'd pinned Darby up in the fight. "That man's a known public nuisance."

"Maybe so." Ringil sidestepped, eyes still on the circling watchmen, and prodded Darby's prone form with his boot. Darby groaned. "But I don't see him in a state to make much mischief now, do you?"

"He assaulted people. He's got a history of it."

"Well, we're none of us historians here. Where are the injured parties?"

Unfortunately, the two law clerks hadn't run off, they were still hiding in the crowd. Now they trod forward, clothes in disarray, faces flushed and bearing some small scrapes. Ringil spared them a glance.

"You got in a fight with this man?"

"He attacked us," spluttered the more distressed looking of the two men. "Unprovoked. Started shoving us in the crowd, screaming abuse for no reason."

"Lying fucks." Slurring tones—at Ringil's heel, Darby had managed to prop himself up on one arm. The motion brought with it a heady stink of unwashed flesh laced with piss and cheap wine. The man had clearly not bathed in a couple of months. "Called me an *animal.* A fucking marsh sloth. Not so long ago it was I fought to keep your mamas from being spitted on a big fucking lizard prick, that's the thanks I get? I made my living with honest fucking steel, not robbing a man's home and family with papers and ink."

"I don't know what he's talking about," said the other clerk, somewhat calmer than his companion. He seemed, perhaps with an eye sharpened by his profession, to have taken stock of Ringil's attire. "But from the state of the man, I think it's pretty clear who you can believe here."

"That's a skirmish ranger's coat he's wearing," Ringil said, trying not to breathe through his nose. "Which suggests he was considered good enough to give his life for the city once. Perhaps there's something in what he says."

The clerk flushed. "Are you accusing me of lying, sir?"

"If you choose to take it that way."

A slight, hanging silence. The crowd watched, lapping it up. The clerks looked uneasily at each other. Neither was armed beyond short ceremonial poniards they clearly had no idea how to use.

"Look," one of them began.

Ringil shook his head. "You don't look worse than shaken up, either of you. Nothing a visit to the baths won't ease. In your place, I'd cut my losses and go home. Think of it as a valuable lesson in manners."

He held their gaze for the time it took to make sure they'd do as he said. Watched them push through the gathered spectators and away, muttering angrily at each other, a couple of backward glances, nothing more. The crowd swallowed them, and chattering broke out in their wake. No one among the spectators seemed too upset by the way things were sliding. Ringil turned his attention back to the Watch.

"Seems the plaintiffs are disinclined to press the matter," he said easily. "So what do you say, shall we show this old soldier here a little civil leniency? Turn him loose with a warning?"

A scattering of murmurs through the crowd. It sounded like agreement.

"Here *fucking* here," croaked Darby, trying to get up. He didn't make a very good job of it; he slipped and fell on his backside, stayed there, bleeding from a bad cut above the eye. The spectators laughed.

Ringil felt a hot stab of anger. Held it down.

"*Honor the unpaid debt,*" Darby mumbled, blinking around at the laughter from his seat on the ground. The air was redolent with his stench now; it wafted with his every move. "*The life and limb in honor given.*"

The young watchmen snorted. "Fucking old soldier, my arsehole. He's quoting that shit off the Grel Memorial. Any beggar with half his wits can do it. And this one's a drunk fucking pervert to boot. Ask anybody around here. Always causing trouble. Exposing himself to the good women of the neighborhood, abusing the citizenry day and night. And as for that coat, the fucker probably stole it off a corpse down at Pauper's Landing."

"Yeah." One of his fellows jeered. "Hasn't washed it since, what my nose is telling me. Some skirmish ranger."

Ringil nodded at the two members of the Watch who were still out cold on the cobbles. "He fought remarkably well, don't you think, for a drunk pervert beggar?"

"He jumped us," said the young one. "He got lucky."

Ringil met the young watchman's eye and held it. "If he'd had a bladed weapon, you'd all be dead men now. You're the ones who got lucky today."

The watchman looked away.

"Just doing our jobs," he muttered.

Ringil spotted the opening. Moved smoothly into it. "Yes, and I'm sure it's thirsty work. Look, I have an idea. I'm a man of some means, and a soldier myself, and I suppose this old warhorse has captured my sympathy. But that's no reason to expect honest men like yourselves to put aside your bound duties in keeping the peace. Perhaps, in view of the trouble you've had, I could stand you all a flagon or two at that tavern I see across the street there."

A hesitant look chased its way around the four watchmen. One of the older ones nodded at their two comrades stretched out on the cobbles.

"What about them?"

"Yes, I imagine they'll need some small medical attention." Ringil spurred the shifting mood on, tossed his commandeered day-club onto the cobbles, and reached for his purse instead. "And I'd be more than happy to foot the bill for that as well. It's only right."

And it's only Ishil's money. Which is only Gingren's money in turn.

Someone in the crowd cheered, and it spread. Ringil forced a smile against the applause until it felt real. He opened the purse and held out a loose palmful of coin.

"Who's in charge here?" he asked.

CHAPTER 10

Robed and hooded astride an undistinguished horse, Poltar the shaman reached the gates of Ishlin-ichan as night was falling. A pair of burly Ishlinak sentries ambled up to meet him, amiably enough but at lance-point nonetheless. Their captain came out of the flicker-lit brazier warmth of the guard hut, grinning and blowing on his hands.

"Twelve," he said, yawning.

"The levy is seven," Poltar said stiffly.

"Well, nighttime rates." The captain stamped his feet, coughed and spat. "Gets cold at night, you know. It's twelve. You coming in or not?"

Ordinarily, the shaman would have used his status to demand free entry, or failing that at least beat the price back down with some arcane threats. But right now he preferred to give up the handful of coins, stomach the extortion, and stay anonymous. He had business in the town not normally approved of in holy men, and besides, with the stories of his shaming at the Dragonbane's hands spreading far and wide, he wasn't sure exactly what status he now had, even this far from the Skaranak tents.

He would not be laughed at, whatever the cost.

The levy paid, he passed under the wooden wall and clopped slowly through the narrow streets of the settlement, cursing Egar ceaselessly under his breath and ducking to avoid the low-level washing lines strung from house to house. Ishlin-ichan, though the name might rather grandiosely mean "city of the Ishlinak," could only by a generous stretch of the imagination lay claim to the title. It was less a town than a sprawling winter camp with walls, a bright idea based on milder climate and a couple of advantageous meanders in the River Janarat. About a century ago, encouraged by these factors and the burgeoning possibilities of trade with the south, a hard core of Ishlinak ancestors started replacing their tents with more static constructions. In time they gave up the nomad life altogether. *Why chase your livelihood across the freezing steppe,* they must have reasoned, *when it may quite possibly come directly to your campfires and offer itself for slaughter.*

In time, they were proved right. The focal point offered by Ishlin-ichan brought merchants out from both the Trelayne League and the Empire, eager for trade and delighted not to have to live under canvas while they were about it. Mirroring the attraction from the other side of the market, the herdsmen from the other Majak clans started bringing their produce to Ishlin-ichan in preference to other, closer but less lucrative temporary venues across the steppe. Secondary industries sprang up, catering to the influx. The essentials at first: bakeries, butchers, whorehouses, and taverns. Then stables, established horse traders, and fixed smithies with decent-sized furnaces, finally supplying high-quality steel. The young men of the Majak came to Ishlin-ichan to outfit themselves and to swagger in the streets. Recruiting officers from the south, once forced to ride the steppes from band to nomadic band and track down promising fighters by word of mouth, now found it infinitely easier to maintain an office in the fledgling town and wait for the recruits to come to them. So the cabins of Ishlin-ichan became stone and mud-brick houses, sometimes even rising more than a single story high. The streets began to be cobbled—a technique taught to the Ishlinak by unemployed Trelayne architects seeking refuge from another economic downturn in the League—and as neighboring clans began to show an unhealthy interest in the rapidly accumulating wealth, the whole settlement was hastily walled and fortified. Finally, the diplomats arrived from the League and the Empire, setting a seal upon the place. They tended to regard Ishlin-ichan as a hardship posting, to be endured in the climb toward more rewarding appointments elsewhere, but while they were there they pushed for anything that might ease their discomfort a little. Plumbing improved; public order patrols were instituted. The more important thoroughfares were torchlit by night, often for their entire length.

The house Poltar wanted was not on one of these streets. It stood in the seclusion and gloom of a darkened side alley by design rather than economic necessity. The alley ran alongside a section of the city wall and Madame Ajana's rose two stories above the parapet, leaning there as if tired by the effort of hoisting itself up to see out across the plain. The height and position were also deliberate—from a mile out on the steppe, you could make out the red glowing lanterns of the whorehouse, beckoning.

In the alley, the brothel was no more subtly appointed. The windows were brightly lit within, and those of Ajana's girls not working were paid to sit in plain view displaying their wares. Incense and softly thudding music smoked out into the street, catching at the throats and ears of those whose eyes were not already captivated by the spread-legged, arch-backed postures of the girls in the windows. A luxurious velour drape curtained the open doors, meant to imitate the drop flap of a yurt, and above hung a wooden sign announcing it as AJANA'S PLACE, a name that in the Majak tongue had a crude and fairly obvious double meaning.

Poltar climbed down off his horse, slipped coins—*more* fucking coins—to the impassive attendants at the door, and let them lead it away. He stepped through into the dimly lit chamber beyond and put back his hood. He was recognized by some of the girls, but none of them smiled at him the way he had sometimes noted that they did with other customers. He gathered in their flinching glances with satisfaction; this was as it should be. He wasn't some drunken herdsman, easily muzzled with a fat tit and coaxed to a bleating climax in a mother substitute's arms. Not some child-hearted brute, content to smother himself in a welter of female flesh.

He was Poltar Wolfeye, Chief Shaman to the Skaranak. He was a man of power, and he had long ago in his initiation broken the bonds that women wove over men.

Ajana came toward him with her painted smile.

"Shaman, you honor us again so soon. What's your pleasure? Will you have the upper room?"

He nodded a curt assent.

"Then I'll have a girl prepared. Come and join me while you wait. A glass of wine? Some sweetmeats?" She snapped her fingers and an effeminate tray bearer came hurrying. Poltar averted his face in distaste. Ajana muttered something in the man's ear as he set down the tray, and he withdrew, nodding. Poltar settled onto the cushioned couch and accepted the goblet Ajana proffered. The vague, restless anger that had consumed him since his confrontation with the Dragonbane began to solidify into something more tangible in the pit of his stomach. He felt a slight shiver of anticipation.

"The new girls are very eager," said the madam, keenly attuned to her customer's moods and massaging where it would do most good. "Hot young sluts from the League, looking for a big Majak prick to suck."

The shaman shifted impatiently. "Just make sure she's not drugged like the last one. I want her to feel what I'm doing."

"Yes, yes, that *was* a most lamentable error." Ajana offered him a plate of spiced cake slices. Her voice purred, soft and cozy as wine from the flask neck. "But it won't be repeated. Ajana's Place draws your pleasure from you exactly as you would most wish to give it up. All preparations are being made to this single end, of that you may lie back and rest assured."

It took half an hour to make the preparations, by which time the shaman was lightly drunk and swollen almost to bursting with Ajana's subtle verbal ministrations. The madam led him up the three flights of stairs with ritual slowness, pausing on each landing so that he could regain his breath and witness through half-drawn curtains scenes of orgiastic abandon that would fuel his arousal. Finally, at the door of the upper room, Ajana took a key from her voluminous robes and handed it to him.

"The lock is oiled and ready," she said. "Enter and enjoy."

She left him facing the door. He paused a moment, then inserted the key, twisted, and let himself into the small perfumed space beyond.

Incense candles burned in the corners of the room, giving off more smoke than light. The shadows on the walls flickered like impatient observers as his entry moved the flames. One tiny window showed faint starlight over the plain beyond the city. In the center of the room, the girl was roped to an inverted Y-frame that hung suspended on a pulley system, her arms bound together above her head, her legs spread along the arms of the Y. Her limbs gleamed with recent oiling, and the mass of dark hair around her face was still damp. She was made up in the southern fashion, eyelids heavy with kohl and cheeks painted with Yhelteth symbols, though she was fairly clearly of Trelayne stock. Beneath it all she was very young and, he saw, afraid.

His grunt of satisfaction seemed to emanate from his stomach.

"You do well to fear me, whore," he said thickly, pushing the door closed with his back. "Because I'm going to hurt you, just the way you deserve to be hurt."

On the stairs below, Ajana winced as the first cries floated down to her, and then hurried away to where she wouldn't have to hear them.

BY THE TIME POLTAR FORCED HIS WAY INTO THE GIRL, HE WAS PANTING from his efforts and the palms of his hands stung from the slaps he'd delivered. He seized the pulleys and worked them, moving both Y-frame and its load down to where he could gloat over the rapidly bruising flesh. The girl's initial screams for help had changed to more intimate pleas when she realized that no one was coming to rescue her from this honored customer—but she still uttered one more little shriek as he stabbed inside her. He came almost immediately, the pent-up pressure gushing out of him before he had completed a dozen thrusts. His hands, which had been clenched around the girl's breasts, relaxed and he sagged forward. A string of spittle drooled out of him and onto her flesh.

"Oh, Urann," he breathed, wiping his mouth. "Oh Ye Gods."

The sudden pain was as intense as it was incomprehensible. It felt as if his prick had been clamped in a swordsmith's vise and someone was tightening the screw. He yelped and tried to pull away from the girl, but that part of his anatomy would not go with him. He looked down at himself in confusion and what he saw in the uncertain light brought a high, womanish scream to his lips. The girl's sex was gone, the flesh between her thighs replaced by a clenched fist whose fingers he could clearly see pulping his shriveling member.

"Don't go so soon," said a voice from the girl's lips.

He looked up and saw that her eyes were open again, that now the kohl and face-paint mask of arousal had smoldered to genuine life. The eyes hooded and looked at him seductively, and then, as he watched, the girl's neck lifted sinuously from the frame against which it lay and lifted the head toward him. He leaned as far away as he could but it came after him like the head of a snake, little crunching and popping sounds emanating from the vertebrae as they stretched. The muscles in the girl's face writhed in the flickering light of the candles, as if whatever was using her had not recently worn human flesh.

"You called upon us," the voice that was not a young girl's said ironically. "To what purpose?"

"Uh-uh-Urann?" the shaman managed, trembling like a man with a high fever.

"Not I." The face glided fractionally nearer, attempting a smile. "But close. I believe you know me as Kelgris."

Even in the extremity of his terror and pain, Poltar had a moment to be puzzled. Kelgris, Mistress of First Blood and the Falcon, belonged to the mewling rituals of the Voronak, was supplicated by young lovers, pregnant women, and the odd, wizened female herbalist. Among the Skaranak, she'd long been ushered into obscurity by the warrior rituals.

Her name cropped up as a curse used by small children and the butt of various lewd jokes about the Majak afterlife, but beyond that . . .

The girl's face hissed at him, very much like the serpent it appeared to think it was.

"*Beyond that* is a level of intelligence, oh Poltar of the dozen mighty strokes, that your kind will need millennia to assemble. What is rather more important here is that you have asked for the intercession of the Dwellers. You begged for us in your prayers and your dreams, you cut the throats of small animals for us at every opportunity—and drank the blood—you burned pots full of that rather overstated incense you seem to believe gets our attention. You wanted the Dwellers, well now you're going to get them, and they won't be the playmates you envisaged, *of that you may lie back and rest assured.*" The thing inside the girl mimicked the words of Ajana an hour earlier with evident relish. "I bring a message from my brother Hoiran, the one you call Urann. That message is *wait and watch.*"

The shaman dropped one hand to the burning pain between his legs. "Will Urann revenge himself on the Dragonbane?" he gritted. "Will I be vindicated?"

"That," said Kelgris sweetly, "depends upon your conduct. If you behave as is fitting in, uhm, a Wayfarer of the Sky Road, you may make some headway. Displease us and I shall make a plaything of your soul in the ice hell beyond the world. Or something. As for *this*—" The fist at the juncture of the girl's thighs unbent its index finger without loosening the vise-like hold it had on Poltar's prick. The finger flicked bruisingly at his fright-shriveled scrotum. "This might conceivably amuse my brother on a bad day, but me it does not amuse. A holy man must be chaste if he is to channel his energy where and when it is most needed. Chaste. Do you remember the meaning of that word?"

The hand squeezed tighter still. Poltar felt skin split, and then the sudden wetness of blood.

"Yes," he shrieked. "Yes, chaste."

"You will not spill your seed in this fashion again without my permission. Do I make myself clear?"

"Yes, yes, yes . . ." Now he was weeping from the pain. The hand released as abruptly as it had clenched, and the shaman reeled backward, stumbling and collapsing to the floor.

"Then abase yourself," said the voice, still sweetly reasonable. "Abase yourself and, uhm, rejoice, that the gods have returned to you."

The shaman flung himself flat before the staked body on the frame. Contact with the rough floor stung his mutilated prick, but he stayed immobile, quivering and gibbering and praying, until voices and an urgent hammering on the door of the little room brought him to his senses.

He looked up, wild-eyed and shaking, and saw that Kelgris had gone, leaving nothing but stillness in her wake. The room was dark, the candles snuffed out. Light from the window made a gaunt silhouette of the Y-frame, where the body of the girl was still tied, neck lolling broken and stretched and twisted to one side, eyes wide open in mute accusation.

Kelgris's smile was still pressed on her dead mouth.

CHAPTER 11

It took the best part of an hour to fix everything up. As with any aftermath, the trick was in the momentum.

You keep everyone moving, Flaradnam had told him that day, from his stretcher in the surgeon's tent. Hoarse breath, face knotted with the pain he was swamped in. Summer rain hissed down on the other side of the canvas. Outside, the slanted ground would be turning muddy and treacherous underfoot. *Don't give them time to think, don't give them time to bitch and moan. They want orders and certainty from you, nothing more. You find that certainty, Gil, fake it if you have to. But you get them out of here. You get them* moving.

He did not survive the surgeon's table.

And out across the mountain's flank, the broken remnants of the expeditionary force huddled miserably against the rain, mail and once gaily colored uniforms like a variegated mold on the landscape. Framed in the tent flap, listening to the gritted shrieks and grating kitchen sounds of surgery at his back, Ringil stared out through the downpour with no earthly clue how to get done what Flaradnam wanted. The Kiriath war machines were lost, abandoned in the rout. The injured and dying numbered in the hundreds, the lizards were coming.

Gallows Water was two days' hard march, south and east over steep, exposed mountain terrain.

You keep everyone moving.

So. *Nothing ever changes, huh 'Nam?*

Get the injured watchmen back to their senses and their feet, downplay the obviously quite serious harm Darby's assault had done them. Cold water from Shalak's yard pump, and some judicious slaps. Ferry the whole squad—amid a sudden crowd of well-wishers, backslappers, and general hangers-on—across into the tavern. Get the wine flowing and paid for in quantity enough to keep everyone clustered there. Call for music. Sip at the god-awful vintages the tavern had to offer, keep the smile pinned on your face. Watch the whores move sinuously in on the company, like cats after scraps. Play the role of gracious-noble-with-the-common-touch until memory and rancor for the fight fogged out and faded in the general merriment.

Leave.

Ringil slipped away as the singing took hold, got out to where a soft blue dusk was stealing up the street from the river. Overhead, the band was out in all its shimmering glory. The thoroughfare had more or less emptied now, only a handful of people hurrying home and the lantern-jacks with their ladders to disturb the evening. Compared with the raucous heat of the tavern, it was very cool and quiet. Ringil crossed the street back to Shalak's shop, saw that Darby was sitting huddled on the doorstep. On the way across to the veteran, he scooped up an abandoned day-club from the cobbles and twirled it through the air with absentminded dexterity.

"Souvenir?" he asked, holding out the club.

Darby shook his head, patted the cudgel that was propped between his knees and cuddled into his shoulder like a sleeping child. "I'll stick with Old Lurlin here. She's seen me right enough times."

"Fair enough."

"I'm much obliged to your worthiness. For the intervention, I mean. I think they had the best of me there." A hand rose to touch his bruised and bloodied face. The fingers came away clotted with gore. Darby grimaced. "Yep. Caught me a good one here, and I'd say the ribs are cracked again."

"Can you walk?"

"Oh yes, Darby can always move on, sir. Be out of your sight directly. Only stayed to thank you."

"That's not what I meant." Ringil reached for his depleted purse, dug out a fresh handful of coin. "Look, I want you—"

The veteran shook his head emphatically.

"No, sir. Wouldn't hear of it. The kindness you done me already, that's more than most would dare these days. Those pretty bend-over boy clerks and their sodomite fucking lawyers, they've got this whole city by the balls. Means nothing to any of them that a man once fought the lizards for them all."

"I know," Ringil said quietly.

"Yes, sir, I know you do, sir." The look on Darby's damaged face changed. It took Ringil a couple of seconds to nail the new expression for what it was—shyness. "Saw you at Rajal, sir. I was fighting in the surf not twenty feet from you when the dragons came. Took me some time to place your face this time, my memory's not what it once was, sir. But I'd know that blade on your back anywhere."

Ringil sighed. "Hard to miss, huh?"

"That it is, sir."

The evening gloom closed in on them. Across the street a lantern-jack burned his fingers and cursed in the quiet. Ringil prodded at a loose cobble with the day-club. He was finding it easier to ignore Darby's unwashed stink now he was used to it. He'd reeked that way himself often enough during the war.

"I'm afraid I don't remember you from Rajal at all," he said.

"No reason why you should, sir. No reason at all. There was a lot of us that day. Only wish I'd been there with you at Gallows Gap."

Now it was Ringil's turn to grimace. "Careful what you wish for. We lost a lot more men there than we did at Rajal. Chances are you'd be pushing up daisies now if you'd been in that fight."

"Yes, sir. But we won at Gallows Gap."

From the tavern, suddenly, explosive laughter and a new song. A war song, one of the classics. "Lizard Blood Like Water to Wash In." Stomping martial rhythm, it sounded as if they were pounding on the tables in there. Darby levered himself to his feet, wincing a little as he did.

"Best be off then," he said, voice tight with his pain. A knowing nod toward the noise, a crooked grin. "Wouldn't want to still be on hand when the old patriotic fervor gets beyond feeling up the whores and drinking. They'll be out looking for blood soon enough, someone to take it out on."

Ringil glanced at Shalak's windows, thought that he'd better get in there and help the shopkeeper douse the lights.

"You're probably right," he said.

"Probably am, sir." Darby squared his shoulders. "Well, I'll be going then. It was a real pleasure talking to someone who understands. Only sorry you find me in such straitened circumstances. I wasn't always this way, sir."

"No, I don't suppose you were."

"It's just the memories, sir. Things I saw, things I had to do. Feels like they're branded in my head, sir. Hard to let it go sometimes. The drinking helps, and the flandrijn, when I can get it." He fiddled awkwardly with his cudgel, wouldn't meet Ringil's eye. "I'm not what I once was, sir, that's the plain truth of it."

"We're none of us what we once were." Ringil staved off his own brooding with an effort, looked for something good to say. Something Flaradnam might have approved. "Seems to me you gave a pretty good account of yourself, all things considered. One of those watchmen has smashed ribs for sure, and the other one can't focus on anything. I'd say you gave him a solid brain fuck with Lurlin there."

The veteran looked up again. "Well, I'm sorry for that, sir. They're not bad men, I had an uncle in the Watch myself years ago. It's a tough job. But they meant to have me, sir. You saw that."

"Yes, I did. And like I said, you gave a fine account of yourself."

It got a smile. "Ah, but you should have seen me at Rajal, sir. They had to *drag* me onto that evacuation barge."

"I'm sure they did."

They stood there for a couple of moments. The martial anthem went on, muffled by the tavern walls, but swelling. Darby shouldered the cudgel, thumped his hand to his chest in salute.

"Right sir, I'll be going."

Ringil dug in his purse again. "Listen."

"No, sir. I won't impose on your kindness any further." He kept his free hand clenched and at his chest. "Absolutely not."

"It's not much. Just to get yourself, I don't know, some hot food, a hot bath. A place to stay."

"It's a kind thought, sir. But we both know that's not what I'd spend it on."

"Well." Ringil gestured helplessly, dug out the coin regardless. "Look, spend it on fucking wine and flandrijn, then. If that's what you need."

The fist came halfway uncurled. Something moved in the veteran's face, and this time Ringil couldn't identify what it was. He pressed the handful of money forward.

"Come on, one old soldier to another. It's just a favor in hard times. You'd do the same for me."

Darby took the coin.

It was a sudden, convulsive move. His hand was rough with accumulated dirt and grit, and a little hot, as if from fever. He looked away as he stowed the money somewhere in his rags.

"Much obliged to you, sir, like I already said."

But his tone was not the same as before, and he would no longer look Ringil in the eye. And when they'd said their farewell and Darby walked away up the street, there was a slump to his stance that had not been there before. Ringil watched him go, and belatedly he made sense of the change he'd seen in the veteran's face, could suddenly name the emotion behind it.

Shame.

Shame, and a kind of disappointment. In some way Ringil could not pin down, it seemed he'd failed the man after all.

He stood in the gloom and stared after Darby for a moment more, then shrugged irritably and turned away. Not like he'd just stood by and let the Watch work the guy over, for Hoiran's sake. Not like he hadn't *tried*. He rapped curtly on the shop door at his back for entry, listened while Shalak bustled audibly across from the window and unlatched to let him in.

"All right?" the shopkeeper asked as he closed the door again.

"Yeah, sure. Why wouldn't it be?"

But later, helping Shalak close up the shop, he looked at his hand by lamplight and saw that Darby had left a grubby smear across the palm.

It proved surprisingly hard to wash off.

HE GOT BACK TO THE GLADES LATER THAN HE'D PLANNED, WITH VERY little to show for the day's excursion beyond a couple of scrapes on his hands and face, and a largely empty purse. The ferryman who brought him upriver had no conversation, which Ringil counted a blessing. He sat in the stern of the boat while the man bent to the oars, huddled against the river damp and brooding over Shalak's vague hints and pointers.

They come to us in ghost form, striking snake-swift out of phantasmal mist, and when we strike back they return to mist and they laugh, low and mocking in the wind.

Great.

Eskiath House was ablaze with lanterns when he came up the drive, and there was a carriage standing outside the main doors, horses quiescent in the traces, coachman sharing a flask of something with another attendant. Ringil eyed them up and down, didn't recognize their livery or the crest painted on the sides of the coach. Something colorful, a stylized wave on a background of marsh daisies. He shrugged and went in through the door, which stood slightly ajar as was customary this early in the evening. One of the house's own attendants met him inside.

"Who's the visitor?" Ringil asked, as he handed over cap, Ravensfriend, and cloak.

"The Lord Administrator of Tidal Watch, sir." The attendant piled up the sword and clothing in his arms with practiced ease. "He has been waiting in the riverside library for two hours."

"Sounds like a fucking sinecure post if I ever heard one," Ringil said grumpily. "Who's he waiting for?"

"For you, my lord."

Ringil shot the man a sidelong glance. "Really?"

"Here he comes now, sir."

Ringil followed the direction of the attendant's nod and saw a richly dressed young man storming toward him out of the library doorway. He had time to take in russet tunic and cream breeches, sea-stained leather boots and a court rapier rigged at one hip, features that looked vaguely familiar under the flush of rage and a neatly trimmed beard.

"Eskiath," he bellowed.

Ringil looked elaborately around the entry hall. "Are you talking to me?"

The Lord Administrator of Tidal Watch reached him and lashed out with his left hand. The move caught Ringil by surprise; it was unlooked for, there was no weapon apparent, just a pair of gloves. The rough-patterned leather stropped his cheek, and stung.

"I demand satisfaction, Eskiath."

Ringil punched him in the face. The Lord Administrator went reeling backward, hit the floor, and floundered there, bloodied at the nose. He touched his upper lip, looked wonderingly at the blood for a moment, then clapped a hand to his rapier hilt.

"You show that steel in my house," Ringil told him grimly. "I'll take it off you and shove it down your fucking throat."

He hadn't moved forward, but the Lord Administrator let go of the weapon anyway, got rapidly back to his feet instead. It was smoothly done, too, an athletic levering motion that Ringil recognized as blade-salon drilled. He readied himself to step in and block the rapier's draw if necessary. But the younger man just drew himself up and spat on the floor at Ringil's feet.

"What I'd expect from a degenerate like you. Street brawling in place of any real sense of honor." He wiped at the blood from his nose again, dripped some on the floor. He looked down at it and nodded, smiled hard and tight. "But you won't avoid the reckoning that way, Eskiath. I call you out. Before witnesses. Brillin Hill Fields, day after tomorrow at dawn. Unarmored, unshielded, light blade standards. We will settle this with clean steel, whether you like it or not."

By now a small crowd was gathering in the hall. Nearby servants drawn from their duties by the sound of raised voices, and behind the Lord Administrator another liveried attendant, who now quietly proffered his master a handkerchief.

"I don't suppose you'd care to tell me what this is about?" Ringil asked. "Why you're in such a hurry to get yourself killed, I mean."

The Lord Administrator took the handkerchief and pressed it under his injured nose. The attendant tried to help and was shrugged off.

"Degenerate, and coward, too! You presume to put me off with your insufferable arrogance?"

Something about the formality of speech twitched at Ringil, some trace of similarity to go with the oddly familiar features. He covered for it with a roll of his eyes and a brief, mannered sigh.

"If we're to do this by the book, Lord Administrator, then it is customary in a challenge to announce the origin of your grievance. I haven't been in this city since the war, at which time you look to have been barely out of your cradle. It's hard to see how I may have given you offense."

The other man sneered. "You offend me by your simple existence, Eskiath. With the corruption and vileness you exude in breathing Trelayne air."

"Don't be fucking ridiculous."

"How *dare*—"

"There are boy whores at the harbor end for you to vent your righteousness upon, if that's what you're looking for. They're young and destitute and desperate, easily frightened and easily hurt. Should suit you down to the ground."

"You laid hands on my father!"

The shout was agonized, echoing in the hall's vaulted ceiling. Silence settled after it like goose down from a ripped pillow drifting to the floor.

In the quiet, Ringil saw the Lord Administrator's face again, as if for the first time. Saw the resemblance, heard the similarity in the overworked speech patterns.

"I see," he said, very softly.

"I am Iscon Kaad," the Lord Administrator of Tidal Watch said, trembling. "My father's position on the council does not permit him to seek satisfaction by duel. He is unwilling—"

"Yes, of course, that's right." Ringil put on a slow-burning, derisory smile. "Not your father's style at all, that—actual risk. He'd much rather cower behind the city walls and his robes of rank, and have others do his killing for him. As he did back in the 'fifties, in fact, while the rest of us were up to our knees in lizard blood in the marshes. Your father was conspicuous by his absence then, just as he is now. Perhaps he was busy in the bedchamber, siring you from some floor-scrubbing wench or other."

Iscon Kaad made a strangled sound and launched himself at Ringil. Unfortunately, he never made the gap. The attendant pinioned him and held him back. The Eskiath doorman twitched toward Ringil in preventive echo, but Ringil gave him a hard look and he twitched right back again. Kaad subsided in the attendant's grasp, then shook himself imperiously free. The attendant let him go. In the interim, the coachman and the other attendant had rushed in from outside, and the Lady Ishil had finally appeared to see what was going on in her hallway. Her face was unreadable.

Ringil folded his arms and cocked his head.

"You want me to kill you, Iscon Kaad? Fine, I accept. Brillin Hill Fields, day after tomorrow at dawn. As the challenged party, I believe it's actually *my* right to the detail of combat, and not yours." He lifted his right hand and examined the trim of his nails, a gesture he'd stolen from Ishil while they were still both young. Across the hall, his mother saw it, but her face didn't change. "But of course, I wouldn't expect you to know that. Someone with your breeding, I mean. You can't be expected to have mastered all the finer points, now can you?"

For a moment he thought the younger Kaad might try him again, but either the man's rage was temporarily spent or he had it more firmly leashed now that Ringil had given him what he wanted. The Lord Administrator merely peeled his teeth in a gritted smile, and waited.

Or maybe, Gil, it's just that Iscon Kaad is nothing like his sire. Ever think of that? Maybe growing up wealthy and secure, the son of a noted and influential city councilor, he just lacks his father's thin skin for social insult and instead he's turned out exactly the way you once were—an arrogant, overconfident, overmannered young thug with delusions of knighthood.

Not quite delusions. You see the way he got up? This one's been through the Academy, or something similar at least.

Well, so have you, knight graduate Eskiath. So have you.

Wonder if he had to take it up the arse from his pledge guardian as well. A lingering glance up and down the Lord Administrator's slim frame. *Wonder if he liked it.*

Stop that.

Still. Wouldn't do to underestimate him at Brillin day after tomorrow.

If it comes to that.

"Are you finished checking your manicure, degenerate?"

Ringil looked up at Kaad and had to mask a sudden, unwanted sense of vertigo.

"Very well," he said coldly. "We'll do it your way. No mail, no shields, light blades only. Seconds to attend. Now get out of my fucking house."

WHEN KAAD HAD GONE, THE GRAVELED CRUNCH OF HIS CARRIAGE fading down the drive, Ringil crooked a finger at one of the attendants nearest to him, a shrewd-faced lad who couldn't be much over a dozen years old.

"What's your name then?"

"Deri, sir."

"Well, Deri, you know Dray Street in Ekelim, right?"

"Up from the river? Yes, my lord."

"Good. There's a shop there that sells Aldrain junk, on the corner of Blubber Row. I want you to go there first thing tomorrow morning with a message for the owner."

"Yes, my lord. What message?"

"I'll write it for you later." Ringil gave him a coin from the bottom of his depleted purse. "Come and find me in the library after supper."

"Gladly, my lord."

"Off you go then."

"And perhaps now," the Lady Ishil declaimed icily from the other side of the hall, "everyone would care to get back to the tasks for which they are retained in this household. And someone clean up that blood."

It set off a scurry of motion, servants dispersing via the various doorways and the staircase. Ishil trod measured steps across the emptying floor space until she was in front of her son. She leaned in close.

"Is it your intention," she hissed, "to offend *every* male of rank in this city before you are done?"

Ringil examined his nails again. "They come to me, Mother. They come to me. It wouldn't do to disappoint them. Or perhaps you'd prefer the name of Eskiath insulted with impunity in your own home? I can't see Father going for that."

"If you had not *assaulted* Kaad in the first place—"

"Mother, for your—" He stopped, cranked down the force and exasperation in his own voice. He looked daggers at the two remaining attendants by the door, who both immediately found a pressing need to step outside. When they were gone, he started again, quietly. "For your information, neither Murmin Kaad nor your beloved husband wants me anywhere near Etterkal. I don't think it has much to do with Sherin, but we've stirred up a marsh spider burrow with this line of inquiry. Kaad showing up here yesterday is just a consequence."

"You did not need to *scald his face*. To, to"—Ishil gestured—"half *blind* the man."

"He exaggerates."

"Oh, you think so? Gingren bribed one of the Chancellery physicians to talk to him after they examined Kaad. He says he may never regain full sight in that eye."

"Mother, it was a flagon of *tea*."

"Well, whatever it was, you've caused both your father and me a great deal of embarrassment we could have well done without."

"Then perhaps you should not have dragged me back to this shit-hole to do your bidding in places you will not go yourself. You know what they say about summoning up demons."

"Oh, for Hoiran's sake, Ringil. Act your age."

Their voices were rising again. Ringil made an effort.

"Listen Mother, Kaad hates me for what I am. There's no way to change that. And he's up to his eyes in whatever's going on inside Etterkal. Sooner or later, we would have collided. And to be honest with you I'd rather that happened face-to-face than that I had to walk about waiting for a knife in the back instead."

"So you say. But this is not helping to find Sherin."

"Perhaps you have an alternative strategy?"

And to that, as he well knew, Ishil had no reply.

LATER, IN THE LIBRARY, HE WROTE BY CANDLELIGHT, FOLDED AND SEALED the parchment, and addressed it to Shalak. The boy came to find him, stood twitchily in the gloom outside the fall of the candle's glow. Ringil handed him the letter.

"I don't suppose you read, do you?"

The boy chortled. "No, my lord. That's for clerks."

"Yes, and couriers sometimes." Ringil sighed. "Very well. You see this? It says Shalak Kalarn. Shalak. You can remember that?"

"Of course, my lord. Shalak."

"He doesn't open early, but he lives above the shop. There's a stairway at the back, you reach it through an alley on the right. Go at first light, wake him up if necessary. He's got to find someone for me, and it may take him the day."

"Yes, my lord."

Ringil considered the boy. He was a sketch in untried eagerness, sharp-featured and not yet grown into his adolescent's frame. The arms and shoulders lacked muscle, he stood awkwardly, but you could see he was going to be tall. Ringil supposed that in a couple of years he'd be fetching enough in a lanky, street-smart sort of fashion.

"How old are you, Deri?"

"Thirteen, sir. Fourteen next spring."

"Quite young to be in service in the Glades."

"Yes, sir. My father's a stable manager at Alannor House. I was recommended." A quick jag of pride. "Youngest retainer on the whole Eskiath estate, sir."

Ringil smiled at the boast. "Not quite."

"No, I am, my lord. Swear to it."

Ringil's smile leached away. He didn't like being lied to. "There's a girl down in the kitchens who's not much more than half your age, Deri."

"No, sir. Can't be, I'm the youngest." Still buoyed up on the pride, maybe, Deri grinned. "I know all the kitchen girls, sir. No one that young down there."

Ringil sat up abruptly, let his arm drop onto the table. Flat thump of the impact—the inkpot and sealing wax jumped with it. The boy flinched. Shadows from the eddied candle flame scuttled over the walls of books.

"Deri, you keep this up, you're going to make me angry. I *saw* this girl with my own eyes. This morning, early, first thing. She served me tea in the lower kitchen. She was tending the cauldron fires."

Silence stiffened in the library gloom. Deri's lower lip worked, his eyes flickered about like small, trapped animals. Ringil looked at him, knew the truth when he saw it, and suddenly, out of nowhere, he felt a cold hand walk up his spine and into the roots of his hair. His gaze slipped, off the boy's face and past his shoulder, into the darkened corner of the room where the shadows from the candle seemed to have settled.

"You don't know this girl?" he asked quietly.

Deri hung his head, mumbled something inaudible.

"Speak up." The chill put a hard, jumpy edge on his voice.

"I . . . said I'm sorry, my lord. Didn't mean to gainsay you, nothing like that. Just, I've never seen a girl so young working in this house." Deri stumbled over words in his haste to get them out. "Maybe it's, I mean, 'course, you must be right, my lord, and I'm wrong. 'Course. Just never seen her, that's all. That's all I meant."

"So maybe she's just new, and you've missed meeting her."

Deri swallowed. "That's it, my lord. Exactly. Must have."

The look in his eyes denied every word.

Ringil nodded, firm and a little exaggerated, as if to a suddenly acquired audience beyond the ring of candlelight.

"All right, Deri. You can go. First light to Ekelim, remember."

"Yes, my lord." The boy shot out of the door, as if tugged on string.

Ringil gave it another moment, then looked elaborately around the shadowed chamber and settled himself back into his chair.

"I could use another flagon of tea," he said loudly, into the empty air.

No response. But memory of the conversation with his mother in the kitchens draped itself over the nape of his neck like folds of cold, damp linen.

Not in front of the servants, eh?

What's that supposed to mean?

And the girl, no longer there. Materializing once more, only when Ishil was gone and he was alone.

Could you not creep up on me like that, please.

He waited, frowning and watching the almost imperceptible tremor of shadows across the spines of books on the shelves around him. Then, finally, he mastered the crawling sensation on the nape of his neck, leaned swiftly forward, and blew out the candle. He sat in the parchment-odored darkness, and listened to himself breathe.

"I'm waiting," he said.

But the girl, if she was listening, did not come.

Nor, at this juncture, did anything else.

CHAPTER 12

Faileh Rakan's find:

A tangled muss of graying chestnut hair, face lined with hardship more than age, and frightened eyes that tracked the Throne Eternal uniforms as they prowled about her or stood and examined their weapons as if they might soon need use. Her hands were scabbed and scraped and still bled in a couple of places, coarse contrast with a worked gold band on one of her fingers. Her lips had cracked during her privation; now they trembled with half-voiced mutterings, and she cradled her own right arm in the left as if it were a nursing infant. Her clothing stank.

"She's not injured," said Rakan bluntly. "It's some kind of shock."

"You don't say."

They had her draped in a horse blanket and seated on a double-folded tent groundsheet in the angle of two shattered low stone walls, pretty much all that was left of a harbor storage shed smashed apart by whatever energies had gotten loose during the attack. The timbers remaining at the least wrecked corner were charred back to angled, black stumps above the woman's head—Archeth thought involuntarily of a gallows. The ghost-reek of burning still hung in the air. She glanced around reflexively.

"Where's the invigilator?"

"His holiness has retired to camp," Rakan said tonelessly. He nodded up the slope of emptied buildings and rubble piles. "In the main market square with the rest of the men. He left before we found her, said it was important that he go to pray for us. It *is* getting dark, of course."

It was elaborately done, in true Yhelteth fashion. The captain's dark, crop-bearded face stayed inexpressive as tanned leather. There was just the hint of creasing in the lines around the jet eyes to match the momentary contempt in the last few syllables he'd spoken.

Archeth took it and ran with it, met Rakan's eyes and nodded. "Then let's keep him up there. No sense in disturbing his prayers for something like this, right? I can ask any questions we need answering right here."

"We've already tried questioning her, milady." The captain leaned in closer, as if to demonstrate something, and the ragged woman flinched back. "Not getting any sense out of her at all. Tried to feed her, too, but she'll only take water. I guess we could—"

"Thank you, Captain. I think I'll take it from here."

Rakan shrugged. "Suit yourself, milady. I need to get a picket organized for the camp, just in case we have visitors tonight. I'll leave you a couple of men. Bring her up to camp when you're done, we'll try to feed her again." He nodded up past the charred timberwork at the sky. "Best if you don't take too long. Like the invigilator said, going to be dark soon."

He made brief obeisance, turned and gestured three soldiers to stay. The rest followed him away up the street. Shanta stayed, hovering on the far side of the broken-down wall like a hesitant buyer outside a shop. Archeth crouched to the woman's eye level.

"Can I get you anything?" she asked gently.

The woman gaped at her, fixed, Archeth supposed, on the intensely black skin.

"Kiriath," she mumbled. "Look at your walls, Kiriath. Look what they did. Get between a swamp dog and its dinner, look what it gets you."

"Yes." Archeth had no idea what a swamp dog was. The woman's accent was not local; she had a way of eliding the Tethanne sibilants that suggested it was not her cradle tongue. "Can you tell me your name?"

The woman looked away. "How's that going to help?"

"As you wish. I am Archeth Indamaninarmal, special envoy of his imperial radiance Jhiral Khimran the Second." She made the Teth horseman's gathering gesture, formally ornate, right-handed across her body to the shoulder. "Sworn in service to all peoples of the Revelation."

"I'm not of the tribes," the woman muttered, still not looking at her. "My name is Elith. I'm from Ennishmin."

Oho.

Archeth's lips tightened as if against pain, way before she could beat back the reflex. Her eyes darted across the woman's clothing, found the frayed edges of orange at the breast where the kartagh, the sewn badge of nonconvert citizenry, had been ripped away. No mystery as to why Elith would have done that—marauders and criminals throughout the Empire took nonadherence to the Revelation more or less as license for their depredations; in any raid or other low-grade thuggery, the infidel was an easy mark. Imperial courts tended to concur: Outrages against the property or persons of nonconverts were consistently underpunished, occasionally ignored. When iron clashed and hooves thundered through your streets, you were well advised to tear off the legally required identification of your second-class citizenship quick, before anyone with a blade and a bloodlust-stiffened prick spotted it.

"We came south," Elith went on, as if blaming Archeth for something. "We were told to come, told we'd be safer here. The Emperor extends his hand in friendship. Now look."

Archeth remembered the long limping columns out of Ennishmin, the desolate tendrils of smoke from the burning settlements they left behind, scrawled on the washed-out winter sky like a writ in accusation. She'd sat her warhorse on a scorched rise and watched the weary faces go by, mostly on foot, the odd cart piled with possessions and huddled children, seemingly washed along on the flow like a raft on a slow river. She'd listened to the boisterous clowning and squabbling of a group of imperial troops at her back as they rooted through piles of loot gathered out of the hundreds of homes before they were put to the torch. Shame was a dull heat in her face.

She remembered the rage on Ringil's.

"Listen to me, Elith," she tried again. "Whoever did this will face the Emperor's justice. That's why I'm here."

Elith gave up the choked edge of a sneer.

Archeth nodded. "You may not trust us, I understand that. But please at least tell me what you saw. You lose nothing by it."

Now the woman looked directly at her.

"What I saw? *I saw the end of the world, I saw angels descending from the band, to make good the prophecies told and lay waste all human endeavor and pride.* Is that what you want me to say?"

They were words out of the Revelation. "On Repentance," fifth song, verses ten to sixteen or thereabouts. Archeth seated herself tiredly on the stump of the wall.

"I don't want you to say anything," she said mildly. "I could use the truth, if you feel like telling it. Otherwise, we could just sit here for a while. Maybe get you some more water."

Elith stared down at her own hands for what seemed like a very long time. The sky grew visibly darker against the fire-blackened timbers. A soft breeze wandered into the harbor and scuffed at the water there. Rakan's men shifted about on the quay.

Archeth waited.

At one point Shanta opened his mouth, but Archeth shut him down with a savage glance and a single tight gesture.

If the woman from Ennishmin saw any of this, she gave no sign.

"We prayed for them to come," she said finally. Her voice was a wrung-out whisper, all emotion long since scorched away. "All through that winter, we sacrificed and prayed, and your soldiers came instead. They burned our homes, they raped my daughters, and when my youngest son tried to stop them, they hung him on a pike by his stomach, in the corner of the room. So that he could watch."

Archeth leaned elbows on knees, pressed her palms together, and rested her chin on the blade it made.

"When they were done, they took Erlo down, because the soldier needed the pike back, and they left him there on the floor, bleeding to death. They didn't kill him, they said it was imperial mercy. And they laughed." Elith never looked up from her hands as she talked. It was as if they fascinated her, just by still being there at the ends of her wrists. "They killed Gishlith, my youngest, because she bit one of them when it was his turn, but they let the others live. Ninea killed herself later, she was pregnant. Mirin lived, she was always the strongest."

A long, almost silent sigh scraped its way up Archeth's tightened throat. She swallowed.

"Did you have a husband?"

"He was away. Fighting the Scaled Folk, with our other sons. He came home after, burned and broken from the dragonfire at Rajal Beach. He saw our sons die there, that's what really broke him, not losing his arm and face like they said. He never." Elith stopped and glanced up at Archeth. "Mirin left, she's in Oronak now, she married a sailor. We don't hear from her."

Which meant nothing good. Reliable mail was one thing the Empire was good for, the couriers ran like clockwork since Akal's father's time, and Oronak wasn't that far down the coast. Archeth had been there a couple of times, it was a shit-hole. Damp, salt-scoured wooden buildings and boardwalks across gray sand, no paved streets beyond the port frontage. A raddled street whore for every corner, and plenty of business for all of them streaming from the merchant ships that jostled for berth space in the harbor.

"He ran." Elith held Archeth's gaze this time, eyes suddenly flaring, offering to share a disbelief the black woman didn't yet understand. "They came, they finally came, and he ran. With the others, into the hills. I stood in the street and I screamed at them, I screamed for a reckoning, or death if they'd give it to me, but Werleck ran. He ran."

Archeth frowned. "A reckoning?"

"We *prayed*." As if to an idiot, as if to someone who hadn't been listening to a word she'd said. "I *told* you. All winter, we prayed for them to come. The Scaled Folk closing from the north, the imperials from the south and east. We prayed for intervention, and they *did not come*. We sacrificed, and they left us to our fate. And *now* they come, *now*, after ten years, with my sons and daughters dead in the stolen soil of Ennishmin, now when we're scattered like flaxseed in the lands of our despoilers. *What fucking use now!*"

Her voice splintered apart on the last words, as if something had torn in her throat. Archeth glanced up at Shanta. The engineer raised an eyebrow and said nothing. Rakan's men stood about and affected not to have heard. Archeth leaned forward, offered her open hand in a gesture whose symbolism she wasn't entirely sure of herself.

"Elith, help me to understand this. You prayed for these . . . creatures to appear. You uh . . . you summoned them? To protect you."

"Ten fucking years gone," Elith mumbled desolately to herself. "What fucking use now?"

"Yes, ten years ago, in Ennishmin. And now they've come, finally. But what are they, Elith? What are we talking about here?"

The woman from Ennishmin looked up at her, and in the grimed, careworn damage of her face, something almost crafty, almost malicious, seemed to pass behind her watery bright eyes.

"You won't stop them, you know," she said.

"Okay, we won't stop them." Archeth nodded along, playing reasonable. "Fair enough. But tell me anyway, just so I know. What are they? What did you summon up?"

Elith's mouth twisted, hesitant. She seemed to twitch at the end of a rope Archeth couldn't see.

And then.

"*Dwenda*," she enunciated, like someone teaching the word.

And sat back and grinned, a trembling, staring, broken-toothed rictus that Archeth knew she'd need krinzanz to get out of her head that night.

CHAPTER 13

The next morning, he went out to the eastern gate. It probably wasn't a good idea, but he hadn't been having many of those since he got back anyway.

The gate was one of the oldest in the city, built a pair of centuries ago along with the great causeway that led to it, back before Trelayne had sprawled as far as the sea, and so serving at the time as the main entrance for visitors. In a blunt, old-fashioned way, it was very beautiful; a fair portion of the city's rapidly burgeoning trade wealth had once gone to finance the import of glinting, southern-quarried stone and to pay the finest masons in the region to shape and dress it. Twinned arches rose twenty feet over the heads of those entering and leaving Trelayne by the gate, mirror-image ends to a long paved courtyard with crenellated walls and statues of guardian marsh spirits at the corners. When the sun shone on it, the stonework winked and gleamed as if embedded with newly minted gold coins. By night, bandlight turned the currency cool and silver, but the effect was the same. The whole thing was widely acknowledged as one of the architectural wonders of the world.

Pity they have to use it as a torture chamber.

Yeah, well. Got to impress the visitors.

There was grim truth behind the sneer. No one entering Trelayne for the first time by the eastern gate would be left in any doubt about the attitude of the city toward lawbreakers.

He knew as soon as he passed under the inner gateway that there had been no executions recently—there would have been a crowd otherwise. Instead, livestock, carts, and pedestrians all went back and forth unobstructed along the worn center section of the courtyard. Stalls were set up along the side walls; grimy children ran about touting handfuls of cut fruit or sweetmeats. A couple of marsh dwellers had set up a brightly colored fortune-telling blanket in one corner. Elsewhere they were juggling knives or acting out tales from local legend. There was a pressing odor of dung and rancid cooking oil.

Could be worse, Gil.

The cages hung overhead in the sunlight, raised on massive bracketed cranes from the courtyard walls, five to a side. They were onion-shaped and seemed quite delicate at a distance, narrow steel bars billowing down and out from the suspension stalk at the top, curling in at the base and meeting in the central crankspace, where the bleak mechanism of the impaling spike rose back into the body of the cage. As he drew closer, Ringil saw he hadn't been quite right about the lack of an execution. One of the cages still held the remnants of a human form.

Abruptly his vision scorched across, like muslin drapes on fire. He couldn't see for the past in his eyes. The memory came on like the glare of a sudden, desert sun.

Jelim, screaming and thrashing as they carried him into the cage in his execution robe. Condemned criminals were sometimes drugged before sentence was carried out, as a mercy or because someone somewhere had put enough coin in the right hands. But not for this crime. Not when an example was to be made.

And Gingren's hand, clamped shut on his wrist. The mail-and-leather press of his men-at-arms around them both, in case someone in the avid crowd might have heard whispers, might make an unwanted connection with the pale Eskiath youth there on the nobles' viewing platform and the doomed boy in the cage.

You'll watch this, my lad. You'll stand here and you'll watch every last fucking moment of it, if I have to pinion you myself.

Ringil hadn't needed pinioning. Fortified with self-loathing, with the reserves of sardonic contempt he'd absorbed in his time spent around Milacar, he'd gone to the gate tight-lipped and filled with a strange, queasy energy, as if walking to his own execution as well as Jelim's. He'd known at some deep, cold level that he would cope.

He was wrong. Utterly.

As they held Jelim in place over the lowered spike, as they forced him down and his thrashing abruptly stopped and his eyes flew open, Ringil held out. As the long, gut-deep shriek of denial ripped out of him, as the executioner below the cage began to crank the mechanism and the barbed steel spike rose inch by cog-toothed inch and Jelim shuddered in the grasp of the men who restrained him, as the shrieks began to peel out of him at intervals broken by inhuman sounds like someone trying to inhale thick mud, as Jelim rose slowly to his feet as if at some kind of obscene attention before the crowd, as his shudders went on in rolling sequence, as blood and shit and piss began to drip below and the cage . . .

Ringil came to on the boards of the platform, throat raw with his own vomit, one of the Eskiath men-at-arms slapping his face. They'd cleared a space for him, the rest of the assembled nobility probably not wanting to get his sick on their finery. But no one was looking down at him in disgust.

No one was looking at him at all.

All eyes were pinned on the cage, and the source of the noises that came from within it.

Gingren towered above Ringil, arms folded and crushed to his chest, and held his head up as if his neck were stiff. He did not look down at his son, even when Ringil gagged and the man-at-arms stuck a gloved finger in his throat and twisted his face roughly to the side so he wouldn't choke.

The noises Jelim was making came to find him on the wind. He passed out all over again.

"*Oi!* What's the fucking . . ." The peasant voice died away on the curse, came back conciliatory. "Oh, my apologies your worthiness. Didn't see you there."

Ringil shivered back to the present. He'd jammed to a halt in the thoroughfare, was blocking passage. He found he'd closed his eyes without realizing it. He shook his head and stepped sideways, out of the flow of traffic and into the shadow of the cages. The drover who'd sworn at him hurried past behind a brace of donkeys, eyes on the ground, not wanting trouble. Ringil ignored him, forced himself to look upward instead.

The man in the cage hadn't been dead all that long. There were still no outward signs of decay, and the birds had not yet taken his eyes— something that Ringil knew could sometimes happen even before the last vestiges of life guttered out in the victim. In fact, there was something unpleasantly life-like about this corpse. Aside from the head, now rolled bonelessly sideways and forward on the neck, the man still stood erect to the demand of the steel spike that held him up. At a glance, and but for the stained ankle-length cream-colored execution robe, he might almost have been a soldier on duty caught rolling his neck around to loosen midwatch stiffness. Even the spike, where it emerged through blood-drenched cloth at the man's right shoulder, might almost have been the pommel of a slung broadsword.

Ringil edged unwillingly a few steps closer so he could see up through the curving bars and into the face. The sun blocked out behind the head, gave it a soft halo. He felt himself grimace as he met the frozen eyes.

"Fuck are you looking at?"

He staggered back, rigid with shock. The corpse lifted its face to follow, kept the sun behind its head, the dead eyes on him. The lips drew back from blackened teeth. He saw a dry shred of tongue flicker between them.

"Yeah, you, pretty boy. I'm talking to you. Pretty fucking brave back in the comfort of your own home last night, weren't you. So now what?"

Ringil locked his teeth behind lips clamped shut. He breathed hard through his nose. He thought he caught the faintest sickly sweet hint of the charnel house.

"Who are you?"

The corpse grinned. "Don't you know?"

Ringil's hand slid up toward his neck and the pommel of the Ravensfriend. The corpse's grin widened to snarling, inhuman proportions.

"Come off it, Gil. This is a krinzanz flashback. You know that."

And gone.

The corpse stood unmoving on the spike, head hanging once more, silent. Autumn sunlight spilled down over its shoulder, through the cage, and laid the shadows of bars across Ringil's face. He drew a deep, shuddering breath and let his sword hand drop. He glanced around surreptitiously and saw no one paying him any attention.

Well, almost no one.

"Oh, he was my daughter's husband, my lord." A shawl-wrapped marsh dweller woman had appeared beside him, one of the ones with the fortune-telling gig in the courtyard corner. She carried with her an odor of salt and damp, and her hand was already out for coin. Ringil reckoned her no older than Ishil, but life out on the marsh had turned her into a crone. The characteristic dweller delicacy of her features was not yet completely worn down, but the hand she held out was already knobbed and wrinkled with age, and her voice was cracked and coarse. "Woe is upon us, he left nine hungry mouths to feed, eight little ones and my own widowed daughter, no help for us but—"

"What was his name?"

"His name, uhm, was Ferdin."

Out of the corner of one eye, Ringil almost thought he saw the corpse shake its lowered head in sanguine and slightly weary denial.

"Right." He ignored the outstretched hand, gestured at the blanket laid out by the wall and the other old woman sitting on it. "I'm curious, madam. Could you read me my future?"

"Oh yes, my lord. For no more than . . ." Her eyes flickered about. "Seven . . . florins, I shall cast the scrying bones for you."

"Seven florins, eh?" It wasn't quite daylight robbery.

The woman lifted one grubby, sunburned arm so her shawl fell back from it. She touched a long vein in her wrist. "The blood that flows here belongs to the marsh clans at Ushirin, the children of Nimineth and Yolar. I am not a cheap spell-chanter from the stalls at Strov."

"You're certainly not cheap, no."

It was water off a duck's back, no impediment at all to the fortune-teller's pitch now it was rolling. As he watched, she freed her other arm from the wrap of the shawl and crossed her wrists in front of her, palms cupped upward. "I trace my family line back eighty-six generations, undiluted, to those among the People who mated with the Aldrain. I have the eye. The shape of things to come opens before me, it is no more mystery than the shape of that which has already been."

"Hmm. Pity you didn't throw the bones for your son-in-law then, isn't it?" Ringil nodded up at the corpse. "He could have used a little insight into the shape of things to come, don't you think?"

It brought the woman up short. Her eyes narrowed, and he saw the hate come up in them. No surprises there, he was almost pleased to see it. Beneath their garish, played-for-the-crowd affectations of fey, the true marsh dwellers had a thin spine of pride that was mostly extinct in the rest of the Naom clans. They lived outside the city in more senses than the merely physical, and that brought its own detachment. There was a marked lack of deference in their manner when confronted with the trappings of wealth or political power. It was the one quality that Ringil could find to admire amid what was otherwise a fairly grubby and brutal cultural hangover from Naom's pre-urban past. Like most kids, he'd dreamed often enough, smarting from a tanning Gingren or one of his tutors had given him, of running away to live out on the marsh with the dwellers. Often enough, he'd seen the faint flickering lanterns of their encampments out across the plain, had felt the distance and escape under open sky that they promised, just like any other kid.

Nice image. But the reality was altogether too backbreaking, damp, and smelly to seriously entertain.

And fucking freezing in winter.

The fortune-teller dropped her crossed wrists abruptly. Her arms hung at her sides, her shawl fell back and covered her hands. Her eyes nailed his. Nothing of her moved but her lips as she spoke.

"I'll tell you what," she said softly. "I'll tell you what I see, and at no charge. You know much of war, you carry its spirit stabbed deep inside you, just as he up there has the steel within him. Just as deeply buried, just as hard and unyielding to all the softer things you are and want and own to. And just as bitter in its wounding. You think you'll be free of it one day; you carry it as if the wound will someday heal. But for you, just as for him, there will be no healing."

"Wow." Ringil reached up left-handed and tapped the pommel of the Ravensfriend with his fingers. "Nice guesses. I'm sorry, Granny. It's still no sale."

The old woman's voice rose slightly. "Mark me. A fight is coming, a battle of powers you have not yet seen. A battle that will unmake you, that will tear you apart. *A dark lord will rise, his coming is in the wind off the marsh.*"

"Yeah. I lost a pocketknife a couple of weeks ago. I don't suppose you'd know where that is?"

She bared teeth at him.

"Among the dead," she said savagely. "Forgotten."

"Right." He made her a brief bow, began turning away. "Well, I have to be going."

"You have killed children," she said to his retreating back. "Do not think that will heal, either."

He stopped dead.

Once again, his vision seemed to burn out and be replaced. He stood in the courtyard again, amid a thin crowd of rubberneckers at Jelim Dasnel's dying. The viewing stand had been taken down, the cage hoisted high. The stains on the stonework below were drying.

Day two.

It had taken that long for him to get out from under the house arrest. Ishil's decision. When Gingren finally brought him home on the first day of the execution, pale and trembling, vomit-stained, Ishil had taken one look at her son and snapped. She sent Ringil to his room with icy aplomb, and as soon as he was gone she turned on her husband like a storm. The whole house heard her bawling him out. It was the only time Ringil could remember that she'd truly unleashed her anger at Gingren, and though he was not there to see the results, the lack of marks on his mother's face the next day suggested Gingren had withered in the blast. In the aftermath, the servants crept about the place, and the orders stood in no uncertain terms—Ringil was not to leave the house before the end of the week. Jelim had been a husky boy, and it was well known that Kaad's executioners could, on request, draw out the suffering of an impaled criminal for a good three or four days, if the victim was strong.

Ringil got out at dawn, out of his bedroom window, along fingertip ledges of stone to the corner of the house, and then over the roof to the stables. He went wrapped in a nondescript brown cloak that didn't show what it was worth, squeezed through the hole in the fence, and fled toward the eastern gate.

When he got there, Jelim was still conscious.

And children were throwing stones.

It wasn't unheard of, wasn't even uncommon. If your aim was good and you had a decent-sized stone, you could jolt the condemned man on his spike and make him scream. In the absence of the Watch, enterprising souls among the urchins had been known to bring a supply of rocks and sell them for pennies from a tray.

The first child Ringil noticed was about eight—fresh-faced and grinning, hefting his stone as he stepped forward and cocked his arm. Comrades of a similar age offered jeering advice. Numb and dizzy, Ringil failed to grasp what was happening until the missile flew, and clanged off one of the cage bars.

Jelim made a girlish, shrilling noise. Ringil thought he heard the raw edge of the word *please* submerged in the agony.

"Oi, you kids," someone shouted. "Pack that in."

Laughter, some of it adult.

"Yeah, *fuck* off, Granddad," said the fresh-faced boy, and squared up for another throw. His arm came back.

Ringil killed him.

It happened so fast no one, Ringil himself least of all, realized what he was doing. He grabbed the raised arm at the elbow, locked his hand into the boy's neck, and wrenched. The boy screamed, but not loud enough to drown out the hollow, meaty sound as his shoulder joint snapped.

It was not enough.

Ringil bore him struggling to the ground and smashed his face into the paving. Blood on the dung-strewn stone, and a wet mewling. He thought the kid was still alive when he dragged the head up the first and second times, thought he heard him still wailing, but on the third impact he went abruptly silent. And by the fourth and fifth, it was definitely all over.

He kept on pounding.

Thin, high screaming in his ears like a steam kettle left on the stove.

By the time they dragged him off, the kid's features were pulp, barely recognizable as human. It was only then, as they hauled Ringil bodily away, thrashing and snarling and lunging out at the openmouthed terror of the other urchins, that he registered the high-pitched shriek in his ears for what it was—his own voice, like nails scraping at the doors of madness.

You have killed children.

He shook it off. *Lizardshit and safe guesses, Gil, just like the rest of it. The war is furniture—anyone able-bodied your age or older was in it.* A man with a blade on his back and a warrior stance, a man with the distance in the eyes that he knew he had. A shrewd fortune-teller could read the implications of it all, just the way you'd read a path through the marsh.

He walked away.

At his back, he thought he heard her cursing him.

HE WAS ALMOST BACK TO THE GLADES WHEN HE REMEMBERED THE last time he'd seen that pocketknife.

He'd put it in a pocket of his leather jerkin in Gallows Water, the night of the corpsemites. The jerkin he wore out to the graveyard and lost there in the fight.

Left there among the dead.

CHAPTER 14

It was on Greasing Night—night of masking and unmasking, night of Ynprpral Walking and the cold that strikes through like a blade, night of acknowledging the wheel of the seasons and inevitable change—that the sign Poltar had been waiting for finally arrived. He supposed it was appropriate in its way; he grudgingly approved of the symbolism it drove home.

Mostly, he was just glad the waiting was over.

He'd watched the sky for weeks after his encounter with Kelgris, gnawing on his hate and his lurid dreams of vengeance. *The Dwellers make their will known for those with eyes to look above,* his father had schooled him, long before Poltar had properly understood that he, too, would one day wear the wolf-eye robe. *Where other men see only to the rim of the world, you must learn to look beyond. You must look to the sky.*

Deeds followed words not long after—Olgan was a shaman in the old tradition, and he intended his son to one day wear his robes with the same conviction. From his father, Poltar learned the seasons and moods of the Sky Road, its colors and the sparks that Urann's iron-shod steed sometimes struck from its surface when the Gray Master rode in haste from the Sky Home to earth or back. He learned why the band might wrap itself in cloud and hide, why it would at other times stand clear and bright from horizon to horizon like a promise in shimmering gold. Learned the humor of storms and the visiting aurora, what they intended and whose business they were habitually about, learned the meaning of each wind across the steppe and what it could tell those with ears to listen. He learned where to find the sky iron, to know when it was most likely to fall to earth, and in what season it could be safely touched. He learned the names and the tales and the invocations and once, when he was still very young, he saw his father raise Takavach the Many Faced from the surface of a crystal mirror tilted to face the darkening eastern sky at dusk.

Look to the sky.

But for weeks, the sky had given him nothing.

And then Ergund came to call.

"MY BROTHER ERGUND?" EGAR FROWNED, NOT REALLY FOLLOWING THE sudden digression, not really wanting to. "Well, why should he? Pay you respect, I mean? You're barely sixteen, and you're a milkmaid, for Urann's sake. You're nothing to him."

"To him, maybe not, or to that clamp-mouthed bitch wife of his. That's not the point." Sula laced fingers that had until a moment ago been otherwise—*and better*—employed, and sat back where she straddled him just above the knees. The view was superb—she was naked but for bangles and the bone-carved necklace he'd given her a couple of weeks ago. But above it all, her face had turned suddenly sulky. "Ergund knows damn fucking well what I am to *you.* Fuck it, I was on my sky-fisted way to your fucking yurt when I passed him. And, like I said, he just fucking *shoves right past me,* without a sky-shat word. Piece of shit wouldn't even fucking look at me. Face all fucking screwed up like he's pissed off about something *I've* fucking done to him."

Egar sighed. His abruptly untended erection slackened, flopped sideways across his thigh. He reached out for the rice wine flask by his head, swigged at it, grimaced and swallowed.

"Look, he's probably just jealous," he said. "I doubt he ever had his hands on a pair of tits as gorgeous as yours his whole fucking life."

That seemed to work. Sula sat forward again with a grin, tilted her shoulders at him, side-to-side, and back again. Like most of his conquests, she was a well-endowed girl. Her breasts swung heavily in the warm, speckled light from the yurt's iron-mesh brazier. A coiling snake tattoo she had from collarbone to cleavage seemed to wriggle on her flesh with the motion. She licked her lips.

"Yeah, and a wife with a mouth closed that fucking tight won't be much for blow jobs, either, right?" She chortled delightedly. "Bet he's lucky if he gets three of those in a fucking year."

"Strictly feast nights only," agreed Egar, reaching up and cupping a callused hand to each of the breasts under discussion. He thumbed the thick, rope-end nipples back and forth, squeezed gently at the jellied weight with his palms. Dropped another broad hint. "And of course, she's a woman of leisure, so, you know, probably got no strength at all in her fingers like you have."

Sula's eyes smeared wide with renewed lechery. She put her hands back on him, gathered up his prick, and began to work it slowly up and down. Ahhh, milkmaid's fingers. He felt himself slam back to fully erect in seconds. Sula felt it, too, grinned again, leaned down and brushed one breast softly back and forth across the head of his prick, then across his face. He gaped after the nipple, twisting his head to catch it and suck it in, heaved up and grabbed after her hips. She swayed sharply back up and shook her head.

"Oh, no. First things fucking first. We're going to get the edge off. I'm not looking for a two-minute drunken herder's fuck out of you, just so you can head off to the ceremonies in fine fucking form. You just fucking lie there and do as you're told, *Clanmaster*. I—" In time now with her slow, rippling strokes. "Am going to *milk* you fucking *dry*. Just like one of my fucking buffalo, yeah? You like that? *Then* we'll see what you can do for me."

Egar chuckled. "You make me suffer, bitch, you know I'm going to hand it straight back. I'll have you yowling like a steppe fox."

Sula lifted one hand from her work, made a flapping mouth with fingers and thumb. "Yeah, yeah—talk, talk. You're all the fucking same, men. Clanmaster or herdboy, you tell me where's the fucking difference."

The clanmaster tipped a meaningful glance around the trappings of the yurt, the rich tapestries and rugs, the brazier in the corner.

"Bit cold to be sneaking out and tumbling herdboys in the grass this time of year, I'd say. That's one big difference."

A shadow crossed Sula's face, a light, watchful tension, and her hands slackened a little in what they were doing. She didn't know him well enough to read his moods yet, to know rough humor from genuine displeasure, a growl from a drawl. He had to force a smile, stick his tongue out at her and clown the moment away before she eased.

In the end, he had to remind himself. *Tits and milkmaid's fingers notwithstanding, this is just one more foulmouthed Skaranak herdgirl you've got here milking your cock for you, Clanmaster.*

It made him unaccountably sad. Sula was gorgeous, supple, succulent in his mouth and hands, utterly joyous and abandoned in her fucking. *But afterward, afterward . . .*

Afterward, as they lay sweat-stuck together, the inescapable truth would seep back in. That Sula was less than half his age, had been nowhere, seen nothing, *knew* nothing beyond the big sky limits of the steppe—and was eminently content to stay that way. That she had nothing much to say about anything but herding or fucking or the current clan gossip or the *endless fucking squabbles* of her extended family.

That she could not even read. And—he'd broached the subject once—that she did not much want to learn.

Oh, you were hoping for book-learned pussy, perhaps? Some Yhelteth-bred courtesan with an astrolabe out on the balcony and an illustrated binding of Tales of the Man and the Woman *on the table beside the bed?*

You were hoping for Imrana, maybe?

Fuck it.

Yeah, fuck it. You can take Sula to Ishlin-ichan when the ceremonies

are done. She'll love that, marching into all those fabric places down Rib
Whittle Row with a clanmaster's purse at her disposal. You can bask in her
reflected squealing joy as she buys everything in sight, and call it happiness.

And now she had him up in the near reaches of his own brief joy—
the heat of orgasm pulsing and pooling in his groin, the strong-fingered
strokes coming shorter and harder, his own grunts and gasps in his ears,
his thoughts fading out in the clamor for ecstasy and release.

C'mon, how bad can it be, Clanmaster? As the feeling rushed him,
stormed up the column of his prick and he exploded, splashed hot salt
white into her hands, and she cackled and smeared it over her throat
and breasts and belly with one hand, the other still pumping at him
hard. *How fucking bad can life be?*

"YOU SEEM UNHAPPY, ERGUND."

"Yeah, well . . ."

Poltar stifled a sigh. He didn't much like Ergund, any more than he
did any of the clanmaster's other brothers. But they were influential and
must be catered for, the more so given Egar's demonstrated blasphemy
and lack of regard for the traditions. And Ergund did at least show a
modicum of respect. The shaman put aside his flensing knife, nodded at
his acolyte to go on with the work, and wiped his hands clean on a rag.
He indicated a curtained alcove at one side of the yurt.

"In here, then. I can spare a few minutes. But the ceremonies are
almost upon us, I have to get ready. What is it you need?"

"I, uh." Ergund cleared his throat. "I had a dream. Last night."

This time, Poltar could not entirely hold back the sigh. It was a
major effort, in fact, not to roll his eyes. In a couple of hours, he had to
go out into the chilling northern breezes and caper about dressed only
in buffalo grease, his wolf-skin robe, and a Ynprpral mask that weighed
as much as an ax. He had to squawk and screech himself hoarse, and be
chased around by small children, and submit to being ceremonially
driven out of the camp, where he'd have to squat for at least an hour in
the cold until the celebrations got well under way, and everyone was too
drunk to notice him slip back in.

In his father's day, of course, the shaman stayed out on the steppe the whole night. But in his father's day, there was respect. In his father's day the self-same children who chased Ynprpral from the camp went out later with food and wine and blankets for the shaman's vigil. Later still, the younger warriors might come and keep Olgan company, shyly ask him advice on how to garner or keep the attention of this girl or that, how to bid shrewdly for a horse or a sword, how to resolve tricky issues of honor and family and ritual.

But Olgan was long gone on the Sky Road, and there would be none of that old respect in these times. Stay out all night for vigil, the most Poltar was likely to get was some stumbling drunk herdboy come out to take a piss and driveling inebriated nonsense at him. Everyone else would be busy cavorting. Since Egar returned from the south, the old ways simply held no sway. There was no sense of honor or tradition now, no *respect.* Ishlin-ichan beckoned, the young men went there often, and the girls around camp acted like the whores they mostly were these days. No one felt the need to listen to the shaman anymore; they'd rather have cheap advice and tales of the south from those Skaranak who had been there and returned, as if riding a horse over the horizon and back was some kind of fucking *achievement.*

And this moping idiot wanted to talk about his dreams.

Poltar got them both seated in the alcove, pulled the curtain, and put on a show of patience he didn't feel.

"Dreams are the path onto heights we may see afar from," he intoned tiredly. "But the view can be uncertain. A rock may look like a horse and rider, a river like beads of glass. Tell me what you have seen."

"It was outside the camp. At night." Ergund was clearly uncomfortable with all this. He was, Poltar knew, a blunt, pragmatic man, a herdsman all his life and pretty much content to stay that way. "I think I'd gone out, you know, for a piss. But the weather was warm, like spring, maybe even summer. I was barefoot and I kept going, kept walking into the grass, trying to find a good spot."

"A good spot to piss?"

"Well, that's what it felt like, yeah. Then I turned around and the campfires were gone, there wasn't even a glow on the sky where they'd been. It was cloudy, so there was no bandlight, or not much anyway. There's this cold wind blowing, I can hear it in my ears all the time. And there's something in the grass, and it's watching me."

"Watching you?"

"Yeah, I could feel its eyes on me. I wasn't worried at first, you know, I had my knife. And I got the feeling this thing was a wolf, and they generally leave you alone unless it's a bad winter." Ergund stared at the ground, held up his hands. He seemed to be trying to frame his thoughts between the blades of his palms. "But then I see it. I see the eyes in the dark, and just like I thought, they're wolf eyes, but they're, like, way above the height of the grass. I mean, four or five feet off the fucking ground."

He shivered a little. Tried on an unconvincing little smile.

"That's got to be the biggest fucking wolf anybody's ever seen, right?"

Poltar made a noncommittal sound. He'd heard sightings of every kind of monster out on the steppe in his time, from the long runners to spiders the size of horses. A gigantic wolf wasn't all that original.

"So now I'm worried, right? I pull my knife, I stand there, and then this fucking thing just comes walking right out of the dark toward me."

"And was it a wolf?"

"Yeah. No. I mean." Ergund's expression was still queasy. "It looked like a wolf, a she-wolf, I think. But it was *walking on its hind legs, man.* You know, like one of those beggar's trick dogs you see in Ishlin-ichan. But—big. Tall as a man."

"Did it attack you?"

The herdsman shook his head. "No. It fucking *talked* to me. I mean, its mouth didn't move or anything, but I could hear this voice in my head, like really soft snarling. It just stood there all reared up on its back legs with its paws held out like it wanted me to take hold of them, and looking me in the eyes the whole time. Close enough I could smell its fur. Close enough to lick my fucking face if it wanted."

"So it spoke. What did it tell you?"

"It told me to come to you. Told me that you were waiting for a message."

Poltar felt the faintest shiver of his own now.

"It called me by name?"

"Yes. It said it knew you. That you'd been waiting for a message, a second message, it said."

Kelgris's words, in the shadowed upstairs room, out of the dead girl's throat. *I bring a message from my brother Hoiran, the one you call Urann. That message is wait and watch.* Poltar recalled the languor in that voice, the searing pain as his prick split and bled, the tethered helplessness. He felt an inexplicable stirring in his groin at the memory.

He moistened his lips.

"So tell me the message."

Ergund looked down at his hands again. "It said . . ."

His voice died on the syllables, the breath hissed out of him unused. The shaman felt a slow pounding begin in his chest. He held himself in check, and waited.

Finally, Ergund looked up, and now there was something almost pleading in his face.

"It said my brother's time as clanmaster has come and gone," he muttered.

The quiet descended like the finest muslin cloth, coating everything in the curtained alcove and, as it seemed, beyond. Poltar felt it tick through his veins, settle in his ears, send everything commonplace away.

He sat rigid.

Ergund opened his mouth. The shaman raised a hand for silence, then got up quickly and went back into the main space of the yurt. The acolyte looked up from his flensing, saw his master's expression, and set down his tools immediately.

"Master?"

"That knife looks as if it could do with sharpening. Why don't you take it over to Namdral and see if he can't put a decent edge back on it. Or better yet, see if he'll dig you out a couple of fresh blades and edge them up for us. Tell him I'll settle with him after the ceremony."

The acolyte frowned. There was nothing wrong with the flensing gear, and they both knew it. And new knives weren't cheap. But he knew better than to argue with Poltar or expect explanations. He bowed his head.

"As my master desires."

Poltar waited until he'd gone, watched from the yurt's entrance as the man moved away through the firelit bustle of the camp, then pulled the hangings tight and went back to Ergund. He found the clanmaster's brother getting to his feet.

"Where are you going?"

"Look, it's . . . I shouldn't have come. Grela talked me into it, she said you'd know what to do."

"Yes. She's right. I do."

"Well," Ergund grimaced. "I mean, it was just a dream, right?"

"Was it?"

"It *felt* like a dream."

The shaman trod closer. "But?"

"But I . . ." Ergund shook his head. It was like watching a buffalo only halfway stunned by some incompetent butcher. "When I woke up, there was grass matted on the bottom of my feet. Still damp. Like I'd really been out there."

"You *were* really out there, Ergund."

"In this cold?" The herdsman snorted, common sense shouldering through the press of arcane fear. "In bare feet? Come on, I'd have fucking frostbite by now. My toes'd be turning black."

Poltar crowded him back to his seat, stood over him. Kept his voice low and hypnotic.

"The dream world is not this world, Ergund. It echoes this place, but it is an otherness, another aspect. It has its own seasons, its own natural laws. You *did* walk there; the grass on your feet is a sign. It's the Dwellers' way of showing you that what you dreamed is real. It's a warning to take this seriously. Your wife was right to send you to me. This is a path we must walk together."

"But, I mean, this thing, the upright wolf. It might have been a demon, sent to trick me. Sent to sow discord in the clan."

Poltar nodded as if giving it consideration.

"That's a good point. But demons do not have the power to cross the expressed will of the Dwellers. If it was a demon that drew you out there and spoke to you, then it did so with the Sky Home's blessing."

And inwardly, he recalled something his father had once said, in an unguarded moment as they sat out at vigil together one spring night. Poltar's mother had passed away the previous winter from the coughing fever, and Olgan had changed with her passing in ways the young Poltar was still trying to fathom.

Common men make a distinction between gods and demons, Poltar, but it's ignorance to talk that way. When the powers do our will, we worship them as gods; when they thwart and frustrate us, we hate and fear them as demons. They are the same creatures, the same twisted unhuman things. The shaman's path is negotiation, nothing more. We tend the relationship with the powers so they bring us more benefit than ruin. We can do no more.

And quickly, glancing guiltily up from his brooding, *Never speak of this to anyone. Men are not ready to hear this truth—though sometimes I think women may be. Sometimes, I think . . .*

But he lapsed into brooding silence again, staring at the fire and listening to the ceaseless wind off the steppe. And he never spoke of the matter again.

"You really think," said Ergund uncertainly, "that the Sky Home has taken against my brother?"

Poltar seated himself with care. He leaned forward. Spoke softly. "What do *you* think, Ergund? What does your conscience tell you?"

"I . . . Grela says . . ." Ergund stared down at his hands, and his expression suddenly turned harsh. "Fuck it, he doesn't *behave* like a clanmaster anymore. You know, coming here, I passed that little slut Sula on her way to his yurt again. I mean, she's what, fifteen? What's he doing with a girl like that?"

"I don't think you need a shaman to answer that," Poltar said drily.

Ergund didn't appear to hear him. "It's not even like it'll last. This is going to end up just like that half-Voronak bitch that threw herself at him last year. Couple of months, he'll get bored and drop her. If there's a child, he'll use his mastery privileges to claw settlement for it out of the clan herds, and then he'll move on to whichever big-titted slut next widens her eyes at him across a feasting board."

He stopped, appeared to rein himself in. He got up and tried to move about in the alcove. He threw out the blade of one open palm.

"Look, if that's how Egar wants to piss his time away, I won't gainsay him. A man pitches his yurt where he will, and then he has to lie in it. I'm not some fucking southern priest, trying to nitpick every ball-scratching moment of every other man's life. But this isn't just about Egar and how he lives. I mean, it's fucking Greasing Night, for Urann's sake, it's a ceremony. He should be out there with his people, showing himself, setting an example. Showing the children how to do their faces for the cold. Inspecting the masks. Not . . ."

"Getting greased in private between the legs?"

It got a weak laugh out of Ergund. "That's right. Taking Greasing Night all the wrong way, isn't he?"

"He is neglecting his duties, yes." More seriously now. "Not all men are born to lead, there is no shame in that. But those who are not must accept the fact, and cede to those who can carry the responsibility better."

Ergund's eyes darted to the shaman's face, and then away.

"I don't want it," he said quickly. "I'm not, this isn't—"

"I know, I know." Soothing now. "You have always been content to tend your herds and your family, Ergund." *And be driven and harried by that nagging, malcontent bitch of a wife.* "To raise your voice in council only where necessary and otherwise stay out of such matters. You are a man who understands his strengths, the paths the powers have laid out for him. But don't you see, that is what makes you the perfect intermediary for those powers."

A hard stare. "No, I don't see that at all."

"Look." Poltar tried to quell a rising sense of moment, of destiny that must be handled with painstaking care. "Suppose one of your brothers had come to me with this, Alrag, say, or Gant. Then, I would have to question whether this dream were true or—"

"My brothers don't lie!"

"Right, of course. You misunderstand me. I say true in the sense of *meaningful.* Truly sent by the Dwellers. Alrag is an honorable man, of course. But it's no secret he's always wanted the clan mastery for himself. And Gant, like you, questions Egar's suitability to lead, but he is not circumspect like you. He speaks openly of these things. The word in camp is that he is simply jealous."

"Ungoverned women's tongues," said Ergund bitterly.

"Perhaps. But the fact remains that both Gant and Alrag might well dream such a dream because it speaks to their own personal desires. With you, I know that's not true. You want no more than what is best for the Skaranak. Through such vessels, the Dwellers speak best."

Ergund sat, head down. Perhaps he was dealing with the weight of Poltar's words, perhaps simply with the unwelcome idea that a steppe wolf really had gotten up on its hind legs and walked out of the darkness to find him. When he finally spoke, his voice shook slightly.

"So what do we do?"

"For the moment, nothing." Poltar kept his tone carefully neutral. "If this is the Dwellers' will, as it seems it is, then there will be other signs. There are rites I can perform for guidance, but they take time to prepare. Have you spoken to anyone else about this?"

"Only Grela."

"Good." It wasn't—you could trust Grela about as far as you could herd campfire smoke. But Poltar knew she had little enough love for Egar. "Then let's keep it that way. We'll talk again, after the ceremonies. But for now, let all three of us be servants of the Sky Home with our silence."

LATER, WHEN THE CHILDREN HAD FACED DOWN YNPRPRAL WITH THEIR grinning, freshly greased firelit faces and their pummeling barrages of half-delighted, half-terrified shouting and their running about at their parents' urging, when they'd chased the ice demon from his flapping, haunting circuits of the great bonfire and back out into the cold dark he belonged to, when all that was done and the Skaranak had settled to their customary drinking and singing and tale telling and staring owlishly into the spit-crackle warmth of the flames . . .

. . . then Poltar crouched out in the windswept chill of the steppe, staying later away from the camp than he could remember himself doing for a dozen or more years, biting back his shivers and hugging himself beneath his father's wolf-skin cloak, muttering under his steaming breath and waiting . . .

Out of the darkness and bending grasses and the wind and the cold, she came walking. Bandlight broke through cloud and touched her.

Grinning, tongue lolling, all sharp white puncturing fangs and eyes, balancing back on legs never made for walking upright, wrapped head-to-foot in wolf the way she had in Ishlin-ichan wrapped herself in whore.

She did not speak. The wind howled on her behalf.

He rose, the chill in his bones and on his face forgotten, and he went to her like a man to the marriage bed.

CHAPTER 15

Gingren was installed in the western lounge when Ringil got in, pacing noisily up and down and barking at someone whose responses were much softer. They'd left the door ajar, which seemed invitation enough to eavesdrop. Ringil hovered for a moment in the corridor outside, listening to his father's gruff tones and a low, diffident voice that he made as that of his oldest brother, Gingren Junior. A cold memory gusted through him at the sound.

A long corridor . . .

He was about to slip away when Gingren, showing a quite remarkable sixth sense, looked up and caught him there.

"Ringil!" he bellowed. "Just the man. Get in here, will you!"

Ringil sighed. He took a couple of steps inside the room and stood there, barely over the threshold.

"Yes, Father."

Gingren and Gingren Junior exchanged a glance. Ringil's brother was sprawled on a couch by the window, rigged for the street in boots and court sword, clearly on a visit from his own family home over in Linardin. It was the first time Ringil had seen him in nearly seven years, and changes weren't flattering. He'd put on weight and grown a beard that didn't really suit him.

"We were just talking about you."

"That's nice."

His father cleared his throat. "Yes, well, Ging's been saying, we can probably nip this idiocy in the bud. Kaad doesn't want it any more than we do, looks like Iscon just went overboard on his own account. It's not the right time for the notable families of Trelayne to be squabbling over trivia like this."

"The Kaads are a notable family now, are they?"

Gingren Junior chortled, then shut up abruptly as his father glared at him.

"You know what I mean."

"Not really, no." Ringil looked at his elder brother, and Gingren Junior looked away. "You come to offer yourself as a second, Ging?"

An awkward silence.

"I didn't think so."

His brother flushed. "Gil, it's not like that."

"No?"

"What your brother is trying to say is that there is no need for seconds, or any other element of this ridiculous charade. Iscon Kaad will not fight, and neither will you. We will resolve this with intelligence."

"Yeah? What if I don't want to?"

Gingren made a noise in his throat. "I'm getting tired of this attitude, Ringil. Why would you *want* to fight?"

Ringil shrugged. "I don't know. It's your family name he insulted coming here the way he did. Threatening steel on the premises."

Gingren Junior bristled forward in his seat. "It's your family, too."

"Good. We're agreed then."

"No, we are *not fucking agreed*!" Gingren yelled. "You cannot just fucking *cut* your way through everything with that cursed sword of yours, Ringil. That's not how we do things here in the city. Not anymore."

Ringil examined his nails. "Well, I've been away."

"Yeah." His father clenched a fist at his hip. "Maybe you should have fucking stayed away."

"Hey—blame your gracious lady wife."

Ging came to his feet. "Don't you dare talk about Mother like that!"

"Oh, *shut* up." Ringil closed his eyes briefly in exasperation. "Look, I'm fucking sick of this. Are you in on this Etterkal thing as well, Ging? You keen to stop me looking for our cousin Sherin, too, in case it puts too many lucrative backstreet deals in the lamplight? Upsets too many of our scummy new harbor-end friends?"

"Sherin always was a stupid little tart," said Ging bluntly. "We all told her not to marry Bilgrest."

"Stupid little tart or not, your honored mother wants her back."

"I told you—"

Ringil grinned wolfishly. "Shame she had to work her way down all three brothers before she found one with the balls to do what she asked."

Gingren Junior surged forward. Ringil went to meet him. He was still shaken up from the events at the gate, would welcome the chance to hit something.

"Ging! Ringil!"

At the sound of their father's voice, both brothers stopped, arm's reach apart in the center of the lounge, gazes locked. Ringil watched his brother's furious face, distantly aware that there was nothing in his own expression to match, nothing there at all but a faint smile and the blank promise of violence.

"Well?" he asked gently.

Ging looked away. "She never asked me."

"I wonder why."

"Hey—*fuck* you." Ging doubled his lowered fists, unconscious echo of his father's anger. Ringil remembered Ging picking it up, back in their shared youth. "I came here to see if I could help."

"You can't help me, Ging, you never could. You were always *soooooo* fucking obedient."

A long corridor . . .

A LONG CORRIDOR IN THE ACADEMY DORMITORY WING, AND COLD winter-afternoon light slanting down through the row of side windows. Dark reek of the waxed wood floor he was pinned to, stinging in his bloodied nose. The reflection of the windows shimmered up out of the polished surface for him, made a receding line of pale pools in the wood, down the corridor to the unattainable door at the end. There was weight on his back from the little knot of seniors holding him down. They were too many to fight, and they were dragging him back from the doorway he'd made a break for, back into the gloom and seclusion of the dormitory. He remembered the chill around his thighs and arse as they forced his breeches down.

He remembered his brother, stopped dead in the corridor coming the other way and staring, just staring.

Most of all, he remembered the look on Ging's face, queasy and weak, as if he'd just eaten something that was going to make him sick. Ringil knew, looking at that expression, that he'd get no help.

The seniors knew it, too.

"Fuck are you doing here, Gingren?" Mershist, the pledge guardian and ringleader, breathing heavily, climbing up off Ringil's neck and squaring up in the corridor. He got his breath back, seemed almost amused. "This isn't your affair. Get the fuck back to drill where you belong. Before I put you on report."

Gingren said nothing, didn't move. He had no weapon—outside of the training yards and salons, the Academy didn't permit the cadets to go armed—but he had some of his father's build about him, was bulkier than Ringil would ever be, and three years into the Academy program was getting a reputation as a canny fighter.

The moment hovered for heartbeats, like a crow on beating wings the instant before it lands. Even Ringil paused in his attempts to thrash free, eyes suddenly on Gingren's face. Hope quavered up in him like small, newly kindled flames.

Then another of the seniors came and stood at Mershist's shoulder, and something indefinable changed about the setting. Even with his face pressed hard to the floor, Ringil felt it. Perhaps Ging might have faced Mershist down alone. But not this. The balance tipped, the moment sideslipped, skidded, and landed on its black-feathered arse. Mershist glanced sideways at his supporting companion, then back to Gingren and grinned. His tone turned conversational, reasonable.

"Look, mate. Little Gil here's getting initiated, whether he fancies it or not. What did you think, your little brother'd get a pass for some reason? You know that's not going to happen. You know how this place works."

Ging's mouth twitched. He was going to try for talk. "It doesn't—"

"I'm doing him a fucking favor, Ging." Mershist let a tinge of exasperated warning seep into his voice. "Gil hasn't exactly made a lot of friends since he matriculated. There's seniors over in Dolmen House want to do him with a fucking *mace head*. And to be honest with you, I can see their point. He took Kerril's eye right fucking *out*, you know."

Ging swallowed. It made an audible click. "Kerril shouldn't have—"

"Kerril was doing what needed to be done." Now the reasonable tone was shredding thin and through. Playtime was coming to an end. Mershist stabbed a finger at Ringil where he lay on the floor. "Your little brother here thinks he's something special, and he fucking isn't. We all go through this, Ging, and we're all stronger for it. You know that. It binds us together, it makes us what we are. Hoiran's fucking balls, it's not like you didn't have old man Reshin's prick up your arse three years ago, just like the rest of us."

Something shifted in Gingren's face then, and the last hope in Ringil guttered out for good. His elder brother's eyes flickered to meet his, skittered away again. He'd flushed with shame. When he spoke again, his voice was almost pleading.

"Mershist, he's only—"

Mershist trod down the words. His voice rasped like steel coming out of the scabbard.

"He's a little fucking pansy, is what he is, Ging. You know it, and so do I. So now he's going to get what he probably secretly wanted all along, from all of us. And *you* will not fucking stop us. So unless you want to join in or watch, I suggest you fuck off back to practice."

And Gingren went.

Just once, as he faltered and turned away, he looked at Ringil, and Ringil thought, later or at that moment, he could not recall which, that it was like meeting someone's eyes across jail cell bars. Ging's mouth worked again, but nothing came out.

Ringil stared back at him. He would not beg.

And Gingren went away, down the dark wood corridor, slowly, like a man carrying an injury, and the declining afternoon lit him coldly at each window he passed.

Ringil closed his eyes.

They dragged him back in.

NOW, IN THE RIVERSIDE LOUNGE, HE LOOKED AT GING OUT OF THE welter of memories, and he saw that his brother was pinned there, too.

Those memories, and all that came after.

The pain, and the bleeding that he kept thinking had stopped but then found hadn't. He didn't need the infirmary the way some initiates did; Mershist and his crew had known what they were about to that extent at least. He supposed he had that much to thank them for. But he had to bite back screams at his toilet for a week.

Then there was the sniggering. The whispered stories about the way Ringil's body had reacted to the rape. No big surprise, it was a fairly common occurrence and cadets at the Academy were used to seeing it. But coupled with the gossip about Ringil's preferences, it provoked an entirely predictable set of minor myths. *Should have seen him*, they would mutter as Ringil limped past on the other side of a courtyard. *Came like a fucking fountain, man, all over everything. You could fucking see he was loving it, every minute of it. Didn't even scream once.*

That much was true. He hadn't given up a single cry.

As they crammed brutally inside him, one after the other, as he was at first just scraped, and then torn, and then for what seemed like a long time, far too long, searingly raw at each stroke, and then finally just increasingly numb to it all, as they dragged clawed hands through his long dark hair and caught it up in savage fistfuls, as they grunted into their own climaxes and spat on him and whispered excited filth in his ears—through it all he gritted his teeth and ground his tongue against the tiny serrated gaps where they met, he fixed his eyes on the weave of the blanket under his face, and he remembered Jelim, and somehow he kept silent.

"I came to help," Ging repeated. His voice sounded hollow, used up. Ringil just looked at him.

"Don't underestimate Kaad," Gingren rumbled. "That'd be a big mistake. Ringil, he may *look* like a fop on his father's sinecure, but he took a silver medal at the Tervinala salons last year. They let imperial bodyguards compete in that one. It *means* something when you take a medal there."

"All right."

Brief pause. Ging and his father exchanged glances again.

"What's that supposed to mean?" Gingren asked.

"It means I won't take any chances tomorrow, and I'll make sure I kill him the first opening I get. Happy now?"

"You really expect me to second you in this duel?" Ging asked him.

"No."

The monosyllable hung there. It silenced both father and brother for longer this time. They both stood there waiting for it to lead somewhere, to an explanation, Ringil supposed.

Fuck that.

Sometimes it seemed that his whole life had been that silent wait, that cold-eyed, staring demand from someone or other, from everyone, that he explain himself. Explain himself away.

The Scaled Folk, at least, had not wanted that much from him.

The tableau broke, to the sound of servant's footsteps. A face peered diffidently around the door.

"My lord Ringil?"

Ringil sighed with relief. "Yes."

"A messenger for you. From the Milacar residence."

CHAPTER 16

They got back into Yhelteth just as the lamps were coming on across the city. Archeth, saddle-sore and stuffed with questions she couldn't answer, would have willingly gone straight to her apartments on the Boulevard of the Ineffable Divine, and to bed. But you didn't do that kind of thing when you were about the Emperor's business. She compromised, sent Shanta and the others on ahead to the palace, and stopped off at her apartments with Elith. She handed the old woman over to her major-domo, told him to put her up in the guest chambers.

"Milady, there is already—" the man began, but she waved it off.

"Later, Kefanin, later. His imperial radiance awaits my presence at the palace. I speed to do his will, y'know."

She swung back on her horse and clattered back out of the house's courtyard, under the arch, and onto the main thoroughfare. Sunset made a dusty furnace glow in the west, backdrop for the blackening silhouettes of minarets and domes across the city. The evening crowds pressed around her, trudged onward toward the end of their laboring day. She felt a twinge of envy. If she knew anything at all, Jhiral would probably keep her waiting a couple of hours before he'd even see her, just to make a point. And even without that expected pettiness, his imperial radiance didn't habitually rise much before noon anyway; it wasn't uncommon for him to hold long counsel with bleary-eyed advisers right through to dawn, then send them directly off to their usual daily duties while he retired to bed. He'd likely have Archeth telling and retelling the details of her report a dozen different ways until the small hours.

She stifled a yawn with the back of a gauntleted hand. Dug in her pouch until she found a small pellet of krinzanz, slipped it into her mouth, and chewed it down to thin saliva-laced mulch. Grimace at the bitter, granulated taste, and swallow. She rubbed the residue against her gums with a leather finger and waited for the gloom of evening to recede a little from her eyes, for the drug to prop the weariness away and lend her its counterfeit lust for life.

DOORS BANGED BACK FOR HER, PIKE-MEN CAME TO ATTENTION AS she passed them down long marble halls. She tugged off her gauntlets impatiently, muttering to herself as she strode the familiar path to her Emperor's presence. From the walls, representations of the Prophet and other notables of imperial history glowered down at her. The krin buzz made some of the better-executed portraits quiver with a simulacrum of hostile life around the eyes. It was scrutiny she could have done without, and it didn't help that there was not a single Kiriath face among those pictured.

You'll have to make it work without us, Grashgal had told her, toward the end. *I can't hold the captaincies any longer. They want out. They've consulted the Helmsmen, all the stable ones anyway, and the answer keeps coming back pretty much the same. It's time to go.*

Oh come on. Hiding her desperation in a snort. *Fucking Helmsman'll give you sixty different answers to the same question depending on how it's phrased. You know that. We've been here before, at least twice that I can remember, and I'm only a couple of hundred years old. It'll pass.*

But Grashgal just stood there at the balcony's edge and stared down into the red glow of the workshops.

The engineers already have orders to refit, he said quietly. *They'll have a fleet that works by year's end. I'm sorry, Archidi. This time it's real.*

But why? Why now?

A shrug that came close to a shudder. *These fucking humans, Archidi. If we stay, they're going to drag us into every squalid fucking skirmish and border dispute their short-term greed and fear can invent. They're going to turn us into something we never used to be.*

These fucking humans.

"The Lady *kir*-Archeth Indamaninarmal," bellowed the herald as the last set of doors opened before her, and across the vaulted and pillared space of the throne room, all the fucking humans turned to stare as she came in.

"Ah, Archeth, you grace us with your presence after all." Jhiral was propped at a sardonic angle in the grandiose architecture of the Burnished Throne, one heel laid four-square over his knee. Light from the Kiriath-engineered radiant stones set into the walls of the chamber behind him conferred the borrowed glow of divine authority. He flashed her a boyish grin. "Almost on time for once, as well. I understand you had to go home before coming to see us. Did you find everything there to your satisfaction?"

Archeth shrugged it off. "I thought it best to come before you fully prepared, my lord. I am ready to deliver my report."

"Oh, good. We have in fact already been hearing from my other, loyal servants." A casual gesture to where Mahmal Shanta, Faileh Rakan, and Pashla Menkarak stood before him in a loose arc. Just the hint of a pause after *other*, the lightest of accents on *loyal*. It was done with masterful subtlety, and Archeth saw how secret smiles flickered among the courtiers. "It seems there's some disagreement about how the situation in Khangset was handled. Some question of you overstepping the limits of your authority?"

Shanta slid her an apologetic glance. She could already guess how things were going. Menkarak had raged all the way back, had in fact been fulminating from the moment he woke up in the camp at Khangset and found Archeth had been busy all night without bothering to secure his approval for anything she'd done.

"It was my understanding, my lord, that the expedition was placed exclusively under my command."

"Within the framework of the Holy Revelation," snapped Menkarak. "To which all secular rule is subordinate. *There can be no light to outshine the radiance of truth, and the servants of truth must brook none.*"

"You were fucking asleep," said Archeth.

"And you abroad by night in the company of an infidel sorceress."

Jhiral lounged back in the throne and grinned again, toothily. "Is this true, Archeth? A sorceress?"

Archeth pulled in a deep breath, held it, let it out. She tried for authoritative calm.

"The woman Elith *believes* she is a sorceress, that much is true. But her claims are suspect to say the least. I do not think she is wholly sane. She and her family suffered greatly in the war, she was forci—... she became an imperial resident under very difficult circumstances. She lost almost her entire family in the war. I would say she was probably half mad with grief well before this raid took place. What she saw when Khangset was attacked may simply have pushed her the rest of the way."

Menkarak exploded. "*Enough!* She's an infidel, a faithless stone-worshipping northerner who would not convert when the hand of the Revelation was extended to her in friendship, and who persists in her stubborn unbelief deep within our borders. The evidence is plain—she has even torn the kartagh from her garb to blind the eyes of the faithful she dwells among. She is steeped in deceit."

"Well now, that is a crime, Archeth," Jhiral said reasonably. "And crimes are usually committed by those with criminal inclination. Are you sure that this woman had nothing to do with the raid?"

Archeth hesitated. "There's no evidence to connect her directly, no."

"Yet Pashla Menkarak here says you incited her to perform out-landish rites on the bluff overlooking the town."

"Well." She affected an icy disdain. "His holiness was not actually present when we went to the bluff, my lord. So it's hard to see how he could know. Perhaps he suffers from an overactive imagination."

"You blackened whore!"

And the world seemed to rock briefly on some unseen axis around her. The krinzanz slugged in her veins, pounded for release. Her palms twitched. Almost, her knives were in her hands.

But she heard the rustling murmurs run through the courtiers as well, saw the way even the urbane Jhiral blinked, and she knew Menkarak had overreached himself. Knew that in some hard-to-define fashion she'd won whatever ritualized combat Jhiral had wanted to see here.

She went in for the kill.

"It's also hard," she said evenly. "To imagine where his holiness learned his court manners. Must I and the memory of my people be insulted in this fashion, my lord, in the very throne room they helped build?"

From among the crowd on the right hand of the throne, a senior invigilator detached himself and came forward to Menkarak's side. He took the younger man's arm, but Menkarak shook it off angrily.

"This woman," he began.

But Jhiral had had enough, at least for one day. "This woman is a valued adviser to the court," he said coldly. "And you have just cast aspersions on her character that may require answer before a magistrate. You came highly recommended, Pashla Menkarak, but you disappoint me. I think you had better retire."

For one insane moment, it looked as if Menkarak might defy the Emperor's command. Archeth, watching keenly, saw something in his eyes that was at best poorly moored to any sense of self-preservation. She recalled Shanta's words to her on the ridge overlooking Khangset. *They say it's a whole new breed coming through the religious colleges now. Hard-line faith.* She wondered if that included aspiration to martyrdom, something the Revelation had flirted with on and off in the past but hadn't seen much of recently.

The senior invigilator muttered intensely at his colleague's ear and his fingers sank into Menkarak's arm just above the elbow, this time with talon-like tenacity. Archeth saw the moment pass, saw the defiance in Menkarak's eyes go out like a doused campfire. The younger invigilator went down on one knee, perhaps forced there by the clawed grip on his arm. He bowed his head.

"My deepest apologies, majesty." The words didn't quite emerge from between clenched teeth, but the tone was ragged—Menkarak sounded like a man slightly out of breath. Archeth surprised herself with a sudden spurt of fellow feeling for the man. She knew well enough the greasy, soiled feeling behind that bent knee and struggling voice. "If my zeal to serve the Revelation has in any way offended you, I beg your indulgence for my lack of courtesy."

Jhiral played it for all it was worth. He sat forward, rubbed at his chin in kingly reflection. Assumed a stern expression.

"Well, Menkarak, that indulgence is not really mine to give." A blatant lie—in the context of the throne room, all and any failure in decorum was a direct insult to the Emperor, whether he was present or not. "Your offensive comments were, after all, to my adviser here. Perhaps you could abase yourself to her instead."

More grabbed-breath gasps around the hall. The senior invigilator looked startled. Menkarak's head came up out of the bow in disbelief. Jhiral held the moment like a long note on the horse bugle he was famed for playing with such virtuoso skill. Held it, expanded it.

And let it collapse.

"Well, no. Maybe not. That'd be extreme, I suppose. Perhaps, then, you could just take your disagreeable presence somewhere it won't offend again." Jhiral nodded at the senior invigilator, voice hardening. "Get him out of my sight."

The senior invigilator was only too happy to comply. He practically dragged Pashla Menkarak back to his feet and then, bowing repeatedly, away down the hall to the doors at the far end. Jhiral watched them out, then he rose without ceremony—a minor breach of etiquette that his father, too, had been fond of using to upset the court—and raised his voice to cover the whole throne room.

"Leave us. I will speak to Archeth Indamaninarmal alone."

It took a minute or less to clear everyone out. One or two hung back, throwing curious glances at the throne; there were a few men among them whose concerns ran a little deeper than palace sinecure, but they were a minority, winnowed down in the years following the accession. Wherever he could afford to, Jhiral had nudged his father's most loyal courtiers out to exile postings in the provinces, occasionally to jail, and in one or two memorable cases to the executioner's chair. A rump of essential competence remained, but it was cowed and dispirited just as Archeth supposed Jhiral had intended. The vast majority of those present were only too glad to follow the imperial will and vacate the chamber.

Faileh Rakan had not moved, awaiting direct command from his Emperor as befitted his rank among the Throne Eternal. And it seemed Mahmal Shanta wasn't going to be sent home, either—he'd begun to back away, but Jhiral caught his eye and made a tiny beckoning gesture with a cupped hand.

The brush and rustle of expensive clothing faded into the hall outside; the doors banged closed. Quiet settled into the throne room. Jhiral gusted a long, theatrically world-weary sigh.

"See, that's what I've got to contend with these days. These new graduates from the Citadel, I'm going to have to do something about them."

"Only give the order, majesty," said Rakan grimly.

"Yes, well, maybe not right now. I've no desire for that kind of bloodbath in the run-up to the Prophet's birthday."

That's right, my lord, we had better avoid a bloodbath. Krinzanz pushed the words forward on her tongue; it was a conscious effort to hold them back. *Not least because, given the choice, the vast peasant mass of the Yhelteth faithful might just decide that fuck it, they've had enough, they'll damn well take fanatical adherence to the tenets of the Revelation over venal exploitation of the throne and top-down decadence. Give it a whirl and see if it doesn't deliver for them.*

And when it doesn't, of course, it'll be too fucking late.

She remembered street battles in Vanbyr, the advancing lines of imperial halberdiers, the screams of the ill-equipped rebels as they broke and were butchered. The shattered homes of collaborators and the lines of shaven-headed captives afterward. The shrieks of women dragged out of line at random and raped to death by the side of the road. The ditches piled with corpses.

After the savagery of Ennishmin and Naral, she had sworn she would not take part in any action like it again. She'd sworn to Ringil, as she talked him down, it was *the last fucking time*.

She rode through Vanbyr and tasted her own lie like the ashes in the air.

And now here was Jhiral, contemplating the same thing in his own capital.

"Perhaps, my lord, we'd do well to analyze the new tendencies in the Citadel and aim to block them at a legislative—"

"Yes, yes, Archeth, I'm well aware of your liking for legislation. But as you've just seen, the Citadel is not currently breeding men with much respect for the niceties of a civilized society."

"Nevertheless—"

"God damn it, woman, will you just shut up." It was impossible to tell if Jhiral was genuinely aggrieved or not. "You know, I expected a little more support out of you, Archeth. It was you he insulted, after all."

Yes, he insulted me. But only after you gave him cause to believe I was out of favor with that snide little comment about loyal servants. You built Menkarak a gangplank he thought was secure, and then when he set foot on it, you kicked it away from the ship and watched him get wet. You play your little games, Jhiral, you play us all off against one another for your greater security and amusement. But someday, you're going to kick someone's gangplank away and they won't go down alone. They'll grab your ankles and pull you down with them.

"My apologies, my lord. I am of course deeply grateful for the protection you extend to my honor at court."

"I should bloody hope so. I don't go up against the Citadel lightly, you know. There's a balance to be played out here, and it's ticklish at the best of times."

She bowed her head. Anything else would have been risky. "My lord."

"They don't like you, Archeth." Jhiral's tone had shifted, taken on a pettish, lecturing tone. "You're a final reminder of the godless Kiriath, and that upsets them. The faithful don't react well when they run up against infidels they can't conquer or condescend to—it starts to look like a nasty little flaw in God's perfect plan."

Archeth sneaked a look at Rakan, but the Throne Eternal captain was impassive. If he heard his Emperor's words as the borderline heresy they so patently were, he gave no sign that it bothered him. And the two guardsmen on either side of the throne might have been carved from stone for all the reaction they offered.

Still . . .

"Perhaps we should discuss Khangset, my lord."

"Indeed." Jhiral cleared his throat, and she thought that for just a moment he looked almost grateful for the interjection. She wondered how much of his guard he'd let down in that last outburst, how much self-pity there was along with the sympathy in the words *they don't like you, Archeth.* Rule from the Burnished Throne was, for all its brutal potential, very much the ticklish business Jhiral described.

"We were discussing, my lord, the—"

"Yes, I remember. The madwoman Elith, and these rites you say she didn't perform. Let's have it, then."

"She did perform the rites, my lord."

"I rather imagined so. Menkarak, whatever his other deficiencies, doesn't strike me as a liar. And was this at your instigation?"

"Yes, my lord."

Jhiral sighed and sank back into the arms of the throne. He leaned an elbow on the arm, put his hand to his brow, and looked at Archeth wearily from under it. "You are going to explain all this in a satisfactory manner at *some* point, I assume."

"I hope so, my lord."

"Then could we perhaps accelerate the process? Because at the moment I appear to be listening to a member of my inner court admitting to sorcery in collaboration with an enemy of the realm."

"I don't believe there was any sorcery, my lord."

"Ah."

"Khangset was certainly attacked by some force with technology we don't have access to, and Elith thinks she helped summon them. But her involvement in these matters is coincidental at best. I encouraged her to repeat the rites she thinks communicate with the attackers, and of course nothing happened."

Nothing, that is, if you don't count the creep of flesh on the back of your neck as Elith stands erect before the crudely hewn stone figure on the cliff's edge in the hour before dawn, arms held out to mimic its patient cruciform beckoning, singing a wild, arrhythmic incantation, fluid northern syllables stretched to shrieking and thrown out into the whoop and roar of the sea wind, until it's hard to tell anymore who's making which sounds. You heard a lifetime of suffering and grief poured out in song there, Archidi, and for more than just a moment or two it seemed to you, didn't it, that something stony and violent must answer from beyond the curtains of gloom and gale.

"Archeth, come on." Jhiral shook his head. "That doesn't in itself prove anything. Perhaps these forces she attempted to summon just weren't interested in an encore. Hmm? Sorcery is an unreliable business, you've said so yourself enough times. And Rakan and Shanta here both say the destruction was pretty overwhelming, the worst they've seen since the war. Who'd come back after a successful sacking like that? What point would there be?"

"My lord, what point would there be in attacking a garrisoned port in the first place, if nothing of value is taken and there is no onward assault?"

Jhiral frowned. "Is this true, Rakan? Nothing was taken?"

"No, majesty. It appears not. We found the interior possessions of houses untouched where they had not been destroyed by fire. And the port authority strongrooms contained silver bullion, paymaster's bagged coin, and several crates of confiscated valuables, all of which were still in place." A hint of emotion crept into the Throne Eternal's dispassionate voice, the faintest tinge of confusion. "Though each door had been ripped off its hinges as if by a team of horses."

"And I take it," said Jhiral drily, "that you could not possibly introduce a team of horses in the lower levels of the port authority."

"No, majesty."

"Shanta? Any alternative explanation you can think of?"

The naval engineer shrugged. "Perhaps some system of pulleys. Sufficiently well anchored, they might—"

"Thank you, I think we'll take that as a no." Jhiral scowled and looked at Archeth again. "It seems to me we're back to the sorcery that you're so firmly of the opinion did not occur."

"I don't say that sorcery—or some form of science of which I'm ignorant—did not occur, my lord. I say only that the woman Elith had no hand in it, that I did not see her perform sorcery at any time, nor do I believe that she has ever had the ability to do so. She is merely a spectator to these events, a spectator with just enough specialized cultural knowledge to give the impression of involvement."

Jhiral made a small, exasperated noise in his throat and threw himself back in the arms of the throne. "You see? I didn't follow any of that last sentence, Archeth. Can you—*please*—spell it out for us in terms a pure-blood human would understand."

She ignored the veiled insult, swallowed it, marshaled the facts at her disposal, and once more built up the façade of professional detachment that kept her sane and out of jail.

"Very well. Elith, in common with a lot of the transplanted peoples from annexed territories in the north, believes in a broad pantheon of different gods and spirits. It's a tradition that bears some resemblance to the Majak nomads' framework of faith, but it's far more ordered. It's been written down, modified, embellished, and shared among the Naomic tribes for long enough to become codified. Among this pantheon, there is a figure, or more correctly a whole race, called the dwenda."

"Dwinduh?" Jhiral mangled the unfamiliar word.

"Dwenda. Or the Aldrain, depending on which tribe's tales you prefer. It comes to the same thing. A race of beings, close to human in form, with supernatural powers, access to realms beyond human reach, and close links to or even shared blood with the gods."

Jhiral coughed a laugh. "Well. I mean, that could be the Kiriath you're talking about there. I've heard the same things said about them enough times. Human-type races with unexplained powers. Are you saying the Kiriath or some of their cousins are back, that they've taken to sacking my cities?"

"Clearly not, my lord." Though she found suddenly she could not make herself hate the idea, the return and the final exasperated turning on *these fucking humans.* And she wondered fleetingly where Jhiral had derived the idea *from,* out of what guilt and half-suppressed fear of the race who had served his father but turned their backs on him. "The Kiriath are gone, yes. But they are probably not the only near-human race ever to have visited this world. In the Great Northern Chronicle, the Indirath M'nal, there is some mention of an enemy that fits the description of Elith's dwenda. I'm not overly familiar with the text, I'll need to look back through it, but one thing I do recall is that these dwenda were reputed to have a specialized relationship with the elements; they could, for example, summon up storms or command the earth to open and vomit up its dead. And certain types of stone and crystal were supposed to have powers they could draw out."

"Crystals?" Jhiral's face was a study in disdain. "Oh, come on Archeth. No one, I mean *no one* with a halfway decent education believes that power-of-crystals shit. That's for the peasants on the northern march, the ones who never learned to read or add up."

"I agree, my lord. But at the same time, it is a known fact that my own people were successful in utilizing certain structural peculiarities of geology for navigational purposes. It simply occurs to me to wonder if the dwenda might not have done something similar."

"Navigation, eh?" Jhiral glanced shrewdly across at Shanta, who looked embarrassed. Archeth had run her theory by him, but he hadn't reacted all that well to it. "Go on, then. I'm listening."

"Yes, my lord. On the bluff overlooking Khangset harbor from the north, there is—there was, I've had it removed now—a stone idol. Very roughly human in form, about the size of a small woman or a half-grown child. It is made of a black crystalline rock called glirsht, commonly found in northern lands, but almost unknown farther south. Elith brought the figure with her from Ennishmin in a cart with her family's other possessions. She set it on the bluff, and periodically she climbs the coastal path to make offerings to it."

The look of disdain flowed back, this time on Rakan and Shanta's faces as well. The Revelation and its adherents had scant time for idol worship. At best it was primitive nonsense, to be discouraged with a more or less heavy ecclesiastical hand; at worst it was a first-category sin, and deserving of death. Imperial conquest was built on a centuries-old assumption of the right to suppress the practice and instruct those conquered in the error of their ways. Specifics varied from Emperor to Emperor, and how well financed the levy was at the time.

"The way I see it, my lord, this idol may have acted as some form of beacon. Elith believes it was her prayers and offerings that brought the dwenda to Khangset. I'm inclined to think those rituals are beside the point. But the stone itself, the glirsht, may have some kind of . . ." A shrug; she had not fully convinced herself of all this, let alone Shanta. ". . . a structural resonance, perhaps. Something for the dwenda to steer by."

Even in her own ears, the words sounded limp. Jhiral looked back at her for a couple of moments, then down into his lap, then back up. When he spoke, his voice was weary, almost plaintive, imploring the simple explanation.

"Look, Archeth—could this not just be a case of pirates? Albeit sophisticated pirates, pirates with a flair for disguise, for exploiting the terrors of our less worldly citizens? Maybe even pirates with some sorcery adept crewing with them." The imperial fingers snapped—abrupt inspiration. "Come to that, they might even have been in league with this northern bitch you brought back with you—what if she was spying for them on shore, going up to the bluff to signal to them."

"They took nothing, my lord," she reminded him. "And no pirate vessel I've ever heard of mounts weaponry sufficient to damage Kiriath-engineered defenses."

"If it were the dwenda," said Rakan, perhaps in an attempt to back up his Emperor, "then they also took nothing. Why would that be?"

Jhiral nodded sagely. "That's a very good point. Archeth? Are these creatures not interested in gold or silver?"

She bit back a sigh. "I don't know, my lord. I'm barely familiar with the mythology as it is. But it does seem clear that these raiders, whether they were dwenda or human, came for something other than loot."

"Such as? Not their local priestess, that's for sure. They left her high and dry for us to pick up."

"Revenge, perhaps?" said Shanta quietly.

There was a brief, prickly silence, during which you could see the naval engineer transparently wishing he'd never spoken.

"Revenge, on whom?" asked Jhiral with dangerous calm.

Archeth cleared her throat. Someone had to say it. "Elith was not well treated by imperial forces during the war. Members of her family were brutalized. One died, and the rest were resettled against their will."

"Well, we all suffered in the war," Jhiral said, in clipped tones of affront. "We all had to play our part in the struggle. That's no excuse for treachery or betrayal of the realm."

Jhiral's part in the struggle and the suffering had been confined, Archeth seemed to recall, to riding behind his father at troop inspections and saluting. For all his training, he never saw combat.

"I don't think Mahmal Shanta is referring—"

"I don't care what you think he's referring to, Archeth." Affront now building to genuine anger. "We've pussyfooted around this long enough. If there is even the slightest suspicion that this woman Elith might have given aid or comfort to our enemies, sorcerous or otherwise—then I want her put to the question."

Archeth's flesh chilled.

"That won't be necessary, my lord," she said rapidly.

"Oh, won't it?" Jhiral leaned bodily out at her from the throne, voice an inch off shouting. It was the most aggressive stance he'd taken all evening, the confrontation with Pashla Menkarak included. "How refreshing that you're suddenly so certain of something. Perhaps you could explain to us, in this mess of mythological mumbo-jumbo and conjecture you've cooked up, *how you can be so bloody sure of that?*"

Seconds ticked away; she could almost hear the clockwork of their passing. Behind her eyes, the seared memory spread itself, of interrogations she'd been required to attend in the past. She forced herself not to swallow.

"I have gained this woman's trust," she said truthfully. "In the days since we found her, her madness has begun to recede. She talks to me freely, not always making sense, but that is improving. I don't believe any degree of inflicted pain will help the process—if anything, it will simply thrust her back into her delusions. I need more time, my lord. But given that time, I am wholly confident I will discover everything of value that she can tell us."

More quiet. But she no longer heard the clockwork in it. Jhiral still looked skeptical, but in a mollified sort of way.

"Rakan?" he asked.

Archeth's gaze leapt to the Throne Eternal's face. She should have known better—there was nothing to hang on to in that impassive face. Faileh Rakan considered for a moment, but the only indication that there was anything going on behind the narrow features was a slight distance in the normally attentive eyes.

"The woman is talking," he said finally. "The Lady *kir*-Archeth does appear to have won her trust."

Yes, you fucking beauty, Rakan. Archeth could have kissed the Throne Eternal captain's impassive face for him. Could have punched the air above her head and whooped.

She held it down and watched her Emperor.

Jhiral saw her watching. He made a tired gesture.

"Oh, very well. But I want regular reports, Archeth. With something substantial in them."

"Yes, my lord."

"Rakan, who did you say you'd left in charge at Khangset?"

"Sergeant Adrash, majesty. He's a good man, northern campaign veteran. I detailed two-thirds of the detachment to stay behind with him, and he has the remains of the marine garrison to work with as well. They're shaken up, but he'll whip them back into shape fast enough."

"How many men does that give him?"

"About a hundred and fifty, all told. Enough to put a cordon around the town, make sure word doesn't get out about the raid until we want it to. We've posted penalty warnings about seditious talk and unlicensed meetings, built a gallows in the main square, and set a dusk-to-dawn curfew. Should have the place back on its feet inside a couple of weeks."

"Good. *That* sounds like solid progress at least." A sour glance at Archeth. "Can I take it we'll be hearing some more about these dwenda?"

"I will begin the research immediately, my lord."

"Fine. Let's just hope the Helmsmen are feeling a little more cooperative than usual, eh?"

The same worry had been dragging at her ever since they left Khangset. She forced it down and manufactured a confidence of tone she didn't feel.

"This raid represents a substantial assault on the realm, my lord. I believe that with those parameters, the Helmsmen will revert to wartime attitudes." *Yeah, Archidi—those we can still consider sane, that is.* "I expect fairly rapid progress."

"Rapid progress?" A raised eyebrow. "Well, I shall hold you to that, Archeth. As you say, this is an assault on the realm, and at a time when relations with our neighbors in the north are fragile, to say the least. We cannot appear weak. I will not permit a repetition of what has happened at Khangset."

Archeth thought of the damage to the Kiriath harbor defenses, and wondered sardonically how Jhiral planned to exercise that particular point of imperial will if the raiders returned.

"No, my lord," she intoned.

If, for example, the dwenda sailed up the river to Yhelteth, came ashore, and stalked the streets of the city as they apparently had at Khangset, phantasmal and to all appearances impervious to any harm human force could achieve. If they put to flight or slaughtered all *these fucking humans,* and then came like vengeful demons to the gates of the palace, and would not be kept out.

What would happen to Jhiral Khimran, Emperor of All Lands then?

Her own sudden ambivalence mugged her, jumped in her veins and belly like a fresh intake of krin. Unnerved, struggling with the jagged new thoughts, she forced recall of the shattered rib cage of a child, buried beneath charred and fallen timbers. Forced herself to remember that *these fucking humans* had once included her own mother.

It helped—but not as much as it should have.

CHAPTER 17

Grace-of-Heaven had two soldiers for him—sun-darkened, sinewy men of indeterminate age who stood around in the upper room at the tavern with arms folded and a latent threat of violence oozing from them like slow smoke. Ringil made them for Marsh Brotherhood muscle, on loan to Milacar no doubt as some kind of lodge-approved favor. Neither was visibly armed, but their loose black burglar's garb could and probably did hide an assortment of close-quarters weaponry. They spared a couple of surprised glances for the Ravensfriend when Ringil first came in wearing it, but neither man passed comment. Thereafter they were closemouthed and watchful in the lamplit gloom, respectful enough to both Ringil and Grace, but without overdoing it. There was no discussion of payment and, interestingly, no mention of the *dwenda*.

"Your main problem," Milacar warned them, "is going to be getting past the urchins."

Which wasn't a surprise, for Ringil at least. He'd had the realities of the landscape laid out for him that first night at Milacar's place. Grace-of-Heaven, staring off the balcony with him, voice discouraged and faintly tinged, perhaps, with envy. *Anywhere else, you'd only have the Watch to worry about, and they can be bought for a harbor-end blow job. Since the Liberalization, that's all changed. The slave lobby had the Watch run out of Etterkal altogether, paid them all off at Chancellery level.*

Ringil grinned. *That's a lot of blow jobs.*

Yeah, well. Sourly. *What I hear, it was Snarl that did the deals, so maybe she's found her level. Anyway, the Watch get to mount nominal guard at the quarter boundaries, especially over by Tervinala, basically because that's where the Empire merchants and diplomats hang out, and right now, despite all this mob xenophobia and shipbuilding, we are still supposed to be looking after them as valued mercantile partners. Meanwhile, Findrich and a couple of others I don't know handed the streets of Etterkal over to the urchin gangs; they're all on a retainer for news of anything out of the ordinary, and some fairly hefty beatings for failure to report. You wander into the Salt Warren alone with that chunk of Kiriath steel strapped to your back, the first street brat that sees you is going straight to Findrich, and you'll have an honor guard taking you to see him shortly thereafter.*

I'll talk to Findrich, if that's what it takes.

Yeah—you will if talk's what he wants out of you. And what I hear, Findrich isn't any more into conversation these days than he ever was. More likely he'll just have them chop your fucking head off and give it to the dwenda. A long sigh. *Look, Gil, why don't you make life a little easier for us all and stay out of Etterkal for another couple of days, give me some time instead. I'll get you your list.*

Fair enough. He kept it carefully casual. *But I'm still going in there, Grace. You know that, right? One way or the other, sooner or later, with or without your help.*

Milacar rolled his eyes. *Yeah, I know. One way or the other, last stand at Gallows Gap, all that. Look, just leave it with me, Gil. I'll see what I can do.*

What Grace could do, it turned out, was supply high-end clothing and even a few forged documents identifying Ringil as a Yhelteth spice merchant, domiciled in Tervinala for the winter, and in the market for something to sweeten his stay. It was a pretty good cover. With his mother's blood and the years of rural living in Gallows Water, Ringil was dark-skinned enough to pass. And Yhelteth merchants of any means would hire local enforcers to accompany them through the streets as a matter of course, so Milacar's on-loan muscle wouldn't look out of place, either.

"And neither, fortunately, will that ridiculous sword of yours. Practically every imperial in Tervinala is wandering around with some kind of Kiriath knockoff on their belt these days, and most people can't tell the difference from the real thing. Common as muck. Half the time, they're selling them to pay off their gambling debts or clear the rent till spring. You've got one somewhere haven't you, Girsh?"

The bulkier-built of Milacar's two soldiers inclined his head. "Took it off some guy's bodyguard in a fight. Piece-of-shit court sword, you couldn't chop an onion with it. Not even half the weight of good steel."

Grace-of-Heaven chuckled. "The demands of fashion, eh. Girsh here isn't very impressed with the imperials."

Ringil shrugged. "Well, merchant class, you know. Shouldn't judge the whole Empire by them."

"Watch it, Eskiath. You're talking to a merchant, remember."

"Thought I was talking to a city founder."

The other soldier stirred, addressed himself to Ringil. "Do you speak Tethanne?"

Ringil nodded. "Well enough to get by. You?"

"A bit. I can do the numbers."

Girsh glanced across at his companion, apparently surprised. "You know Tethanne numbers, Eril?"

"Yeah. How else you going to take money off these people at cards?"

"Well, you shouldn't need it anyway," was Milacar's opinion. "The clothes and the blade should be enough, unless you run into some fellow imperials, and this time of night, that part of town, it isn't likely."

"You think the Watch are going to let us through? This time of night?"

Eril made a significant gesture with one open hand, thumb rubbed across fingers. "If we treat them right. Sure. They'll be amenable."

Ringil thought briefly of his scuffle on Dray Street, the way his purse had cleared up what his fighting skills could not. He nodded.

"Nothing ever changes in this town, huh?"

Which proved accurate. At one of the makeshift street barricades on Black Sail Boulevard, where Tervinala nominally ceased and the Salt Warren began, a squad of six watchmen stood about in war-surplus hauberks and open-face helmets, yawning and looking so amenable they practically had their hands out. Their barricade was cobbled together out of old furniture; its most useful function seemed to be as a place to lean and pick your teeth. Street glow from the lamps on the Tervinala side picked out the dents on the men's superannuated helms, and painted their faces faintly yellowish. They mostly wore short skirmish swords, though one or two had pikes, and to a man they were all visibly sick of the duty. Not a shield between them. Ringil, whose calculus for these things was reflexive, reckoned he could probably have taken the whole group in close-quarters combat and suffered not much more than scratches.

Eril approached the sergeant in charge and coins changed hands, subtly enough that Ringil almost missed it. Most of him was focused on the gloom on the other side of Black Sail Boulevard, where there were no lamps and the ancient torch brackets were either empty or held torches long since burned down to a blackened wick. The Watch had set up a couple of braziers beside the barricade, presumably more to ward off the gathering autumn chill than to throw light; the light they gave barely stretched across the paved street. The houses beyond were sunk in shadow. Vague shapes moved about in windows at the second and third floors, in all probability urchin gang lookouts, but the darkness and the distance painted them shifty and unhuman, all hunched posture, sharp features, and oddly angled bones.

Well, here are your dwenda already then, Gil. And all it took to see them was an overworked imagination.

But his smile faded as soon as it touched his lips. He could not shake the memory of Milacar's fear. The story of the amputated, living heads.

The Watch sergeant called out orders to a couple of his men. Eril turned and beckoned to Ringil and Girsh. The sergeant gestured to one side of the barricade, where one of the pike bearers stood aside to let them through. For show, Ringil muttered a string of ornate thanks in Tethanne, then, turning to Eril, the first couple of lines of a Yhelteth nursery rhyme.

"Eleven, six, twenty-eight," replied Eril with a straight face, and they were on their way, moving across to the darkened side of the boulevard.

Behind them, perhaps trying to be helpful, a watchman stabbed vigorously at one of the braziers with his sword, stirring up the dull glowing coals. But all it did was set long shadows dancing past their feet and up the brickwork ahead.

"YOU EVER KILL A CHILD?"

Girsh asked it idly as they passed under a narrow covered bridge—the third or fourth so far—over whose unglassed stone gallery ledges urchins hung their arms and chins and stared down with unblinking calculation.

But he wasn't joking.

Ringil remembered the eastern gate.

"I was in the war, remember," he evaded.

"Yeah, I don't mean *lizard* pups. I mean humans. Kids, like those ones back there watching us."

Ringil looked at him curiously. He supposed it wasn't Girsh's fault. It was a common enough conceit in Trelayne that the war had been a straightforward battle for the human race—with a little technical support from the Kiriath—against an implacably evil and alien foe. And Girsh, for all his quiet enforcer's competence, wouldn't be any better informed or educated than the next street thug; in all probability, he'd never been outside the borders of the League in his life. Possibly, he'd never even been out of the sight of Trelayne itself. And quite clearly, he had never been within a hundred miles of Naral, or Ennishmin, or any of the other half a dozen fucked-up little border disputes the war had degenerated into at the end. Because if he *had*—

No point in getting into that now. *Let it go,* Archeth had urged him last time they met, and he'd tried. Really tried.

Was still trying.

"I won't have any problem, if it comes to it," he said quietly.

Girsh nodded and left it alone.

Others were less compliant.

No, you never really did have a problem, did you, whispered something that might have been Jelim Dasnel's ghost. *Not when it came to it.*

He shook it off. Tried letting go of that as well.

In doorways, from windows and the lowest of the rooftops, and from a few dozen furtive steps behind them in the street, the urchins kept track.

As if they knew.

Ah, come on. Stop that shit.

He focused on the street, moored himself back to its realities. They wouldn't have to kill anybody tonight, adult or otherwise, if they just kept it together. Etterkal, despite Milacar's ghost stories, was no more alarming than any other run-down city neighborhood he'd walked through at night. The streets were narrow and infrequently lit compared with the boulevards in Tervinala or some of the upriver districts, but they weren't badly paved for the most part, and you could navigate easily enough by the lights in windows and the handful of shop frontages still open at this hour. For the rest, it was just the darkness and its usual denizens—the garish, inevitable whores, breasts out and skirts raised, faces so worn and blunted that even heavy makeup and shadow could not disguise the damage they contained; the guardian pimps, hovering and gliding in doorways and alley mouths like half-summoned dark spirits; the occasional sharkish presence that could have been a pimp but was not, emerging from convenient gloom to cast a speculative eye over the passersby, sinking just as rapidly back when the nature of Ringil and his companions became apparent; the broken, piss-perfumed figures slumped low against walls, too drunk, drugged, or derelict to go anywhere else, among them no doubt a fair few corpses—Ringil spotted a couple of the more obvious ones—for whom all concerns of commerce, livelihood, shelter, or chemical escape had finally ceased to matter.

They came to the first address on Grace-of-Heaven's list.

For a slave emporium, it didn't look like much. A long, rambling frontage, three stories of decaying, badly shuttered windows, lights gleaming through here and there, but most of it in darkness. The plaster walls were stained and wounded back to the brick in patches, the roof sloped down like a lowered brow. There were a couple of doors at ground level, each caged shut behind solid barred gates, and a large carriage entry stood snugly closed up with heavy, iron-studded double doors that looked fit to stand against siege engines.

Back before the crummy little fishing harbors at the mouth of the Trel were dredged to any serious depth, Etterkal had been a warehouse district for the landward merchant caravans, and this was a pretty standard example of that heritage.

Over time, the increasing commerce by sea had stomped all over the caravan trade, and Etterkal fell apart. Poverty came and ate the district; crime snapped and snarled over the remaining scraps. It wasn't anything Ringil had direct experience of—the process was well and truly ingrained by the time he was born, the corpse of Etterkal already rotted through. But he knew the dynamic. Where municipal authorities in Yhelteth had a textually delineated religious obligation to maintain any town or neighborhood with a majority population of the Faithful, the great and the good of Trelayne were more in favor of benign neglect. No point nor profit in swimming against the tide of commerce, they argued, and in Etterkal that tide was ebbing fast. The money went looking for somewhere else to live, and all those who could went with it.

But the warehouse blocks remained, big and brooding and impossible to rent. Some were carved up into lousy accommodations for labor overspill from the newly burgeoning shipyards—not a strategy that ever really worked out; some were demolished to clear out the vagrant bands they were found to be housing. A few burned down, for reasons no one was clear on, or cared very much about. With the war, the low-rent space became briefly useful again, for billeting and the marshaling of matériel, but the area saw no long-term benefit from it. The war ended, the soldiers went home. No one who wasn't ordered to was going to move into Etterkal.

That left slaves, and those who traded in them.

Girsh found a small hatch cut into the body of the carriage entry door, and commenced banging on it with a compact, well-worn mace he produced from his burglar's clothes like a conjuring trick. Ringil stood by and affected an aristocratic disdain for the proceedings, in case anyone was watching from one of the casements above. It took a good five minutes of repeated pounding, but finally there was the clanking sound of bolts being drawn, and the hatch hinged inward. A disgruntled, scar-faced doorman stepped out into the street, short-sword drawn.

"What the fuck do you think you're doing?" he barked.

Eril had taken the lead. He turned toward Ringil and reeled off a string of numbers in Tethanne. Ringil inclined his head and pretended to consider, then spoke back a couple of random sentences. Eril turned back to the doorman.

"This is my Lord Laraninthal of Shenshenath," he said. "He's here on recommendation, to examine your wares."

The doorman let a sneer creep across his face. He put up his sword.

"Yes, well, my master doesn't do business at this hour," he told them. "You'll have to come back."

Stone-faced, Eril punched him in the stomach.

"And *my* master," he informed the downed minion as he curled up on the floor whooping for breath, "does not like to be told to come and go like a common stevedore. Especially not by harbor-end curs like you."

The doorman made gagging sounds and groped around on the cobbles for his sword. Girsh kicked it casually out of his reach. Eril crouched down and grasped the man by his collar and balls.

"We know," he said conversationally, "that your master deals in the exotic end of things. And we know that he likes to conduct that business at exotic hours, if the price is right. Get up."

The doorman really had very little choice in this last instruction. Eril dumped him onto to his feet and shoved him back against the iron-studded wood of the gate.

"My Lord Laraninthal is in the market for your stock in trade, and he's impatient. The price he's prepared to pay is substantial. So go and fetch your master, and tell him he's missing a very special opportunity."

The doorman groaned and cupped at his groin. "What opportunity?"

"The opportunity not to have his business burned down around his ears," said Girsh, deadpan. "Now fuck off in there and tell him. No, leave the door. We'll come in and wait."

The doorman abandoned his halfhearted attempt to close the hatch on them, and they followed him through into a long, well-lit archway with a courtyard beyond. A side door was open in the wall of the arch, and the doorman disappeared into it, limping and muttering to himself. The three of them stood in the flickering torchlight after he'd gone, eyeing up the surroundings with identical professional interest.

"Think they'll kick?" Ringil asked.

Eril shrugged. "They're trying to make a living, just like everybody else. No percentage in bloodshed if you can deal instead."

Girsh slapped the head of his mace into his palm a couple of times. "Let them kick. I've got a couple of cousins lost family to the debtors' block since Liberalization. I won't mind."

Ringil cleared his throat. "Let's not get carried away here. I need information from these people, not broken skulls."

"Everyone's got cousins seen family auctioned," Eril said quietly. "It's the times, Girsh. Nothing you can do about it."

They waited in silence after that.

The doorman came back, accompanied by a larger and uglier colleague who wore a knotted leather flail at his belt and a long knife at his boot. He didn't look as if he'd need either in a fight.

"My master will see you now," the doorman said sullenly.

IT SEEMED THEY'D GOTTEN TERIP HALE OUT OF BED.

The slave trader sat behind his dark oak desk in a silk robe, slippers on his naked feet, graying hair tangled and matted from the pillow. Lamplight gave his skin a yellowish tone. Ringil didn't know him, but he fitted Grace-of-Heaven's thumbnail sketch well enough. *Greasy old fuck, got eyes like a dead snake.* It was true, he did. Once a small-time trafficker working various illicit trades through little-known marsh routes in and out of the city, Hale had apparently done well under Liberalization. Legacy of his prior success as a supply-and-demand criminal, he knew men's appetites inside and out. A shrewd buyer's sense at the auction blocks gave him his initial edge, it seemed, and a tightly maintained web of onward contacts in other cities of the League kept him out ahead of the pack. He was dangerous in his way, Milacar reckoned, but he wasn't an unreasonable man.

He fixed the expressionless black eyes on Ringil.

"This had better be good," he said mildly.

"I thank you, honored sire, for the—"

For the sake of appearances, Ringil had begun in Tethanne. Now he coughed diffidently and switched to Naomic, stamping it through with a guttural edge common to imperials who'd learned the Trelayne tongue but never lived in League territory. He spotted the doorman and the flail-equipped muscle smirking at each other as he spoke.

"Honored sire, I thank you, for seeing me at this late hour." He shuffled his feet, playing up a timidity of stance and tone he'd sometimes liked to put on in games with Grace-of-Heaven. Silk-skinned kidnapped Yhelteth youth begs his captor—in vain, of course—not to corrupt him. "I, uhm, would not have come so late, you see, but this visit is not one my father would countenance if he knew of it. I am Laraninthal, eldest son of Krenalinam of Shenshenath, attached—uhm, we both are—to the Yhelteth trade mission in Tervinala and recently arrived in your gracious city, which I must say—"

"Yes, yes." Hale waved it away as if swatting an insect. "*What* exactly is it that your father would not countenance about your visit?"

Ringil hesitated for a calculated couple of seconds. "Its purpose, sire."

Hale rolled his eyes and made a signal to the doorman, who slipped out of the room without a word. The slave trader bridged his hands.

"Yes. Let's talk about this purpose, shall we?"

"Gladly."

Another pause. Hale visibly repressed a sigh.

"So what *is it*? Your purpose? What do you *want*, Laraninthal of Shenshenath?"

"I desire." Ringil cleared his throat and looked about the room. "A bedmate. A woman, for my use here in Trelayne."

A small smile leaked out of the corner of Hale's mouth.

"I see. And your father wouldn't approve of this?"

"My father is a conservative man. He would not wish me to spill my seed among women not of the tribes."

"Well, fathers can be difficult like that, can't they?" Hale nodded sagely. "Of course, at a price, I could probably provide you with a Yhelteth girl. Perhaps even of your specific tribe. You'd be surprised how easy—"

Ringil held up a hand. "I am not . . . drawn . . . to women of the south. I want pale skin, paler than mine. I want . . ."

He gestured graphically. Terip Hale grinned.

"Indeed. That's something the girls up here are usually good for, isn't it? Not the first time I've heard one of your countrymen remark on the matter, either. Difference is the spice, I always say." A small sound from the door. "Ah, speaking of which, here we are."

The doorman came back in the company of a girl carrying a gaudily painted wooden tray laden with goblets and a flagon. She wore not much more than three fistfuls of cloth and a couple of thin cords holding it all together, and she walked to accentuate what was on display. She was too young for the makeup she wore, and there was a worried crease around her eyes like someone trying to remember the right way to perform a complex task, but she conformed more or less to the specifics they'd just been discussing. Ringil made his eyes stick to her curves in an appropriate fashion as she crossed the room. Hale saw, and smiled.

"So. You like?"

"Yes. This would be, uhm, suitable, but—"

"Oh, I'm sure it would." Hale, dreamily, watching as the girl laid out flagon and goblets on the desk. "Unfortunately, Nilit here isn't for sale. I've taken a bit of shine to her. But really, she's nothing special, and she has sisters."

He glanced up.

"I mean that quite literally. Sisters, two of them. All sold together. But the others are still in training. That can take awhile, especially if the girl is . . . spirited."

Nilit's hand knocked the flagon against one of the goblets she'd already set down. The cup toppled and rolled off the edge of the desk, clattered hollowly on the floor. Hale's lips pressed together in exasperation. Nilit scrambled to retrieve the still-rolling goblet, and her eyes flashed on Ringil's. The worry was gone, wiped out by a more immediate terror. She set the goblet back in place, hung her head, and mumbled something inaudible to Hale. He raised a finger at her and she shut up instantly.

"Just get out," he snapped.

The girl hurried away, her wagging display-walk forgotten. Hale poured from the flagon, two goblets only. He beckoned Ringil forward.

"Please, be my guest. Choose a cup. This is one of the best wines the League territories have to offer. Before one becomes a customer of Terip Hale, one becomes an honored guest in his house. How else will we bind trust in our dealings?"

Ringil selected one of the goblets and held it up. Hale matched the gesture for a moment, drank first, as host ritual required. Ringil followed suit, swallowed a mouthful, and made an appreciative face.

"Fine vintage, eh?" purred Hale.

In fact, it wasn't all that impressive. A dark Jith-Urnetil grape, late-harvest pressing of course, you couldn't mistake *that* taste; but really a little too sweet for Ringil's palate, and cloying on the aftertaste. He'd never been a big fan of the coastal range vintages anyway, and this one lacked far too many middle notes. But it would certainly have been expensive, and that counted for a lot with men like Hale.

"Well, then." The slave trader finished his drink and put down the goblet. There was an anticipatory gleam in his eye. "I'd say that since it's fairly clear what your requirements are, maybe we should just go down to the stable together and see if something doesn't catch your—"

Ringil put in a mannered cough. "There is another matter."

"Oh?" A politely raised eyebrow. "And what would that be?"

Ringil cradled his goblet and peered into it. Put on a sheepish expression. "I have mentioned already how my father feels about these things, about my . . . preferences. This uh, this behavior . . . of mine."

"Yes." Hale could not quite keep the weariness out of his voice. "Yes, I believe we've covered that. Go on."

"Well, there is one thing I need to be certain of before I buy from you—there must be no issue from this woman. She must be barren."

And something drained abruptly out of the room.

It was bizarre. Ringil felt the change the way he usually felt the prelude to combat; slight pressure at his lower back, the faintest of crawling across his shoulder blades. Somehow, it seemed, he'd said the wrong thing. In the sudden quiet that had opened behind his words, he looked up from his drink and saw that something indefinable had shifted in Terip Hale's demeanor.

The slaver picked up his emptied goblet again, studied it as if he'd never seen it before and couldn't imagine how it had gotten into the room with him.

"That is a very . . . specific requirement," he said softly. He looked up and met Ringil's eyes. The anticipatory gleam was gone. "You know, my Lord Laraninthal, I'm really not sure we shall be able to accommodate you so easily after all."

Ringil blinked. This was unlooked for. The way he'd put the Laraninthal character across—wealthy but diffident, recently arrived in Trelayne, uncomfortable in his desires, and fearful for his father's good opinion—he was offering Terip Hale an irresistible opportunity. First off, if Laraninthal was new to the city, he'd have no real sense of the market here, and thus no clear idea of what his pale, well-endowed sex slave ought to cost him. The fact that he was embarrassed about wanting her in the first place would only compound the matter. Hale could overcharge him to the mast tips. And that was just the start—do the deal right, and the slave trader was opening the lid of a whole treasure chest in genteel blackmail. *You see, my lord, it appears there are rumors. We wouldn't want your father hearing them, would we? Now, don't worry, I'm sure we can stanch the chatter—but it will cost a little something, these arrangements always do . . .*

And so forth. For the duration of his stay in Trelayne, this Laraninthal could be discreetly bled for whatever he was worth.

It was a lot to pass up.

Yeah, but looks like old Terip here is getting ready to throw it away with both hands. And throw you out, too, Gil, you don't get a grip on things pretty fucking fast.

"If this—" His accent had slipped with the surprise—he tugged it back into place, cleared his throat, and improvised off a tone of insulted pique. "If this is some trick to increase your price, then I am not—"

"We have not discussed price yet," observed Hale, still in a tone like silk. But Ringil's feigned outrage seemed to have had the desired effect. A little of the tension went out of the slaver. He set the goblet down and steepled his fingers. "In any case, it isn't that which concerns me. It's merely that I don't see why you should be so concerned with the wench in question's breeding capacity. It really is neither here nor there. If she swells with child, we can soon find you a replacement, well before she becomes unsightly. And meanwhile, by law you will own the offspring if it survives. You can sell it, along with the mother if she no longer pleases you, or separately, if that improves your price. The market is flexible in these matters."

"I, uh, I would not know how to go about—"

"Oh, you may be assured of my diligence in such a case. I'll gladly pledge you any assistance you require."

Yeah, I'll bet—for a small consideration. But at least Hale seemed to be tipping back in the right direction. Ringil put in another diffident clearing of the throat.

"You see, in imperial law, slave offspring cannot be—"

"Yes, I'm sure." A faint impatience curled into the slaver's tone now. "But you're not *in* the Empire now, my lord. We have League law here, and I assure you, I know it to the letter where my business is concerned."

"Well, then." Grudgingly. "I suppose that—"

"Excellent." Hale clapped his hands. "Well, I think what we'll do is, instead of talking all night, we'll go down and see some flesh right now. That'll give you something to sleep on, eh, my lord."

A lewd wink. Ringil tried hard to look enthusiastic.

"Oh, and perhaps before we do that, my Lord Laraninthal could give me any other specifics he has in mind. The stable we hold is extensive, and it may save time if we can narrow the field. Is there perhaps a particular hair color that draws you? Height? I understand your women in the south are quite small-boned."

Ringil called Sherin to mind, his own faded childhood memories and what Ishil had told him about her lineage. He had the charcoal line sketch of what she looked like in his pocket, but better right now to play it looser than that. He didn't want to tip his hand too early.

"You have in this city, I'm told, a race who live out on the marsh. Is it so?"

"Yes." Hale was watching him warily. "That's so. What of it?"

Ringil cleared his throat. "Numerous countrymen of mine have told me that the marsh women behave uhm, well . . . differently in bed. You know. That they, uhm, abandon themselves to the act. Utterly. Like animals."

It was flat-out fabrication—the marsh dwellers had no such reputation in Yhelteth, in fact most untraveled imperials would have no knowledge that they existed at all as a discrete group. As far as the Empire was concerned, the whole of the Trelayne territory was filled with backward, marsh-grubbing peasants. Only the very well informed knew enough to make distinctions. But no matter—it would play well enough. You could hear the same basic whisper of abandoned sexuality about women from any brutalized or excluded race under the band. Ringil had sat and listened to soldiers repeat it around campfires in every disputed piece of territory he'd fought in after the war with the Scaled Folk was done. It was a basic justification for rape.

He sometimes thought they would have said it about the lizard females as well, if the Scaled Folk had not been so unremittingly alien.

Well, I wouldn't rule that out, either, Archeth once told him, huddled against the coastal wind in Gergis, watching the camp below them. *These men would fuck mud if it was warmed to a decent temperature.*

She was talking about her own command.

"Marsh dwellers, eh?" Terip Hale rolled out a slow smile. "Well, I've not heard that one before, exactly. But of course, if that's your preference. Janesh."

The doorman took a step forward. "My lord."

"We'll be paying a visit to the joyous longshank girls. Go down ahead of us and see that everything's opened up. So to speak."

The doorman's face split in a fierce grin. "Yes, sir."

Hale watched him go with a sober expression at odds with the joke. He seemed to be working through something in his head.

"We don't deal that much in full-blood dwellers," he said reflectively. "Though if what you tell me is true, perhaps we should. But it's problematic, you see. Their families are mostly very tightly knit, and as a people they're a stubborn, unthinking lot. I've seen cases where a man on the marsh would rather starve than sell his children. I mean, what can you do with people like that?"

Ringil hid his face in his goblet.

"Fortunately, though, marsh dweller blood isn't quite as uncommon among our ordinary citizens"—Hale permitted himself a thin smile—"as those same citizens would have you believe. It's been known to leak into even the noblest of Trelayne families. Don't worry yourself, Laraninthal of Shenshenath, I'm quite sure we'll be able to find you a girl with suitable blood."

They made small talk after that, while Ringil finished his wine, played the diffident imperial fop, and kept his feelings masked. Inwardly, a cautious optimism was rising through him. He didn't really expect to find Sherin here—even if she had passed through Hale's stable, and not one of the others that specialized in concubinage, that was a month ago. Despite the slave trader's comments about the difficulties of training spirited girls, Ringil didn't think it would require that long to break a young woman who probably already considered herself worthless for her lack of child-bearing ability; who had already been shunned by her whole family and then, finally, betrayed by the man who'd taken her away from them.

But if she had been here, there'd be traces. Memories among the other girls, among servants and handlers. There'd be documents of sale, somewhere. It was a legal trade now, all above board. Part of the brave new world they'd all been fighting for. If this was the place, the door was halfway levered open, and Ringil could do the rest in easy stages—even if that meant taking Terip Hale somewhere secluded and getting what he needed out of him with hot coals and iron.

If this was not the place, well, he had the other names on Milacar's list. He could start all over again.

"Shall we go down?" Hale asked him.

He smiled and nodded in eager, foppish assent.

IT SEEMED THE JOYOUS LONGSHANK GIRLS WERE KEPT ON THE OTHER side of the building. Ringil followed Hale down to ground level and out to the courtyard. Eril and Girsh brought up the rear, along with Hale's flail-equipped muscle. Everybody watched everybody else with hardened calm. The night had turned clear and cold while they were inside—they crossed the courtyard in silence under sharp stars and the long cool arc of the band. Ringil saw his breath puff ice white in the air.

If the cold bothered Hale, in his silk dressing gown and slippers, he gave no sign. He led them through another side door in the courtyard wall, down three sets of stone steps and into a semicircular basement chamber with five curtained alcoves along its curving wall. Janesh the doorman was already there, the grin still plastered across his face—apparently he'd been enjoying his work. Bandlight spilled in from small barred windows near the roof, but most of the illumination came from two lanterns set down in the center of the room. There were Majak rugs on the floor, lewd murals etched into the curving wall—though rather prim of content compared with Grace-of-Heaven's ceiling—and a vast black iron candelabra hanging from the vaulted roof.

Terip Hale turned to face them.

"Allow me to present," he said gravely. "The joyous longshank girls."

The curtains whisked aside in their alcoves. Armed men stood there grinning. Short-swords and hatchets, maces and clubs. Two men to an alcove, at least. Ringil saw at least one crossbow, raised and cocked.

The doorman caught his eye and winked.

"Now," said Hale. "Perhaps, Laraninthal of Shenshenath, you'd like to tell me who exactly the fuck you *really* are."

CHAPTER 18

Egar rode out a couple of hours before sunset.

He didn't really need the extra time; the Skaranak buried their dead relatively close to wherever they happened to be camped at the time, and their migrations across the steppe were roughly seasonal. As the anniversary of his father's death swung around each year, so did the proximity of the grave Erkan was laid in. Egar could track it by the changes in the sky and the few windswept landmarks that marked the steppe, could feel it circling beyond the horizon as the seasons turned, curving slowly inward as the warmth ebbed from each year and winter crept in, closing on him like the anniversary itself.

He didn't need the extra time.

But Sula was driving him up a fucking guy rope right now with her youth and her breezy nomad matter-of-factness; she was blunt and clumsy around his feelings, would not give him space, thought sucking him off was the solution to pretty much everything.

Can hardly blame the lass. Not like you've given her any reason to think any different, is it?

So he told her lies as he dressed.

"I'll do the last league on foot," he said. "For respect."

"But that's stupid!"

He held down his temper with an effort. "It's a tradition, Sula."

"Yeah." A throaty snort. "Not since my fucking *grandfather* died, it isn't."

"Well, that wasn't all that long ago, was it?"

She stared at him, stricken. "What's that supposed to mean?"

It means I remember your grandfather as a young man about the camp. It means I'm easily old enough to be your father. It means you're sixteen fucking years old, girl, sitting in my yurt like you own it, and beyond all of that it means that at my age I really should know better than to keep doing this.

"Nothing," he muttered. "Doesn't mean anything. But traditions are, uhm, important things, Sula. They're what holds the clan together."

"You think I'm too young for you," she wailed. "You're going to pack me in, just like you did that Voronak bitch."

"I'm not going to pack you in."

"Yes, you are!"

And she dissolved in tears.

So then of course he had to go to her, had to hold her. He had to nuzzle at her neck and murmur in her ear as if she were a horse he hadn't quite broken yet, had to tip back her chin with one hand and wipe away her tears with the other. Had to shelve the chilly, swelling sadness under his own ribs, had to force a grin as she stopped crying, had to tickle her and grope her through the red felt overshirt she'd appropriated from his clothing chest. Had, in fact, taken to wearing around the camp like a blazing fucking declaration of what she spent her time doing in the clanmaster's yurt.

Have to talk to her about that.

At some point.

"Look," he said finally. "It's fucking freezing out there, right? Riding doesn't keep you warm. That's the real point. If I walk, I warm up. Chances are, that's where the tradition comes from in the first place, right?"

She nodded doubtfully, sniffed, knuckled at one eye. He mashed his tongue hard into the back of his grin and wished she didn't look so much like a fucking child when she did that.

How come they all start out hot-eyed temptress minxes and all end up crying into your shirt like babies?

Isn't it enough I have to carry the weight of the whole fucking clan on my back? Urann's aching balls, isn't it enough that I came back, that I left Yhelteth and everything it held and rode home to be with my fucking people? Isn't it enough that I'll probably fucking die up here just like my father and never see Imrana's face again?

No answer that he could hear.

You whine like a girl, Clanmaster. Worse than a girl—this girl wearing your shirt is at least weeping about the future, about something she might be able to change. She's not the one moping around full of bitterness about a past you can't do any fucking thing about.

Now get a grip.

He tilted her chin back again.

"Sula, listen. I'll be back as soon after dawn as I can make it. You wait for me, you keep things warm." He clowned it, raised brows, grabbed after a buttock and a breast again. "Know what I mean?"

He got a choked laugh out of her, and then a long, wet kiss. He got out pretty fast after that. Marnak had his horse saddled and waiting outside in the ruddy evening light, shield and lance and small ax slung, a bundle of blankets, firewood, and other provisions tied securely on. The older man stood a discreet distance off from the clanmaster's yurt, beside his own horse and in grave conversation with a pair of camp guards. He glanced over as Egar pushed back the yurt door flap, left the other two men immediately to their own devices, and strode across. He surveyed his clanmaster without comment.

"All right?" he asked.

"Been better. You still want to ride along?"

"With you in that mood?" Marnak shrugged. "Sure, should be a bundle of fun."

IN FACT, EGAR'S MOOD LIGHTENED SOMEWHAT AS THEY RODE OUT ACROSS
the steppe and the camp fell behind. Slanting rays from the low winter
sun turned the grassland a deceptively warm reddish gold, gave the
sense that the evening might hold itself like this forever. The sky was
clear and hollow blue, the band arched through it at a tilting angle,
tinged a scintillating wash of ruddy shades to match the sunset. A keen
wind came scything out of the north but the grease on their faces kept
back its bite. The horses made an ambling pace, occasional clink or
jingle from metal parts in the rig and the small iron talismans braided
into their manes as they tossed their heads. Once or twice, a returning
pair of herd minders would hail them as they passed, headed in for the
evening meal.

It all felt a little like escape.

"You ever miss the south?" he asked Marnak eventually, when the
quiet between the two of them had loosened to a wayfarer's ease. "Ever
think about going back?"

"Nope."

He glanced across, surprised by the spike of vehemence. "Really?
What, *never*? You don't even miss the whores?"

"Got a wife now." Marnak grinned in his beard. "And they got
whores in Ishlin-ichan, you know."

"Yeah, I know."

"Even some Yhelteth girls there these days, if that's your thing."

Egar grunted. He knew that, too.

Marnak raised up a little in his saddle, gestured around at the
steppe. "I mean, what's not to be happy with here? Grazing that never
ends, plenty of waterholes, slow-flowing rivers we don't have to fight the
Ishlinak for, plenty of space for everyone. Practically no raiding
anymore, now the young guys all head off south instead. We don't see
the long runners much this far south and west, the wolves and steppe
cats mostly leave us alone as well. We've got more meat on the hoof
these days than we know what to do with. Got the clan, the people
around us. What's in Yhelteth to stack up against all that?"

Where'd you want me to start?

Views over the harbor, sunlight shimmering off endless ruffled blue to the horizon. Tall white towers at the headland, the slow spiral of a dozen big lizard raptors riding the thermals. The carping of gulls down on the wharf, the bang-bang on wood of fishermen repairing their boats.

Patios, sun-blasted and riotous with some flowering crimson creeper whose name you never did learn to pronounce right. Ornate ironwork on windows and doors, narrow white-walled streets that tricked away the sun's assault. Cunningly crafted meeting nooks and warm stone benches set in deep pools of shade, the music of falling water somewhere beyond a screen.

Market stalls heaped high with brightly colored fruit you could smell at a dozen paces. Philosophers and verse-makers declaiming from their pitches in the less pricey corners of each square, teahouses spilling out with the noisy back-and-forth quarrel of voices disputing everything under the sun: the advisability of trade with the western lands, the existence or not of evil spirits, the urban horse tax.

Books—the warm, leather-skinned weight of them in your hands, the way they smelled when you lifted them close to your face. The unfeasibly heart-jolting shock once, as a tome fell heavily open at some much-visited page, divided itself neatly in two blocky halves along the spine—and you thought, guiltily, that you'd broken it.

The lines and lines and lines and lines of squiggling black text, and Imrana's long-nailed finger leading him along them.

The stir and billow of translucent window drapes as a sea breeze wandered in from the balcony and carried away some of the midday heat, cooled some of the sweat on your skin and hers.

The ebbing bustle of the day, the cries of street sellers growing somehow ever more mournful as the light thickened and a yellow-glow sprinkle of windows lit up across the city.

The aching, dusk skyline lament of the call to prayer—and ignoring it in slim, dark, orange-blossom-perfumed arms.

The riding lights of fishercraft out on the evening swell.

"Yeah, well," he said.

Marnak concentrated on the grasslands ahead for a while. Maybe he could feel some of what was smoking off Egar.

"In the south, they paid me to kill other men," he said tonelessly. "That's well and good when you're young. It seasons you, and it wins honor for your name, for your forefathers in the Sky Home. It brings you to the Dwellers' notice."

"It gets you laid."

A chuckle. "It gets you laid. But the time comes you're not a young man anymore. You start to lose the pleasure in it all. Truth is, I would have gone home long before I did, if the Scaled Folk hadn't come."

"*Humanity's finest hour,* eh?"

The quote didn't come out quite as sour as Egar intended. Despite everything, the clarion ring that Akal the Great had given to it still clung in faint echo. Marnak nodded to himself, so slightly it might have been the motion of the horse that caused it.

"For a while, it was."

"Yeah, until you end up facing your own fucking people across a line of lances."

Marnak shrugged. "That never bothered me much. You take imperial coin, chances are sooner or later you're going up against the League. You go up against the League, chances are sooner or later you're going to find yourself facing Majak. Just the way it is. No different from squabbling with the Ishlinak up here like we used to. I fought for the League myself once or twice, back in the day, before the Empire really started hiring. And yeah, it always figured if we did ever beat the lizards, everyone'd go back to fighting each other again, just like before."

"So why not stay and make some more coin?"

"Don't think I didn't give it some thought. I had a line commander's commission by then. But like I said, it's all well and good if you're young. I just *wasn't* anymore, wasn't anything close to young." Marnak shook his head bemusedly. These weren't places his mind habitually went. "I don't know, you get older and each battle you survive starts to feel like luck. You start wondering why you made it to the end of the day, why you're still standing when the field is clogged with other men's blood and corpses. Why the Dwellers are keeping you alive, what purpose the Sky Home has laid out for you. Like that. When the Scaled Folk came, I thought I'd understood that purpose. I thought I knew why I'd survived, thought I'd probably die fighting them, didn't even mind that much so long as it was a good death."

"But you didn't die."

"No." Egar thought he heard something that was almost disappointment in the other man's tone. "I didn't. Not even at Gallows Gap, and Urann knows we came close enough there. Now, that was a perfect place for a good death, if ever I saw one."

And now it was Egar's turn to chuckle. But it was a grim sound he made, not much humor in it.

Marnak's lips bent in silent echo. "Instead of which, we all became heroes. You, me, even that fucking faggot friend of yours."

"Look, he wasn't exactly my—"

"And next thing you know, we're back to fighting humans again. And that's fine, you know, like I said, but . . ." Another helpless gesture. "It got *old*. Felt like some kind of massive wheel coming right the way back around to start. There were all these new Majak kids flooding into Yhelteth on the recruiting wagon, looking to fill the gaps in the ranks, no fucking clue what it was all about—"

"Yeah, I remember." Mostly, what Egar remembered was wanting to break their shiny, enthusiastic faces for them. The fact that they reminded him so much of himself a decade earlier only made it worse. "Weird times, huh?"

"You know what it felt like?" Marnak slipped off his cap, scrubbed vigorously at his scalp with the nails of a half-clenched fist. "You remember those round-and-round-about machines the Kiriath put into the tea gardens at Ynval? The ones with the wooden horses?" ·

"Yeah. Been on them a couple of times."

"Yeah, well, you know what it's like when the ride's finished, then. Everything comes to a halt, you're sitting there, getting used to the whole world not spinning around you, and you've got a whole new set of people, mostly kids, all swarming to get on. You don't know whether you want to give up your seat or not, and then it suddenly hits you." He slipped his cap back on again, shot Egar a sidelong glance. "You realize you don't *want* to go around again. In fact, you're not even fucking sure anymore whether you really enjoyed it the first time around."

They both laughed this time, and loud. Quick bark of tension released, then the looser, more reflective stretch of genuine amusement, shared under the massive sky. The small, human sounds it made held briefly against the landscape, then soaked away into the vast quiet and the wind, like piss into the ground.

"You know," Marnak said, maybe loath to let the silence win. "I broke one of those horses once. I ever tell you that? I mean, broke its neck right fucking off, hanging off it when I was blasted on pipe one time. They were going to make me pay for the fucking repairs, too, about half a week's wages as it happens. Called the City Guard on me when I wouldn't cough up. I ever tell you that story?"

In fact, he had, but Egar shook his head amiably and the other man launched into the tale. There was an easy pleasure to be had from hearing the escapade again, all its wall-scaling, roof-leaping, harem-invading chases and shocks and reversals, plus a couple of fresh embellishments added into the mix, just to keep it sharp. It was like sitting around the fire and listening to a skilled storyteller run through the Tale of Takavach and the Mermaid's Virtue, or something equally well worn.

When the tale was done, with Marnak safely back across the river and into barracks before dawn, when their laughter had soaked away once again, the clanmaster nodded and told another Yhelteth story from his own stock. How a noted imperial knight had once come home to find the young Egar in bed with his wives, all four of them at once. *And you know, more than anything, that seemed to be what he was so pissed off about. Standing there, yelling at me with that fucking stupid court sword in his fist. Apparently, the Revelation says yes, you can have up to six wives, but it absolutely forbids you doing it with more than one of them at a time.* Egar let drop the reins, spread his hands wide. *Hell, how was I supposed to know that?*

More laughter.

Another tale.

And so, eventually, they came to Erkan's grave. They quieted and looked at each other. For a while they'd been able to forget where they were going, but that was over now. Egar dismounted.

"Thanks for the company."

"Yeah." Marnak cast glances around. A slight rise, a single stooped and gnarled tree with the ball of the declining sun tangled in its leafless branches. It was a bleak place, not made for the living.

"I'll be fine," Egar said quietly. "He was a good man in life, he isn't going to hurt me now."

Marnak grimaced. It wasn't the received wisdom among the Majak that good men made good ghosts. A spirit must be placated, regardless of its origins; rituals must be honored. So said the shaman. No one ever explained exactly why, but the implication was that if you didn't get that stuff right, there'd be a heavy price, for you and your people.

"Go on, get moving. You ride hard, you'll make it back not much after full dark." Egar watched the other man wheel his horse about. "Oh yeah, and if Sula asks, you left me half a league out, doing the last stretch on foot. Right?"

Marnak grinned back over his shoulder. "Right." He clucked and heeled his horse into a gathering trot, canter, finally a full gallop back the way they'd come.

Egar watched him go, until horse and rider were a single dot that faded slowly into the gloom. Then he sighed and turned to his father's grave.

It wasn't much to look at. Steppe soils made for hard digging at this time of year, and the grave was shallow, piled over with rocks it took them the whole day to gather. They'd built the traditional cairn end pile at the buried man's feet, warded it about with daubed symbols in the Skaranak colors and iron talismans hung off the stones on buffalo-hide thongs. They shredded tundra rose and crocus petals over the stones and set a dwarf oak sapling in the ground at Erkan's head, so in a couple of years' time he'd have shade when summer swung around.

Now the clan colors were bleached with age, and the branches of the grown tree were naked and skeletal overhead. Only the shaped iron ornaments remained, though—Egar squinted suspiciously—it looked as if even one or two of those might have been stolen from the grave over the past year.

"Motherfucking Voronak tinks," he muttered.

Yeah, this far south and west it's just as likely Skaranak renegades, or even some bunch of fuckwit explorers from the south. He'd seen Skaranak grave wards in more than one imperial museum over the years, had never quite been able to drive home to anyone the rage it aroused in him. In Yhelteth, in the city itself at least, they tolerated a variety of beliefs well enough, but behind that there was always the base assumption of a civilized superiority in the Revelation that never failed to piss him off. In the end, the imperials didn't much care whose sensibilities they trampled on.

Let's stick to the task at hand, shall we.

He left his horse to crop the grass a short distance off, unstoppered the rice wine flask he'd brought with him, held it lowered in clasped hands, and stood a moment looking down at the grave.

"Hey, Dad," he said loudly. "Brought you something special this time."

The quiet wind keened. There was no other reply for him.

"It's good stuff. Used to drink it in the south all the time. This tavern down by the harbor had it, not far from Imrana's place. I think you would have liked it in there, Dad. Noisy, full of all these tough guys off the docks. You could see the sea from the front door." He paused, stared down at the cairn. "I would have liked to show you the sea, Dad."

He blinked hard a couple of times. Cleared his throat.

"Can't believe they're selling this stuff in Ishlin-ichan these days. Bringing it all the way up here. Cost me a ball and an eye, of course, but hey, I'm the fucking clanmaster these days, right?"

Got to relax, Eg. Loosen off. You've got a full night out here, and the sun isn't even down yet.

He lifted the flask and tipped it, poured slowly and steadily, working little circles into the action. The rice wine splattered and darkened the stones, ticked and dripped in the dark places between. When the flask was empty, he upended it and shook out the last drops, then placed it carefully against the base of the cairn. His fingers lingered on it awhile, kept him bent there, face turned slightly away, listening to wind. Then, abruptly, he straightened up. A grimace chased across his face—whether from the brief, flaring pain of holding the posture too long, or something else, he couldn't say. He cleared his throat again.

"So—I guess, we're going to build this vigil fire."

He unsaddled the horse, set out his weapons, blankets, and provisions with drilled, soldier's neatness. Unbundled the firewood and put the fire together on the scorched and balding patch of grass that marked the previous vigils. The sun dropped free of the tree branches, hung increasingly low at the horizon. He shivered a little, gave it the occasional glance as he worked. He went about collecting a few storm-torn branches he'd noticed lying in the grass earlier, dragged them over and stamped them into manageable lengths, stripped the biggest of the twigs from them, and piled it all up beside the waiting fire. He reckoned the bundle he'd brought with him should last until dawn, but the extra couldn't hurt. More importantly, the work had shaken some of the shiver from his bones.

He knelt by the unlit fire. Like most Majak, he carried kindling grass and flint in a dry pouch under his shirt. He now dug them out, struck sparks into a wiry fistful of the kindling until it caught, and then poked it carefully into the hollow heart of the fire pile. He tipped his head sideways, almost to the ground, and peered in. Smoke and tiny flames licked upward at the underside of the wood. The smaller pieces began to catch, smoldering and then popping alight. A cheery yellow light spilled out. The warmth of it washed his eyes and face, felt a little like tears. He hauled himself quickly upright again, back into the gathering gloom and chill of the air around him. He stowed the kindling pouch, brushed off his hands. Glanced back at the gnarled marker tree and the declining sun.

"Well, Dad, I—"

A figure stood there.

It was a hammerblow to his heart, an icy clutch of fear that dropped his right hand reflexively to the hilt of the knife at his hip.

It was not his father.

At least, not in any form that made sense. He saw a drab, full-length patched leather cloak of the sort favored by League sea captains, a soft-brimmed hat tilted forward to shade the face, though the sun was behind and in any case almost gone. Erkan, colorful, boisterous, a Majak to the bone, had never owned anything remotely resembling either item.

No. Wouldn't have been seen dead wearing them, either.

Egar felt the corner of his mouth quirk. The humor pushed out the shock, brought in a shrewd skirmisher's calculation instead. The cloaked figure looked to be alone. No visible companions or weapons, no horse nearby. Egar sidled a glance across to where his own mount stood, still placidly cropping the grass and apparently unaware of the newcomer, then to the neat piles of his gear on the ground—staff lance and ax, both well out of reach. He could not believe he'd allowed himself to be ambushed this easily.

He kept his hand loose on the hilt of his knife.

"I'm not here to harm you, Dragonbane."

The voice came across the distance between them as if from much farther away, as if carried on the wind. Egar blinked at the effect.

"You know me?"

"After a fashion, yes. May I approach?"

"Are you armed?"

"No. I have no real need for such accoutrements."

Egar set his mouth in a thin line. "You're a shaman?"

Abruptly the cloaked figure loomed a scant two feet in front of him. It happened so fast, Egar would have sworn he never saw the newcomer move at all. A hand clamped brutally on his wrist, held it down so he could not have drawn his knife if his life depended on it. The face beneath the brim of the hat loomed, gaunt and hard-eyed. A gust of acrid chemical burning swirled in the wind, something like the smells that sometimes blew off the Kiriath brewing stacks south of An-Monal.

"There is not much time," the voice admonished, no less distant sounding than before. "Your brothers are coming to murder you."

And gone.

Egar jumped, and nearly fell down with the sudden release of the pressure on his arm. He cleared his knife from its sheath, belatedly, whirled about. The figure was nowhere to be seen. It was gone, into the chill of the air and the long grass, like memory of the voice into the wind, like the acrid chemical tang into the sweeter smell of wood smoke from the fire. Like the fading pressure on his wrist.

He wheeled about once more, breathing tightly, knife balanced on his palm.

Quiet, and thickening gray gloom across the steppe.

The band like a hoop of blood. His father's cairn, the emptied flask laid beside it. The blackening silhouette of the tree.

"My brothers are in Ishlin-ichan," he told the silence. "Getting drunk."

He jerked his head westward, roughly the direction you'd take. Threw a glance out to the setting sun.

Saw silhouetted riders there, approaching.

CHAPTER 19

Ringil tried, just the once, on fading hope, for the outrage of imperial nobility.

"Just what is the meaning of this? You intend to *rob* me, like common criminals? My father will have you—"

Terip Hale shook his head. "Let it go, friend. I don't imagine that accent is any more real than the rest of this charade, so drop it, why don't you. This is going to be painful enough for you as it is. Now, like I asked you before, who the *fuck* are you? What are you doing here, asking after barren marsh dwellers?"

Ah.

"All right," Ringil said, because he guessed he had perhaps another half a minute, at most, before Hale did the obvious thing and had them all disarmed.

Yeah, and after that, it's down to whatever disciplinary facilities Hale keeps around here for recalcitrant slaves. Where we'll be put to the question repeatedly, until Hale gets what he wants to hear from us, and then, if we're lucky, they might put us out of our scorched and mutilated misery with a quick slit throat.

Nice going, Gil.

Ringil measured the possibilities. Eril and Girsh had both frozen when the trap was sprung, arms well out from their bodies so as not to invite a crossbow bolt for twitching a hand the wrong way, faces taut with concentrated tension. They looked like men wading belly-high across an icy river, like adults caught out midstep in a children's game of closer-closer-statue. They would have already assessed the odds. Now they watched for Ringil's lead.

There were three crossbows leveled at them, as far as he could see. The rest was hand-to-hand cutlery.

"All right *what*?" grated Hale.

"All right, you win. I'm not Laraninthal of Shenshenath, and I'm not an imperial. My name's Ringil Eskiath."

Hale blinked. "*The* Ringil Eskiath? Yeah, right."

But Ringil had seen how that same taken-aback flinch ran around the armed men in the alcoves. He felt the way their casual thug focus gave way to curious stares. He saw a couple of them mutter to each other. The siege of Trelayne was eight years in the past, the triumph at Gallows Gap a year older than that. The war itself had been over now for more than half a decade. But the stories lingered on, attenuated maybe, yet still there in the city's consciousness.

"Eskiath died at Ennishmin," someone sneered. "Fighting imperials."

Ringil forced a calm he didn't feel.

"Heard that one before a couple of times," he said lightly. "And it's almost true. Still got the scars. But it takes more than three Yhelteth sneak assassins to put me away."

Another of the men voiced a faint cheer. His companion elbowed him savagely to shut up. Ringil pushed as hard as it would go. He raised a cautious thumb, well out from his body so it wouldn't be misinterpreted, gesturing up at his left shoulder.

"This is the Ravensfriend," he said loudly. "Kiriath steel. Forged at An-Monal for the clan Indamaninarmal, gifted to me by Grashgal the Wanderer. Rinsed in lizard blood at Rajal Beach and Gallows Gap and the siege of Trelayne. I *am* Ringil of the Glades house of Eskiath."

Another voice from one of the alcoves. "He does look kind of—"

"Yeah?" Terip Hale wasn't having this. "Well, you know what I heard? I heard Ringil Eskiath was a fucking queer. That true as well?"

Ringil bent him a smile. "Would I have come to you looking for slave girls if it were?"

"I don't know why you're here." Hale nodded at the muscle with the flail. "But we are going to find out. Varid."

The big man moved across to Ringil, stepped in close enough to block any attempt to bring the Ravensfriend out of its scabbard, far enough off to beat a grapple move. It was done with sober professional care—no grin like the doorman's, no jeering. Just a custom-hardened watchfulness in the eyes. Chances were that Varid had been a soldier once.

He nodded at the sword pommel. "Unstrap that. Make it slow."

A tiny breeze got in from somewhere and made the lantern flames flicker behind their metal mesh. Shadows danced and shivered across the floor.

Ringil dropped the dragon knife from his sleeve. He took one rapid step left.

The Majak had made them, in the last years of the war, once the tide had turned. Mostly they were ceremonial, a statement of the victory to come, not ideal for fighting, even close in. Egar had given him his in a drunken fit of affection one campfire night on the Anarsh plain. *Fucking useless thing,* he'd mumbled, looking away. *You might as well have it.* It was basically an infant dragon fang, triangular in section, serrated up the two back edges, razor-sharp and smooth at the front. The artist, whoever he was, had carved a serviceable hilt into the base, weave-patterned it on both sides for grip. The whole thing was barely nine inches long—small enough to conceal, long enough to prick the life out of a man's heart. It shone a dirty amber in the lanternlight as it came clear.

Ringil pivoted from the hip, rammed the knife home under Varid's chin.

"*Noooooooooooooooo!*"

Someone bellowing with hysterical fury. It certainly wasn't Varid—his tongue was nailed to his palate on the fang, his mouth was jammed shut. The best he could manage was a strangling agonized grunt, and his eyes were already turning up in their sockets as the rest of the dragon knife ripped his brain in half from below. Blood burst through his locked teeth in a gurgling crimson spray. Ringil held him up, stayed close in to his bulk, blinking the blood from his eyes, made the yell for Hale's—no one else could have seen quite what was going on yet, probably no one else would be giving orders . . .

"*Shoot, fucking shoot, will you!*"

What Ringil had hoped for happened. He heard the flesh-cringing *twang-clatter* as the crossbows went off at close range. All three—skirmish-schooled, he counted them off and knew. Varid jolted with the impact. A quarrel head tore through the big man's shoulder and nearly clipped Ringil's nose off. The other two went somewhere else, Ringil couldn't tell where. *Crossbows—now, there's a fucking useless weapon for you.* He grinned—quick, pulse-jumping relief. Sensed rather than saw Hale's men come storming out of their alcoves. Bolts shot, the advantage thrown away—it was down to the steel. He shoved Varid's corpse away, left the dragon knife where it was. Gained a scant few necessary feet of space as they rushed him. The combat moments seemed to float loose of each other, spun out and unreal . . .

Freed hands both rising for the pommel now, so natural, so smooth, it was like Kiriath machinery, as if he *were* machinery, a cunningly crafted clockwork Kiriath mannequin, built to complement the steel.

He felt the accustomed kiss of the grip on his palms, felt the grin on his face turn into a snarl.

Cold chime as the scabbard gave up its embrace.

And the Ravensfriend came out.

YOU WANT TO KNOW HOW IT ENDS, GIL? GRASHGAL, CRYPTIC AND rambling and more than a little drunk one evening at An-Monal, holding up the newly forged Ravensfriend in scarred black hands and squinting critically down the runnel. Fireglow from the big room's hearth seemed to drip molten off the edges of the steel. The carved beam-end gargoyles leered down from the gloom in the roof space above. *I've seen how it ends. Someday, in a city where the people rise through the air with no more effort than it takes to breathe, where they give their blood to strangers as a gift, instead of stealing it with edged iron and rage the way we do, someday, in a place like that, this motherfucker is going to hang up behind glass for small children to stare at.* Grashgal hefted the Ravensfriend one-handed, made a couple of idle strokes through the air, and the sword whispered to itself in the firelit gloom. *I've seen it, Gil. They look at this thing through the glass it's kept behind, they put their noses up so close to that glass their breath fogs it, and you can see the small, slow-fading print of their hands in the condensation after they've run off to look at something else. And it doesn't mean a thing to them. You want to know why that is?*

Ringil gestured amenably from the depths of the armchair he was sprawled in. He wasn't hugely sober himself.

No. I mean, yeah. Can't guess, I mean. You tell me.

No one in that city understands, Gil, because it doesn't matter to them anymore. They've never learned to fear the steel and the men who carry it, and none of them ever will, because they don't have to. Because in this place I've seen, men like that don't exist anymore. We don't exist anymore.

Sounds like a beautiful fucking place. How do I get there? Ringil grinned fiercely up at the Kiriath clan captain. *Oh wait—you're going to tell me the rents are sky-high, right? And how am I going to earn a living if they keep their swords in a museum?*

Grashgal looked back down at him for what seemed like a long time. Finally, he smiled.

You don't get to go, I'm afraid, Gil. Too far off, and the quick paths are too twisted for humans to follow. And on the straight road, you and I will be dust and half-remembered tales before they even start to build that city. But it will come, and when it does, this sword will still be there to see it. Kiriath steel—built to harm, built to last. When all the damage it's done and the grief it's caused have been forgotten, even by the gods, when the Kiriath themselves have passed into discredited myth, this murderous fucking . . . thing . . . will hang unused, and harmless, and gaped at by children. That's how it ends, Gil. With no one to remember, or care, or understand what this thing could do when you set it free.

Ringil met the first of Hale's men in a blur of eager motion and the blue sweeping arc of the blade. The man was hacking down with a hand ax, and Ringil already had the Ravensfriend at high guard. He blocked, two-handed, hard, angled not for the hatchet but the arm that held it up. The Kiriath blade took the man's hand off cleanly at the wrist. Blood gouted from the stump, rained on him, and something savage in Ringil's heart shrilled with joy. The arm completed its downward arc, still spurting, painting them both, and the hatchet hit the ground with a thud. Its owner gaped dumbly at his own hand still gripping the haft, the yell dried up in his throat. Ringil chopped down at the juncture of shoulder and neck, severed artery and sinew, finished it.

The next man was close behind, short-sword in one hand, mace in the other. Ringil feinted high and right, let his opponent raise both weapons to the misdirection, dropped the Ravensfriend low and almost horizontal, swung in for the belly. No broadsword made of human steel would have allowed the abrupt shift of vector; the Kiriath alloy not only allowed it—it *sang.* The stroke opened the other man up from side to side and carved a notch off the base of his spine before the blade tugged clear.

Fuck.

Sudden cold sweat—it was sloppy bladework, and against better men it might have gotten him killed. He'd been off the battlefield too long.

But these were not better men, and the edge on the Kiriath steel was forgiving of such errors. Ringil got clear, stepped past. The gutted man wallowed in his wake, not yet fully aware of what had been done to him, tried muzzily to turn and follow as his attacker slipped away, and then his intestines and the contents of his bisected stomach fell out on the rug, and he tangled in it all and went down screaming like a child.

Ringil's third attacker flinched back, hampered by his gutted comrade. He had an ax and a club, but didn't seem to know quite what to do with either. He was young, no older than seventeen or eighteen, and he looked sick with the sudden fear of combat. Ringil darted forward, boot on the dying man's chest to close the gap, put a straight thrust into the youth's throat and watched his face contort as he tried to cope with the pain. The blood rushed out, drenched his clothes dark from neck to waist. Then, as if the weight of all that soaking cloth was pulling him down, he sank gracefully to the floor. He was still clutching the weapons he had never gotten around to using. His gaze clawed upward after Ringil's face, his mouth worked for words.

Ringil was already turning away.

It was the breathing space, the first moment he'd had to assess the field. Taste of the blood he'd spilled metallic warm on his tongue, the paint of it on his face. Discordant yelling all around, the fight in its various splintered, snapping pieces. He saw Eril backed to a wall, a knife in each hand, fending off two attackers with kicks and slashes. A third lay bleeding on the floor at his feet. A short distance away, Girsh was down, a crossbow bolt through the thigh. A bulky figure stood above him, sword raised. Girsh rolled away as the blade came down, slammed his mace backhand into his opponent's shin. The man howled and staggered, wagged his sword about ineffectually. Girsh belted the blade aside, propped himself up on an elbow, and chopped sideways into his attacker's knee. The swordsman collapsed in a heap beside him, still howling. Girsh rolled again, came up on top, and started smashing in his attacker's face and forehead with the mace.

Peripheral flicker from the right—Ringil swung and saw Terip Hale stabbing at him with what looked like a fucking *fruit* knife, for Hoiran's sake. Bad angle, no time. He jerked aside, let go of the Ravensfriend with his left hand, and fended off the blow with a Yhelteth empty-hand chop. He hit Hale in the face with the pommel of the Ravensfriend at the same time. The slaver yelped and fell down. Ringil left him there, turned back just in time to block a looping mace attack from Janesh the doorman. He caught the mace on the edge of his blade, turned the attack crossways on its own momentum, and kicked Janesh's feet out from under him as he swayed. The doorman hit the floor, rolling desperately to get away. Ringil followed impatiently, hacked down and severed his spine. He looked back to see how Girsh was doing, saw instead two more of the joyous longshank crew rushing him at once.

He bared his teeth and yelled in their faces, grabbed the momentary gap it gave him to dance sideways, across the chamber toward Girsh, and drag the fight's center of gravity with him. The two men came around, squared up to him again, but you could see in their faces they'd lost a lot of their initial bloodlust to that one feral snarl.

"Come on then," Ringil spat. "Don't you want to know what Kiriath steel feels like in your vitals? Do I have to bring it to *you*, you fucking *pansies*?"

They came on then, flushed and angry at the insult, but far too late. The momentary flash of fear had already tripped them, sapped their commitment to killing this blood-splattered sneering maybe-hero with the blurring blue Kiriath blade in his hands. They came in clumsy and shaken, brandishing their weapons without strategy, and Ringil took them apart. One sweeping circular block sent the man on the left stumbling into his comrade's path. Ringil followed through on the spin, slammed into the man, hip and shoulder, sent him sprawling. It put the other fighter almost in front of him with his back turned, and by the time the man worked out where Ringil had gone, Ringil had the Ravensfriend up and through his neck in a shallow-angled slash from the side. The man tried to turn, as if to find out what the *fuck* had happened that hurt so much, and his head flopped almost off with the motion. He was dead before he hit the floor.

Ringil cast about, found the first man gamely getting back to his feet; he kicked him in the face with the instep of his boot, then again with the toe. Solid crunch of the jaw breaking on the second blow. There wasn't time for more—a couple of feet away, Girsh was about to get brained by some giant with a spiked club. Ringil stepped closer, hacked low and hamstrung the man, watched as he fell—

And abruptly, before he could consciously register it, the fight was done.

Ringil stared around as his senses caught up. It really was over. Eril was off the wall, driving back a single opponent. On the ground, Girsh was killing the hamstrung giant with his mace. The rest was blood-painted carnage and crawling forms and moans. Between them, they'd accounted for a dozen men, at least. He became vaguely aware that he was panting.

Right.

He strode heavily up behind Eril's opponent, swung tiredly at the man's sword arm, and stopped the fight. The man screamed, dropped his weapon, and spun about, mouth gaping wide in shock and betrayal. Then Eril stepped in like a dance partner, hooked him with one arm, and buried his long knife upward under the sternum. The man gagged and thrashed and Eril hugged him close, twisting and gouging with the knife, finishing it. Over the dying man's shoulder, teeth gritted, half his attention still on the killing, he nodded at Ringil.

"Thanks, man. Thought I'd never fucking get an opening with this one."

Ringil waved it off and went to take care of Girsh.

THE CROSSBOW BOLT HAD GONE IN THROUGH THE FLESHY PART OF THE thigh at a downward angle and stuck there. It showed a clear two inches of blood-streaked shaft behind the blunt octagon of the quarrel where it protruded out the other side. To Ringil's battle-schooled eye, it suggested that either the weapon had misfired or the owner hadn't racked up the tension enough—at that range, it should by rights have gone straight through an unarmored limb, ripped a hole the width of the brutal iron fletching on the thing. Instead, the damage seemed to be quite limited. The entry and exit wounds were messy, sopping and treacly with blood, but there was none of the telltale heavy-duty welling-up that would have signified major blood vessels torn apart.

"Looks like you got lucky."

"Yeah," gritted Girsh. "Fucking feels like it."

Ringil went and retrieved his dragon knife from Varid's chin—a glutinous, messy business in itself—and set about using the serrated edges to cut cloth from the dead man's shirt for a tourniquet. Eril went upstairs to the door into the courtyard and listened for signs that the fight had been heard by anyone who cared to do anything about it. He came back looking satisfied.

"All quiet up there. Looks like we got the lot of them. I guess that *joyous longshank* number means all hands to the killing chamber. Cute."

Ringil grunted, preoccupied with knotting the tourniquet tight on

Girsh's thigh. The Marsh Brotherhood man bit back a groan. Eril came over to watch.

"We need to get that out of his leg," he said soberly. "If there's rust on it—"

"I know. But if you pull it back as it is, we're going to rip up the wound and maybe open a major blood vessel. We need something to cut the quarrel off."

Eril nodded. "Okay, then. It's a slave house. They've got to have ironwork tools around here somewhere. Manacle cutters, something like that."

"I can walk," Girsh rasped. Attempting to push himself upright and prove it. He turned white with what it cost him, sagged back to the horizontal again.

"Not far, you can't," Ringil told him.

He sat back on his heels and looked around. Thought about time remaining and what they'd come here to do. Despite the subsiding pulse in his veins, the relative quiet of the aftermath, they were not even close to done with Hale and his household. He wasn't much looking forward to the next part.

He stifled the waking qualm like an infant in the crib.

"All right," he said finally. "Eril, you take care of the wounded. I'm going to see if we can't get some answers out of our gracious host over there."

Girsh grinned savagely, biting down on his pain. "Yeah, now *that* I'm going to fucking enjoy."

"You stay put," Ringil warned him. "I don't want you moving that bolt about any more than you have to. And I don't need the help. This isn't going to be difficult."

Right, Gil. Hardened Etterkal people trafficker, lifetime criminal success before he got legal. Should be a pushover.

While Eril went around checking bodies and slitting the throats of the injured, Ringil heaved Hale's semiconscious form off the floor and into a sitting position against the curve of the chamber's back wall. The slaver was bleeding from where the Ravensfriend's pommel had smashed into his face earlier, and his right eye was already swelling shut.

Blood had splashed down onto his silk robe and into the hair on his chest where it was exposed. Ringil cut a piece out of the garment with his dragon knife, cleaned up Hale's face, and then started slapping him methodically back to wakefulness. Across the room, someone squalled weakly as Eril pulled back his head by the hair, ready for the knife. It was Janesh the doorman, flopping snap-spined and desperate between the Marsh Brotherhood soldier's booted feet.

You did that, Gil, some perpetually unsoiled, disbelieving part of him whispered. *That was you.*

"Hold it."

Eril paused, looked up at him expectantly.

"Just give me a minute here." He peered closely at Terip Hale as the slaver started to come around, slapped him a couple of times more to speed the process up. "Figure we could maybe use the leverage."

"Got it." Eril lowered Janesh's head almost gently back to the floor. He settled into a patient crouch above the injured man. Janesh barely moved beyond a couple of twitches in one arm. He'd maybe passed out from the pain of his wound, or just into the realm of quiet delirium.

Terip Hale, meanwhile, woke to a vision of carnage strewn across the joyous longshank chamber, and a small fixed smile on Ringil Eskiath's face.

"Welcome back. Remember me?"

To his credit, Hale snarled, made fists, and came almost off the wall with rage. There was a lifetime of street fighter's venom in the twisted lines of his face. His legs flailed free of the robe's silken folds. But he wasn't a young man anymore. Ringil shoved him back with a palm heel in the chest.

"You just sit there and behave."

"Fuck you!"

"No, thank you. But I have got some questions I want answered. It'd really be in your best interests to tell me what I want to know."

"Yeah, well fuck your questions." Hale's voice drawled slower, contemptuous. He gathered his mutilated robe back around him, covered the parts of his body the disarray had exposed. "And fuck you, too, you fucking queer."

Ringil glanced around at the bodies and the blood. "I think you're missing the specifics of who won here."

"You think you're going to get away with this?"

Ringil tilted his head, put a cupped hand to his ear. "You hear that? On the stairs? That's the sound of no one coming to stop us, Terip. It is over. You pulled the joyous longshank girls on us, and it didn't work."

He nodded at Eril, who yanked Janesh's head back up. The doorman shrieked as he realized what was happening, woke maybe from a dreamed escape to something better. Eril's knife dipped in, did its severing and opening—dark crimson gush of blood and Janesh's face went suddenly idiot-soft and pale. Eril let go of his head, and it hit the floor with an audible bump.

Ringil masked himself in what felt like stone.

"You want to live?" he asked Hale quietly.

Hardened or not, the slave trader had gone almost as pale as his murdered minion. Respectability, or perhaps just age, seemed to have sapped some of his edge. His mouth twitched over words he didn't appear to know how to voice.

"I'm sorry, you'll have to speak up."

"The cabal." Hale licked his lips. "They won't let this stand."

"The cabal." Ringil nodded. "Okay. Why don't you scare me with some names? Who are they? Who do they represent?"

"Oh, I think you'll find that out soon enough."

"I'm not a patient man, Terip."

The slave trader scraped together an awful, lopsided grin. "It doesn't matter what you do to me, if you kill me here or not. They'll find out about this either way."

Ringil, out of nowhere—some combination of twanging battle-comedown nerves, general weariness, who knew what besides—took a blind leap.

"Going to stick your head on a tree trunk, are they?"

He saw the jolt go through Terip Hale, almost as if the slaver had been struck by one of his own men's crossbow bolts. He saw the fear in the one unswollen eye.

"You—"

"Yeah." Grab the advantage, run with it. "I know all about it. That's why they sent me. See, Terip—I used to kill lizards for a living. One time in Demlarashan, I helped take down a whole fucking dragon, me and just one other guy. So I got no problem putting away your pet dwenda if he gets in my way. Now, you tell me—what's so fucking special about Sherin Herlirig Mernas that you've got to try to kill me when I ask after her?"

"Who?"

"You heard."

"I don't know that name."

"No?" Ringil produced the dragon knife and held it up in front of Hale's good eye. He breathed deep. "You remember well enough that she's barren, that she comes from marsh dweller stock, but you don't know her name? That's lizardshit. Now *where the fuck is she?*"

And something seemed to break in Hale. Maybe the talk of sorcery, maybe Janesh's murder, or maybe he just wasn't as tough as he used to be. He flinched back from the tip of the fang.

"Don't . . . wait, listen to me. I can't—"

Ringil tapped his eyelid with the knife. "Yeah, you can."

"I don't fucking *know,* all right." Hale seemed to see an opening, to grab at it. The desperation in his voice scaled down a little. "Look. This marsh bitch you're looking for, how long ago was she sold?"

"About a month."

"A *month?*" A harsh, high-pitched laugh—the slaver's bravado was seeping back in. "A fucking *month?* Are you insane? You got any idea how much cunt comes through this place every month? You think I got nothing better to stuff my head with than their fucking *names?* Forget it. Give it up, man."

Ringil slammed his palm against Hale's forehead for purchase, dragged the dragon knife tip down the man's cheek, and tore the skin open to the bone. Blood spritzed everywhere. Hale shrieked and flailed. Ringil let him go, as if he were hot to the touch. He felt his own face twitch, felt a deep pounding start somewhere in his chest. The moment was an unbroken Yhelteth horse, bucking under him, taking him away, body and soul. With shaking hands, he fumbled in his pocket, found the charcoal sketch of Sherin and rolled it open in both hands, still holding the dragon knife at the top edge of the parchment like some ornate scroll end. He tried to get his breathing back.

"You *are* going to tell me," he said tightly. "One way or the other. Now. Let's try again. This girl. You bought her, right?"

Hale cupped a hand at his wounded cheek, staring.

"You know she's barren." Ringil was shouting now, somehow couldn't stop himself. Could barely stop himself, in fact, from going back to work on Hale with the knife right now. *"You know she's got dweller blood. You give her to me, or so help me Hoiran, I'll take your guts out hand-over-hand right here and now."*

"It's not her."

Ringil seized him by the throat. The sketch of Sherin fluttered away. "You fucking piece of shit, that's it—"

"No, no." Babbling, working weakly at Ringil's grip with both hands, voice gone almost sleepy with terror. "Don't, don't—it's not her."

"*What's* not her?"

"It's not . . . I didn't think you . . . not one girl—it's *all of them, fucking all of them he wants. He takes them all.*"

Something portcullis-heavy seemed to clank down behind Ringil's eyes. Abruptly the rage drained out of him and he felt the shiver of an apprehension he couldn't name in its place. He let go of Hale's throat.

"He? You're talking about the dwenda?"

Hale nodded brokenly, still trying to edge away from Ringil along the curve of the wall. Ringil took a handful of silk robe and dragged him back. He leaned close.

"Talk to me." Voice trembling from the sudden collapse of the fury. Blood singing in the depths of his hearing like the sea. "You want to live, you talk to me. You tell me about this dwenda."

"They'll kill me if I do."

"And I will kill you if you don't, right here and now. Make a choice, Terip. The dwenda. What's he doing here?"

"I don't know." The slave trader made a peculiarly morose gesture. "He talks to the cabal, not me. Word came down. Any marsh cunt, anything looks like it might have the blood, make sure the warlocks check it out. If it can't breed, you set it aside. Count it as a tithe."

"Right. And anyone comes asking after a woman like that, you show them the joyous longshank girls. Right?"

Hale stared downward, would not meet Ringil's eye. The silence stretched. Blood dripped off the slaver's face and into his soiled silk lap.

Eril came over and crouched at Ringil's side. "We're done here," he murmured. "No one breathing left. You want me to do him, too?"

Ringil shook his head. "Get me that mace over there. We need a messenger. I don't want to leave Findrich and the rest in any doubt about what happened here." He raised his voice. "You hear that, Terip?"

The slave trader twitched at the sound of his name. He would not look up. Ringil leaned in and took Hale's skull firmly in his two cupped hands. He tilted it with a lover's care, until the slaver was forced to meet his eyes.

"You pay attention," he said quietly. "You tell this to Findrich, or Snarl, or whoever it is you report to in this idiot cabal of yours. You tell them Ringil Eskiath wants his cousin Sherin back. Soon, and unhurt—it's not negotiable. If I don't get what I want, I'm coming back to Etterkal to ask again. Believe me, they don't want that, and neither do you."

Hale jerked his head out of Ringil's hands. Outrage at the intimacy, or maybe just the knowledge he was not going to die, seemed to kindle a new fire in him.

"Fucking touch me," he muttered. "Piece-of-shit queer."

Silently, Eril handed Ringil the mace. Ringil smiled faintly, beat it very gently in the cup of his palm.

"You're missing the point, Hale."

"And you're fucking insane." The slave trader managed a shaky laugh. "You do know that, don't you, Eskiath? Come in here talking like some relic out of the prewar, some gang tough from harbor end. Don't you get it? Things aren't like that anymore—we're *legal* now. You can't come around here acting like this. You can't touch us."

Ringil nodded. "Go on telling yourself that if it helps. Meantime, tell the others I want my cousin back. Sherin Herlirig Mernas. There'll be records, and I'll leave you the sketch. You make sure they get the message. Because if I do have to come back to Etterkal and ask again, I promise you it'll make what happened tonight look like a minor toothache. I'll kill you and your whole fucking family, and I'll burn this place to the ground around the corpses. Then I'll move on to Findrich, and Snarl, and anyone else who gets in my way. I'll torch the whole fucking neighborhood if I have to. You think things changed after the war, fuckhead?" He reached out and chucked the slave trader hard under the chin. He hefted the mace. "Got news for you. Things just changed back."

CHAPTER 20

Jhiral let them go home not long after midnight. He appeared to have satisfied himself that everything possible was being done and, perhaps more importantly, that his grip on his advisers was no less secure than it had been before the Khangset pot boiled over. He nodded them out with the minimum of ceremony. Faileh Rakan disappeared into the bowels of the palace without a word beyond the necessary honorifics, and Archeth walked out to the front gates with Mahmal Shanta.

"Seemed to go well enough," the naval engineer said when they got outside.

She couldn't tell if there was an edge of irony on his words or not. Krinzanz was good for a lot of things, but it was not a subtle drug. The finer points of human interaction tended to go out the window. She shrugged and yawned, checked the immediate vicinity for nosy minions, habitual caution so ingrained it was reflex.

"Jhiral's not stupid," she said. "He knows we've got to nip this in the bud. If word gets out the Empire can't protect its ports, we're going to have a southern trade crisis on our hands."

"Which our competitive little city-state friends in the north will be only too pleased to exploit."

"Wouldn't you?"

Shanta did his own reflexive sweep of the surroundings. "What I would do, my lady, is not fit conversation for environs such as these. Perhaps some other time, over coffee aboard my barge?"

"Perhaps."

"Did you mean what you said about the Helmsmen? *Will* they view this as a war context?"

"How the fuck would I know?" Wearily now, despite a residual wakefulness. Her eyes felt gritty and smeared open. "The one down in dry dock I was trying to debrief last week talks about as much as a Demlarashan mystic in midfast. Makes about as much fucking sense as well."

They reached the gates and had to wait in the slightly chilly air while slaves brought Archeth's horse from the stables, and a carriage was summoned for Shanta. She pulled on her gauntlets and shook off a tiny shiver. Winter was creeping in early this year. It'd be good to get home, peel off her travel-stained clothes, and stand barefoot on heated floors in the cozy warmth of her apartments. Let the last of the krin burn away, give in to sleep. Along the shallow zigzags of the Kiriath-paved approach causeway, pale lamps studded a seductive path down through the darkness the palace mound was sunk in, and into Yhelteth's carpet of lights at the bottom. The firefly clustering of the city's illumination spread wide in all directions, split down the center by the dark arm of the estuary. Closer in, Archeth picked out the Boulevard of the Ineffable Divine, lit in bright double rows and straight as a sword blade laid across the more haphazard patterning of the other streets. It seemed almost close enough to touch.

Shanta was watching her keenly.

"They say the ones that stayed are angry," he murmured. "The Helmsmen, I mean. They feel abandoned, resentful that the Kiriath would not take them."

She looked at the lights. "Yeah, they say that."

"That's got to affect their attitude to the Empire as well, I'd imagine. Got to put pressure on any kind of loyalty they might have."

"Oh, look. They got Idrashan out already." Archeth nodded to where a slave was leading her horse out of the stable block. "So that's me, then. G'night, Mahmal. Hope your carriage doesn't take too long. Thanks for coming along."

The engineer smiled gently at her. "My pleasure. It has certainly been instructive."

She left him there and went to meet the slave halfway. Mounted up, waved a final, wordless farewell to Shanta, and urged her horse out the gate.

On the first sloping downturn of the causeway, she stood in the stirrups and looked back. The naval engineer was an indistinct figure through the railed iron of the gates above, backlit into silhouette by bright-burning torches behind him on the palace walls. But she knew beyond doubt that he was still watching her.

So fucking what? She left the palace behind and let the horse find its own way home through the stew of streets on the south side. *Shanta's no fucking different from the rest of the old guard. Holed up in their positions of privilege and moaning in their little cabal corners about how much better it was when Akal was still around.*

Well? Wasn't it?

Akal was still around when we smashed the rebels at Vanbyr. Let's not forget that inconvenient little blemish on the face of prior glory.

He was on his sickbed by then.

He still gave the fucking order.

Yes. And you obeyed it.

She passed a sleeping figure, curled into the angle of a darkened smithy's yard. Ragged cloak and hood; emblazoned on its folds she recognized the sable-on-white horse insignia of an imperial cavalryman. Hard to know if you could take that at face value or not—the city was full of demobbed and damaged soldiery sleeping in the streets, but military garb elicited more pity when you were begging, whoever you might actually be, so it was well worth the risk of stealing it if you got the chance. It could get you fed, even taken in on winter nights if the cold bit hard enough or it rained. Archeth knew a brothel near the harbor whose madame prided herself on letting derelict veterans sleep in her laundry shack. She'd even been known to send out girls from the more raddled end of her stable to provide free hand jobs on feast days.

You found patriotism in the strangest places.

She slowed the horse to a halt and peered hard at the cloak-wrapped form, trying to decide. Something about the posture rang true, the laconic efficiency in the way cloak and hood were used. But without waking the man up . . .

She shrugged, dipped in her purse, and found a five-elemental piece. Leaned over and tossed the coin so it clipped one wall in the corner and hit the paved floor with a loud *chink*. The figure grunted and moved, and a right hand groped out from under the cloak until it found the money. Ring and little finger gone, along with most of that half of the hand. Archeth grimaced. It was a common enough injury among the horse regiments: Yhelteth cavalry swords were notoriously badly provided with protection for the hand. One powerful, well-judged slice down the blade from a skilled opponent, and you were a cavalryman no longer.

She tossed another five elementals down onto the drape of the cloak, and clucked Idrashan onward.

A couple of streets later and nearly home, she passed through a small, leafy square once called Angel's Wing Place but now renamed for the victory at Gallows Gap. It was a place she'd walk to sometimes when she needed to get out of the house, both before and after the war, though she'd preferred it before. Then it had hosted a bustling fruit market. Now they'd built a self-important little three-sided stone memorial in the center, grandiose bas-relief images of exclusively imperial soldiers standing on piles of reptile dead, a central column designed to look vaguely like a sword thrusting skyward. There were stone benches built into the structure and lettered homages in rhyme to OUR GLORIOUS IMPERIAL COMMANDER, OUR SONS OF THE CITY INSPIRED. Archeth had read the compositions enough times to have them, unwillingly, by heart, had even, once, at a court ball, been briefly introduced to the poet who'd penned them.

Of course, one was not actually there *at the battle,* this smirking minor noble had told her, and sighed manfully. *However much one might have desired it. But I did visit Gallows Gap last year, and one's muse can always be relied upon in such cases to catch the echoes of the event in the melancholy quiet that remains.*

Indeed. But there must have been something in her face despite her best efforts, because the smirk slipped a little, and the poet's tone turned anxious.

You, uhm, you were not there yourself, milady? At the battle?

Oh no, she managed urbanely. *But my father died on the expeditionary retreat, and two of my outlander friends led the final Gallows Gap charge.*

He left her alone after that.

Home, in the courtyard, she handed Idrashan over to the night watchman and let herself in through a side entrance. The house was lit with lamps turned low, and it was quiet—she kept servant numbers to a minimum, and manumitted the slaves she occasionally bought as soon as custom and city regulations would permit. Kefanin, she guessed, would be dozing in his cubicle by the front door, waiting for her return. She saw no reason to wake him and went directly upstairs to her chambers.

In the dressing room, she hung up her knives, wrestled her boots off one after the other and tossed them into a corner, shucked the rest of her clothes like an old skin and stood there a minute luxuriating in the feel of the warm air on her body. Then, as she bent to scratch an itch on her calf, her own smell mugged her. She wrinkled her nose, glanced at the tapestried bellpull by the wall.

Ah, come on. Fucking Scaled Folk campaign veteran. You bathed under a waterfall in the upper Trell, winter of '51. That so long ago?

It was ten years, truth be told, time that had crept up on her somehow; but the fading edge of the krin was a blessing, a twitching impatience under her skin, and she let that carry her. She left the bell unrung and went through to the bathing chamber, not relishing the thought of a cold-water scrub but unwilling to go through the rigmarole of calling down to the basement, getting the slaves to stoke up the furnace, fill the boiling pans, waiting the time it took while the water heated and they carried it upstairs and—

The water in the big alabaster bathing jugs was not cold.

She blinked, stirred a hand loosely through the water in one of the jugs again to make sure. No question, it was still lukewarm. Kefanin, proving himself once again worth his weight in precious gems, she supposed. She grinned and went through her ablutions with a small measure of relief, scrubbed the worst offending portions of her body, and rinsed herself off. She took a towel from the rack, wrapped herself in it, and wandered through to the bedchamber.

There was someone in her bed.

As she slammed to a halt in the doorway, the scent on the towel she wore caught up with her. She knew it from somewhere, but it was not her own.

"Hoy," she snapped. "You're supposed to be in the guest wi—"

But it was not Elith.

It took her a moment to place the candlewax-colored hair and the pale features, blurry with sleep, as the woman propped herself up in the bed. It was the scent that triggered the recall, the tight wet grip of Jhiral's hand on her jaw five days ago, the salt-smelling damp of the slave girl's juices drying on his fingers. Archeth felt her nostrils flare slightly at the memory, and abruptly she didn't trust herself to say anything else.

"I—" The girl was clearly terrified. She pushed herself upright in the bed, slipping on the silk sheets. Babbling in Naomic. "I was commanded, milady. The Emperor himself, it was not my doing, I would not wish . . ."

And now Archeth remembered Jhiral's smug face when she showed up in the throne room. *I understand you had to go home before coming to see us. Did you find everything there to your satisfaction?* His prurient, conspiratorial intimacy in the Chamber of Confidences five days earlier. *She's new. What do you think? Would you like me to send her to your bedchamber when I'm finished with her?* And then, the throwaway decision, the whim. *Come, I shall send the girl to you as soon as you return.*

It didn't do to underestimate Jhiral's whims. They were all still learning that, up at the palace and across the city below. You'd think the lesson would have sunk in by now, but it seemed that—even for Archeth Indamaninarmal, most shrewd and pragmatic of imperial advisers—it hadn't.

Archeth had a moment of retrospective sympathy for Kefanin. She recalled the mayor-domo's face when she handed Elith over, his single, swiftly overridden attempt at a warning. *Milady, there is already . . .*

. . . an unexpected guest in your house.

. . . an unexpected young female slave awaiting your approval and command.

Tiny, trickling tingle in her belly at that particular thought.

Stop that.

. . . an unexpected and gracious gift of the Emperor, delivered and imposed with no possibility of demurral.

It explained what the girl was doing in her bedchamber. Jhiral liked his commands to be carried out to the letter, and didn't mind detailing what would happen if they were not. The imperial messenger who brought the girl would have instructed Kefanin minutely, she supposed; and Kefanin, outlander by birth and slave from age five up, summarily castrated at fifteen, less than four years of manumission and citizenship to his name, mayor-domo or not, would have sprung to obey.

Archeth cleared her throat. Mumbled. "All right, fine. I see. You can—"

But the girl threw back the covers and came out of the bed anyway, naked, curve of hip and pale, bisected arse, soft, heavy swing of breasts, and crawled on her hands and knees across the rug to Archeth's feet, and knelt there.

Archeth gritted her teeth.

"I was told to please you, milady." Accent thick and intoxicatingly exotic as it softened and slithered on the Tethanne syllables. Her hair fell over her face. "In any way you see fit."

It had been so long, so very, very long.

She let one hand fall toward the girl's bowed head—

—*she's a slave, Archeth*—

—snatched it back. Her heart felt abruptly like a panicked bird in a cage. She closed her eyes with the force of it. The blood thumped through her veins at jolting, krin-notched speed.

You are not human, Archidi. Tears in Grashgal's eyes as he stood on the fireship's gangway at the An-Monal dock. *Never think, because we cannot take you with us, that you are human. You are Archeth, daughter of Flaradnam, of the Kiriath clan Indamaninarmal. Remember it in adversity. You are one of us, you always will be. You are not like them.*

And then, of course, it was easy.

She swallowed and opened her eyes. Summoned a dry, self-possessed irony into her voice.

"The Emperor is generous beyond all bounds. It's truly fortunate he is not here, for I am unsure what words I would find to thank him."

She tucked the towel a little tighter around her. Self-possession or not, she did not trust herself to have the girl rise and stand facing her.

"I will no doubt be able to find work for you in my household, but for now I can think of nothing obvious. You should sleep until morning and then we will talk. What is your name?"

"Ishgrim." It was barely a murmur.

"Good. Then go back to bed, Ishgrim. It's late. I will summon you tomorrow."

She turned and headed rapidly back into the dressing room, so she would not have to watch all that long-limbed, full-breasted flesh get up off the floor and move away from her.

SHE FLUNG ON A DRESSING GOWN, STABBED HER FEET INTO SLIPPERS. Faced herself in the mirror with a scowl, and then went loudly down the staircase. It woke Kefanin up and brought him hurrying out of the cubicle by the door.

"Oh, milady. You are already—"

"Yeah. Already home, already seen what's in my bed. The Emperor is most pressing in his generosity, is he not."

Kefanin inclined his head. "Just so, milady. I would have preferred—"

"Yeah, me too. Did our other guest settle in okay?"

"I believe so. She ate shortly after sunset and then retired."

"Good." She yawned. "I'm going to the east wing study. Can you bring me a decent bottle of wine from the cellar and something to eat?"

"Immediately, milady."

"Are the lamps lit there?"

"No, milady. But I have a lantern here that—"

"Good enough." She swiped up the lantern from its rack by the door, tinkered with it until the flame brightened. "Oh yeah, and get me some krinzanz while you're at it, would you? There's a bottle of tincture on top of the right-hand cabinet in the larder. The blue one."

Kefanin scrutinized her face in the glow from the lantern. "Is that wise, milady?"

"No, it's not. Your point is?"

A grave, deeply made bow, the sort she only got out of Kefanin when he disapproved mightily of a decision she'd made. She grunted, set off along the hall to the east wing, got there in a couple of minutes, a little out of breath. She worked the bolts. A faint, musty chill puffed out at her as she hauled the door open. It had been a while since anyone was in here.

Shadows capered on the walls while she moved about, lighting lamps from the wick of the lantern with a paper spill. A warm yellow glow spread over the untidy piles of books and less easily defined junk that owned the floor. The study emerged by increments from the gloom. Her desk in the center, stacked with papers and more books. The curtained window. Paintings of An-Monal on the walls, a map etched on Kiriath glass.

The Helmsman.

"Hello there, Archeth Indamaninarmal."

"Hello Angfal." She cleared off one side of the desk so she could put her feet up, pulled out the chair and sat down. "Been a while, hasn't it?"

"You should not concern yourself on my part." The Helmsman's voice was deep and melodious, warmly avuncular and at the same time very slightly unnerving at the edges, as if at any moment it might suddenly scale upward into an inhuman scream. "You know time doesn't have the significance for me that it does for . . . humans."

Archeth grinned at the calculated insult. It wasn't the first time. She cocked one ankle over the other on the corner of the desk and stared through the angle between her feet at the thing she shared the study with.

"Good to see you again, anyway."

It took up most of the space near the wall, a span of nearly twenty feet and a height of at least ten. Mostly it looked like guts, riotous loops and coils of dark iron intestine all across the pale plasterwork and trailing down onto the floor, seemingly at random. But there were other parts, too, segments that hung fatly off the wall like lungs or tumors, and the whole thing was speckled with a series of weak green or yellowish lights behind what appeared to be thick glass optics each no larger than a thumbprint. Near the center and high up, two symmetrical sets of angled ribbing gripped the wall and ceiling, braced outward from a swollen oval the width of a man's arms at full stretch. Not for the first time, Archeth thought that the arrangement was uncomfortably arachnoid—it gave the impression that some giant spider out of a child's nightmare was somehow oozing through the wall prior to springing down on whoever happened to occupy the study at the time. Or, perhaps, that the same monstrous creature had simply been embedded there in the plaster like some grotesque hunting trophy.

It didn't help that there were clusters of the little green and yellow lights gathered at the lower end of the oval like eyes.

She knew—because the Kiriath engineers who ripped Angfal out of a derelict fireship's hull and installed it here had told her—that the Helmsman's consciousness existed within the whole organic-looking mess at once, but that didn't help much. Like it or not, she found herself habitually, instinctively, addressing herself to this hanging half-spider central structure, focusing on it whenever—

She was doing it now.

"So what do you want?" it asked her.

"Why should I want anything from you?" She unfixed her gaze from the clustered lights, made a point of gazing off toward the window instead. "Maybe I just stopped by for some light conversation."

"Really?" Angfal's voice didn't change all that much, but Archeth thought there was now an accent of cruelty in the inquiring tone. "Come to reminisce, then, have we? Talk about all those good old times when your father and Grashgal were still alive, and the world was a finer, nobler place?"

She held down the hurt, the old familiar ache.

"Far as I know," she said tonelessly, "Grashgal's still alive. Far as *you* know as well, I'd have thought, given that when they cut you out of the wreckage, they left most of your sense organs behind in the hull."

A tiny beat of silence.

"Archeth, daughter of Flaradnam, you come to me with elevated pulse, dilated pupils, swelling of blood in breasts and labia—though that's ebbing now—and a fractionally unsteady vocal range, all clear symptoms of mingled sexual arousal and krinzanz abuse, a combination that is, incidentally, not ideally suited to your physiology, or indeed any physiology beyond the very youthful. And you're staring out of a window that has a curtain drawn across it. So you see, as we both already know, my sense organs were not all left in the wreckage, and you did not come here for light conversation."

The quiet seeped in again. She thought maybe one or two of the lights in Angfal's coils had shifted color or maybe just brightened.

"I'm two hundred and seven years old," she said. "That is youthful in Kiriath terms."

"Yes, but not for a half-breed."

Her temper snapped across, shiny steel rage at the break. "Hey, *fuck you!* Grashgal's alive and laughing, somewhere better than this."

"Grashgal is dead," the Helmsman said patiently. "They all are. The Kiriath barely survived the voyage through the quick paths on their way here, and then their strength was at full flow, their science honed, and their minds undamaged. The forces they encountered undid all of that. They did not choose to come here, Archeth, despite anything the chronicles might claim to the contrary. They were shipwrecked here, and if they stayed four thousand years, it wasn't because they liked the scenery. It was because they were afraid that the return would break them."

Her rage failed her—she found herself looking at the bright jagged edge of it with weary disenchantment. This wasn't the way to get what she wanted.

"Some say the passage opened their minds," she offered. "Gave them the gift of a new vision, an insight across time. They say it didn't corrupt, it enhanced."

"Yes, that's right," Angfal jeered. "So much so that the most enhanced among them, those most *gifted,* as you put it, went off into the desert to contemplate their insight and apparently forgot to eat."

"Not all of them."

"*Most* of them."

"You're talking about the extreme cases. As a race, we learned to cope."

"We? *We* as a race?"

"Figure of speech. The *Kiriath,* as a race, adapted. And in the end their adaptation made them stronger, better able to resist the effects of a return voyage."

"Oh, is that a thesis you're developing? I'd be very interested to see your evidence."

"I'm sorry they left you behind, Angfal."

It broke the rapid parry-riposte pattern of the exchange better than if she'd screamed. A longer silence this time. The lack of motion in the Helmsman's frozen iron coils and bulges seemed suddenly wrong, ridiculous, some impossible constriction of a natural emotional order and its responses. She looked for a shift in the lights, but they held their color, they burned steadily back at her.

The Helmsmen are not human, Archidi, her father had told her once, when she was still quite a small child. He spoke High Kir, and the word he used for "human" was one the Kiriath used about themselves. *They aren't like you or me or your mother at all, not even like the spirit of one of us in a bottle or a box. They are something . . . other. You must remember that in your dealings with them. They are not human, for all that they might sometimes do a good impression of one.*

At the time, it sounded to her awed child's ears like a warning about demons.

"They left you, too," said the Helmsman finally.

"Yes, they did."

More silence. Memories swarmed through her in the space it left, adding their weight to the krinzanz crash. She stared at the fleck-lit, dismembered iron monster on the wall, the way it bulked and coiled there, and she tried to find a similar stillness in herself.

"Well, then." Angfal's voice broke smoothly back into the quiet, to all appearances as if none of the previous conversation had happened. "What can I do for you, Archeth Indamaninarmal? What is it you wanted to talk to me about?"

CHAPTER 21

They smashed both of Terip Hale's legs below the knee with the mace, got the whereabouts of the tool shop out of him fairly quickly thereafter, and then let him sink into semiconsciousness where he lay. They got Girsh settled as comfortably as possible against the opposite wall, put a freshly cranked and loaded crossbow in his lap, and went to fetch the manacle cutters.

"Is it true, then?" Eril asked him as they loped rapidly down a darkened corridor on the other side of the courtyard. "That stuff about you killing the dragon?"

"Pretty much. Why?"

"Uhm—but they don't call you Dragonbane?"

"No."

Short pause, the other man not wanting to leave it alone, not knowing how to press the point without offense.

"Never seen a dragon," he said finally.

"Yeah, well, believe me, that's the way you want to keep it."

More quiet. They reached the end of the corridor, found stairs downward.

"He, uh, he kept calling you a queer."

"Yeah."

"Well, uh . . ." With an audible sigh, Eril gave it up. "Fucking scumbag, right?"

"Indeed."

At the bottom of the stair, as they'd been told, there was a door sporting a modest padlock. Eril kicked it in with a poise and economy of motion that looked extensively practiced. A couple of shattering blows at the latch with his heel, the door sprang inward on its hinges, and they found themselves in a long underground chamber lined along one wall with cage-fronted cells. Bandglow seeped in from windows set up near the heavy-beamed roof, much the same construction as the joyous longshank chamber and the same effect: There was just enough pale silver light to make out figures huddled to the back of each cell on the floor. Mostly young women, one or two more androgynous forms that might have been boys—the difference, shrouded in any case beneath each clutched-up, moth-eaten gray blanket, tended to drown out in the low light. Hollow, terrified eyes and curled defensive postures created an unsexed uniformity. Each captive cringed visibly as the booted feet went past their cell, clung harder to the blanket as if it might be torn away from them. One or two started to make a tight-racheted keening, but you couldn't really tell which of them it was—the sound crept out past the bars and filled the whole chamber like the relentless drip of water. It put Ringil's teeth instantly on edge. He hadn't heard anything like it since the war.

"Good thing Girsh isn't here to see this," Eril murmured. "He'd probably want to let them all out."

"Yeah."

They found the tool section at the end of the row, a long alcove set with three workbenches broad enough to take a human body and lined along the back wall with hanging racks for the tools. Ringil scanned the racks, spotted a couple of delicately finished branding irons and some other suggestively shaped implements whose applications he didn't want to think about; then his eyes fastened thankfully on what they'd come for. Four identical, long-handled manacle cutters dangling side by side. He lifted one off its hook and flexed the scissor motion a couple of times.

"Should do the trick."

"Right. Let's get out of here."

Ringil hesitated. He tossed the cutters across the chamber to Eril, who fielded them one-handed with a knife fighter's precision.

"You go. I'll catch you up."

"What?" Eril looked from the cutters in his hand to Ringil, and then, with dawning realization, down the long line of cells. "Oh, come *on*. We haven't got time for th—"

"I said you go. I won't be long."

For a moment it looked as if Eril might argue. He held Ringil's eye, face unreadable, hefted the cutters a couple of times. Finally, he shrugged.

"Your call. But Girsh is in no state to hang about. Soon as I get that bolt out of his leg, we're leaving. Don't miss the boat."

"I won't."

Eril nodded, turned, and headed back up the line of cells to the door. He didn't look at any of them, didn't turn his head at all.

Admirable focus.

Yeah. What are we doing here, then?

Ringil took another pair of manacle cutters from the rack and went to the first cell in the line. The lock was a simple affair, two bolts and a cowled fastener. It took him less than a minute to mangle it apart with the cutters. He opened the cage door and stepped hesitantly into the space behind. Instantly the girl on the floor recoiled into one back corner of the cell, as hard and as fast as the walls would let her. It was almost as if she'd been thrown there by some external force he was radiating. He saw, even in the low wash of bandlight from the windows, that she was trembling violently.

"You're free to go," he said, feeling foolish.

She just stared back up at him, eyes and knuckles and the blanket edge. The awkward way she'd sprawled in the corner revealed one thigh to the hip, a small triangular glimpse of buttock and waist beyond— pale, naked flesh and the small weave-patterned discoloration of a brand on the hip bone. The blanket was her only clothing.

Fuck.

He left her, went mechanically along the row of cells, wrenching the locks apart with a rising fury that made him clumsier each time, made the cutters slip and turn as he used them, as if they had a mind of their own. His teeth gritted tighter, his breath came harder, the locks buckled and tore, hung off each door like mangled body parts, or else they slipped and clanked on the floor at his feet. And he knew, all the time, even as he was doing it, that he was wasting his time.

What are they going to do, Gil? Weary, reasonable voice in his head. *They're naked, traumatized, trapped in the middle of Etterkal. They aren't going to make it a hundred yards down the street outside before some bunch of fucking urchins blows the whistle on them.*

Shut up.

And even if they do make it to Tervinala or the river, even if they can find some way back to the homes they came from, even if they don't get raped and murdered or abducted all over again by whatever scum they'll find prowling the streets at this time of night, uniformed or not—

I said shut up.

—even if their families haven't also been sold, or thrown into the street, or hounded out of the city by their creditors, even if they are still clinging on somehow, who's to say they'll want or be able to take them back.

Shut up, shut up.

Thing is, Gil, they've been legally sold. Times have changed, remember. Everybody says so, Hale, even your old saddlemate Grace. It's a brave new age. They go back to their families, the debt reengages. The Watch comes for them all over again. Back to the Chancellery, back up for auction, all over again. With compensation demanded, no doubt, by the brokers, and paid for out of the skins of the family.

I said—

Yeah, all told, it should make for some really beautiful family reunions, Gil—if any of them ever make it that far in the first place.

"SHUT THE FUCK UP!"

The words jumped him, out of his head and suddenly echoing off the walls of the chamber as he yelled. Metallic clang, he'd wrenched the last lock apart and hurled the cutters back down the row. The slaves flinched and moaned and huddled in the cells. None of them had ventured even as far as the broken-open doors.

See, you're up against the system here, Gil. The reasonable voice again, it could almost have been Archeth, back in Ennishmin, talking him out of putting his dagger through the throat of an imperial commander. *It's pretty much an endless supply of enemies, something you'll never finish as long as you live. You burn Hale, you've got to pretty much burn down the whole of Etterkal. And these scum-fucks are legal now. You burn down Etterkal, you've got to take on the Chancellery, the Watch, and Kaad's fucking Committee, probably most of the upriver clans as well.*

Hell, Gil, in the end, you'll probably have to burn the whole of Trelayne into the fucking marshes.

For one fleeting moment, it was what he wanted to do. All he wanted to do. He could taste it, like old iron in the back of his mouth. He could smell the smoke.

"You all stay here," he heard himself say. "I'm going to find clothes for you."

He retreated from the cells, up the stairs and along the corridor, no clear idea how he was going to do this. The voice in his head jeering at him now . . .

And crossing the courtyard, he heard Girsh scream.

Terror and pain, loud enough to carry up out of the joyous longshank chamber, eldritch enough to raise the small hairs at the back of his neck. Not the sound of Eril's make-haste surgery in progress, not anything remotely so prosaic.

Plans, considerations, the complications he faced all evaporated like river mist before the morning sun. His acceptance wiped every other consideration away. It was like seeing an old friend, like picking up an old, much-loved weapon. It was easy. Simplicity itself, the old, clean, steel call to death, or something very like.

His hands rose and unslung the Ravensfriend from his back once more. He paced across what remained of the courtyard space.

He found he was grinning in the cold.

Eril met him on the stairs. The Marsh Brotherhood enforcer came flying up the steps, face contorted with panic in a way Ringil would not have believed possible a few minutes ago. He saw Ringil and brandished his knife like a madman.

"It's got him," he shouted. "It took Girsh."

Chilly tingle along Ringil's spine.

"What did?" he asked.

"It's a fucking—a wraith, a marsh demon, a—" Eril's eyes were staring with what he'd seen. He tried to push past. "It came right out of the fucking wall, man! Girsh shot it with the crossbow, the bolt went through, fucking let me *go*."

Ringil put a hand on Eril's chest and slammed him hard against the wall. His gaze cut sideways and nailed the enforcer where he was.

"You stand!" he hissed. "Running isn't going to help now. You stand there, you get a fucking grip, and tell me what happened."

But he already knew what had happened. Knew what it had to be. *Dwenda.*

He thought he heard laughter ghost upward from the chamber below. Eril swallowed hard, trembling, mastered himself.

"Listen, we've got to get out of here," he said shakily. "You can't fight this, it's fucking sorcery, man. The bolt went right through, didn't stop it, didn't even *touch* it. It's glowing fucking blue."

"What makes you think this thing is going to let us run?"

The laughter again, unmistakable this time, echoing from the bottom of the stairs. Eril shuddered.

"That's it," he hissed. "That's the noise it made."

Ringil eyed the confines of the stairwell. It was knife-fighting ground at best, no space to wield the Ravensfriend. He nodded over his shoulder.

"Back outside. If it can come through a wall, we need some open ground."

"Open ground?" Eril managed a choked laugh. "I told you, the bolt went *right fucking through it*. What are you going to do to it with a *sword*?"

Ringil ignored him, backed up the four or five steps he'd come down, through the door and out once more into the courtyard. Eril came with him, but he could see at a glance the enforcer was too close to breaking to be much help. It was a look he knew well enough, had seen on countless faces, League and imperial alike, at Rajal Beach and Demlarashan when the dragons came. It was in the eyes. Men were like blades, they would all break sooner or later, you included. But you looked around at the men you led, and in their eyes you saw what kind of steel you had to hand, how it had been forged and tempered, what blows, if any, it would take.

He sighed.

"Go on, get out of here."

"What?" Eril's grip on his knife shifted. He wet his lips. "Look—"

"I said go. You're right. You can't fight this." Ringil suffered a sudden, overpowering urge to put a hand on Eril's shoulder, on the point where it met the soft rise of his neck. He settled for a tight-lipped smile. "But I think I can."

Faint bluish glow now, spilling up what he could see of the stairwell and staining the interior wall with its radiance. Ringil settled into a two-handed guard with the Ravensfriend. Eril was still hovering at his side, wavering on the edge of his own barely controlled terror.

"All right, I'll stand wi—"

"No." Sharper now; the time for gestures was past, and Ringil's own fear was starting to eat into his resolve. "You get the fuck out of here while you still can. Get back to Milacar alive, tell him what happened here. Make sure the Brotherhood pay Girsh's family their blood dues."

"You—"

"Just fucking *go*, will you." Ringil shot him a single angry glance, all he could spare from the will it took to face the doorway and whatever might be coming through it. There was a faint, melodic hum rising through the air now, and it put his teeth on edge. "You've already lost this one. Can't you feel that? All you're going to do if you stay is *die*."

The thing that had killed Girsh spilled out into the courtyard.

There was a kind of relief in the moment, a letting go of other options that he knew well enough from the half a hundred battlefields in his past. But beside that old familiar slide, Ringil felt an icy blast of terror spike up his spine and into his head. The dwenda was nothing like he'd imagined it would be.

Hoiran's twisted cock, you should be here to see this, Shalak. You and your circle of Aldrain enthusiasts. They'd shit milk and sugared biscuits.

It walked toward him like fire on paper, the dwenda, like a dancing blue rainstorm a dozen feet across, radiance falling and splashing back up off the floor again, jagged little fissures of brighter light in amid the general glow, eating up the normality of the courtyard paving and the chilly air like the sun chasing out shadows. And it laughed as it came, it chuckled and hummed to itself like a craftsman bent to a task he knew well, like a mountain stream or a well-fed fire, like all of these—the comparisons came to Ringil fully formed—but with an edge to the sounds that invaded his ears like stinging insects, set up a vicious, ringing echo, and left a tight, indefinable ache under his ribs.

"*Run!*" he screamed at Eril. It was the last breath he could spare.

It was not a man, it was not anything like a man. The eldritch, lordly creatures in Shalak's manuscript scraps and illustrations, dropped away in his mind like puppet theater mockeries as the puppet master rises from behind his curtained façade for applause. The dwenda came on, it murmured at him, it sang to him and it shivered, it would have him for its own, and now he identified the ache that lay behind it all.

Loss.

It was the blue-tinged taste of a regret so deep you could never plumb its depths. It was the victory at Rajal that never came, it was his brother walking away down the long dark wood corridor, it was a life he might have had in Yhelteth if disgust and fury had not sent him away in disgrace instead. It was the slaves he could not free, the screaming women and children of Ennishmin he could not save, the piled-up, silent dead and the smashed-in, ruined homes. It was every wrong decision he'd ever made, every path he'd failed to walk, fanned out and held up for him to understand, and it *hurt*. It ate into him like dragon spit as he stared it down. There was a flickering heart to the dwenda, he now saw, shadows rippling through it, curves that might have been dancing limbs, a lithe, broad torso maybe, the long, leaping straight edge of—

The Ravensfriend swung to guard.

Impact stung down his arms, snagged in his joints. It felt eerily as if the sword had done the work without him. Sparks showered, flung off something he couldn't fully make out in the glow. A long, echoing chime rang across the courtyard. The dwenda stopped singing.

Oho. The thought pulsed through him, savagely exultant. *That shut you the fuck up, didn't it?*

As if in answer, the barely seen straight edge came rippling back. He twisted and blocked it again, easier now the ringing in his ears had stopped. This time he saw the meeting of blades for what it was. The dwenda was armed with an unfeasibly slender long-sword whose edges gave up light like the jamb of a door cracked open onto a room filled with blue fire. Behind the sweep of the blade, he made out a tall, long-limbed figure, flowing hair, maybe the glint of eyes. The glow still flickered everywhere, but Ringil thought it might be fading.

And the ache was ebbing with it, the whole fan of failed options he'd seen now folding away, reduced to abstract, fleeting acknowledgment, and then to nothing at all. Regret vanished, shriveled up like paper in flames. The fight came on inside him like a stoked furnace. He put on the snarl he'd used to kill Terip Hale's men. He readied the Ravensfriend.

"Come on, then, you *pixie-faced piece of shit.* You think you can take me?"

The dwenda bellowed—its voice was like a tolling silver bell—and came in swinging from the left. Ringil parried, locked the blades up, stepped through and kicked out savagely at knee height. Thuggish, tavern-brawl technique—amid the soaking blue radiance, he felt the edge of his boot connect. The dwenda shrilled and staggered. Ringil whipped his blade clear of the clinch and slashed in at midriff height. His opponent leapt back to avoid the cut. Ringil came on, reversing the swing for a higher-angled assault. The dwenda blocked, whiplash-swift. It stopped the Ravensfriend cold. The riposte came slashing down, faster than Ringil could get his own sword in place. He jerked his head back, felt the dwenda's blade whicker down the side of his face, leave cold air and a faint crackling sensation in its wake. The ghost laughter bubbled—but Ringil thought there was a harder edge on it now, the fading amusement of someone driven to unexpected effort.

Better get used to that, motherfucker.

Long lunge, all the speed that he had, right for the eyes or where he assumed they had to be. His opponent caught the Ravensfriend, hooked it aside, and sliced back down the blade, scraping up sparks—Ringil had to disengage to save his hand. He fell back. The dwenda came at him again, long-sword all flickering, flirting half cuts and feints. With human steel, Ringil would have been outclassed, reduced to full retreat and broad defensive swings. But the Ravensfriend seemed to rise to the occasion like a trained hound. It rang chimed warnings off the more extended of the dwenda's attacks, chipped the glow-edged long-sword back, gave Ringil a speeded, feverish battle fervor to match the unearthly poise of his attacker. He was panting with the effort it took, but there was a lifting, grinning passion behind it as well.

He had, he recalled in the midst of the fight, been *good* at this.

And the glow was dying, no question now. The shadow at the heart of the light was thickening, becoming less a blur of hinted form and more the bulk of a solid opponent he could kill. Now he saw eyes, oddly shaped, still faintly radiant, but recognizable for the organs they were. The blue flickering uncertainties were giving way, the spill of light from the edge of the dwenda's blade damping down to little more than a gleam. More and more, it was the cold fall of bandlight that lit the duel. More and more, he saw his opponent's face behind the clash of steel edges—stark-boned and pale, eyes narrowed, teeth bared, the combat rictus to mirror his own. The fight emerged from dream and became what it was—the man-dance, the steel measure, the promise of blood and death on cold courtyard stone.

Let's get it done, then.

The dwenda might almost have heard him. Shadowy black and silver by bandlight now, it leapt in at him with redoubled speed. Ringil turned the blows, got in weak ripostes, could not break the attack momentum. He staggered back. The dwenda blade got past at the tip, touched his face, dropped and licked across his shoulder and breast. He felt sudden heat, knew he'd been tagged. He yelled and struck back, but the dwenda was ahead of him, had seen the move, and the Ravensfriend skidded off a neat upper block. Ringil twisted, tried for the eyes again, failed, had to fall back.

The dwenda came on.

How do I take him down, Shal?

And the myth vendor in his junk shop, brooding, doubtful. *You'd have to be very fast indeed.*

Ringil launched the counterattack without warning, out of a parry posture that looked like retreat. It was the last thing you'd expect, and it had every sprung inch of reflexive speed he could muster behind it. Blade up and inward, lean forward instead of back, savage chop for one thigh. The dwenda wallowed, caught out, wrong-footed for an attack it now had no way to deliver. The block came late, would not turn the force of the Ravensfriend . . .

It almost worked.

Almost.

Instead, the dwenda yowled and leapt, went nearly chest-high straight into the air, crouched like a cat. The Ravensfriend whooped through empty space beneath, Ringil staggered, splay-legged behind the blow, and the dwenda whirled and shrilled and kicked him in the head coming down.

The courtyard swooped and spun around him, dimmed out, swam with tiny purplish points of light. The band looped overhead, across one corner of his vision, trailing blurry white fire. The stone floor tilted and came up, grabbed him by the shoulder, cuffed him across the side of the head, tore the Ravensfriend from his grasp.

FOR LONG, GROGGY MOMENTS, HE CLUNG TO CONSCIOUSNESS.

The courtyard seemed to have upended itself, was trying to dump him off its surface and into a warm waiting darkness below. He fought it, smeared vision and ebbing strength, groped across cold cobbles for his lost sword, twisted and curled about like some half-crushed insect on a tavern tabletop.

A shadow fell across him.

He managed to turn his head; he struggled for focus.

A towering black figure stood over him, etched in bandlight and the soft blue gleam from the edges of the long-sword in its hands.

The blade came up.

Someone blew out the candles.

t can't be, it can't be it can't fucking be . . .

He knew it was.

Egar saddled his horse again with numb competence, slung ax and shield, pegged the lance upright in the ground. Noticed his fingers trembling. The leather-cloaked figure fluttered in memory behind his eyes. He forced it down, no time for that now, or the icy shivering questions cramming into his head alongside. He scanned again for the riders, found them, down off the horizon now and almost invisible against the twilit flank of the steppe they were crossing. Drab colors, not a common thing among the Majak unless a sneak raid was the order of the day.

Or a brotherslaying.

Egar's mouth tightened. He counted heads. Seven, maybe eight of them, in single file. Long odds, and time running out. The riders weren't moving particularly fast, but there was a steady purpose to the motion and to the path they picked out. And you didn't have to watch them for long to know they were heading for the tree and Erkan's grave.

The fire crackled to itself, unconcerned. It was gaining strength now.

Oh, you faithless motherfuckers.

He stared blindly across the horse's back for a moment, eyes defocusing on the riders, remembering Ergund's face.

I'll go with him, Eg. You know what Alrag gets like when he thinks about Dad, when he drinks. He'll get in a fight as soon as spit, if I'm not there to drag him out.

Yeah. Egar, recalling his own drunken brawl with the quiet imperial, nearly two decades gone. *Getting a bit old for that shit, isn't he?*

Ergund gave him a strange look. *We all find different ways to live with it, Eg. Who's to say yours is the best?*

I wasn't saying that.

No, but—

Okay, skip it. Whatever. You keep an eye out for him.

And off to some meeting of herd owners he hoped he could choke down to a couple of hours, by which time Sula should have gotten her chores done and her hot little body across to the yurt, and would no doubt be admiring herself in the big Kiriath mirror he kept there. He was going to come up behind her there and—

He remembered that, staring out at the riders now, how that feeling had snaked tight across his belly, how he'd watched Ergund slope off to Ishlin-ichan, and been glad to see him go.

Glad the vigil called for a single son, glad for once that rank and tradition demanded he fulfill the role. He badly didn't want to have to spend the night in the company of Ergund and Alrag, or any of his other brothers, come to that, whether sunk in the reeking, steaming, bellowing chaos of an Ishlin-ichan tavern or out here on the cold quiet sweep of the steppe, with nothing at all to say to one another.

He swung himself up into the saddle, wheeled the horse about, and yanked the staff lance up out of the ground. His lips peeled back off a grimace.

Well, there'll be no shortage of things to say now, I expect.

He nudged the horse up the rise until it stood just clear of the tree. He rested the lance across the saddlebow at a slanting angle and waited for the riders to reach him.

HE SPOTTED ALRAG WHILE THE NEW ARRIVALS WERE STILL A GOOD hundred yards out—his eldest brother had a cockerel swagger in the way he sat a horse, and for all he was swathed in a heavy cowled cloak, Egar would have known him anywhere by stance alone.

The others—he now saw it was seven, not eight, *thank Urann for small fucking mercies*—also went cloaked and cowled. Their weapons made vague lumps in the cloth, could in some cases have been anything, mace, hand ax, who knew. But four out of the company carried broadswords, naked blades jutting clearly down below the hem of their outer garment. Mercenaries, then. The Majak didn't have much time for broadswords; too expensive, too southern-showy, and only really good for the one thing—killing men. It offended the steppe nomad soul to wield a weapon you couldn't hunt with or use around the camp for chores. So it seemed Alrag had hired for the occasion—either southern freebooter scum too low-grade to hack it in the south, or wannabe Majak renegades aping the manners of those they aspired to be.

Something in Egar eased a little. These he could probably kill without too much trouble. He sat motionless, head tipped down, and let them draw near. When the distance was down to easy hailing, he looked up. Only his eyes moved.

"Well, *brother*," he called. "Are you going to take that priest bollocks hood off and show me your fucking face?"

Three different hands twitched at the reins; one even rose halfway, then fell back. Egar nodded bleakly to himself. The three without swords. The betrayal was almost complete, then. Alrag and Ergund, without question. One other, Gant or Ershal. Had to be Gant, he'd mouthed off enough in the past about what a shit clanmaster Egar was, he'd want to be here for this.

The party drew to an ill-coordinated halt less than twenty yards away. Egar held his posture.

"What about you, Ergund? You come to murder me, but you won't look me in the eye? Father would be proud."

One of the cloaked figures reached up and tugged back its cowl. Ergund's face emerged, helmeted for battle. In the failing steppe light, he looked pale beneath the metal, but determined.

"We haven't come to murder you," he shouted. "If you'd just—"

"Yeah, we have." Now Alrag shook off his hood as well. He, too, wore a helmet, a little more ornate than Ergund's, with a low horsehair crest. "He's too fucking stubborn to bow out gracefully. Anyone can see that."

"It doesn't have to—"

"Yes, it does, Ergund." Ershal's quiet tones from beneath one of the other cowls. He did not unmask. "Alrag's right about this. There won't be any half measures."

Egar forced down his surprise, and a little unlooked-for hurt.

"Hello, little brother. Didn't expect to see you here. I thought better of you."

"Yeah, well we all thought better of you, too," Ershal snapped. "Once upon a time, when it still looked like you deserved it. Seven years we've given you, Egar. Seven fucking years! And what have you done with our fealty? You pissed it away, man. Made us the laughingstock of the Majak, made our family the laughingstock of the clan. You're not fit for the mastery. That's the truth, and everybody knows it."

"Everybody, huh? So what happened to Gant? He break a leg getting on his horse? Or has he just not poured as much tavern courage down his throat as the rest of you?"

Ershal put back his hood. Of the three brothers, he was the only one who had chosen to ride bare-headed.

"We're not drunk," he said calmly. "And Gant will not involve himself in this, but he will approve the outcome. He knows as well as anyone, the mastery must pass to safer hands."

Egar stared back at him, unmoving.

"You do know you're going to have to kill me," he said.

"That choice is yours." Ershal held his gaze. "But you have left us no choice at all. The shaman is right. If we don't act, you'll bring the ruin of the Gray One on us all."

"The shaman, eh? Been listening to that dried-up old buzzard, have you? You *stupid* fucking—"

"We've been vouchsafed a vision," shouted Ergund. "You profane the names of the Dwellers for all to hear. You snub the respected men of the clan as if they were hirelings, so you can rush back to your yurt, get pissed, and shove your prick into whatever teenage slut takes your fancy. You barely bother to honor the rituals, you drink and brood and sit alone instead, or you get out of your face and stumble about all night telling everyone how fucking wonderful it was in the south, how much you miss it, how *we've* all got to fucking change and be more like the imperials, be more *civilized*. You've sired no honorable heirs, nor given any good example for our young men to follow except to escape their obligations and go adventuring in the south. Oh yeah, and to fuck whatever piece of cheap milkmaid arse they can get the leggings down on."

"Jealous much, Ergund?"

"Hey, *fuck* you!"

Egar snapped a glance at Alrag. Their gazes locked.

"And you, brother. Do I get to hear your list of complaints, too? Some hallowed boundary I've overstepped in your eyes as well, is there?"

Alrag shrugged. "I don't care who you fuck. You're in my way."

It was like a cowl thrown back from everything, the truth of the moment exposed and grinning skullishly at them all. The mask of talk peeled off, discarded somewhere in the quiet. The chill of what had to be done stood waiting.

Ergund must have felt it more than the others.

"Listen, Egar. It doesn't have to be like this. You can walk away. Just give up your weapons and your horse. Give an oath on father's cairn that you won't come back. They'll take you as far as the mountains and turn you loose."

It was almost worth laughter—Egar made do with a thin grin. "Is that what they told you, Ergund? Is that how they got you saddled up for this?"

"It's the *truth*."

"It's a fucking lie. It's not even a very imaginative one." Egar nodded at the hooded, silent sword carriers. "These men? They'll slit my throat as soon as you're over the horizon, just to save themselves the ride. I'm surprised they even agreed to show up before you had me disarmed. I hope you haven't paid them in advance."

A couple of growled oaths from the freebooters—one of them cleared his sword from its straps, leveled the blade one-handed at Egar. But his mount skittered a couple of steps at the movement and ruined the gesture. His voice came across young and tense.

"You shut your fucking mouth."

"I think I'll wait till you come over here and make me." Neither the clanmaster nor his Yhelteth warhorse had shifted more than a statue. Egar saw the sword tremble as the mercenary worked to hold its weight out horizontally. Saw the tip waver and grinned into the blank shadow under the hood. "Son, you have been misinformed. Did they not tell you who I am?"

The young freebooter swiped back his hood, used the move to drop his sword and leave it at an easier angle to maintain. In the space cleared by the fallen cowl, Egar saw a crude metal helmet but only leather at his shoulders and throat, perhaps at most some kind of thin wood-slat cuirass. No shielding steel. The face above the collar matched the voice—wispy-bearded, acne-scarred, pale features out of the free cities or somewhere close. No more than eighteen or nineteen years old. Mouth stretched wet and wide to let out all the youthful rage.

"I know you're a fucking dead man," he yelled.

"We all are, sooner or later. But I think you'll be on the Sky Road before me. I used to kill *dragons* for a living, son. You, I'm going to use for a toothpick."

"We're going to fucking *gut* you!"

"In your syphilitic whore mother's dreams, you are."

And then, of course, it all came apart.

He heard Alrag yell, wasn't sure if it was an attempt to stop the slide toward slaughter, or just impatient incitement to get on with it. Either way, it was irrelevant—the young freebooter had already kicked his horse into an untidy charge, mouth working, face contorted. Another of the mercenaries went with him, tugging his sword up and out as he came, hood still up and flopping in his eyes. Yelling a name. Maybe the word *son;* in the tilt of the moment it was hard to tell.

Fucking amateurs.

Egar met the two men head-on. He cut out low with the lance, slashed open the throat on the younger man's horse, let it thrash past in panicked agony. Blood loosed on the air, splattering off the lance blade, the scream of the dying animal and the rider's wild yell as he came off. Egar's horse stepped delicately sideways of it all, as if avoiding a lady's carriage on the Boulevard of Grace Foretold. The second mercenary reined hard and right, trying to avoid the mess in his path, thoughts of attack apparently forgotten. Egar leaned, took his cowl and most of his face off with a savage upward slash. The man shrieked and flailed blindly about with his sword. His helmet was gone, flipped off and away like a mug off a tavern table. Raw flaps and shreds of flesh hung in place of his features, blinding him the way the hood must have earlier. His terrified mount spun about beneath him, screamed along with him, then flung him to the ground. Egar whistled and nudged his warhorse, and it stamped forward, put its steel-shod hooves through the fallen freebooter's rib cage with the same trained delicacy it had danced aside before. Egar heard the crunch it made, felt it right through the horse's frame and up into his own groin. He threw back his head and howled.

And there was Alrag, teeth bared, hurtling in with his own staff lance swung high in one hand for spearing. It wasn't a thrust you could block.

But . . .

Egar danced the Yhelteth destrier aside, put himself on Alrag's unweaponed flank. His brother spotted the move, couldn't swap the lance about in time and had to settle for a clumsy double-handed defensive block. Egar met it with his own lance double-handed as a staff. The two weapons struck each other a glancing blow and then Alrag was past, wheeling his mount tightly about, turning the charge. Egar knew the animal from camp, it was well trained and spirited, and his eldest brother was a consummate horseman. He didn't have much time.

The two remaining mercenaries had huddled their mounts together as if for comfort. One of them brandished his sword; the other had a small, horseman's crossbow, was trying desperately to crank it back for action. Egar urged his horse into a gallop, right at the two of them, venting another long berserker scream as he came.

As he'd hoped, their horses panicked and split apart. He ignored the man with the sword, charged down on the crossbow artist before he could get his horse back around and bring his weapon to bear. The lance blade shocked into the freebooter's back with enough force to unseat him, must have gone right through the thin wood-slat armor, if he was wearing it, and severed the spine beneath. Egar yanked back fast and tight so as not to lose the lance as the man went to the ground. The blade came free, the body toppled bonelessly sideways off the horse and onto the ground. Egar never saw it complete the fall—he was already turning his own mount about.

Alrag was right on his tail.

Egar roared and brought his lance swinging around, stabbed out as his brother rode in at him. Alrag flinched, both lances went wide. The two horses passed each other again in the dusk. The clanmaster gathered himself, grabbed glimpses of the steppe left and right, saw the final mercenary in full flight, spurring his horse toward the horizon as if pursued by demons. He snarled a grin.

"Just family now," he yelled against the darkening sky. "Cozy, isn't it?"

Something hissed through the air. The Yhelteth warhorse screamed and bucked beneath him. A black-fletched arrow sprouted from its shoulder. He whipped about, saw Ershal, recurved short bow in hand, arm reaching down to the saddle box for the next shaft. Remembered too late his younger brother's chief prowess ever since they were children.

"Oh, you little *shit*!"

He urged the destrier forward with his thighs. It wallowed as it tried to obey. A second shaft took it deep in the flank. Blood welled up. It screamed again, staggered forward half a dozen desperate steps, neck arched, stumbling. Egar screamed with it, hefted his lance, willed himself and his mount closer to his brother.

"I'll rip your motherfucking heart out for this, Ershal!"

The third arrow put out the animal's eye. It went mad, reared and tumbled, hurled Egar from its back. He hit the ground and rolled, somehow kept the lance, somehow else managed not to spike himself on it, came to a halt in the grass clutching at its shaft. Behind him, he heard the crash as his horse hit the ground, the sound of it curling and trying to get up, falling back. The endless heart-ripping cries it gave out as it struggled and thrashed.

He got muzzily to his hands and knees. Soft pulsing snarl in the base of his throat. *Back on your feet, back on your fucking feet, Majak.* The horse screamed again. Egar cast about in the gloom of near dark, found Ergund and Ershal a couple of dozen paces away, edged in bandlight. Alrag farther out but trotting back toward them and erect in the saddle, pleased with himself. None of them close enough to take down with a thrown knife.

Off to the left, the young mercenary staggered about groaning, fell down abruptly, lost to view in the grass. It looked as if he'd taken a bad blow to the head when he was unhorsed. He didn't get up again.

Ershal put another arrow into the stricken warhorse. It screamed again, but weakly now.

"Urann's sake, fucking *kill* it, will you."

Ergund—all his life, he'd hated it when the animals suffered. Egar remembered when he was ten and . . .

The *hiss-thump* of another arrow. The horse snorted and quieted. Egar slipped through the grass in a low raider's crouch, knuckles white on the staff of his lance, a pulsing vein of fury through his brain like a spike. Whatever else happened now, he was going to take Ershal apart before he died.

"That's far enough, Egar."

His brother's voice, calm against the fading agony of the destrier. Egar looked up through the night breeze sway of the grass and saw Ershal upright in the saddle, the bow bent on him from less than ten yards. Cold, quailing horror as he waited for the impact—his brother would not miss, and at this range, off the recurved bow, the shaft would go right through him.

"That's it. Up where I can see you."

Egar straightened from his crouch. A bitter smile touched the corners of his mouth. He heard the snuffling his horse made as it died. He thought maybe his knife would reach from here. He dropped the lance.

"Go on then. You traitorous little fuck. Get it done."

"You were given every chance to—"

"Oh, *fuck* off."

Alrag rode up, reined his horse to an unnecessarily savage halt, and glanced back and forth along the line the arrow would take.

"What are you fucking waiting for?" he inquired acidly.

Ershal flickered a glance at Alrag, then Ergund. But his attention never shifted from the draw he had on Egar.

"We're all agreed, then?"

Egar clawed for his knife.

Ershal loosed the arrow.

The world went dark.

NO, *NOT DARK*, HE REALIZED.

Had *time* to realize.

The arrow had not hit him.

Not dark, just dim, like the dimming of your eyes when you'd stared too hard at the sun before you ducked into a yurt. Like the sudden steeping of gloom in a Yhelteth theater house before the curtains ran back.

The wind across the steppe seemed to hold its breath.

Out of nowhere, there was a figure standing in the path of Ershal's shot. Leather-cloaked, face shadowed beneath a soft-brimmed hat. It reached up and took the arrow out of the air with no more effort than a man grabbing a lance pennant in the breeze. The fingers of the hand seemed—Egar squinted hard—to elongate and flex in places no human hand could have. A voice whispered out to them in the still spaces left by the wind, distant and intimate at once.

"Can't allow that, I'm afraid."

And suddenly the wind came back, buffeting, and in it Egar caught the wash of chemical burning once more. His brothers' horses scented it, too—they whinnied in terror and tried to back up. Ershal cursed and dropped his bow as he fought his mount for control.

"Harjalath!" spat Alrag.

"Not as such, no." The apparition lowered its arm and snapped the arrow deftly in half, one-handed. It let the pieces fall. "Harjalath is . . . other, when he cares to manifest himself. Though for your purposes, the end difference here will be negligible."

Ergund spared one hand from calming his horse, made a hasty ward. "We are about Kelgris's business, demon. Begone. You may not hinder us."

"It's not that simple," whispered the thing. "You see."

With the hand that had snapped the arrow apart, it brushed through the grass as if stirring the surface of water. Waves raced out from its touch, seemingly random, certainly in defiance of the prevailing breeze from the north. The grass bowed, it shivered and whipped about, it made mounds like the racing backs of sea creatures just below the surface.

"*Do* you see?"

In the space around the figure, the mounds grew suddenly still, rose silently and took on stricter form. Half a dozen separate shapes, maybe more. Egar felt the breath stop in his throat as he realized what he was looking at. The creature in the leather cloak had surrounded itself abruptly with men—but men woven out of the grass itself, and moving restlessly around on its surface like bathers immersed to the waist in a river.

"No corner of the steppe," murmured the figure. It sounded oddly distracted, almost sleepy. "But that the blood of men has fallen there and fertilized it. Occasionally, the steppe can be made to recall these things. Kill them."

And the grass men flung themselves forward.

They had no weapons, nothing beyond their ill-formed stringy tendril hands, but they surged up at the terrified horses like ill-intending waves, and where they gripped, Egar saw blood spring out on the animals' hide. He saw them pull Ergund's mount right over in a flounder of limbs and rolling eyes, saw Ergund stagger briefly upright and make frantic warding signs, shrilling the name of Kelgris until they dragged him down into the grass as well, and his screams turned choked and gurgling. He saw Alrag hacking about him with his lance, yelling and cursing, Ershal wheeling his beleaguered horse about in the chaos, face a mask of horror . . .

There was little enough time for more—a pair of the grass things came at Egar as well, and he was busy grabbing his lance back up off the ground where he'd dropped it. Grass came with it, blades of the stuff folding over and wrapping and clinging stubbornly to the shaft, trying to pull it back down. For one insane moment, it was like a tug-of-war for the weapon with some surprisingly tenacious toddler around the camp, and then Egar had the lance free and was swinging it up to defend himself against a long thin slashing arm and the empty eye sockets of the grass-formed head behind it. He scythed off the arm at what might have approximated an elbow joint, saw it simply re-form as more grass stalks slithered up into place. A ragged gap opened in the thing's head where a mouth would have been on a man. The rustling, keening noise that came out of it turned his blood to ice.

"Not him."

The leather-cloaked figure spoke without turning, hissed, furious words, made a rapid whiplash gesture back across its shoulder that would have dislocated the limb on a normal man. The two forms slopped like waves collapsing up a beach, and were abruptly gone. Melting motions in the grass and an errant gust of wind, and then nothing at all. Egar drew harsh breath and gaped around him in time to see Alrag hauled, lance still flailing, down to a bellowing death in the grass, and Ershal spurring his horse away at the gallop, lashing wildly behind him with his knife, chopping at the empty air alongside his mount's rump like a man deranged. The summoned forms surged about for a moment or two, perhaps looking for more victims, then they, too, sank back into the grass that had spawned them and Egar stood panting, alone with the thing in the leather cloak.

It turned slowly to face him. That the features below the brim of the hat were no more than nondescript human seemed like the final impossible thing. The voice that drummed around the inside of his skull hit him like the pulse of a bad hangover.

"You were supposed to run, Dragonbane. That's the purpose of a warning."

"Who—" Egar struggled to master his breathing. "—the *fuck*. Are you?"

The eyes beneath the hat glinted, another warning in them for him. "That's complicated."

"Well, hey, everybody's fucking dead. We've got some time."

"Not as much as you think. You heard your brother Ergund call upon Kelgris? She is awake and abroad. Poltar the shaman has her favor. All I have done here is hold back the tide a little."

Egar found his rage still had the better of his fear. He clenched fists on the staff of his lance, drew clamped breath. Grimaced.

"Listen. Don't think I'm not grateful to you, because I am. You saved my life. By sorcery or not, I still owe you a blood debt for that, and you won't find me stingy on the payback. But I will have a name for my debt, or it can't be called honorable."

It was hard to tell in the poor light, but he thought the figure rolled its eyes. It turned away from him for a moment. It seemed to be staring out across the steppe, or maybe just at the thin plume of smoke rising from Egar's fire.

"Can't fucking believe it's come to this," it muttered. "Negotiating with a fucking herdsman—you know, sometimes it's—listen, I was the thief of *fire* once, you goat-shagging thug. You know that? The fucking doom bringer to kings." An arm thrown out in exasperation. "Back when the earth was young, back when there was still a *moon* in the fucking sky, I pulled on whatever flesh was needful and I struck terror into the hearts of the powerful and enthroned all across this mudball world, and an-other dozen like it. I took the spirit form and strode across measure-less . . . ah, *fuck* it, never mind. All right, a name. You *know* my name."

And, abruptly, he did.

It was as if someone had taken a binding from his eyes, as if he'd suddenly shed the blurry fog of a fever. He saw the sea captain's cloak as if for the first time, remembered tales and associations from a lifetime of Majak myth. A traveler, by land but more often by sea, a master of disguises and stratagems, a murderous, barely discriminate force when unleashed, a wry borrower of the human form. The least predictable, most violently capricious of the Sky Dwellers.

The chill of it blew through him.

"Takavach," he whispered.

The hat-brim-shadowed visage tipped back toward him. There might have been the glimmer of a cold smile. "Good. Are you happy now, with your name, with your *knowing*?"

"What?" Egar swallowed. Voice still a whisper. "What do you want with me?"

"That's better. First and foremost, I want you to shut up and listen. Your brother Ershal has escaped. In a matter of hours he'll have roused the whole camp and told them that you are possessed by demons."

"Demons? There's no fucking way they'll be—"

"The next time you interrupt me, I'll sew your fucking lips up with grass. And don't think I won't." The thing that claimed to be Takavach drew a deep breath. "Now *listen* to me. Ershal will say that he and your other brothers, perhaps drunkenly—which would explain the impropriety of the matter—rode out to greet you at your vigil. That you flew into a fury, summoned demonic forces, and slaughtered Alrag and Ergund; that he barely escaped with his life. Poltar will vouchsafe his story with the usual superstitious horseshit about your southern manners polluting your Majak purity, which is a line he's been spreading about you for some time now, incidentally. And at dawn, they'll all ride out here and see for themselves. Would you like to take a closer look at how your brothers died?"

The question appeared to be rhetorical. Takavach was already drifting through the grass to where Alrag had fallen. Egar went after him, mouth pulled tight for what he was about to see. They came upon the occluding bulk of his brother's murdered horse first, collapsed massively sideways, streaked everywhere with blood and clinging blades of grass. Egar stepped around it at the rump end and saw, mingled with the animal's spilled entrails, the ruined mess that lay beyond.

Alrag lay in a flattened, blood-drenched patch of grass, and he was roped to the ground. The blades and tendrils had lashed around his limbs and trunk at every juncture and pulled him down so tight that at his wrists and neck they had sunk through the skin and into the flesh beneath. They'd burrowed into his eyes and nose and ears, had turned the eyes themselves to bloodied mush in the process. Had twisted his head and neck sideways, wrenched his mouth down to the ground and so wide that the jaw was dislocated. Had crowded inside and down his throat in a twisted rope of grass as thick around as Egar's forearm and now slick with blood.

Bandlight turned the image unreal, like an acid etching on metal. Egar made himself stare at it, unblinking until his eyes began to hurt.

Brotherslayer.

He was not sure whom the voice in his head was accusing.

At his side, Takavach shot him a curious glance, then went and crouched by Alrag's head. His leather cloak pooled around him, made him seem hunched and unhuman. Egar thought of a solitary vulture settling to feast. The Dweller looked back up over his shoulder at the clanmaster.

"Would you like to see Ergund as well?"

"No," Egar heard himself say thickly. "That won't be necessary."

"No, I suppose not." Takavach took hold of the woven rope emerging from Alrag's broken mouth and tugged at it experimentally. It didn't move much. "Well, I think you'd agree that outside of sorcery, this is going to be hard to explain."

"Explain?" Egar drank in the sight of his eldest brother for one more measured moment, then turned on his heel. He slung his lance across one shoulder, cast a glance at the sky, and gauged a straight line back to camp. "I'll fucking explain it. I'll cram that bow down Ershal's throat the exact same *fucking* way."

"And the—where do you think you're going?" Takavach's words came hurriedly after him. "And the *shaman*? *Kelgris?*"

Egar didn't look around or stop walking. "I'm going to gut that scrawny motherfucker, the way I should have done months ago, and then stake him out for the buzzards, still living. And if Kelgris shows up in support, I'll do the same fucking thing to her."

Faint rumble of thunder walking at the horizon. The clouds there lit briefly from within with a malevolent mauve radiance.

"So." Takavach was suddenly at his side again. "Now it's Egar the fucking Godbane, is it? Do you not think you're biting off a little more than you can chew here, herdsman? Kelgris is a Sky Dweller. You don't know how to kill her, you wouldn't know where to start."

Egar kept walking. "So tell me."

Brief silence. Takavach kept pace with him. "I'm not at liberty to do that. There are certain . . . protocols that have to be observed. Agreed rules, if you like. Oaths and ties that bind."

"Fine. Then don't tell me. You've already done enough."

"And what's *that* supposed to mean?"

"Nothing," Egar said violently. "It means *nothing*. Two of my brothers are dead back there, I'm on my way to finish the job. That's all. Now will you *stop fucking following me!*"

To his surprise, the Dweller did exactly that. He stood in the grass and watched the clanmaster stride away. The thunder at the horizon came again, and if Egar had looked back then, he might have seen Takavach shiver.

"Fine. Go to your fucking death, then, if that's the way you want it. Kelgris will put a legion of steppe ghouls between you and the camp, a legion of rabid fucking wolves, maybe even a flapping wraith or three if she's feeling inventive. And you're on *fucking foot!*"

Egar ignored it. The image of Alrag's death danced behind his eyes.

"So," the Dweller shouted furiously after him. "This is what it means to be owed thanks and a blood debt by a Skaranak clanmaster, is it?"

It stopped him like a crossbow bolt. He lowered his head for a moment, breathed deep. Nodded to himself and turned back to the cloaked figure that stood behind him.

"What do you want from me, Takavach?"

"At the moment, I want to help you stay alive. Would that be so terrible?"

His brothers lay dead and cooling in the grass behind him, scant yards from their father's grave. Marnak's words floated back through his mind. *You start wondering why you made it to the end of the day, why you're still standing when the field is clogged with other men's blood and corpses. Why the Dwellers are keeping you alive, what purpose the Sky Home has laid out for you.*

Thunder rattled at the chained doors of the world.

Egar's face twitched as he heard it. Closer now, and out across the steppe the clouds were massing. He felt his own future come and touch him with one cold hand at the neck. The long purpose of the Sky Home was rarely beneficial to those who served as its instruments, heroes least of all. You only had to look at the legends.

He spat in the grass.

Went back to where the cloaked god stood waiting for him. He met the glimmering eyes beneath the hat brim and discovered that in the strange storm blowing through his heart now, there was no longer any room for fear.

"All right," he said.

CHAPTER 23

Waking up felt like riding one of the huge iron navigation buoys in the channel at Yhelteth port. The taste of rust in his mouth, a cold, black watery rushing around him, and a wavering patch of light on the surface of the dark above. He felt a hot twinge through shoulder and chest, wasn't surprised to feel it but couldn't quite recall why. Through the jagged glimmer of approaching consciousness, he thought he saw a dark figure waiting for him.

Don't you fucking get it, Dad. Mumbling through an oddly aching jaw. *It's all a fucking lie, the whole stinking edifice from the marsh up . . .*

And awake.

He lay on smooth, cold stone. Limestone drip of water somewhere in the gloom. A pale light danced on raw vaulting rock overhead. The dark figure stood against a dressed stone wall to his left.

"Why did you do it?"

But the voice came from the right. Ringil blinked and propped himself up on one shaky elbow. Pain lanced up from his jaw and through the right side of his head. Memory crashed in on him. The fight—the dwenda—the damage he'd taken. He peered around, saw little beyond the vague loom of overhanging rock and stalactites.

"Do what?" he asked groggily.

Shadows moved on the stone floor where he lay. It was paving, he noticed, dressed to match the wall on his left. He squinted and made out a cross-legged form seated just beyond the fall of light around him. Whoever it was seemed to be staring down into cupped hands.

"Why did you fight for them?" There was a music to the voice, a deep-toned, melodic vibrancy, for all that the words themselves came quietly across the gloom. The language was Naomic, but tinged with archaisms from old Myrlic and a quaint grammatical ornateness. "They'd execute you on a spike for your choice of bed partner, and call it righteousness; they'd watch it done and toast your agony with tankards and songs, and dedicate it to their idiot gods. They're brutal, moronic, they have the ethical consciousness of apes and the initiative levels of sheep. But you took the field against the reptiles for them nonetheless. Why?"

Ringil sat up with an effort. Tried to speak, coughed instead. Got it under control, finally, managed a weak shrug.

"Dunno," he croaked. "Everyone was doing it, I just wanted to be popular."

Arid laughter, echoing in the cavern. But the question still hung there in the silence that followed, and the figure did not move. An answer was required, a real one.

"Okay." Ringil took his jaw between thumb and forefinger, flexed it and grimaced. He cleared his throat. "I wouldn't swear to it after all this time. But looking back, I think it was probably the children. I saw a couple of towns hit by their raiding parties early on. You know, the Scaled Folk tend to eat their prisoners. And for children, well, that's got to be the ultimate nightmare, right? Being eaten. Chained up watching, knowing it's going to happen to them next."

"I see. For children." The seated form cocked its head. The voice stayed soft and silky, but somewhere it held the underlying tensile strength of Kiriath skinmail. "Children who would in all probability grow to be just as ignorant and brutal and destructive as those that spawned them."

Ringil pressed fingers to the throbbing side of his head. "Yeah, probably. When you put it like that, does seem kind of stupid. So what about you people? You eat your prisoners at all?"

The figure rose smoothly to its feet. Even in the gloom, Ringil could see the physical power and grace the motion implied. The speaker came forward into the light.

For a moment, Ringil forgot to breathe.

Throbbing pain in his jaw and head, the twinges from the sword-tip slash on his shoulder and chest, a messy, soiled feel to his consciousness and clothes, and behind it all a vague, disconnected sense of fear—still, Ringil felt the spurt of nascent lust in the base of his belly. Grace-of-Heaven Milacar's words spilled back through his head.

He's beautiful, Gil. That's what they say. That he's beautiful beyond words.

Whatever questionable source had carried that word to Milacar, you couldn't fault their powers of observation.

The dwenda stood over six feet tall, slender almost to boyishness in hips and limbs but with a sudden breadth and power in chest and shoulders that made his upper body look more like a stylized cuirass than anything living. He—you had to assume it was male from the bulge in the loose black breeches and the flat planes of the chest—stood with the same effortless poise that he'd shown getting up. Long, tapering hands hung pale and slightly crooked, as if they remembered a hawkish past life as talons. The nails each gave up a minute rainbow sheen in the light.

The face that topped it all was everything Shalak's Aldrain enthusiasts could have wished for—bone white, mobile and intelligent, long-lipped, and just fleshy enough in chin and nose to offset the high, cadaverous cheekbones and broad flat forehead. Long black hair hung straight on either side, met the wide shoulders and spilled back over them like dark water. The eyes—

The eyes were pits of pitch, just the way the legends had it, but even in this low light Ringil saw how they flung back the same faint rainbow glimmer as the dwenda's nails. He had a sudden flush of absolute certainty that in daylight the whole eyeball would blaze like sunrise over the Trell estuary.

The dwenda inclined slightly over him. It was at one and the same time something like a reverence, something like predatory intent.

"Would you *like* me to eat you?" it asked.

Ringil felt the squirm in his guts again.

Get a fucking grip, Gil. This is your enemy, you nearly killed him last night—

Tonight, still? Some part of him needed, for some reason, to know.

—you might still be able to manage it.

Instead, he managed an ironic clearing of the throat and a manufactured lightness of tone belying the *trip-trip* that went up along his arms and down into his groin.

"Maybe later. Right now, I've got this motherfucker of a headache."

"Yes." The head slightly cocked again. Splinters of light danced across the inky eyes. "I apologize for the pain. The damage is slight, and in this place you will heal much faster than you would in your world. But even here, a physical price has to be paid. And it was the only means I had of ending the fight without killing you."

"Then I suppose I should thank you."

The dwenda grinned unexpectedly. Teeth. It wasn't an altogether reassuring sight. "I suppose you should."

"Thanks."

The dwenda dropped abruptly into a crouch, faster than Ringil could react, and its hand shot out to cup the side of his face. The long fingers slid up into his hair, tangled in its strands, and tugged his head forward.

"I'm afraid in the end I'm going to want more from you than that, Ringil Eskiath."

Its lips were cool and firm on his, the subtle pressure split his mouth before he realized he'd wanted to open it, and a slick, flickering tongue met his own. There was the sudden press at his chin of a stubble so soft it was almost like velvet pile. The trickling in his belly flared up like a bonfire. He felt himself hardening.

The dwenda drew back.

"You are not healed yet," it murmured.

Ringil's lips peeled off his teeth. "I'm feeling a lot better."

But the dwenda was back to its feet again, just as rapidly, its grip on him gone, fading to a sense memory; he could still feel the tips of the fingers on his skull, the slip and press of the tongue in his mouth, like a promise of more. The slender figure turned away from him, rather hurriedly, he thought. Like wincing.

"Let me be the judge of that," it said harshly.

Ringil raised an eyebrow at the change. "Well, it's your place."

"Not mine, exactly." A glance back across one shoulder that he could not read. "But near enough. You'd do well to let me guide you here."

"Okay." Ringil got himself upright with rather less grace than his host had shown. He stood at the dwenda's back, close enough to pick up scent. It wasn't exactly new territory, he'd been here enough times before and to spare: the last-minute panic of a novice partner not sure what it was he really wanted. He'd learned at Grace-of-Heaven's knee— *so to speak, Gil*—the patience and guile of when to force the issue, when to back up and wait.

He waited.

Silence. Long enough for him to notice that the dwenda gave off a faint musk whose constituent parts he could not quite—despite a tantalizing familiarity—pin down.

"Where are we?" he asked. "Under the city?"

"In a manner of speaking." The dwenda seemed to have regained a little of its previous poise. It drifted away a couple of steps, turned to face him at what it apparently judged a safe distance. "Though it's not a version of Trelayne you would recognize, I think. In your version, it will take millions of years for the river to lay down the sediment that goes to form this rock."

"Then did we take the quick paths to get here? Travel through the pressured places under the earth like the Kiriath?"

"No." A thin smile. "The Black Folk are engineers. They take the long way around to get to everything. Much like humans, in fact. In time you will come to resemble them more than you know."

"That's going to upset a few Majak purists I know."

The dwenda shrugged. "They won't live to see it. As a culture or as individuals. For that matter, nor will you, the League cities or the Empire."

"You sound irritatingly superior when you talk like that." Ringil offered up a smile of his own. "If you don't mind me saying."

"Why should I mind? The superiority is evident."

"So it's true, then. All the stories they tell, all that Aldrain lore they babble. You are immortal."

Another shrug. "So far."

Ringil laughed out loud. He couldn't help it. "Just like that barking black dog, eh? How the hell would anybody *know* something like that?"

The echoes flapped at the chamber roof, then chased each other away through the dark. The dwenda frowned. "Black dog?"

"Doesn't matter. Just something I heard the other day." Ringil stared around in the gloom, groping after memories of the evenings spent in pointless discussion at Shalak's place. Speculation run wild amid cheese and wine and easy company. "So, this place, then. This has to be part of the Aldrain marches. The places between, *where the constraints of time are not felt.* The Ageless Realm."

"It has been called that, yes. Among other things."

"And you brought me here with, what? Sorcery?"

"If you like. It might be simpler to say I carried you. When the aspect storm, the maelstrom gate of alternatives, is summoned, it translates everything within its radius. As it wrapped around me, so it brought you as well."

"Neat trick. You think you can teach it to me?"

"No. You would have to . . . *evolve* before that became possible."

Ringil's eyes fell on the black figure against the wall. He saw now that it was a suit of something like armor, hung a couple of feet up on the stonework in some fashion he couldn't work out. He moved closer, scrutinizing the smooth oval curves of a helm that showed no external decoration at all, that in fact resembled nothing so much as the head of some sleek sea mammal coming up for air.

"This yours?" he asked.

"Yes."

Ringil reached up and touched the suit at one hip. The material it was made of felt cool and smooth, more like leather than mail. He imagined it would mold to the wearer like a second skin. And the visor—he could only now make it out—was a simple sweep of glass as black as the rest of the suit, set in the helm with a precision he had only ever seen before in the finest workings of the Kiriath engineers.

He felt the dwenda draw closer behind him. He lifted one slack leg of the armor in his hand, let it swing gently back against the wall.

"You weren't wearing this when you came for me."

"No. There wasn't time." Ringil thought the voice turned ironic. "Nor much need, in the end."

It was like a touch, soft at the nape of his neck. He turned about in the dark drip-sounding damp of the air, and found himself eye-to-eye with his companion. This time the bonfire in his belly was instant, a roaring, sheeting heat that rushed upward and licked at the underside of his ribs.

"You got lucky," Ringil said unsteadily.

The dwenda seemed to move forward, a single seamless step. His bulk crowded at Ringil's chest. "Did I?"

And Ringil—Ringil couldn't do anything at all now with the slippery smile that played around his lips like smeared grease, and would not come off. He felt his breathing deepen, his pulse go dripping like hot wax along the insides of his arms and down his thighs. His prick was a hot iron bar pinned up against his stomach by the suddenly constricting cloth of his breeches. The dwenda's arms lifted to his sides, a gossamer caress of motion that he felt with shivering intensity, for all that the thing's hands never touched him.

"What time is it?" he asked, thickly.

The question came out of nowhere. He couldn't fathom a reason for it at all, couldn't understand it in any way but that it felt like the last flailing of a drowning man.

The dwenda stepped into him again, drenched his face in its shadow. The candle gleam in the eyes, oh ye gods the pressure of a huge iron-hard erection to match his own pressing against his thigh, and now the dwenda's hands on him.

"It's no time at all," the voice told him in a whisper. "I am time here, I am all the time you need."

And then the cool mouth fastened on his, levered his lips apart once again, lozenges of light and dark seemed to slide across and through him, and then the whole world went over sideways in sparks, like a tabletop candelabra swiped flat amid the laden plates of a feast abandoned in the gloom and waiting for anyone with the inclination to come and plunder.

IF THE DAMP AIR WAS CHILLY, HE DIDN'T NOTICE AS HIS CLOTHES CAME off, as the dwenda's heated kisses bit their way down his neck and over his exposed chest, as impatient hands tugged down his breeches over boot tops, tore undergarments down to match, as the dwenda knelt and plunged the head of Ringil's cock into his mouth.

He gasped and flexed at the sudden heat of it, and then as the friction of teeth and tongue set in, he grabbed at the dwenda's shoulders, sank his fingers into its hair and twisted. A long moan forced its way up out of him, counterpointed by the small grunting noises the dwenda made as it pumped its lips up and down. A cool hand weighed his balls in their sack, and then one long finger split off from the grip and angled up into the whorl of his anus. From somewhere, the dwenda had conjured the slick wetness of spit or something like it onto the fingertip and Ringil felt himself opened and gently impaled with a sly controlling competence that made his heart turn over.

Stable boys in Gallows Water had never been like this.

And then, somehow, the dwenda took him softly to the floor and if the stone was cold under them, Ringil didn't notice that, either. He heaved up and stared down the length of his body, the tangled breeches and boots still not off, the dark form hunched and coiled over his legs and hips head-down like a feeding beast, and somewhere seemingly distant beyond vision, the delirious timed motions of mouth up and down, of the probing finger twisting in and out. The scent of the dwenda's body, that maddening mingle of spices and somewhere, the faintest hinted odor of shit in the air from his opened anus. And the mouth and the finger that went on and on, driving him forward, inches at a time, toward the precipice—

And threw him off.

Shuddering, hinging force as he came into the dwenda's sucking mouth, it stormed through him, it seemed to want to snap his spine. It hooked him up, then flung him back down on the stone, flapping and twitching and—he realized it with sudden, cold shock—laughing and bubbling out the words *oh no, no, no, no . . .*

It brought the first tears to his eyes he could remember since his youth, since the carnage of his first battlefield aftermath.

When he was done, when he lay there drained and hollowed out, and utterly still, he felt the dwenda unfasten itself from him, glide upward, and straddle his chest. It reached down and took hold of its own swollen cock by the shaft, rubbed the glans roughly against his cheek and across his face. The mingled-spice scent came with it, headily concentrated now. Ringil followed the soft dragging blows of the prick over his features, opened his mouth and made gentle biting motions after it with his lips. The dwenda hunched over him a little more. He thought it smiled in the gloom as it fed the glans into his mouth, but he couldn't be sure.

He reached up awkwardly past the body on his chest with his hands, found the skin-thin velvet of the shaft, and gently displaced the dwenda's fingers with his own. He tried to meet the dark, glimmer-touched eyes above his. He sucked and nipped, was about to go to work in earnest when the dwenda said something in a language he had never heard, and then it pulled clear of him.

"But I want—"

Pulled back down his body, perhaps grinning still.

Reached down with both hands and spread his legs, pushed them hard apart and up, hinging and folding them at the knees. Did something with its hands at the juncture between, the soft sound of spitting, and then there was pressure at his sphincter again, but harder now, thicker, more insistent than the finger had been. The dwenda reared up over his spread and hinged legs, working itself into place inch by remorseless inch, jaw working—he saw it in the dim light—talking to him in the same odd cadenced tongue as before. And he was helping, hugging his legs up and out to make way, thrusting up his hips, his own jaw tight on the repetition of *yes, yes, yes, yes* . . .

And the dwenda fell on him, brought its face down to within inches and grasped his skull with both hands and split his mouth with another kiss. The thrusting built, gathered a hungry, gulping momentum, and with it Ringil felt himself growing rock-hard once more, saw the dwenda feel it, too, saw a glinting grin in the gloom, and knew suddenly beyond question that what the dwenda had said to him was true, there was no time here, there need be none, none that meant anything at all beyond the surrender to this, all this, the thrusting, the pumping, the fucking, clenched jaw *yes, oh yes, oh fuck me yes, yes, yes* . . .

And the bonfire in them both now, sheeting through them, turning flesh incandescent with sensation and skin unbearably delicate, stretched to breaking—

And lost, to time and all that mattered in other places that were not this and were not here.

Lost.

THIS TIME, RINGIL WOKE TO HAZY DAWN LIGHT THROUGH NARROW windows, and small garden sounds beyond. He lay in silk sheets, balls and body muscles stung to a pleasant ache, the alkaline odor of his own body fluids mingled with something more spiced and nudging at the edge of his awareness, tugging a faint smile onto his lips. He grinned up at the architecture of the window arch, breathed in the garden air. There was a soft and easy familiarity to it all; it felt like a return to youth. He had one long moment of complete peace, too profound to permit the intrusion of conscious thought.

He smiled again, harder, and turned over.

Dawn.

Recollection slammed him upright amid the sheets.

Dawn. Fuck!

And then it was all gone, the peace and the unthinking bliss, taken jaggedly away from him like Jelim, like home, like the victory they all once thought they'd won.

He kicked himself clear of the silk that wrapped him up, cast about on the floor of the chamber for clothes.

Found them tidied and carefully folded on top of a wooden chest under the window instead.

The Ravensfriend propped casually against the wall nearby in its scabbard.

He stood and gaped at it. Outside the windows, birds made stupid, early-morning noises to counterpoint the sudden stillness. It felt, in some aching way, as if he already knew the room he was in.

What the fuck . . . ?

"Thought you'd have to fight your way out, did you?"

He spun about, one hand groping back after the weapon. The dwenda leaned in the arch of an entryway on the other side of the chamber, grinning, dressed. His hair was gathered back from his face, his arms folded over a doublet of black and sapphire-blue weave. His feet were booted in black to match; his breeches were no lighter, and they clung to the lines of his legs before they tucked in. He was not armed.

If you ignored the blank dark eyes, he might almost have been human.

Ringil made himself turn away from the empty gaze. He picked up and started to unfold his clothes.

"I have to go," he said, not quite firmly.

"No, you don't."

Ringil fumbled his way into his shirt. "You don't understand. I have an appointment. I'm going to be late."

"Ah, just like the estranged princess of fairy tale." A whip-crack snapping of fingers behind him, to jog memory that must, Shalak had always argued, stretch back through thousands upon thousands of years. "Now what's her name? You know, the one who loses track of time at the ball, the one who stays and dances all night, until the night wears thin, as thin as the soles of her shoes and then she finds—"

"You know." Underwear, breeches. Bending to pull them on, breath held tight. "I could probably do without the fucking fairy-tale jokes right now."

"All right." And the voice so suddenly close, the cold-water shock of it on his neck. Right behind him. He spun about and found the dwenda standing two feet away in the light from the window. "Try this. You're not going anywhere."

"Try and stop me."

"I already have. What time do you think it is really?"

Ringil met the Aldrain gaze and he saw the eyes glow, just as he'd known they would, with the rinsed-out rosy tints of the approaching sunrise. He felt the spike in his heart, felt how he sagged as the realization hit. The dwenda nodded.

"Dawn itself, properly speaking, has come and gone while you slept. You are out of time. They waited for you at Brillin Hill Fields a full half hour, as custom apparently dictates these days. Then your second, a man named Darby, stood in for you and was duly killed by your opponent. He gave a good account of himself, it seems, but was simply not well enough versed with a court sword to hold his own."

Ringil closed his eyes, bit his lip until he tasted blood. Behind his curtained-off vision he saw it, the little gathered knots of men on the open ground down by the fish pools. Gray sketched figures, not enough light yet to color them in. And the two men between, the back-and-forth shunt of the duel. He heard its miserly metallic tones on the cool air, the clink and scrape of the court sword blades. Saw Darby drawn in, wrong-sided, feinted out. Riposte—the grating blade goes home. Bright crimson on the graying pastel palette of a day that Darby now won't live to see.

How long did it take Iscon Kaad to find the opening? Was Darby sober, had he made that much effort for the man that might have been his commander once?

Ringil opened his eyes. Whatever the dwenda saw there, it didn't like much. It swayed back a fraction.

"Easy there."

"You knew. You fucking knew."

The dwenda nodded. "So did you. But you allowed yourself to forget."

Ringil wrenched his shirt straight. "You take me back. Back into the Aldrain marches, back before it happens. You—"

"I'm afraid that can't be done."

Through clenched teeth now. "You fucking take me back or—"

"Or what?" Abruptly the dwenda's arms whipped out. A grabbed handful of shirt, Ringil was jerked forward. A flat palm came at him like stone, slapped palm-first into his forehead, and suddenly he was on the floor, arms and legs robbed of anything resembling motive force. He flopped like a landed fish.

The dwenda stood over him, arms folded.

"*Ageless Realm* is a misnomer, you see," it said somberly. "We can swim to the shallows, yes; with practice we can step into places where time slows to a crawl, slows almost to a stopping point, even dances around itself in spirals. It's a matter of gradient relative to, well . . . never mind, it's not something you're equipped to understand. But however slow the crawl, we cannot actually *stop* time, and nor can we turn it back. What is done, cannot be undone. You will have to accept this as truth."

Ringil managed to get onto his front and force his knees under him. The room rocked and shifted around him, ice trickled down his limbs. He struggled for strength to push himself upright.

He heard the dwenda sigh.

"I was afraid it might come to this, Ringil Eskiath, but not so soon. We are none of us used to dealing with humans after so long. It's a constant learning experience."

A booted foot came out and gently shoved him over on his side. Getting up faded to a distant dream. Ringil summoned what breath he could.

"Who sent you?" he panted.

"I am not sent, as you put it." The dwenda knelt beside him. "But you do have your petitioners for my favor. There are those, it seems, who have no wish to see your grim but still rather beautiful face get slashed to ribbons in squabbles of petty honor."

He raised his hand again, palm-down, fingers lightly flexed. The gesture blocked light from Ringil's eyes.

"Wait, *wait.*"

It took Ringil a moment to understand that the dwenda had obeyed.

He could not read the sudden flurry of expression that chased across the unhuman face as it hung there. He thought he saw impatience, but impatience with whom it was hard to tell.

"Well?"

"Tell me." Faintly. Ringil's voice was almost emptied out, no stronger now than his limbs. "One thing, I need to know. It's important."

The palm hovered. "Yes?"

"What's your name? We fucked all night, and I never asked."

Another hesitation, but finally it gave way to a curious smile. "Very well. You may call me Seethlaw, if that will serve."

"Oh, it will." And now Ringil smiled as well. "It will."

Silence dripped between them. The dwenda's palm stayed where it was.

"You mind telling me why now you suddenly want to know my name?" it asked him finally.

Ringil nodded weakly. Summoned some last fragments of breath and made his lips move.

"Simple enough," he whispered. "A cheap fuck doesn't need to have a name. But I like to know what to call the men I'm going to kill."

Then the dwenda's hand came down, touched his face, lifted gently off again. It seemed to lift consciousness away from him as well, like a delicate mask he'd been wearing and hadn't noticed until now.

The last thing he saw, as his own vision inked out, was the dwenda's gaze as it raised its head to face the windows; the featureless empty eyes, now washed the color of blood by the rising sun.

S he went up to the palace at first light.

Earlier would have invited arrest. While the lower echelons of palace life—the lighting of stoves, the cleaning of acres of marble flooring—got under way well before dawn, courtiers did not present themselves before breakfast. It was a rule of thumb with strong precedent. Two years ago, a provincial governor had made the mistake of bringing his concerns before Jhiral while the Emperor was still in bed. The occasion was a local revolt by resettled eastern nomads who'd jumped their reservation and reverted to banditry against the trade caravans, so there was some justification for the urgency, at least in the eyes of the governor's special envoy, who rode up to the main gate at the head of a cavalry squad just as the sun was rising, and started yelling for the Emperor's immediate attention.

He got it. Jhiral had him thrown in jail for a week, along with his men, summary sanction for lack of respect before the imperial throne. Protests by senior advisers at court were in vain; the punishment stood. By the time the man was brought into the imperial presence and formally reprimanded, the revolt had more or less sputtered out, and the issue was moot. Proving, Jhiral observed drily, that there'd been nothing to get so worked up about in the first place. He took a rhetorical turn about the throne room to drive the point home, gesturing, pitching his voice for effect in the vaulted space. *These are not the days of my father's reign, my friends. Not the days of bitter warfare and privation, however much various of my father's faithful friends and advisers in that struggle appear, inexplicably, to wish otherwise. Give it a rest, gentlemen. We are no longer at war, we face no implacable enemies or unhuman threats. There is no need for panic-stricken counsel and steely decision before the dawn comes up. Our Empire is prosperous and at peace. Our difficulties in these times are small and undramatic, admitting of equally small-scale solutions, which, though they may offer scant chance of wild glory, should nonetheless be effective. I, for one, welcome that change. It has been given to us to* enjoy *the legacy of all those who sacrificed for us—not to imitate their suffering. I am glad and grateful for that fact, as I am grateful for their sacrifices, and I would have* thought *that those of you who went through the horror of the war with my family would feel the same.*

Does anybody here not *feel the same?*

Eloquent silence in the gathered ranks of the court. Somewhere off to the right, someone cleared his throat, then evidently thought better of speaking up. The sound turned magically into a cough. Jhiral heard it, knew what it meant, and smiled. He waited the echoes out, then clapped his hands.

Excellent. I am, as ever, indebted to you all for your loyal support. Now—next order of business, and please tell me it's a simple budget for city sewer repairs.

The laughter was largely sycophantic, but Archeth had found her mouth stretching to echo it anyway. Privately, though she commiserated with some of her friends from the old guard, she felt there was a lot in what Jhiral said. She knew the provincial governor who'd sent the emissary, and didn't hold him in much regard. Quite conceivably, he'd overreacted to a situation a shrewder man could have handled without rising from his desk. The revolt very likely could have been extinguished with relatively little fuss—could perhaps even have been avoided altogether, with a little intelligent foresight. You kept your finger on the pulse, you picked up the warning signals well before matters reached boiling point. You made a few examples, you made a few concessions, nine times out of ten the combination paid off. She'd done it herself enough times in the past, when Akal was still on the throne.

Panic and overreaction—the late response of fools.

Now, waiting in an antechamber for Jhiral to get out of bed, going over what the Helmsmen had told her, she couldn't be sure if, sleepless and churned up and raw from the krin, she wasn't giving in to a similar fool's impulse herself.

But:

The dwenda are gone, Archeth. Thousands of years ago. They fled the parameters of this world when they couldn't defeat us.

Apparently, they're back.

One of the Helmsman's unnerving silences. Then, severely:

That's really not funny. The dwenda are not something you joke about, daughter of Flaradnam.

I'm not trying to be funny, Angfal. I've got better things to do with my time than come down here and tell you jokes.

You certainly have. To start with—if you're right and the dwenda really have returned, now, with the Kiriath gone—then you have graves to dig. About a hundred thousand ought to do it—you might want to get started ahead of time.

"The Emperor will see you now."

She glanced up and saw the smirk on the chamberlain's face. She supposed there weren't a lot of courtiers receiving audience in Jhiral's bedchamber. It begged a rather obvious question, and court gossip would doubtless provide a dozen different salacious answers by lunchtime.

"You can wipe that fucking grin off your face," she told him as she got up. "Or I'll come back and cut it off for you."

The smirk vanished as if dragged downward off the man's visage with a claw. He shrank from her as she passed. The krin made her glad.

Better get ahold of that temper, Archidi. His radiance Jhiral Khimran II won't bully as easily as his servants.

She stepped through into a room that reeked of sex.

The imperial bedchamber faced east by careful design and had floor-to-ceiling windows for the view. The sun flooded in, struck deep into the back of the room, and gilded what it touched—the drapes on the huge four-poster bed, the rumpled covers, and the three tousle-haired sleeping forms that lay amid them. Archeth registered the curves, made herself look carefully away.

"Archeth! Good morning!" Jhiral was over by the wood-paneled partions on the far side of the room, wrapped in a long silk robe and picking at an extravagant spread of breakfast platters set out on three separate tables. He turned to face her, put a quail's egg into his mouth and chewed vigorously. Lifted a wagging finger. "You know, when I said I'd hold you to your promise of rapid progress, I didn't intend you to take it quite *this* hard. Sometime this afternoon would have been fine."

She bowed. "I must apologize for intruding on your rest so early, my lord, but—"

Jhiral waved it away, still chewing. "No, it's fine. Educational." He swallowed and gestured at the breakfast spread. "Some of this stuff, it's the first time I've ever tasted it when it's still hot. So what's the news? Did you have a good night in the sheets with my little gift?"

"Your generosity . . . overwhelms me, my lord. I have not yet actually been to bed."

"What a pity." Jhiral picked up an apple and bit into it. His eyes met hers across the top of the fruit, and the look in them was suddenly hard and predatory. He gouged the chunk of fruit loose with his teeth, chomped it down, and wiped his mouth on the back of his hand. "I'd rather hoped we could compare notes, actually. Maybe even share young Ishgrim's training between us."

"My lord, the reaction of the Helmsmen to my news about the dwenda incursion has been . . . disturbing."

"Yes. Well, you certainly look disturbed." Jhiral stared down at the bitten apple for a moment, then tossed it back among the platters on the middle table. "Oh, very well then. You'd better come through."

He forced the slides of the partition apart at the join and walked through into the chamber beyond. There was a surfeit of sunlight in here as well, though diluted down and tinged in various colors by stained-glass panels set into the lower half of each window and depicting scenes of historic triumph from imperial history. Vibrant little smears of pink and blue lay across the wooden floor and paneled walls, and the green leather surface of a large writing desk in one corner. Armchairs were set up at the back of the room around another, low table covered to match the desk.

"Sit." Jhiral gestured her to a chair and took the one opposite. He covered a leonine yawn with one hand, sank back in the arms of the chair, put a slippered foot on the edge of the low table, and steepled his fingers. The robe split and gave her a narrow view of an impressive—if you liked that sort of thing—prick and balls. She couldn't tell if it was deliberate. "So—disturbing. In what way?"

Archeth hesitated. "I think the Helmsmen are afraid, my lord."

"Afraid." Jhiral coughed up a short, uncertain laugh. He shifted in the chair and straightened his robe. "Come on. They don't understand things like fear. You told me yourself, they aren't anything like human. Anyway, suddenly you're talking in plural here? How many Helmsmen have you actually spoken to?"

"Two, my lord. Angfal, who is installed in the study in my home, and Kalaman in the fireship *Toward the Candle of Vigil Maintained* at the Kiriath Museum. Their attitudes are somewhat different, Kalaman is more pragmatic, less inclined to drama, but their basic responses are the same. Both give extensive warnings about what the dwenda are capable of; both are of the opinion that if these creatures are returning to this world, then the results will be catastrophic."

"Hmm." Jhiral stroked at his chin. He seemed to have been doing some thinking of his own since the night before. "Catastrophic for *whom*, though? The way you've explained it, this is a northern thing, this dwenda mythology. Is it possible these creatures might confine their depredations to that part of the world?"

"They came to Khangset, my lord."

"Yes, in response to either the prayers and idolatry of a northerner or the presence of a type of stone found only in the north."

"Found *mostly* in the north, my lord." Holding down a tremor of alarm, because she could see where this was going. "Glirsht deposits are to be found in various parts of the Empire as well."

Jhiral gave her a shrewd look. "But you don't really believe it's the glirsht itself, do you, Archeth? If the dwenda use this stuff as a beaconing device, it would need to be shaped in some way, crafted to its purpose. The way our little friend from Khangset crafted her idol."

"I don't believe th—"

"Don't interrupt your Emperor when he's thinking aloud, Archeth. It's rude."

She swallowed. "My apologies."

"Oh, accepted. Accepted." A languid gesture. "Now look; our trade ships don't just steer down the coast by any old fire they happen to see on a clifftop, any piece of brightly colored junk floating in the water that they might pass. They look for lighthouses and marker buoys. The dwenda are going to be the same—they're going to be looking for a specific form of this rock, something shaped. Something prepared by their acolytes, by those who worship them."

Got to nip this in the bud, Archidi. He'll do it, this little shit trying to fill his father's boots, he'll sign an order to get it done without a second thought, and you'll watch the refugee columns form from horizon to horizon all over again . . .

"The dwenda have been gone for several thousand years, my lord." Voice as smooth as lack of sleep and krinzanz would let it get. "I think it's safe to say that any *acolytes* they may once have had among humans are now dead. And this woman Elith certainly did not herself craft the idol she owns. She refers to it as an heirloom of her clan, and it certainly has the look of something many centuries old."

"But perhaps, Archeth," the Emperor said softly, "Elith herself is many centuries old, as well. Did you think of that? Perhaps she's been kept alive by the sorceries of her dwenda masters, gifted with eternal youth in return for her services. Perhaps she is a witch. Or even, a creature crafted from stone and given sorcerous life."

Archeth sat as if poised on the edge of the An-Monal crater. Lives spun past in her head, held in a balance whose mechanism she had only the slightest influence over. She saw Elith, screaming her lungs out on the rack or pincered apart, opened and probed with red-hot steel. Thousands like her, driven from their homes, no food or water beyond what they could carry, starving on the roads, brutalized and extorted of what little they still owned by the soldiery supposed to watch over them.

She was accustomed to reading Jhiral's face, but could make nothing of the bland expression he wore now.

"Do *you* believe that, my lord?" she asked with knife-edge caution. "That this woman is a . . . a witch? Or some kind of golem even?"

The Emperor studied his hands, gazed critically at his manicure for a few moments before he would meet Archeth's eyes. He sighed.

"Oh, I suppose not. Not really, no."

"Then—"

A sudden jabbing finger. "But—and I told you before about interrupting me, *God fuck it, Archeth*—what I *am* beginning to think is that maybe my father's policy of resettlement after the war was a mistake. It wouldn't be the first mistake he made, would it? You remember that god-awful mess in Vanbyr. So, the way I see it, we've got tens of thousands of these people living among us, refusing to convert, most of them, turning their backs on the civilized benefits the Empire offers, going on with their idolatry and who knows what else besides. I don't want to start sounding like that little twat Menkarak, but if permitting the kind of religious freedom we do is going to bring down some millennia-old curse on us all, well, then maybe we need to rethink our values. And maybe we don't want these people inside our borders after all."

She sat and waited.

"Well?" he snapped.

"Do I have your majesty's permission to speak?"

"Oh, Mother of the fucking Revelation, Archeth, don't *sulk*! Yes, speak. Speak. It's what I pay you for, isn't it?"

She marshaled her words with care. She'd come to the palace with the avowed intention of scaring the shit out of Jhiral. Now she wasn't so sure it was a good idea.

"My lord, according to the Helmsmen, the dwenda were a race with mastery of worlds that lie parallel to our own, worlds that in some way seem to occupy almost the same space as ours, that are no farther away than your bedchamber is from where we sit now. I can't say I understand how this is supposed to work, but it does correspond to some of the common Aldrain legends in the north, which claim that certain places are inhabited by otherworldly creatures in a way that is hidden from human eyes. An isolated mountain crag becomes a fairy-tale castle at certain hours of the night, or in the midst of a powerful lightning storm; you can knock on a forest oak and it will be opened to you like a gate, but only on certain nights of the year; and so forth. I find in these stories an echo of the Kiriath tales of voyaging here from another world, which is why I am inclined to take them seriously, but there is one major difference. My people were forced to seek out the deepest, hottest, most pressurized places in the bowels of the earth before they could find a way to pass between worlds." She paused, measured her tone again before she plunged on. "The dwenda, it seems, can effect this passage anywhere they choose. They can enter this world at will, at any given point."

Her words seemed to evaporate into the quiet. Small, domestic sounds seeped in from elsewhere in the palace. Banging of doors, voices giving instructions. Behind the wall, water gurgled in pipes. The Emperor looked at his hands again.

"You're saying this isn't just a northern problem, then," he muttered.

"I'm saying, my lord, that until we have a clear idea of what the dwenda want, geography as we understand it is largely meaningless. These creatures could show up anywhere from the Demlarashan wastes to the palace gardens right here in Yhelteth. We simply do not know."

Jhiral grunted. "And this stone idol? You seemed pretty fucking convinced last night that it was the key to the incursion. Changed your mind all of a sudden?"

"No, my lord. I still believe it is important. But it's the first of its kind that I've ever seen." *Though both Angfal and Kalaman recognized it from my description and nearly shit rivets when they did. But you don't need to know that right now, my lord.* "Elith brought it with her when she was resettled, but she was already at that point a deeply disturbed woman. It is heavy, bulky, and far from attractive in aspect. I think it's safe to say such things are not a common possession of Naomic peoples, either here or in the north. A few might exist, here or there, but—"

"We could always institute a search. House-to-house, immigrant districts throughout the Empire."

Hoiran's fucking balls. "We *could* do that, my lord, but I am not convinced that it would be an efficient use of manpower. In fact, I have an equally direct but somewhat smaller-scale plan of action that perhaps my lord would—"

"Yes, all right." Jhiral gestured wearily. "Don't sugarcoat it to death. I already guessed you wouldn't have come all the way up here at this time of day unless you wanted something. Come on then, let's hear your bright idea."

It felt like stepping off a bobbing coracle and onto a slippery but solid jetty. Archeth tried not to let her relief show. Carefully, then, very carefully:

"The woman Elith and the idol she brought with her are originally from Ennishmin, more precisely from the eastern fringes of that province."

The imperial lip curled. "Yes, that's a godforsaken corner of the world. You'd think she'd have been glad to get south to some decent weather."

"Uhm—yes, my lord."

"That was a joke, Archeth."

"Yes, my lord." She patched together a smile. "Ennishmin is not blessed with ideal weather."

The look in Jhiral's eyes hardened. "Don't fucking humor me, woman. You really think I'd have put up with your drug-soaked insubordination and superior airs this long if I didn't value you for something other than sycophancy? Revelation knows, I get enough of that from the rest of the court. You, Archeth, I trust to tell me the truth, even if it upsets me. So get on with it. Upset me, if that's what you're planning to do. What about Ennishmin?"

"Yes, my lord." The krin was building a shrill desire to scream in his face. She held it down, barely. "When I mentioned the origins of the idol to the Helmsmen, both of them independently concluded that the

Khangset incursion was probably a navigation error on the part of the dwenda. That they had intended to arrive in the east of Ennishmin and the relocation of the idol threw them off. Imagine trying to follow a map that's thousands of years old. It would be easy enough to make mistakes."

"So these creatures are not perfect, then. Not angelic essences condensed to flesh, the way the Revelation promises. I suppose that's some relief."

"They are very far from perfect, my lord. What the Helmsmen told me suggests a wildly impulsive nature, barely governed by the wisdom they must have accumulated over a million or more years of unchanging existence. And—" She hesitated, because even remembering this next piece of the puzzle still sent a chill scrabbling up her spine. "According to Angfal, they may not even be sane, not as we would understand the concept."

Jhiral frowned. "I've heard that said about outlanders and enemies before, and I don't generally trust it. Just too bloody convenient, the quick and easy way to deal with difference. *Oh, they're not like us, they're insane.* It saves you having to think too much. They said the Majak were insane when we first ran into them, said they were semi-human beasts that howled and ate human flesh, and it turned out they were just a lot tougher than us on the battlefield. Come on, Archeth, I've heard it said on occasion that *your* people were insane by human standards."

"Yes, my lord. Which is precisely Angfal's point. The mental . . . changes . . . that the Kiriath went through on their voyage here appear to have been the result of a single passage through the spaces between worlds, a single exposure. The dwenda, it seems, *live* in these spaces, inhabit them as a matter of course. I don't like to think what that must have done to their sanity. I'm quite certain a human could not survive it undamaged."

Jhiral sat and thought about it for a while. He rested his arm on the chair, put his chin on a loosely curled fist, and stared at Archeth as if hoping she'd go away. He sighed.

"So you're telling me—you seriously believe this, Archeth—that these immensely powerful, possibly insane beings have some special interest in Ennishmin." The coughed-up laugh again, the throwaway gesture. "Well, I mean, they'd *have to* be insane, wouldn't they? A shit-hole northern province that grows turnips or hunts swamp snakes for a living, and barely makes its tax bill each year. What possible earthly use is it going to *be* to them?"

"The Helmsmen have an explanation of sorts, my lord. It seems what is now eastern Ennishmin was once the site of a decisive battle against the dwenda. The swamps at the eastern end of the province are apparently not wholly natural. According to Angfal, they were originally created by some cataclysmic weapon the Kiriath deployed there. I wonder if that weapon didn't have some effect on the barriers between worlds, perhaps make them easier to breach than elsewhere. Stories of hauntings and apparitions apparently persist in the local culture, and there's some kind of trade in so-called Aldrain artifacts, things retrieved from the swamps that are reckoned to have magical powers."

Jhiral snorted. Archeth nodded a measured dose of agreement.

"Yes, it's improbable, I agree. In fact, these artifacts are probably mostly bits and pieces left behind by the Kiriath armies in the past. But there may be an element of truth to the tales as well. In the markets and specialist shops in Trelayne, where Aldrain lore is an affectation among the rich, I quite often saw objects that didn't appear to be of human manufacture, but were not reminiscent of anything my people might build, either."

"You're saying the dwenda have come back to the site of an old defeat. What for, revenge?" Jhiral shook his head. He even smiled, but she thought there was an edge of bitterness on it. "Well, they've come a little late for that. Perhaps someone should go up there and tell them they just missed their ancient enemies on the way out the door at An-Monal. Maybe then they'll leave us alone."

"Or maybe not, my lord. The war against the dwenda was apparently an alliance of Kiriath and human, in much the same way as the war against the Scaled Folk. If your enemy has fled but his dogs remain guarding the hearth, what will you do with those dogs?"

Jhiral nodded. It was logic he understood.

"So you want to go to Ennishmin. Is that it?"

"I think leading an expeditionary force there might be advisable. A thousand men, say, with engineering support, could—"

"*A thousand men?*" Jhiral seemed genuinely aghast. "Where exactly do you think I'm going to snap my fingers and get a thousand men from? This isn't wartime, you know."

"No, my lord. Not yet, it isn't."

"Oh, that's a ridiculous thing to say." The Emperor surged to his feet, stormed to the window, and stood staring out. Came back. "And— look—even if it's not, Archeth, even if this is the prelude to some kind of conflict—the attack came from Khangset, from the west and from the ocean. You're asking me to commit a major force twelve hundred miles away on a completely different frontier, all staked on not much more than some mumblings from senile machinery and a theory you haven't slept on yet."

"My lord, I realize—"

"Well, I don't think you do, Archeth." His voice trod hers down. "I don't think you've noticed, in the depths of your drugged-up self-pity and obsession, that we're trying to run an Empire here. Currently, we've got the Trelayne League stamping their collective feet and making angry diplomatic noises about trade restriction again—those motherfuckers certainly forgot pretty fucking fast who kept them afloat during the war—and by all accounts they're building a new navy into the bargain. We've got an upsurge in piracy along the southern coast, some kind of horseshit religious schism going on at Demlarashan that'll probably need riot control before the end of the year. And on top of that I have provincial governors marching into my throne room every fucking month like clockwork to whinge at me about supply lines and banditry and public health crises, but not one single one of them ever wants to come up with the taxes we'd need to solve those problems. The long and the short of it is, Archeth, I can't fucking give you your thousand men, because I don't fucking have them to spare."

AND THAT WAS THAT.

Archeth collected her horse and wended her way back down into the city, muttering to herself and grinding her teeth; clear indications—*as if*

I fucking needed them—that she'd overdone the krinzanz. The strengthening midmorning sun stung her eyes, layered her shoulders with the promised heat of the day to come. Worst of all was the knowledge within her that Jhiral had a point. The Empire didn't have a lot of excess military capacity. The war dead numbered in the tens of thousands, and the devastation wrought by the Scaled Folk was massive. Across the whole imperial domain, the population was only just starting to get back on its breeding feet. Most farms and manufactures were still desperately short of labor. The levies had been cut back as soon as a workable peace and a stable frontier could be hammered out with Trelayne, not because the Empire was weary of war, but because Akal's economic advisers had bluntly told him that if he didn't slacken the demand for soldiers soon, his harvests would rot in the fields and his subjects would starve. It was that as much as anything else that brought imperial ambitions in the northwest to an abrupt, conciliatory halt.

Bring me some evidence, Jhiral told her as she was leaving. *Something solid. I'll put the army back on a war footing if I have to, but I won't do it for rumor and conjecture and a few trinkets you once saw in a shop window in Trelayne.*

Then give me a reduced force, she'd pleaded. *A few hundred. Let me—*

No. I'm sorry, Archeth. He did genuinely seem to be. *Quite apart from anything else, I need you here. If there is a crisis, I need to be able to point you at it pretty fucking fast, and I can't do that if you've gone haring off to the wrong end of the Empire.*

Perhaps he was even right. Degenerate lifestyle aside, he wasn't a stupid man.

She thought abruptly of Ishgrim's pale curves, thought about owning them the way Jhiral had, the way he owned the three sleeping girls in his bed now. Owning the belief, no not even that, owning the *knowledge* that this was flesh you had a right to use like any other purchased thing you might have in the house. Like the flesh of the fruit you kept in the larder, the leather of a jerkin you liked to wear.

Perhaps you're the stupid one, Archidi. Ever think of that?

She dismounted into the sunlit quiet of the courtyard, beset by her own murmuring, circling thoughts. No sign of the stable boy. Well, he wasn't the sharpest pin in the box, but still, he should have heard

Idrashan's hooves on the cobbles when she rode in. She glanced sourly toward the stables, felt a spike of krin-driven anger, and tamped it back down with great care. *You don't take it out on the servants,* Flaradnam had told her when she was about six, and it stuck. She led Idrashan over to the hitching rail by the stables, looped the reins there, and went to look for Kefanin.

Found him.

Bloodied and crawling on hands and knees, just inside the main door. He'd heard her come in, was trying to get up. The blood made a darkened, matted mass of his hair on one whole side of his head. It dripped off his face onto the flagstones, spotted them in a line where he'd crawled.

She stopped dead, rigid with shock.

"Kef? *Kef?*"

Kefanin looked up at her, mouth working, making the repeated silent gape of a gaffed fish. She dropped to her knees at his side, gathered him up, and got his mouth close to her ear. She felt the blood smear on her cheek.

"I'm sorry, milady," he uttered, voice clicking and breathless, barely audible. "We tried to stop them. But they took her."

CHAPTER 25

For Ringil, the days that followed were like fever dreams from some battlefield injury that wouldn't heal.

He couldn't be sure how much of it Seethlaw was inducing for his own purposes and how much was just a levy-standard human reaction to time spent in the Aldrain marches. Either way, it was pretty horrible. Landscapes and interiors he thought were real would suddenly melt without warning, collapse around him like walls of candlewax bowing to the flame; worse still, behind them was a radiance that glimmered coldly like bandlight on distant water, and a sense of exposure to the void that made him want to curl up and cry. Figures came and went who could not possibly be there, stooped close to him and bestowed cryptic fragments of wisdom on him, each with the chilly intimacy of serpents hissing in his ear. Some of them he knew; others brought with them a nightmarish half familiarity that said he *ought* to know them, maybe *would have* known them if his life had only turned out fractionally different. They at any rate affected to know him, and the dream logic of their assumption was the thing he came to dread most, because he was tolerably sure he could feel aspects of himself ebbing away or shifting in response.

If it's true, Shalak pontificated, one warm spring evening in the garden behind the shop, *if it's really a fact that the Aldrain realms stand outside time, or at least in the shallow surf on time's shores, then the constraints of time aren't going to apply to anything that goes on there. You think about that for a moment. Never mind all that old marsh-shit about young men seduced by Aldrain maids into spending a single night with them and going home the next day to find forty years have passed. That's the least of it. A lack of time presupposes a lack of limits on what* can *happen at any given point as well. You'd be living inside a million different possibilities all at once. Imagine the will it would take to survive that. Your average peasant human is just going to go screaming insane.*

You think about that, he repeated, and leaned in close to whisper. *Give us a kiss, Gil.*

Ringil flinched. Shalak wavered and went away. So did a large chunk of the garden behind him. Flaradnam stepped through the blurry space it left, seated himself opposite as if it were the most natural thing in the world.

Thing is, Gil, if I'd taken that attitude at Gallows Gap, where would we be now? I'd never have made it back in one piece.

What attitude? Ringil shook his head numbly, stared back at the seamed anthracite features. *You didn't* make it back, *'Nam. You never got to Gallows Gap in the first place. You died on the surgeon's table.*

Flaradnam pulled a face, as if he'd just been told a joke in very poor taste. *Oh come on. So who led the charge at the Gap, if it wasn't me?*

I did.

You?

Yes! Me! Shouting now. *You were fucking dead, 'Nam. We left your body for the lizards.*

Gil, what's the matter with you? You're not well.

And so on.

"DO YOU EVER GET USED TO IT?" HE ASKED SEETHLAW ACROSS A SOFTLY snapping campfire in a forest he didn't remember walking into. Thick green scent of pine needles mingled with the smoke. He was shivering, but not with cold. "How long does it take?"

The dwenda cocked his head. "Get used to what?"

"Oh, what do you think? The ghosts, the visitors I'm getting. And don't tell me you don't fucking see them."

Seethlaw nodded, more to himself than to the human he faced. "No, you're correct. I do see them. But not as you do. They are not my alternatives, they mean nothing to me. I see a faint gathering of motion around you, that's all. Like a fog. It's always that way with humans."

"Yeah, well there's no fucking fog around you," Ringil snapped. "How long before I can learn to do that?"

"Longer than you have, I suspect." The dwenda stared into the fire, and its light turned his eyes incandescent. "No human has managed it to my knowledge, except maybe . . . well, but he was not truly human anyway."

"Who wasn't?"

"It no longer matters." Seethlaw looked up and smiled sadly. "You ask how long. In all honesty, I wouldn't know. I was born to it, we all were. Our young flicker in and out of the gray places from birth."

Later, they walked in single file along a worn footpath through the trees and up across the shoulder of the hill. Ringil followed the broad-shouldered figure of the dwenda without question, something that seemed wrong to him, but in some oddly shaped way he could not define. A pale but strengthening glow seeped in between the jagged barked trunks, brought the ground underfoot into clearer view, but it never really got light.

"Where are we going?" he asked Seethlaw's back.

"Where you wanted to go." The voice drifted to him over the dwenda's shoulder. Seethlaw did not turn around or slacken his pace. "I'm going to fulfill your obligations for you."

"And why would you do that?"

A lewd chuckle that put twinges through Ringil's sweetly aching groin. "You have a short memory, Ringil Angeleyes."

"Lucky I've got a fucking memory at all," Ringil muttered. "Place like this."

And he shivered again.

BACK IN THE GARDEN, THERE WAS A GRIZZLED SOLDIER IN IMPERIAL cavalry rig who said he knew him and talked incessantly about campaigns in the desert Ringil had never been a part of.

Not like we didn't warn old Ershnar Kal not to quit the outcrops that time, is it? Fucking coast huggers, got no clue how to fight a desert war. Not much surprise the scale faces took them apart before we got back. You remember what they did to Kal's ribs, the way they left him?

No, I don't. Slightly desperate, because the horrors of a screaming, sun-seared image he had never seen were beginning to trickle into his head. *Like I told you, I was never fucking there.*

Gave me nightmares for months, that. The imperial seemed to be ignoring his protests. But perhaps he had to, perhaps they all had to, the same way Ringil had to resist each apparition's false assumptions about him, in order to go on existing at all. *Still get it sometimes when it's a tough summer, still wake up sweating and screaming, dreaming about the scale faces coming up out of the sand all around us. You ever have dreams like that?*

The Scaled Folk came from the sea, Ringil told him firmly. *They were never in the desert. They came out of the western ocean and we threw them back into it. That's what I remember, that's what fucking happened. And I don't know who the fuck you are, either.*

Surprised hurt in the soldier's eyes. Ringil thought of Darby's face when he offered him the money, thought of how he must have looked when Iscon Kaad skewered him. He dropped his gaze, ashamed.

"You got to hang on, Gil," Grace-of-Heaven said uncomfortably. The unknown soldier was gone, but the garden remained. "It's for the best."

"Yeah?" Ringil slurred. "Whose fucking best is that then?"

"No one wants you hurt."

"Fucking trade-up piece of shit. With your house in the Glades."

"Oh, I see. That's reserved for the Eskiaths of this world, is it? I guess I was just supposed to stay colorful for you here in the slums."

Ringil summoned a defensive sneer. "What's the matter, Grace? You want to be like me? You're trying way too hard."

Milacar turned away. Ringil waited for him to dissolve like the soldier, then discovered he wanted him back after all.

"I'm sorry about Girsh," he called. "But I think Eril had time to get away. I think he made it."

Grace-of-Heaven gestured impatiently—fast, angry motion, face still turned away. He would not look back or meet Ringil's eye.

THEY CAME OUT OF THE CAVERNOUS DARKNESS AND PICKED THEIR WAY over a litter of massive granite boulders embedded in smooth white sand. Ringil couldn't tell how long they'd been walking; the garden was the last thing he remembered clearly, and before that, less clearly, the forest path. Now, overhead, the rough, climbing roof of the sea cave they'd just emerged from made a jagged upper frame for his view down the beach to the surf. Above the sea, the night sky showed a handful of stars and—

Ringil slammed to a halt. "What the *fuck* is that?"

Seethlaw paused between two boulders, spared a brief sideways glance. "That's the moon."

Ringil stared at the softly glowing dirty-yellow disk that sat fatly just above the line of the horizon, the darker patches like stains across its radiance.

"It's like the sun," he murmured. "But it's so *old*, look at it. Like it's almost used up. Is that why the light's so weak here?"

"No."

"Is it the Sky Home the Majak talk about?"

A note of impatience crept into the dwenda's voice. "No, it's not. Now keep close. This isn't wholly our territory."

"What do you . . . ?" Ringil's voice faded out.

There were figures in the surf.

At first he thought they might be statues or just approximately human-looking rocks for all the movement they showed. But then they did move, and Ringil felt a cool gust of fear up his spine at the sudden change. They were some twenty yards distant, and the light was uncertain, but he thought they had breasts, huge luminous eyes, and circular lamprey-like mouths.

"Might help if I had a weapon," he hissed at Seethlaw's back.

"You do," said the dwenda absently. "Your sword is on your back and that grubby little reptile tooth you're so handy with is in your belt. Much good they'll do you if this goes bad."

Ringil clapped a hand to his shoulder, found the strap of his scabbard hung there, the pommel of the Ravensfriend in place and within reach. He would have sworn only moments ago that he had not felt the weight.

"Don't touch it." There was a taut warning in Seethlaw's tone. "Just smile at the akyia, stay away from the water's edge, and keep on walking. Chances are they'll leave us alone."

He led the way out around a tumbled pile of granite blocks. The smooth pale sand was soggy underfoot now, and the surf was closer. The figures in the water shifted about, and one or two of them disappeared beneath the waves, but otherwise they seemed content simply to watch their visitors go past.

"They're not armed," Ringil pointed out.

"No, they're not. They don't need to be."

Along the gently shelving beach, in and out among the half-buried boulders and tilted blocks of stone. Light from the feebly glowing phantom sun made the rocks into black silhouettes against the sand. Now Ringil saw that the—he groped for the name Seethlaw had given them—*the akyia* were keeping pace, diving beneath the surface in sequence, a handful at a time, coming up twenty or thirty yards farther along and waiting for the rest of their companions to catch up. A chittering, sucking noise seemed to come and go faintly on the wind, gusting between the sound of the waves.

Seethlaw stopped and cocked his head to listen. Ringil thought a smile touched the corners of his mouth.

"What's so funny?"

"They're talking about you."

"Yeah, right."

Now their path apparently took them away from the shoreline again. The cavernous overhang of the sea cave had given way to sections where the cliffs above had collapsed altogether into mounds of gigantic rubble. Seethlaw led him in among it all, up through a narrow ravine between drunkenly angled blocks each the size of an upended imperial coach. They began to climb away from the sea. Ringil touched his hand briefly to the pommel of the Ravensfriend again.

"When did you give me the sword back?"

"You've had it from the start. You just weren't aware of the fact. It's a simple enough trick. That one, I *could* teach you."

"I've been carrying this thing all along? Even in the forest, when we camped?"

Seethlaw looked back at him, mouth quirked again. "We haven't reached the forest yet."

Ringil felt the strength run out of his legs like water. The rock wall to his left seemed suddenly to be toppling over on him.

"Then . . ."

"Shut up!"

Seethlaw had locked to a halt in the narrow space ahead of him, one closed fist raised, point-man-style, for silence and stillness. Very gently, without moving any other part of his body, he nodded upward. Ringil followed the direction of his gaze, and stopped breathing.

Fuck.

One of the akyia had not, it seemed, been content to stay in the ocean and watch them leave. It crouched on top of the right-hand block, two yards over their heads, poised lizard-like on arms splayed wide. Powerful-looking hands curled like claws into the fissures and features of the granite.

Ringil's hand flew to the pommel of the Ravensfriend. The akyia's head tilted, lamp-like eyes fixed on the movement.

"I said don't fucking touch that!"

For the first time since he'd known the dwenda, Ringil thought he heard genuine fear in Seethlaw's mellifluous voice. He dropped his hand back to his side. The akyia shifted its head again, met his eyes directly. It felt like a physical blow.

"Don't do anything stupid," said Seethlaw, very softly. "Don't move, don't do anything sudden at all."

Ringil swallowed and remembered to breathe. Held the creature's gaze, stared at it while his mind stumbled after comparisons.

The akyia looked like a harbor-end pimp's nightmare of woman-hood. Like something dreamed into being from the fumes of one too many flandrijn pipes and the constant, stealthy background slap of water against the pilings under the wharf. It was long-haired and full-breasted, pale-skinned in the light from the worn-out moon, and smoothly mus-cled from a lifetime in the water. But the hair straggled back from a skull built out of angles to make you scream. The eyes were the size of clenched fists, and for all that Ringil sensed a ferocious intelligence in their stare, they were set in sockets that had more in common with the skull of a lizard than anything human. Thickly ridged cheekbones forced them back and up, separating the upper features from a chinless lower face that seemed wholly prehensile, and currently held the circular lam-prey mouth aimed at the intruders like another massive eye.

It raised itself on the angle of the rock, scuttled down a couple of feet so it was hanging almost upside down on the wall above them. Ringil watched in fascination as two long, fin-fronded limbs coiled about in dark silhouette behind its head. He could hear them rasping as they sought purchase on the top of the block.

He cleared his throat.

"Just stay where you are," Seethlaw murmured. "If it wanted to hurt you, it already would have."

The akyia claw-walked its way down the wall of rock until it really was suspended upside down almost within touching distance of Ringil's head. It brought with it the salt waft of its body, the fresh blast of ocean water overlaid with more fragrant elements that were curiously similar to Seethlaw's scent. Its hair hung in its eyes like the strings of a wrecked fishing net until, with a motion that was startlingly feminine, it lifted one hand from the rock and swept the strands back behind its head. A nictitating membrane flickered up over the left eye, the circular lip of muscle around the mouth flexed in and out like an iris, and Ringil, staring up with a crick in his neck, saw concentric rings of teeth lift themselves briefly erect and then lie down in the throat again. He swallowed hard, fought down the terrible sensation of vulnerability that crawled in his face and scalp. It wasn't a stretch to assume the akyia could bite open his head as easily as a Yhelteth fisherman's machete taking the top off a coconut.

From deep in the thing's throat came the same glutinous chittering he'd heard earlier. It cocked its head back and forth between man and dwenda as if puzzled by the juxtaposition.

Out of the corner of his eye, Ringil thought he saw Seethlaw nod.

Then, rapid as a fleeing lizard, the akyia whipped about on the rock and was gone, back over the top in a succinct thrash of pale curves and coiling rear limbs. Ringil heard it scuttling away somewhere above them.

He sagged with relief, heart thunderous from the shock of that last sudden move.

Wished he'd been carrying some kind of weapon.

FUCKING, SOMEWHERE, ON COOL, DEW-DAMP GRASS IN A RING OF mist-shrouded standing stones, under stars he did not recognize. There was a flavor to it, a raw abandonment that stung him like a blow across the mouth—Seethlaw sprawled naked and ivory white on hands and knees before him, panting and snarling like a dog as Ringil crouched and thrust into him from behind, hands hooked in and hauling on the hinge of the dwenda's bent body where hips and thighs met. A shivery sense of exposure came and went through his flesh, as if the standing stones were silent but tautly aroused spectators who'd paid to watch what the two of them were doing. Ringil, feverish with lust, reached around for the dwenda's cock, found it stony hard and pulsing at the edge of climax.

The feel of it slipped the final leashes on his own control; he heard himself growling now, saw himself as if from a height outside the standing stones, hammering madly against Seethlaw's split buttocks, pumping the shaft in his hand until it kicked against his grip and the dwenda howled and clawed in the grass and Ringil came in his wake, as if in answer to the call.

And sagging, and collapsing forward, like a burning building coming down into the river, hand trapped beneath the dwenda's body as they went down, still frantically milking Seethlaw's cock into the wet grass, face pressed hard between the broad pale shoulders, laughing and sobbing and the tears again, icy this time, as they spilled onto the dwenda's skin.

ACROSS LOW HILLS UNDER A SKY THICKLY CARPETED WITH STARS, THERE was a road of black stone built for giants. Its surface was broken and weed-grown underfoot, but it extended for a full fifteen or twenty yards on either side of them. Walking it, from time to time they passed under pale stone bridges higher than the eastern gate at Trelayne. Off to the right, there were clusters of towers gathered on the flanks of the hills like sentinels. Ringil's eye kept sliding out to them. There was something wrong with the architecture. The towers had no features, were as basic and flat-edged as a small child's drawing of buildings, only taller, so tall they looked stretched beyond any humanly useful dimension.

"Does anything live in those?" he asked Seethlaw.

The dwenda cast a long glance at the towers. "Not if there's any other option," he said cryptically. "Not from choice."

"You're saying they're prisons?"

"You could argue that, yeah."

For a while, Jelim walked with them on the road, but it was a Jelim that Ringil had never known. The moody good looks were changed, weathered into something older and wiser than Jelim had ever had the chance to become. He looked, Ringil thought vaguely, like a successful young shipmaster, well traveled enough to have grown wise, still not aged enough to seem weary. He chatted away with coffeehouse aplomb, smiled often, and touched Ringil with an open confidence that belonged in some fantasy mural Grace-of-Heaven might commission to go with his bedroom ceiling.

And how's your father keeping these days?

Ringil stared at him. *You've got to be fucking kidding me.*

Saw him in the street a couple of months back. Jelim frowned, reaching for the misplaced memory. *Over in Tervinala, I think it was. But you know how it is, neither of us really had the time to stop and talk. Remember me to him, won't you? Tell him I miss all those fireside debates we used to get into with him.*

Sure. I'll do that.

At some point he couldn't clearly recall, Ringil had given up arguing with his ghosts.

Anyway, this time the ground felt a little more solid. The tenuous image of cheery evenings around the hearth with Gingren might creep in, but it stood no earthly chance of gaining any real foothold in his head.

Still, when Jelim leaned across and tousled his hair up, kissed him casually on the neck as the other Jelim always had—it hurt. And when the alternative left him, no farewell, just a slow fade, exclaiming *Come on, guys, let's up the pace a bit, shall we,* laughing and striding forward first into transparency and then into nothing—when that happened, something ached in Ringil the way it had when he first faced the dwenda and the blue storm it was wrapped in.

Later they camped under one of the huge pale bridges and Seethlaw summoned a fire out of an ornate, broad-bottomed flask he carried. Whatever was in the vessel burned with an eerie greenish flame, but it radiated a comforting wash of heat out of all proportion to the size of the thing. Ringil sat and watched shadows leap about on the pale stone support pillar behind the dwenda.

"When you summon the storm," he said slowly. "How does it feel?"

"Feel?" Seethlaw gave the impression he'd been dozing. "Why would it feel like anything? It's power, it's just . . . power. Potential, and the will to deploy it. That's all magic is in the end, you know."

"I thought there were supposed to be rules to magic."

"Did you?" The long mouth bent into a crooked smile. "Who told you that, then? Someone down at Strov market?"

Ringil ignored the sneer. "It doesn't hurt you? The storm?"

"No." A look of dawning comprehension. "Ah, that. The regret, is that what you're talking about? This sense of loss? Yes, he always talked about that, too. It's a mortal thing, as far as I can tell. The aspect storm is a warp in the fabric of every possible outcome the universe will allow. It gathers in the alternatives like a bride gathering in her gown. For a mortal, those alternatives are mostly paths they'll never take, things they'll never do. At some level, the organism seems to know that."

He?

It was a passing curiosity. There was too much else. The sadness Jelim had left behind still clung around Ringil's heart in creased folds.

"But you don't feel it that way," he said bitterly. "You're immortal, right?"

Seethlaw smiled gently. "So far."

And then his gaze drifted out to the left, eyes narrowed. Ringil heard footfalls across the black stone road behind him.

". . . Seethlaw . . ."

It was a female voice, fluid and melodic but slightly muffled; the dwenda's name was the only word Ringil could pick out, and even that was stretched and twisted almost beyond recognition. He turned his head and saw in the glow from the fire that a figure stood behind him. It was garbed in black, wore a long-sword across its back; its head was sleek and rounded. It took him a couple of seconds to realize he was looking at someone in the suit and helm Seethlaw had shown him under the city. Then the figure lifted a hand to the featureless bulb on its head and pushed back the glass visor. Framed in the space behind was an empty-eyed dwenda face.

A shudder scrawled its way across Ringil's shoulders—he could not prevent it. For just a moment in the eerie unreliable firelight under the bridge, the featureless dark of the newcomer's eyes seemed to merge with the black of the helmet, and the bone-white features took on the aspect of a thin, sculpted mask with empty eye holes, a helmet within a helmet, set on the shoulders of a suit of armor that must, instinct told him, contain nothing but the same emptiness that lay behind the eyes.

Seethlaw got up and ambled across to greet the new arrival. They took each other's hands loosely at waist height, oddly like two children readying themselves to play a game of slap-me-if-you-can. They talked back and forth for a few seconds in what appeared to be the same tongue the newcomer had used, but then Seethlaw gestured back at Ringil and broke into the antique dialect of Naomic he'd been speaking before.

". . . my guest," he said. "If you'd be so kind."

The female dwenda studied Ringil for a moment, showing all the emotion of the mask she had seemed to wear just a moment before. Then her mouth twisted into a crooked half smile and Ringil thought she muttered something under her breath. She lifted the smooth black helm from her head—it came slowly, as if a very tight fit—shook out long silky hair not quite as dark as Seethlaw's, and rolled her head back and forth a couple of times to loosen her neck muscles. Ringil heard vertebrae crackle. Then the new dwenda tucked her helmet under one arm and stepped forward, free left hand extended languidly to make one half of the greeting she had shared with Seethlaw.

"My respects to those of your blood." Her Naomic, aside from being archaic, was very rusty. "I am with name Risgillen of Ilwrack, and sister of already you-know this Seethlaw. How are you called?"

Ringil took the offered hand as he'd seen Seethlaw do, wondering if he was being subtly snubbed with this casual, one-armed variant.

"Ringil," he said. "I've heard a lot about you."

Risgillen shot a glance at her brother, who shook his head minutely and said something in the other tongue. The female dwenda peeled her lips back from something that wasn't really a smile, and let go of his hand.

"You come by unexpected ways, for this the un-, the dis-, the *lack* of proper ceremony. I regret."

"We ran into some akyia on the coastal path," Seethlaw told her. "This seemed like a safer option."

"The merroigai?" Risgillen frowned. "Shown proper respect, they should not have bothered you."

"Well, they did."

"I don't like such event. And with now these other matters, too. Something stirs, Seethlaw, and it is not us."

"You worry too much. Did you come alone?"

Risgillen gestured back the way she'd come. "Ashgrin and Pelmarag, somewhere beyond. But they seek you at different angles, alternatives less than here. None expected you this adrift. I myself, it was by scent only I came to you."

"I'll call them."

Seethlaw moved out from under the bridge and disappeared into the gloom. Risgillen watched him go, then seated herself with Aldrain elegance beside the fire. She stared into the oddly tinged flames for a while, perhaps marshaling the words she needed before she deployed them.

"You are not the first," she said quietly, still looking into the fire. "This we have seen before. This I have done myself, with mortal men and women. But I do not lose myself as my brother can. Clearly, I see."

"I'm happy for you."

"Yes. So I tell you this." Risgillen looked up and fixed him with her empty eyes. "Do not doubt; if you bring hurt or harm upon my brother, I will fuck you up."

OUT IN THE DARKNESS, A LITTLE LATER, HOWLING SOUNDS.

Ringil looked at Risgillen, the perfect geometry of her features in the greenish glow from the flames, saw no reaction beyond the faintest of smiles. The realization hit him, like icy water, that he recognized the sound.

The howling was Seethlaw, calling for his kind.

Risgillen did not look up, but her smile broadened. She knew he was watching her, knew he'd understood, once again, suddenly, where he really was.

A fight is coming, a battle of powers you have not yet seen.

The words of the fortune-teller at the eastern gate, welling up in his mind like chilly riverbed ooze. The certainty in her voice.

A dark lord will rise.

CHAPTER 26

*W*e tried to stop them. But they took her.

For long moments, the words made no kind of sense. Ishgrim was a gift of the Emperor; you'd steal her on peril of a very slow and unpleasant death when the King's Reach caught up with you, which they inevitably would because with Jhiral they themselves would be facing some pretty stiff penalties if they didn't. Sure, she was long-limbed and beautiful, but so were a lot of northern slave girls. You wanted one badly enough, you could pick them up down at the harbor clearinghouses for less than it cost to buy and tax a decent horse these days.

Never mind that. Krin-driven brain, screaming in her head. *How did they even fucking know? Ishgrim's a gift of the Emperor since yesterday. No one knew she was here. You* didn't even know she was here until the early hours of this morning.

She hugged at Kefanin, worried at the impossibility of the situation. "Who? Who, Kef? Who took her?"

The mayor-domo made a grunting noise deep in his throat. Rapid, battlefield-trained assessment told her his wound wasn't fatal, but the blow had stunned him badly. She wasn't sure how much sense he could make in this state.

"Citadel . . . livery," he managed.

And then it all came tumbling into place, like some circus trick performed by a dozen inanely painted, grinning clowns.

Not Ishgrim—*get that pale flesh out of your head, Archidi, get a fucking grip*—not the Emperor's gift at all.

Elith.

Menkarak: *She's an infidel, a faithless stone-worshipping northerner who would not convert when the hand of the Revelation was extended to her in friendship, and who persists in her stubborn unbelief deep within our borders. The evidence is plain—she has even torn the kartagh from her garb to blind the eyes of the faithful she dwells among. She is steeped in deceit.*

The mix of hysterical accusation and cod-legal posturing rang around the inside of Archeth's head like a rolling metal ball. Not much doubt what awaited Elith once they got her inside the Citadel.

"How long?" she whispered.

But Kefanin had lost consciousness again.

Footfalls outside. She spun to her feet, a knife in her hand like magic. The stable boy, dazed looking, hesitant in the doorway, backlit by the blast of morning sun.

"Milady, they—"

"How long?" she screamed at him.

"I—" Now, as he stepped inside, she saw the bruise blackening beneath his left eye, bubbles of fresh blood at his nostril on the same side. "Not half an hour, milady. Not even that."

A map of the south side's maze of streets flared into view behind her eyes. The krinzanz collided with the fury in her veins, inked in the Citadel and the path they'd likely take on their way back to it, stitched it onto the map in pulsing red.

"How many of them?" she asked, more calmly now.

"It was six, I think, milady. In the livery of—"

"Yes, I know." She sheathed the knife, felt a muscle twitch in her cheek. "Get the doctor. Tell him if Kefanin lives, I'll double his fee. If he dies, I'll have him driven out of the fucking city."

Then she took off, running.

SIX MEN, CITADEL LIVERY.

The streets were packed, no way to ride a horse through it faster than a slow clop. She wasn't uniformed, had no baton and whistle or blunted saber to clear her way. And anyway, they'd see her coming a hundred yards off.

She cut left, up a little-used dogleg back alley she knew, sprinting flat out as soon as she had the space. Abrupt relief from the heat of the sun in the narrow angles of the passage. A couple of chickens panicked screeching away from beneath her booted feet as she took the corner, but nothing else got in her way. She hit the teeming cross street of Horseman's Victory Drive—where now, ha fucking ha, you couldn't even *take* a horse unless it was hauling produce—shouldered through the crowd, and got to the whitewashed stone steps that led up onto the roof of the Lizard's Head tavern. From there, she could get her bearings, make a match with the map in her head. Then vault the alley on the other side, get onto the onion-domed rooftop sprawl of the covered bazaar.

"Hoy, you can't come up—"

She shoved the heavy-gutted publican back in his deck chair as he tried to rise. Danced past, ducking and dodging lines of washing. Grabbed a look amid the glaring white of hung sheets and rooftops beyond. *Right, Archidi. Think.* Bazaar. Clothmaker Row. The Hustray strait-back Narrows. If they'd taken the most direct route for the Citadel, by now they were headed up Desert Wisdom Drive, off the main boulevard at a forty-five-degree angle. To cut them off . . .

She ran at the lip of the roof, flexed legs into the jump, and over onto the flat top of the bazaar. Pain jarred up into both knees, but she came up running. *No time, no time.* Around the first of the onion-dome protrusions, and *shit, shit,* right onto a broad stained-glass skylight. She—

Staggered, threw herself into an ungainly, flailing leap.

Caught a fragmentary glimpse of shoppers moving fishily through a red-and-blue-tinged crowd below, saw herself crashing through and down among them—

Made the other side instead, cleared the glass by inches, landed awkwardly, swayed back, pinwheeled her arms desperately for balance and—

Upright. Running again, looping between the onion domes and roughly southeast.

It was like sprinting across the top of the world. Sounds of the city lost below, the glinting sword of sunlight and a cooling breeze out of the west. The tall rows of houses that fringed Desert Wisdom Drive angling in, closing from the left.

The market beneath her feet was one of the largest in the city—not quite up to the sprawling grandeur of the Imperial Bazaar north of the river, but it still covered several city blocks. She used its roof to cover ground in minutes that would have taken the best part of half an hour at street level.

Fetched up on the eastern edge, trotted rapidly along the guttering until she spotted a grain cart parked below and leapt down into it. Startled oaths and the slugging pain of the impact along arse and back and one thigh. She rolled up from the fall, stood unsteadily, up to her ankles in the grain. Faces peered in at her.

"Fuck was that?"

"Hey. Listen, bitch, that's my—"

"Oooh, no, but look at 'er, Perg, she's black as a burned bun. It's a fucking keeriass, it is."

"Kiriath," she snarled and jumped down among them. Shoved her way clear and set off at a fast jog along the sparsely used delivery and storage alleys that constituted the Narrows. She dodged among tradesmen laden with trays of produce, past squatting laborers sharing bread. *Six men, Citadel livery.* If Menkarak was playing true to type, that meant an invigilator–advocate general to oversee the legality of the proceedings—he'd be oldish—and five men-at-arms.

In the pulse of the krin, it seemed like pretty good odds.

The Narrows spilled out at various points along a curved and crooked street called Bridle Trail Walk. It was lined with low-end jewelers and curio shops, and busy with citizens browsing the iron-caged windows. Archeth skittered through, pushing and cursing, getting angry looks until her color registered, and then averted eyes and a few wards against evil.

Three blocks up, savage elbows and flat hand shoves, *Come on, come on, Archidi, pick it the fuck up,* and right, into Sailcloth Yard. A few seam-stress stalls set up in corners, otherwise quiet. She sprinted the short, right-angled length of it, slammed into the railing at the end, and stared, panting, down a loose soil slope onto a bend in Desert Wisdom Drive.

Citadel livery, Citadel livery, Citad—

There!

Desert Wisdom was tangled up worse than Bridle Trail Walk or the boulevard. They'd made even less headway than she'd thought. She spotted the invigilator-advocate's robes first, black and gold and the gray silk hood that marked his legal standing. The men-at-arms, a worn, white-clad figure trudging among them, head bowed, arms tied back. If they were in a hurry, it didn't show.

Archeth sucked in a sobbing breath and vaulted the rail.

Her feet hit the slope six feet below, tried to sink in the soil and tip her headlong. She tore loose and ran, long, uncontrolled flopping strides to stay ahead of her own falling weight. Came hammering down into Desert Wisdom Drive hard and fast enough to smash passersby in her path to the ground. She got back control of her gait, swerved through the confusion she'd sown, and started into the crowd. Couple of hundred yards to close up, at most.

"From the palace, from the palace!" Chanting it at the top of heaving lungs. "Move! Get out of the fucking way!"

Slowly at first—the cry met only with jeers and unresponsive backs turned. But then the people she cannoned into started to look around, saw what she was, and almost fell over themselves to obey. They opened passage for her, and the scramble transmitted itself through the crowd ahead like a wave on water. A hundred yards on, she barely needed to push.

"From the palace, from the—"

Two of the men-at-arms had turned back, stood now squarely in her path. She saw wolfish grins, a short-sword drawn, a raised club, went for her knives with less thought than it took to blink. In the crowd beside her, someone screamed. Panic in all directions, the scream found a mate, and then another. The crowd swayed apart, scattered like frightened fish.

Archeth threw left-handed, put the knife in the sword wielder's right eye. It was Bandgleam, narrower than the rest, eager and skipping white in the sun. It went in up to the hilt. The man staggered back, squalling like a scalded infant, sword gone, scrabbling at his face and the worn metal thing that now protruded from it. Archeth came in behind the throw, yelling, and she had Laughing Girl light and low in her right hand. The second Citadel thug started visibly at the sound she made, panicked like anyone else in the crowd, and swung massively with his club. He succeeded only in knocking down his shrieking companion. Archeth swayed back in and grabbed, rode the momentum of the swing, carried the man to the ground and cut his throat before he could recover.

She came halfway upright, splattered with the blood. Saw the invigilator-advocate at bay fifteen yards off, amid fleeing and stumbling bystanders, one hand locked around Elith's upper arm, staring in disbelief at the bodies of his men and the bloodied black woman crouched over them.

The remaining three men-at-arms bracketed the street, a cordon of sorts around their master and his prize. Two swords, another club. The club wielder had a crossbow, but it was on his back. On the ground, the man with Bandgleam buried in his eye had curled up in the dirt and was screaming.

Left-handed, reflexive, Archeth drew Quarterless from the sheath in the small of her back. She stalked forward, Laughing Girl raised and pointing.

"That's my guest you've got there," she called. "Whether you live or die, you *will* give her back."

The street had cleared—impossible to believe it had been crowded scant seconds before. Archeth came on, boots crunching detritus underfoot. Quarterless glinted as she hefted it in the sunlight. The men-at-arms glanced at one another uneasily.

"Are you *insane*?" The invigilator-advocate had found his voice, if not a very deep timbre for it. His face darkened with rage as he screeched. "How *dare* you impede the sacred work of the Revelation?"

She ignored him, stared down the three men-at-arms instead.

"Sacred?" she asked them, tone rich with disgust. "Among the seven tribes, a guest is sacred. You know this much, or at least your forefathers did. Which of you wants to die first?"

"Fuck you, bitch," said the one with the club uncertainly.

"Mama," screamed the man on the ground suddenly. "It hurts, I can't *see* anything. Where are you?"

Archeth smiled like winter ice.

"Want to join him?" she asked.

"This Kiriath whore is an abomination, an affront to the Revelation." The invigilator-advocate had mustered some depth of tone now, was bellowing at them all. "It's your sacred duty to cut her down where she stands, it's a holy act to take her fucking life."

The injured man gave out an inarticulate, sobbing cry, then trailed off into soft, hopeless weeping. Archeth waited.

The swordsman on the right broke first. Flung himself forward, yelling something garbled at the top of his voice.

Laughing Girl took him in the throat at the second step. He went down choking and coughing blood. Archeth had Wraithslayer in her right hand before he hit the street. The club wielder, surging forward in his comrade's wake, stopped dead as he saw the new knife. Or maybe he spotted the hilt of Falling Angel, still sheathed in her boot. Or both. Archeth met his eyes, showed him the smile again. He broke and ran.

The final man-at-arms hesitated a moment, then fled into the press of the watching crowd with his friend.

Archeth drew a long, deep breath. Over.

The invigilator stood with Elith collapsed in a heap at his side, bawling at Archeth and the bystanders and apparently everyone else in this city of sinners to *get down on bended knees,* to humble themselves before the majesty of the Revelation, to repent, to *fucking* repent before it was—

Archeth strode up to him and slashed his throat open with Quarterless.

He staggered backward a few steps and fell into the arms of the crowd behind. Blood welled up along the line of the knife wound, spilled down his front and soaked into his robes. His mouth worked, chewing, she supposed, on the rest of the unfinished sermon, but no sound came out. Archeth knelt beside Elith, satisfied herself that she was only doped up and with something innocuous. Her breathing was fine. She spared a final glance for the invigilator, whom the crowd was now gathering around as he flapped and bled out, then she went back to the man-at-arms with Bandgleam in his eye. He was still alive, and when she crouched beside him and reached for the knife, he put his hands softly on hers and made a faint mewling sound. She pressed one hand onto his forehead for purchase, and he smiled like a baby at the touch.

When she pulled Bandgleam out, he died.

"GOD DAMN IT, ARCHETH, I AM *NOT* PLEASED WITH THIS MESS."

"No more am I, my lord." She felt sick and shaky, but there was nowhere to sit down and no acceptable way to ask for a chair. "I am at a loss to understand the Citadel's behavior."

"Oh, you are, are you?" Jhiral paced tigerishly back and forth across the floor of the emptied throne room. He'd thrown everybody out in an incandescent display of imperial rage, and now Archeth stood alone with him, still thrumming from the chase and combat, still covered in blood, and chilled in the stomach with too much krin. "Come on, woman, don't be so fucking naïve. This is a power play, and you know it."

"If that's so, my lord, then it's a remarkably unsubtle one."

"No." He stopped and came up to her with one menacing finger raised. "What you *did* about it was remarkably unsubtle. Had you not chased, caught, and slaughtered this little crew of zealots in full view of *half the fucking city,* then we would not be facing this particular crisis."

"No. We'd be facing a different one."

"Precisely." He turned away, went back up the steps to the throne, and dumped himself into its burnished arms. Stared gloomily into space. "We'd be facing a politely impassive Citadel, everybody closing ranks, whether they're happy about it or not, around a clique headed up by that little cunt Menkarak, who'd strenuously deny ever making off with your guest, while at the same time loudly and semi-publicly insisting that the secular powers of Empire apparently just lack the force of will to protect the faithful from outside evil forces."

"That's probably still going to be his line now."

"Yeah. Going to be like the fucking Ninth Tribe Remembrance Brotherhood all over again." Jhiral shot her a brooding look. "You remember those guys, right? I mean, you were around for that."

"Yes. Your grandfather had them all executed."

"Don't fucking tempt me."

It was empty noise, and they both knew it. Those days were over. Akal had long ago mortgaged himself to the Citadel to feed his wars of expansion—loans and blessings and a firm helping hand from prayer towers and pulpits to recruit extra troop strength from the zealous masses. Yhelteth marched to its conquests under Akal the Great with fully a third of its soldiery believing they were holy warriors. Not nearly enough of them were killed in the process for Archeth's liking, not even when the Scaled Folk came. There were still far too many hot-eyed young men out there, trained and hardened in war under false pretenses, looking now for continuance of the struggle. Wouldn't much matter against whom.

Jhiral inherited them all, along with the debts and the solemnly agreed twining of secular and spiritual authority at court.

"How many of the Citadel's mastery can you count on?" she asked him quietly.

"Situation like this?" He shrugged. "Not many. Archeth, you slit an invigilator's throat. In broad fucking daylight, on a busy street. What are they *supposed* to say about that?"

"How many, my lord?" An edge on her voice. She was getting past caring about throne room etiquette.

Jhiral blew out a dispirited breath. "The ones we can bribe, the ones we can blackmail? I don't know, maybe fifteen or twenty. Add in a few of my father's old friends on top of that, men who can see the dangers if things get out of hand. That's half a dozen more at most."

"So—twenty-five, say?"

"If we lean hard, and if we're very lucky, yes."

"It's not a majority."

Jhiral grimaced. "Tell me about it."

"All right, then." The queasiness in her stomach took a new twist. She held out her hands at waist height and stared at them, flexed her fingers wide and willed them to stop trembling. "So let's see. They'll vote, reach an obvious decision, and at a minimum they'll require me at the Citadel to face an inquisitorial court. They'll drag Elith into it as well, if only as a witness. Chances are, they won't get the answers they want and that means further questioning. After that—"

"Don't you fucking worry." The sudden, grim vehemence in his tone jerked her gaze up to where he sat. "I made my father a promise on his deathbed, and I aim to keep it. There's no fucking way I hand you over to that scum."

Shocked gratitude stung tears into her eyes. It was like a different man speaking, a different man sitting there on the throne. She'd have fled the city before she gave herself up for questioning, was already at some level in her mind beginning to lay the first tentative plans for it. But *this* . . . ?

"I . . . thank you, my lord, I have no words to express—"

"Yes, all right." He gestured it away. "I think we can take all that as read, don't you? I wouldn't like to be facing the Citadel's grubby little inquisitors and their toys, either. The question is, how exactly do we get out from under this without having to roll out the troops. It's the Prophet's fucking birthday at the end of the month. Going to be enough breast-beating hysteria in the streets as it is. I don't need a mob marching on the palace as well."

"From a legal point of view—"

He shook his head. "Forget the law. It isn't going to help. They'll cite it where it suits them, ignore it where it doesn't. They're *clerics*, Archeth. They spend their whole fucking lives selectively interpreting textual authority to advantage. We have to hamstring them before they even get started." He bridged his hands and brooded. "Basically, Archeth, you have to disappear for a while."

"And Elith."

"Oh, all right, yes. Fine. Your northern witch as well. Works out better like that anyway, I suppose. With both of you gone, the whole basis for their grievance collapses." He nodded slowly, but with building vigor. "Yeah, that'll work. That will work. We get you out of the city under cover, before nightfall. I'll have Faileh Rakan put together an escort squad to do it. Meantime, I agree to an emergency session of the mastery and field the Citadel's demands. We send for you, you're nowhere to be found. Repeated summons, no result. With a bit of prevaricating—and the Holy fucking Mother knows it's what the court does best—that gets us to some early hour tonight. By the time it's clear that you've fled, it's dark and you could be anywhere. I undertake to have the militia out scouring the streets for you at dawn. When they don't find you, we say we've sent out the King's Reach as well. Might even do it with a few of them I can trust to look in the wrong places and keep their mouths shut about it. Anyway: Rumors of you heading northwest for Trelayne, or maybe into the wastes. Doing all we can, gentlemen, thank you for your time. We'll keep you posted." He wagged a finger at Archeth. "Meantime, we stash you . . . where? Any idea where you'll go?"

And something moved in her head like the oiled components of a fireship hatch mechanism, everything sliding and locking into new configurations. She almost heard the solid clunk as it happened. A fresh excitement shouldered the krin crash aside, picked up the beat in her veins. She cleared her throat.

"I had thought of Ennishmin, my lord."

CHAPTER 27

They emerged into vague, greenish gray light and the overarching striation of winter trees. Faint odor of decay on a slack and sickly breeze.

At first, Ringil registered the change with little more than weary mistrust. His time in the Aldrain marches had shown him far worse, and the shift had not been without its advance warnings. The great black road they'd met Risgillen and the others on had been fading for some time now, either aging at some fantastically accelerated rate as they walked it, or rotting through from beneath as they pressed into new territory that would not permit its existence. Jagged cracks started to appear, some broad and deep enough to put an incautious foot in and snap your ankle. Ringil thought he saw human skulls wedged down into them at intervals, but that might have been another marchland hallucination, and he was getting numb to those.

Well, most of them.

_____

JELIM COMES BACK TO HIM ONE MORE TIME, PERHAPS IN A DREAM WHILE they're camped on the road, perhaps not; in the marches it's hard to tell. This time Ringil is standing above him with the Ravensfriend across his back, though slanted the wrong way, pommel jutting over his right shoulder. The difference feels bizarre, uncomfortable. Jelim stops a short distance away and looks up without speaking. The face is the same, though stained and mottled with weeping, but he's dressed in far finer garb than the real Jelim, minor merchant's son that he was, had ever been able to afford. He stares up at Ringil, meets his eyes, and fresh tears start down his cheeks. Ringil feels a deep aching in his chest at the sight. He wants to speak, but the words are jammed up in his throat.

I'm sorry, *Jelim weeps.* Gil, I'm so sorry.

And now the pain in Ringil's chest will not be contained. It rips through him, upward and downward, right up into the muscles of his shoulder, right down to—

I'm sorry, Gil, I'm so sorry. *Jelim seems to whisper it endlessly, staring up in horrified fascination.* It should have been me.

And the thing that juts from his right shoulder is not the pommel of the Ravensfriend at his back, it's the end of the impaling spike where they drove it through the final nine inches and locked the mechanism in the base of the cage, and the pain is not an ache in his heart, it's an oceanic, white-hot shredding, scalding agony that drives up from between his legs and rips through his guts and then across his chest, neatly avoiding his heart so he need not die for days . . .

I'm sorry, I'm so sorry.

And then he's screaming, as he realizes where he is, shrieking, for mercy, for Hoiran, for his father, for his mother, for anyone or anything to come and stop the pain. Screaming with such force that it seems it must blow his veins apart, explode his skull, shatter it and let his lifeblood drain out through the ruined mess.

But he knows it won't.

And he knows that no one will come, that in the long, slow-leaking agony ahead, there will be no rescue of any kind.

HE STAMPED DOWN ON THE MEMORY, BATHED IN SUDDEN SWEAT, HEART hammering. Focused on where he was instead.

Winter trees. Quiet.

He stood and stared up at the stripped branches. Waited for the panic-flush of sweat across his skin to cool, for his heart to slow back down. He breathed in deep, like a man escaped from drowning.

Not real, not real. His pulse throbbed with the rhythm of the words.

No more real than the thousand other phantoms that had haunted him across the Aldrain marches. He had not died.

Jelim had.

A hand clapped him across the back. His pulse kicked up again for one terrified moment, then eased as he registered the touch. Seethlaw's hand shifted, squeezed intimately at the nape of his neck.

It felt uncomfortably like ownership.

"Nice to be back in the real world, I imagine," the dwenda murmured, and stepped past him across the tufted, swampy ground. Tiny squelching noises in the stillness with each step the dwenda took. Ringil saw water well up in the boot prints he left.

The other members of the party followed, Risgillen with wrinkled nose and a sour glance cocked up at the trees, Ashgrin as watchful and impassive as he'd been since Ringil met him. Only Pelmarag acknowledged the human, turned as he passed and gave him a wink.

"Where are we?" Ringil asked.

"Journey's end," said Pelmarag. "Hannais M'hen the Cursed. Look."

He gestured out to the left, and Ringil felt a tiny start in his pulse as he saw a stunted black figure there. It took him a moment to realize it was a statue, a moment longer to realize—*how?*—that it would not, as the akyia had done in the surf, suddenly move and come to silent, bright-eyed life.

"Tell you a funny story," Pelmarag said, advancing on the statue without any apparent trace of amusement on his face. Ringil shrugged and followed him.

It waited there for them, set at a tilted angle in the marshy ground, stubby outstretched arms raised to shoulder height on either side like a diminutive preacher facing his congregation or a child asking to be picked up. As Ringil got closer, he saw that the thing was hewn entirely out of black glirsht, sculpted crudely so the body wore no obvious clothing and the face was a blunt, asexual approximation of human features. He noticed the shallow-scooped facets that served as eyes were polished so the crystalline stone glinted, but he couldn't tell whether the effect was deliberate or not.

Pelmarag stared down at the statue, brow creased as if it had asked him a difficult question.

"Funny story?" Ringil reminded him.

The dwenda stirred. "Yeah. About a month and a half ago the way you people'd look at it, Ashgrin's brother Tarnval was looking for this place. He was real well equipped, too, came heavy. Never much cared for Seethlaw's stealth strategies, thought we were all moving way too slow."

Pelmarag's Naomic, better than Risgillen's or Ashgrin's from the start, had become positively fluent in the time he'd spent talking to Ringil. He was by far the most gregarious of the group. In fact, he seemed to be acquiring a lot of Ringil's preferred expressions and phrasing. It gave the human a peculiar sensation to hear his own verbal quirks fed back to him this way, and it made him wonder how much time the journey in the Aldrain marches was really taking. How learning and experience might— or even could—function without fixed reference to time.

"Yeah, always one for a frontal assault, Tarnval." Pelmarag grimaced, apparently at something only he could see. "And he talked a pretty fight, too. Pretty enough to get the support he needed. So, he had about three dozen of us at his back, some storm-callers of reputation among the company. All set to take back Hannais M'hen the Cursed, turn back the clocks, undo all the harm the Black Folk wrought here. We unleashed the talons of the sun through the aspect storm before we deployed, clearing a path. We came storming through in their wake. And you know what? We ended up over a thousand miles southwest of here, up to our waists in seawater on the beach at some shit-hole little imperial port. All because some fucking idiot human moved the marker."

Not sure if he was supposed to laugh or not, Ringil made a noncommittal noise. Pelmarag's mouth twisted again with the memory.

"Had to fight our way up off that beach," he said softly. "We lost six or seven dwenda doing it. Across town and up the hill, fucking humans everywhere, running around screaming and jabbering in the dark like the lost souls of apes, you know, cut one down and there's another right fucking behind it. We took another five casualties, and Tarnval himself down by then with a chest wound, searched that fucking town, tore it apart till we finally found our beacon. And when we finally did, we found they'd moved the fucking thing and we were nowhere close to where we were supposed to be. No Hannais M'hen, cursed or otherwise. We were south, way south. And with *that* kind of sun coming up in a couple of hours' time, well . . . nothing to do but collect the dead and injured, let the storm-callers take us back out of there. Tarnval died from the storm-stress on the way out, so did a couple of others. After that?" Pelmarag shrugged. "We all went back to listening to Seethlaw."

"Talking about me again?"

Seethlaw had come up behind them. His expression as he looked at Pelmarag was unreadable.

"Just a little reflection on strategy."

"Yeah?" Seethlaw put a hand on Ringil's shoulder. Something chilly poured into the air between the two dwenda. "Gil here isn't a part of our strategy, Pel. He doesn't need to know anything about it."

Pelmarag held the other dwenda's gaze. He said something short and bitten-sounding in the language they used when Ringil was not included in the conversation, then turned away and went to join the others. Seethlaw grunted and nodded after him, a quick, chin-jutting gesture that had nothing friendly in it.

"So what's that all about?" Ringil asked.

"Nothing that concerns you." Seethlaw's grip on his shoulder tightened slightly. "Come on. We're not there yet."

THROUGH THE WINTER TREES, ALONG PATHS THROUGH THE SWAMP THAT the dwenda either knew by heart or could sense without much effort. Ringil took an experimental detour at one point, around the other side of a rotting tree stump, and found himself abruptly up to his shins in yielding black morass. Gray, soupy water pooled rapidly in the holes he'd made and brought with it a stench like death. He floundered back out, boots liberally streaked and plastered with mud. No one said anything, but he thought he caught Risgillen sneering. He stayed carefully in file after that.

There was no sound other than the squelch of their steps.

In the end, it was this that told him where he was. He knew something about marshland expanse from growing up in a city surrounded by one, and he was beginning to miss the signs of life he should have heard. There were no birdcalls, recognizable or otherwise, and no sudden rustling movements from amid the ground-level vegetation as they passed. Here and there, they saw pools and angled stretches of stagnant water bridged with moss-grown fallen tree trunks and stepped in by small mangroves, but nothing living stirred there, not even insects hovering above the leaden surface.

He'd heard of only one swamp this dead. Had even seen the place, once, from a safe distance to the west.

Hannais M'hen the Cursed, Pelmarag had called it.

Hannais M'hen.

Ennishmin.

Cursed was right, then. Forget the peasant-level legends and ghost stories they liked to weave about this place. He'd lost what little faith in things remained to him at Ennishmin, and for the most prosaic of reasons. Had nearly lost his life as well. Probably would have lost it but for Archeth's prompt medical attention and—he suspected—her intercession with the powers-that-be at camp. *Never tangle with an imperial commander at knifepoint if you plan to let him live,* he'd begun one of the chapters in that treatise on skirmish warfare that never saw print, the chapter headed "Diplomacy."

"Hss-sst!"

Ahead of him, Seethlaw had locked to a halt. He held up one rigid hand and hinged it downward, then sank smoothly into a crouch. The other dwenda froze and followed suit, and Ringil did his human best to copy them. Seethlaw raised a hand and pointed silently through the trees ahead. A broad gunmetal creek opened out there. They had walked almost onto its bank—and something made soft splashing sounds as it moved through the water toward them.

Seethlaw's hand moved again.

It was, Ringil thought later, exactly the way to describe what happened. The dwenda's hand moved, but not in any way that suggested its owner had any control over it. It was as if fingers and palm had each acquired a malicious but not quite coordinated will of their own. The wrist flexed at what looked like an impossible angle, the hand made an odd, repeated clawing gesture with three fingers, and Seethlaw hissed out words under his breath. Ringil caught only a half syllable or two, but his skin goose-fleshed with the sound.

Then something seemed to happen to the light around them.

At the same moment, a long, battered-looking canoe glided into view on the creek. It held five men, bearded and scruffily clad, but all armed to the teeth. Ringil spotted broadswords and axes, recurved bows held loosely nocked, and a huge arbalest strapped across a back. Two of the men wielded the paddles, digging and driving with the ease of long custom, strokes that knifed into the water almost silently and propelled the canoe along with barely a ripple. The other three were evidently the lookouts, heads swiveling, eyes tense and watchful above their bearded cheeks. None of them spoke a word to one another the whole time they were in view.

They passed less than five feet from where the dwenda crouched, and apparently did not see them.

Seethlaw waited what seemed like a long time, and then his hand unclawed itself, the light shifted again, and he started breathing, something Ringil now realized the dwenda had stopped doing completely when he first froze there on the bank of the creek.

"And they were—?"

Seethlaw shrugged. "Scavengers. They scour the swamp for trinkets of the Black Folk, sell them on northward as Aldrain curios. Desperate men, mostly, but they know the swamplands well. They have camps out on the fringes. It pays to avoid them."

"Avoid them?" Ringil frowned, felt an odd tide of mingled hilarity and disappointment rising in him. His mouth twisted with it. "Are you serious? The mighty fucking dwenda, skulking about in the bushes hiding from swamp trash? Hoiran's twisted cock, Seethlaw, they're only human."

"Yes, but some of us," said Risgillen, suddenly, sibilantly, into his left ear as she slipped past him, "are not all that keen on humans. For one thing—they don't wash all that often."

Seethlaw shot her a warning look, and she said no more.

"It's this way," he said, and they pressed on parallel to the creek. The channel broadened out as they walked, and a number of tributary arms opened up along the far bank. Drifts of some tubular, tangled floating weed began to appear on the gunmetal water, and an occasional gust of wind scudded the surface. The scent of decay lifted somewhat. They saw no more water traffic, and nothing else living until the water took a sharp bend to the right and suddenly a smooth-headed black-clad form stood ahead of them, sword across its back. Ringil, by now accustomed to the sleek helm and unornamented design of Aldrain armour, barely spared the new dwenda a glance. Most of him was absorbed in the thing that loomed behind.

It was a bridge, that much was clear, but the term *bridge* struck Ringil as a poor attempt at describing what he saw spanning the creek. By the same token, you could call the Imperial Bazaar in Yhelteth a market. It was true as far as it went, but—

The bridge soared out from buttresses as tall as Trelayne's eastern gate, and appeared to be built mostly of wires and light. He made out spiraling stairways at either end, a shallow sweeping support arc from side to side, and spiderweb patterns of structure beneath. There was a delicacy to the construction that made Ringil think if the sun shone through it strongly enough, the whole thing might almost disappear.

Seethlaw, it seemed, had noticed his awe. The dwenda was watching him closely, almost as if he'd just passed some test.

"You approve?"

"It's very beautiful," Ringil admitted. "The scavengers don't see it?"

"They see something." Seethlaw stepped closer, breathed across his fingertips, and then pressed them gently to Ringil's eyes. "Look."

Ringil blinked and stared upward.

The bridge was gone.

Or . . . not *gone* precisely. The buttresses remained, but now they were composed of pale granite, twin bluffs facing each other across the creek, cracked and seamed with moss and thin-grown lines of yellowish grass, broken apart in places but offering no obvious route up. And where the bridge's span had once been, a pair of slim fallen trees yearned out toward each other from the top of each bluff, branches thinning and then thinning again into twigs as they extended over the gap and grew closer, but never quite touched.

Ringil blinked again, hard. Rubbed at his eyes.

The bridge was there again.

"There are legends, of course," Seethlaw said. "The boy who stumbles on this place at twilight on Padrow's Eve or some other festival night and sees, in place of the rocks and trees, a fabulous fairy-tale bridge. But very few of your kind can actually see it for more than a passing second." A wry smile. "As you say, they're only humans."

They left the helmed and armored dwenda with a brief exchange that sounded formulaic to Ringil, for all he could not understand a word of what was said. Then Seethlaw led them up the spiraling stairs and out onto the span. Ringil, close behind him, took a handful of cautious steps out onto the weave of hairline strands under his feet and then froze. He couldn't help it—it was like walking on the air itself. For long moments, he felt sick with terror of falling. The wind made fluting sounds across the strands around him; the dark water below rippled invitingly. A rift opened in the clouds overhead, and where the stronger light touched the bridge, structure dissolved into the beaded gleam of a dew-soaked cobweb.

He saw the looks he was getting from Risgillen. Swallowed, fixed his gaze firmly ahead, and started walking again. It didn't help that the bridge gave a little underfoot with each step, not unlike the spongy ground they'd been treading on their way through the swamp. And as it gave, the strands seemed to chime very faintly at the upper edge of Ringil's hearing. It wasn't a pleasant sensation, and he was glad when they were over to the other side and coming down the spiral stairs.

At the bottom, they were met by two more armored dwenda. One of them pulled off his helmet and fixed Ringil with a hungry eye until

Seethlaw snapped something at him. The conversation went back and forth a few times, and then the dwenda shrugged and put his helmet back on. He didn't look at Ringil again.

"I'm really not popular around here, huh?"

"It isn't that," said Seethlaw absently. "They're just worried, looking for something to take it out on."

"Worried about *what*? Those guys in the canoes?"

The dwenda looked at him speculatively. "No, not them. There's some talk about the Black Folk still being around here. One of our scouts went into a local camp wearing enough of a glamour to get served and sit unnoticed in the alehouse. He heard men talking about a black-skinned warrior in one of the villages to the west."

"Yeah—come on. That's just going to be some southern mercenary, maybe out of the deserts. Skins get pretty dark once you're south of Demlarashan. Easy mistake to make."

"Perhaps."

"No perhaps about it. The Kiriath are *gone*, Seethlaw. I saw them off myself. Stood and watched at An-Monal until the last fireship went under. Wherever they went, they're not coming back."

"Yes, this is what I have learned in Trelayne. But I've also learned that the tongues of men are not much leashed by concern for accuracy or truth. It seems lies come very easily to your race. They lie to those they lead, to their mates and fellows no matter how close-drawn, even to themselves if it will make the world around them more bearable. It is hard to know what to believe in this place."

Something about the weariness in his tone stung Ringil into defensive anger.

"Funny, that's always what I heard about your people. That the dwenda were masters of deceit and trickery."

"Indeed?" Ashgrin, laconic and grave at his shoulder. Ringil had heard his voice so few times it was a genuine shock now. "And from which four-thousand-year-old expert in Aldrain lore did you hear this?"

Risgillen cleared her throat loudly.

"Are we going to get on, brother? It seems to me that we have more to concern ourselves with than the prattling of—"

Seethlaw swung to face her. His voice came out dangerously low.

"Do you want to lead, Risgillen?"

She didn't reply. The other dwenda watched with interest.

"I asked you a question, sister. Do you want charge of this expedition? Will you abandon the pleasures and comforts of our realm and become earthbound as I have? Will you immerse yourself in the brawling filth of human society to achieve our ends?"

Still no response.

"I'll have an answer, sister, if you please. Or I'll take your silence as the *no* it has always been. Is it *no? Then shut the fuck up!*"

Risgillen started to speak, her own tongue, but Seethlaw slashed the blade of a hand across the flow. He turned slowly about, blank eyes switching from face to face among his fellow Aldrain.

"I hear you complain," he spat, still in Naomic, perhaps, Ringil guessed, to snub them, to shame them before the human. "All of you, time and again, bemoaning what you must endure here, the journeys and sojourns of a few weeks' duration that you must make among humans, tied to time and circumstance. I have spent *three fucking years* tied to time so that we could build a path in Trelayne. I have tasted this world on my tongue for so long I can scarcely remember what it was like not to be tainted by its limits. I have swallowed it down, day after day, sickening from the brute animal stupidity of its ways, all so that I might learn its parameters and its possibilities, all so we may in the end take back what is ours. I have done all of this willingly, and would do it again. And I ask for nothing in return but your allegiance and your trust. Is that so very much to give?"

Silence. Very, very faintly, the sound of the Aldrain bridge humming and whining in the wind above them. Seethlaw nodded grimly.

"Very well. You will not gainsay me in this again, Risgillen. Is that clear?"

A half syllable of Aldrain speech in reply. Risgillen bowed her head.

"Good. Then wait here." Seethlaw nodded at Ringil. "Gil, you come with me. There's something you need to see."

CHAPTER 28

A few hundred yards beyond the Aldrain bridge, as if in some kind of savage architectural riposte, a massive black iron platform jutted out of the swamp at the angle of a sinking ship. It was easily over a hundred feet from side to side, multileveled, six flanges that Ringil could make out as they approached, tipping his head back to count. The top was crowned with spikes and webbed wire assemblies that looked somewhat like fishermen's nets hung out to dry. The whole thing stabbed upward at the murky sky like a blade buried in a wound and then snapped off. In the hanging silence that surrounded it, there was a presence, a heavy tension like the feel in the air before a storm.

"See," said Seethlaw grimly, "what your allies did to this place."

It wasn't hard to make the connection—the design of the platform could only have one origin.

"You're talking about the Kiriath?"

"The Black Folk, yes. Look around you, Ringil Eskiath. This was once the site of the greatest Aldrain city on the continent. They called it Enheed-idrishinir, dwelling place of the joyful winds. You've seen the bridge. Imagine streets and towers made the same way, stretching to the horizon. Sculpted rivers whose waters flow in and out of the real world as easily as a Trelayne canal emerges from a tunnel or passes under a toll station. Trees, and built structures like trees, to echo and worship their form, reaching up to catch the breeze and sing. I was a child the last time I saw Enheed-idrishinir, before the Black Folk came."

He pointed at the platform again.

"It fell from the sky. They say it screamed as it came. You see the six levels? There are twenty-seven more belowground, buried past the swamp and into the bedrock beneath. At the spear-point was a device that tore reality apart. Fifty thousand died or were swept away, out in the wash of the greater march. We still sometimes find their remains today. Some still live, after a fashion."

"Nothing ever changes, huh," said Ringil quietly, and thought of Grashgal's visions of a museum for swords. Children mystified by an edged-steel past that was locked away safe behind glass.

It always had sounded like an unlikely piece of wish fulfillment.

"No, things will change." Seethlaw turned and fixed him with the dark, empty stare. His voice rose a little in the quiet of the swamp, took on faint echoes of a passion Ringil had only previously seen in him when they were fucking. "The Aldrain are coming back, Ringil. This world is ours. We dominated it for millennia before what you under-stand as human history had even begun. We were driven out, but it re-mains our ancestral home, our birth canal. Ours by right of blood and blade and origin. We will take it back."

"How you going to do that then?" Somehow, this new aspect of Seethlaw left Ringil obscurely disappointed. "There don't seem to be that many of you."

"No, not yet. The Aldrain are wanderers by nature, individual by inclination, always happiest at the edge of our known domains and pressing farther outward to see what else lies beyond. But buried at the heart of each of us is an ache for this world, for a unity, a certain place to carry in the heart and to return to at journey's end. When the gates are opened again here, my people will come from every corner and aspect of the marches. They will flock here like crows at evening."

"Is that supposed to cheer me up?"

The blank-eyed gaze bent on him again. "Have I used you so ill then?"

"Oh no. I've seen slaves treated far worse."

Seethlaw's face turned aside as if he'd slapped it. He stared past Ringil at the sunken platform. His voice turned toneless.

"I could have killed you, Ringil Eskiath. I could have taken my pleasure, wiped myself on you like a rag, and thrown you away. Left you to wither from the soul outward in the gray places, or finished our duel as it began, with steel. *You* came into *my* domain, you brought your blade and your threats and your pride that no beauty or sorcery could stem your killing prowess. You stirred up my affairs in Etterkal, killed and mutilated useful servants of mine, forced me to intervene when it was hardly convenient. I ask you again. Have I used you ill?"

Since there was only one fair answer to that, Ringil ignored it.

"Just tell me something," he asked instead. "I see your end of this, you get your sacred ancestral . . . lizardshit . . . blood right . . . *whatever* . . . promised fucking land back. I see that, it isn't what you'd call a fresh concept. But what's in it for the cabal? Looks to me like you've got the whole Chancellery dancing to your tune one way or the other. What the fuck did you promise them?"

The dwenda gave him a thin smile. "What do you think? You see where we are, you know what Ennishmin represents to the League."

The knowledge must already have been there inside him in some shape or form. He felt no real surprise, only an icy sliding sensation in the pit of his stomach.

"You told them you'd take it back for them?"

"Yes, more or less."

"You're going to *invade imperial territory*? Break the accords?"

Seethlaw shrugged. "I signed no accord. Nor did my people. It's a service I'm rendering my hosts in Trelayne."

"But . . ." Now the trickle of ice in his guts was swelling, was filling him up. "The Empire isn't going to sit still for that, Seethlaw. Not the way things are right now. They'll go to war. It'll mean *another fucking war*. You must know that."

"Yes." Another blank-eyed shrug. "What of it? The League and the Empire will go to war over their relative hypocrisies, with my hand on the Trelayne side of the scales to render the struggle evenly matched. They'll fight for years, I imagine. They'll spend their strength and drag each other down, and when it's done, when they're finally sick of the slaughter, when they're tired and broken, my people will walk through the ruins and take up their rightful place once again in this world." Seethlaw's voice turned oddly soft and urgent. "You shouldn't object, Gil. It'll be a far better world for it. No more hysterical hatreds and petty factional bloodshed. No more hypocrisy to cover for the abuse of power, no more lies."

"No, that's right. Just domination by the Aldrain. I think I've got some sense of what that'll be like."

"That's a stupid thing to say." A quick trace of anger in the dwenda's voice, as quickly wiped away. "There is no reason human and dwenda can't coexist as we did once before. Our chronicles are full of warriors from your race, taken in out of pity or love and rising to great stature among us. I myself—"

He stopped. Made a small gesture.

"No matter. I'm not some market trader at Strov, hawking his wares, nor a member of the Chancellery making his empty speeches for funds and a handsgrab more power over his fellow humans. If your own wits and experience will not convince you, then I will not drag you to an understanding you do not want to own." He turned abruptly away. "Come, we are here on other business."

They picked a careful path through the swampy ground, around the massive iron flank of the platform, to where something like a partially roofed corral had been built against the lowest visible flange. There was a fence of some material similar to the wires of the Aldrain bridge, though nowhere near as subtly worked. Woven more thickly, the same webbing went to form three long, low structures like stables, which were backed up to the ironwork of the platform. The ground the corral occupied was firm and looked dry, was perhaps reinforced with the same Aldrain building materials as the rest, but outside the fence swamp water pooled and sat in stagnant, grayish expanses. The path through was twisted and deceptive and ended at a chained gate.

Around the corral, and set back about a yard from the fence, a number of small, blunt objects protruded from the water. Ringil made them for rotted tree stumps until they were almost at the gate, and one of the nearer protrusions made a wet, sucking sound. He looked down at it more carefully.

And recoiled.

Fuck!

The object was a human head, fixed neatly at the neck to the tree stump he'd believed it to be. A young woman's head, long hair trailing down into the soupy gray water in clotted rat's tails. As he stared at it, the neck corded and twisted about, and out of a pale face the woman's eyes found his. Mud-streaked, her mouth twisted and formed a silent word.

. . . please . . .

Grace-of-Heaven's story slammed back through him:

I didn't say these men were dead. I said all that came back were their heads. Each one still living, grafted at the neck to a seven-inch tree stump.

Swamp-water tears started from the woman's eyes, ran dirty down her face.

Ringil's eyes darted out across the swamp, and the other protrusions that studded the surface. It was an arc of the same horror, living human heads staring inward at the corral.

He'd seen dragonfire and the charred bodies of children on spits over roasting pits. He'd thought himself hardened to pretty much anything by now.

He was not.

"What the *fuck* is this, Seethlaw?"

The dwenda was occupied with the chain on the fence, hands laid on and murmuring softly to it. He looked up distractedly.

"What?" He saw the direction of Ringil's stare. "Oh, those are the escapees. Got to hand it to you, you humans are a stubborn lot. We told them where they were, told them there wasn't any easy way out of the swamp, told them it was dangerous to try. We told them if they stayed put they'd be fed and well treated. They still kept trying. So those are a kind of object lesson. We don't have so many escape attempts now. In fact, mostly they stay inside, and certainly well away from the fence."

Ringil's eyes went to the stable construction in the shadow of the Kiriath iron. He pressed his tongue hard against the roof of his mouth.

"These are the marsh blood slaves? You're keeping them here."

"Yes." Seethlaw lifted the suddenly unfastened chain aside and pushed the gate open. He seemed to notice Ringil's expression for the first time. "So what? What's the matter?"

"You." It was as if he suddenly could not draw breath properly. "Did this, to them, just to warn the others?"

"Yes. An object lesson, as I said."

"How long do they go on living like that?"

"Well," Seethlaw frowned. "Indefinitely, given water supply to the roots. Why?"

"You motherfuckers." Involuntarily, Ringil found he was shaking his head. "Ahhh, you fucking piece of shit. You *cunt.* No reason human and dwenda cannot coexist? *What do you call that, then? What kind of fucking coexistence is that?"*

Seethlaw stopped and fixed him with a stare.

"Is it any worse," he asked softly, "than the cages at the eastern gate in Trelayne, where your transgressors hang in agony for days at a time as an example to the masses? There is no pain involved in this process, you know."

Ringil forced down memory of the searing agony he had never suffered. "No pain involved? Would you choose it for *yourself,* you fucker?"

"No. Clearly not." The dwenda seemed genuinely perplexed by the question. "But their path is not mine, nor would I have walked it the way they have. This really is a minor matter, Ringil. You're making far too much of it."

In that single instant, Ringil would willingly have given his soul to have the weight of the Ravensfriend on his back, the dragon-tooth dagger in his sleeve. Instead, he swallowed hard, swallowed down his hate and looked away from the muddied woman's face, through the open gate of the corral.

"Why?" he managed, in a shaking voice. "Why have you brought them here? What purpose does it serve?"

Seethlaw studied him for a long moment.

"I'm not sure you will understand," he said. "You are being very obtuse at the moment."

Ringil bared his teeth. "Try me."

"Very well. They are to be honored."

"Oh, *that* sounds delightful. That's better than the Revelation's *purifying inquisitorial love*, that is."

"As I said, I do not expect you to understand. The marsh dwellers on the Naom plain are the closest to kin that the Aldrain have in this world. Thousands of years ago, their clans were favored retainers to the dwenda, favored enough that we mingled our blood with theirs. Their descendants, in however attenuated a form, carry our bloodline."

"That's a fucking myth," Ringil said disgustedly. "That's the lie they sell down at Strov market so they can jack you twice as much to read your fortune. Don't tell me you fell for that shit. What, three fucking years of politics in Trelayne, rubbing shoulders with the best liars and thieves in the League, and you still can't see a simple street scam like that coming at you?"

Seethlaw smiled. "No. The myth, like most of its kind, is based on truth, or at least on an understanding of the truth. There are ways to confirm it. How strongly the dwenda heritage emerges among the marsh clans varies enormously. But when a female child is born unable to conceive in human congress, there the bloodline is strong. It's harder to tell in males, but something similar applies."

"So you've been creaming them off through Etterkal and bringing them here. Your cousins at a hundredth remove. Come on, what does that *really* mean, *honored*?"

He was aware of the same savage grin, still pinned to his face. He saw the way Seethlaw was looking at him, and in some tiny way it felt like loss. There was another test here, like seeing the bridge, and this time he was failing it.

"I think you know what it means," the dwenda said quietly.

From Ringil's throat came a single, jolting, almost soundless sneer. "You're going to sacrifice them."

"If you care to call it that." Seethlaw shrugged. "Yes."

"That's great. You know, I'm just some scum-fuck human, I've barely seen three decades of life, and even I know there are no gods worthy of the name out there. So what is it you fucks believe in so desperately it needs a blood ritual?"

The dwenda looked pained. "Do you really require an answer to this tirade?"

"Hey, we're fucking talking, aren't we?"

Another shrug. "Well, then. It's less a question of gods than of mechanisms, of the way things are bound up and acted upon. Of ritual, if you like. You may as well ask why humans bury their dead, when eating them would make more sense. There *are* powers, entities with sway in these matters, though the Aldrain do not consider themselves bound by them in any meaningful way. But there is also an etiquette, an observance of hallowed rules, and for this, blood has always been the channel. You might think of it as the signature on the treaties your people make with each other—though we at least honor our agreements once they are made. If there must be blood, we will offer it. The blood of birth, the blood of death, the blood of animals when a minor shift in fate is required, of one's own people when something greater is desired. In our history, those chosen for this honor have always gone willingly to their end, as a warrior goes willingly to battle, knowing what their sacrifice is worth."

"I don't think that's going to be the case with your distant cousins here."

"No," Seethlaw agreed. "It's not ideal. But it will have to serve. In the end, the fact that *we* are willing to spill blood we know is our own, well, that will have to be sacrifice enough."

"Oh, *good.* Glad you've got it all worked out."

The dwenda sighed. "You know, Gil, I had thought you of all people might be able to understand. From what I know of you—"

"You know nothing of me." Through clenched teeth. "*Nothing.* You've fucked me, that's all. Well, that's a crowded hole you're in, darling. And us humans, we're a lying, dissembling bunch, remember. Doesn't pay to trust us between the sheets any more than anywhere else."

"You're wrong, Gil. I know you better than you know yourself."

"Oh, *lizardshit!*"

"I've seen you in the marches, Gil. I see how you handled yourself there." Seethlaw leaned across and seized him by the shoulders. "*I see what the akyia saw, Gil. I see what you could become, if you'd only let yourself.*"

Ringil raised his arms, sharp empty-hand technique, broke the dwenda's hold, shook him off. He felt an odd calm settling over him.

"I've done all the becoming I'm going to in this life. I've seen enough to know where it all goes. Now you made me a fucking promise. Are you going to keep it? Or do you want to give me back my sword and we'll finish this thing the way we started it?"

They stared at each other. Ringil felt himself falling into the dwenda's empty eyes. He locked up the feeling, kept the stare.

"Well?"

"I keep my promises," said Seethlaw.

"Good. Then let's get on with it."

Ringil turned brusquely and shouldered his way past, into the corral. Seethlaw stared after him for a long moment, face unreadable, and then he followed.

Sherin didn't know him.

You couldn't blame her, Ringil supposed. It had been a long time, and there probably wasn't a lot left in him of the little boy who refused to play with her in the gardens at Lanatray. Certainly there wasn't much of the wan little girl *he* remembered in the woman slumped before him. He'd very likely have walked right past her in the Glades without recognition if he hadn't been staring a hole in Ishil's charcoal sketch of her for the last couple of weeks. In fact, even the sketch wasn't such a great match now. Sherin's privations seemed to have melted the flesh from her face, turned her eyes hollow and inward, and added a brutal burden of years she hadn't yet lived. There were streaks of tangled gray in her hair and gathered lines of pain around mouth and eyes that wouldn't have looked amiss on a harbor-end tavern drudge twice her age.

Looking at her, he wondered briefly what marks his time with the dwenda had left on his own face. He hadn't seen a mirror since the night he left the Glades for Etterkal, and now, suddenly, the thought of facing one filled him with unease.

"Sherin?" he said, very gently. He knelt to her level. "It's your cousin Ringil. I've come to take you home."

She didn't look at him. Her eyes were fixed past his shoulder on Seethlaw, and she cowered into the corner of the stall as if the mother-of-pearl weave of the walls would absorb her. When Ringil reached out to touch her arm, she flinched violently away and her hands crept up to clutch and cover her neck. She rocked back and forth minutely in the corner and began a high single-note keening, a sound so divorced from human voice that at first he could not be sure it came from her throat.

Ringil twisted on his haunches, looked up at Seethlaw's pale, Aldrain features.

"You want to get the fuck out?" he snapped. "Give me a minute with her?"

The dwenda's gaze went from his face to Sherin and back again. His shoulders lifted minimally. He turned and slipped out through the half-open door like smoke.

"Listen, Sherin, he isn't going to hurt you. He's . . ." Ringil weighed it up. "A friend. He's going to let me take you home. Really. There's no trick here, no sorcery. I really am your cousin. Your mother and Ishil asked me to come. Been looking for you for . . . for a while. Don't you remember me from Lanatray? I never wanted to play with you in the gardens, remember, even when Ishil made me."

That seemed to do it. Inch by inch, her face came around. The keening broke up, caught on shards of breath, then soaked away into the quiet like water into parched earth. She looked at him out of one eye, shivering, both hands still clasped at her neck. Her voice creaked like a rusty hinge.

"Ri-ringil?"

He put together something resembling a smile. "Yeah."

"It's really you?"

"Yeah. Ishil sent me." He tried the smile again. "You know what that means. Ishil. What she's like. I fucking *had* to find you, didn't I?"

"Ringil. Ringil."

And then she threw herself onto him, collapsed over his neck and shoulders, weeping and clutching and screaming as if a thousand possessing demons were trapped inside her and had decided now, finally, that they'd been there too long, they wanted out, and it was time to let go.

He held her while it lasted, rocking her gently, murmuring platitudes and stroking her rat's-nest hair. The screams ran down to sobbing, then to shuddering breaths and quiet. He peered at her face, cleaned it of tears as best he could with his shirtsleeve, and then he picked her up and carried her out, bits of straw from the stall's floor still clinging to the simple swamp-stained shift she wore.

Happy now, Mother? Have I done enough?

Outside, the sky was moving, thick cloud boiling past overhead at menacing speed. The light had changed, thickening and staining toward a day's-end dimness, and the air reeked of a coming storm. There were no sounds from the other stables or the other stalls in this one; if their occupants were awake, terror or apathy was keeping them quiet. Ringil found himself glad—it was easier to pretend there was no one else kept prisoner here but the woman he now held in his arms.

Seethlaw stood with his back to the wall of the stable and his arms folded, looking at nothing at all. Ringil walked past him without a word, stopped a couple of steps past with Sherin in his arms. She buried her face in his neck and moaned.

"So," the dwenda said at his back. "Satisfied? You have everything you want now?"

Ringil did not look around. "You put us both on a good horse, you point me to the Trelayne road, and you let me get a full day's ride away from this shit-hole. Then we can maybe talk about promises kept."

"Sure." He heard the sound of Seethlaw levering himself off the wall, straightening up and gliding in behind him. His voice fell drab and cold, lifted hairs on the nape of Ringil's neck. "Why not. After all, there's nothing more for you here, is there?"

"You said it."

He walked toward the gate in the stormlight, bracing his steps a little because Sherin was heavier to carry than he'd expected when he first picked her up. Some forever insouciant part of him remembered a time when he could fight all day in plate armor and still stand as night fell, find the energy to go among the conscripted men at camp and build their spirits for the next day's slaughter, talk up victory he did not believe in and share their brutally crude jokes about spending and fucking and hurting as if he found them funny.

Were you a better man then, Gil? Or just a better liar?

Your arse cheeks and belly were tighter, anyway. Your shoulders were bigger and harder.

Perhaps that was enough, for them and for you.

He cleared the gate, working grimly to keep his eyes away from the heads in the water beyond. He almost succeeded. One slippery, sliding glance as he walked out, the corner of his eye grabbed by the despairing muddied features of the woman nearest the gate. He jerked his gaze away before he could glimpse more than one tear-soiled cheek and the mumbling desperate mouth. He never met her eyes.

On through the swamp and the failing light, with Sherin weighing ever heavier in his arms and Seethlaw cold and remotely beautiful at his side, all three of them like symbolic characters from some irritatingly pompous morality-tale play whose original moral had somehow been scrambled and compromised and lost and was now, to audience and participants alike, anybody's fucking guess.

ON THE SOUTHWESTERN FRINGES OF THE SWAMP, THE LAND GREW slowly less hostile to human use, and apparently to life of other kinds as well. It started with the odd mosquito bite and sparse clouds of flies rising around their boots as they plashed through marshy portions of the path. Then, slowly, birdsong began to seep into the silence, and a short time after that Ringil started to spot the birds themselves, perched or hopping about in plain view on branches and fallen tree trunks. Increasingly, water gave up its unpredictable claims to the earth, ceased to ooze up out of the ground wherever they stepped and confined itself more and more to creeks and inlets. The path they walked hardened up; the ever-present stench of the stagnant pools receded to an infrequent wafting. The ground rose and folded itself, while the sound of flowing water over rock announced the presence of streams. Even the sky seemed to brighten as the threatening storm crawled off somewhere else for a while.

Like many other things in Ringil's life, the oppressive stillness at the heart of the swamp had not seemed so hard to endure until he walked away from it.

They followed one of the creeks as it turned into a river, stopping to rest at frequent intervals along the bank. After a while, Sherin was able to walk by herself, though she still shrank against Ringil's side whenever any of the dwenda came close or turned a blank-eyed gaze on her. She didn't talk at all, seemed in fact to be treating the whole experience as if it might at any moment turn out to be a hallucination or a dream.

Ringil sympathized.

Seethlaw, for his part, was almost as silent. He led the group with a minimum of verbal and gestured instruction, and didn't speak to Ringil any more than his fellow Aldrain. If he'd selected the other dwenda who accompanied them, Ringil had not seen him do it. Pelmarag and Ashgrin simply fell in beside them as they crossed the Aldrain bridge, and another two dwenda he didn't know were waiting for them at the other side. Brief snatches of conversation went back and forth among these four as they walked, but Seethlaw was not included, and didn't seem much to care.

At twilight, they came to a scavenger camp built beside the creek.

"There's a ferry across," Seethlaw explained as they stood under trees at the edge of the little knot of cabins and storehouses. "And from there, the road bends northwest. We've come this far south to avoid the worst of the swamp, but the ground from now on is a lot easier. It's a couple of days' walk to Pranderghal, that's a fair-sized village. We'll get horses there."

Ringil knew Pranderghal. He'd watched its original inhabitants driven from their homes and onto the road south, back when it was still called Iprinigil. He nodded.

"And tonight?"

"We spend here. The ferry won't run now until morning." Seethlaw grinned unpleasantly. "Unless you want me to bring the aspect storm and find a way around in the marches."

Ringil held down a shiver. He glanced at Sherin. "No thanks. I don't think either of us is up for that."

"Are you quite sure?" The grin stayed. "Think about it. You could be home in Trelayne in a matter of days instead of weeks. And it won't feel like days anyway; it won't feel like time at all."

"Yeah. I know what it'll feel like. Give it a fucking rest, why don't you?"

They went into the only inn in the camp, an earthen-floor-and-straw establishment with a dozen trestle tables and a long wooden bar at ground level. There was a staircase against the far wall and a railed landing overhead with doors leading off. They forced their way through the din and press of bearded, unwashed-smelling men to the bar and procured rooms for the night. Ringil saw no obvious change in Seethlaw or the other dwenda, but they'd evidently cast some kind of glamour about themselves, because no one reacted to their looks or outlandish garb. The innkeeper, a thickset, swarthy individual hard to tell apart from his clientele, took coin from Pelmarag with a curt nod, bit into it and pocketed it, then gestured toward a trestle table in the corner near a window. They took their seats and were served a hog-rib dinner along with tankards of thick-foamed ale shortly thereafter. It all proved surprisingly digestible, at least to Ringil's stomach, though he saw the dwenda shooting one another wry glances as they chewed.

He found he couldn't remember what they'd eaten in the Aldrain marches. Only that Seethlaw had supplied it, magicked it forth from somewhere, and it had melted like the finest cuts of honeyed meat in his mouth, like the most sought-after of Glades cellar vintages on his tongue. Beyond that . . .

Even that . . .

It was all fading now, he realized, fading fast, the marches and everything he'd seen and done there like fragments of a last dream before waking, pieces of self in action that made no obvious sense, tantalizing images without context and an incoherent tumble of events loosed from any mooring in time or sequence—

He stopped chewing abruptly, and for just that moment the tavern food was a clotted mouthful of sawdust and grease he couldn't bring himself to swallow. The heat and lamplight and noise in the place swelled to a dull, unbearable roar. He stared across at Seethlaw, seated directly opposite, and saw the dwenda was watching him.

"It's fading . . . ," he said through the food stuck in his mouth. "I can't . . ."

Seethlaw nodded. "Yes. That's to be expected. You've returned to the defined world, you're tied to time and circumstance again. Your sanity will suffer if you remember anything else clearly, if the alternatives seem too real."

Ringil swallowed his mouthful, forced it down.

"It's like it's all turning into a dream I had," he said numbly.

The dwenda gave him a small, sad smile. He leaned forward a little. "I've heard it said that dreams are the only way your kind can find their way into the gray places. And that only the insane or the inhumanly strong of will can stay."

"I—"

Someone bumped heavily into Ringil from behind, jolted loose what he wanted say before he could frame it properly. The thought spilled away from him like coins across the street and down a grate, little glints of gleaming meaning, gone.

He snapped around angrily on the bench.

"Why the fuck don't you watch where you're going?"

"Oops, sorry, citizen, sorry. Look, I'll gladly make good any spillage if you . . . Gil? Fucking *Ringil*?"

Egar the Dragonbane.

Out of the lamplight and tavern hubbub like a figure from legend emerging from battlefield mist. Broad and tall and tangled looking, hair a wild knotted mass with little iron talismanic ornaments hanging in it. One leather-sheathed blade of his staff lance jutted up over his shoulder; there was a short-handled ax matched with a broad-bladed dirk at his belt. He smelled of marsh and cold, and had obviously just come through the door. His scarred and bearded face split into a huge grin. He clapped hands on Ringil's shoulders, dragged him up off the bench with no more effort than a father picking up his infant son.

"Urann's fucking balls, let me get a look at you," he bellowed. "What the fuck are *you* doing in this shit-pile dump? *You're* the fucking face from the past I'm supposed to recognize and save? *You're* the one that cloaked fuck was on about?"

And then everything came apart.

For Ringil it was like stepping suddenly back into some aspect of the marches. Time stopped working, slowed to a pace that was like moving in mud. His perceptions stretched and smeared; he saw what was happening as if through some other, entirely more attenuated set of senses.

Seethlaw, slamming to his feet, eyes wide.

Egar, warrior's senses suddenly awake to the tension, hand falling without fuss to the broad dirk at his hip.

Heads turning at neighboring tables.

Ashgrin, seated at Seethlaw's side, turning, reaching down for something.

A faint shimmer on the air. A darkening.

"I think you are mistaken, sir," Seethlaw said, and raised a hand a few inches off the table at his side, fingers spread loosely to make a spider. A ripple seemed to run through the fingers, as if they were suddenly boneless. "This is not your friend."

Egar snorted. "Listen, old man, I'd know this guy any . . ."

He frowned.

"A mistake," repeated the dwenda caressingly. "Easily made."

"You must be very tired," agreed Ashgrin.

Egar yawned cavernously. "Yeah, ain't that the fucking truth. Funny, I could have sworn—"

Ringil, for no clear reason he could later name, screamed and swept an arm savagely across the table. Tavern-brawl tactics, tugged out from some dark pocket of response he rarely went to these days. The lamp in the center went over, oil spilled out. Flame caught and sprinted a line among the platters and tumbled tankards. He came to his feet, heels of both palms under the trestle, upended it at Seethlaw.

"It is me, Eg," he was yelling. "It fucking *is* me. *Get the girl.*"

Later, tears would squeeze into his eyes as he recalled the Majak's reaction. Egar's lips peeled off a snarl, he surged back in at Ringil's side.

The dirk came out, broad dark glint in the dancing light from the flames now loose in the straw on the floor. He brandished it at the stumbling dwenda.

"Right you are, Gil," he roared. "Who wants this right up their fucking arse? Fucking magicking old cunts."

His other hand had already flashed out, seized Sherin by the arm, and dragged her off the bench. As Pelmarag tried to stop him, the dirk flashed out. Pelmarag's arm got in the way, the blade sliced, and blood darkened the dwenda's sleeve. Pelmarag made a wolfish snarling sound of his own and leapt at Egar. The steppe nomad's eyes widened in shock. Whatever he'd seen in Pelmarag before, whatever glamour had sullied his perception, it was gone now.

"Wraith!" he bellowed. " 'Ware spirits! *Swamp wraith!*"

Then he went over on the floor with Pelmarag on top of him.

Weapon, weapon. It gibbered through Ringil's head. *Sell my fucking soul to Hoiran for a weapon.*

He spun and dropped on Pelmarag's back instead. Knew it was a matter of seconds before the other dwenda at the table had him. Did it anyway. Egar was locked up in the knife fighter's clinch, arms braced and straining to bring his blade to bear against Pelmarag's grip. The legs of dwenda and man thrashed about on the earthen floor, looking for purchase. Ringil hooked the fingers of his right hand into the dwenda's eyes and hauled back. Pelmarag howled and flailed. Egar broke the dwenda's grip and shoved the dirk through his throat from the side. Blood gouted everywhere. It smelled, Ringil would later realize, bittersweet and strong, quite unlike anything out of human veins.

For now he was already spinning about, crouched and yelling, looking for the others in the rising smoke. He had one moment to lock gazes with Seethlaw, who was poised to leap the upended trestle, features an awful mask of blank-eyed, snarling rage. Then a surging mass of humanity swept in between them.

"Swamp wraith! Swamp wraith! Get the motherfuckers!"

Out of nowhere, Ashgrin had a terrible blue long-sword blade flashing in his hands. The first humans to reach him went down in butchered pieces. The surge turned chaotic and shrill, some scrambling backward away from the sudden steel, others who had weapons bawling for space and struggling to get to the front.

"Ringil!" Egar, yelling in his ear. "Let's get the fuck out of here!"

He gulped air. "Gladly. Get the—"

"Got her! Just fucking *go!*"

The Majak's hand was firmly around Sherin's arm again, engulfing it just above the elbow. She'd have bruises tomorrow, Ringil knew.

If we live that long.

They made the door somehow, elbowing and tripping others who'd had the same idea. Ringil kicked it open and tumbled out into the cold and dark. The inn was built on a slight rise and he fell over with his own momentum, landed in a winded heap.

Shattering of glass. A dwenda came leaping, shrieking through the window like a lost soul, landed like a cat, and stalked toward them, blade in hand, grinning.

Egar let go of Sherin's arm.

"Get behind me, girl," he grunted.

He freed his small ax, hefted it left-handed, kept the dirk in his right. No time to unship the lance, much though he'd have loved the extra reach. He eyed the creature's sword with professional calm. The empty inhuman eyes had been a shock with the first one, but now his blood was up, he wasn't fussed. No worse than a steppe ghoul, he supposed. A fighting grin licked around his lips.

"Fuck you looking at?" he barked.

The creature ran in, shrilling. Terrifying speed, but Egar had seen that a few times before as well. He hurled his dirk upward, underhand at its face. The long-sword flashed out, deflecting, but it was an awkward block, anyone could see that. Egar was in behind, now with the ax in both hands, hacking sideways under the twisted sword. The swamp wraith yowled and leapt out of the way. Egar pressed in, got the hook-backed edge of the ax on the blade and yanked it out of the way, left-handed. His right hand curled to a fist, smashed his opponent in the face. The swamp wraith reeled. Egar followed through. Another punch, into the face again—*leave the body alone, assume armor of some sort under that weird black leatherish gear*—and he felt the nose break with a solid crunch. The wraith screamed and tried to slash back at him with its blocked blade. Speed it had, but not the brute strength it needed. Egar grinned and reached down, hooked an arm under a thigh, and heaved. The creature went over on its back. Egar dropped on its chest with a knee and his full weight. Something creaked and cracked. The swamp wraith screamed again, weakly. Egar got his ax free, no time to reverse it, and smashed the iron-shod haft down into the empty-eyed face. He put out an eye, shattered a cheekbone. Smashed the mouth and the already broken nose.

Movement behind him.

He whipped around, saw Ringil standing there swaying in the feeble light. Blew out a sigh of relief and eased his grip on the ax.

"Get up," the Trelayne knight said hoarsely. "We've got to get out of here. Before the others get outside."

Egar glanced toward the inn. The sounds of violence raged from the broken window and the doorway, where a mob of men was gathering, torn between the fascination of spectators and the terror of what they'd seen. There was smoke and the jumping light of flames. No one seemed to have noticed the three of them yet, down here in the gloom. All attention was on the building.

"There's got to be better than sixty men in there," he told Ringil. He was breathing hard from the fight. "Even if only two-thirds of them want to mix it up, they'll finish these fuckers, easy."

"No, they *won't*." An awful urgency split Ringil's voice open. "Believe me, we've got minutes at most."

You don't follow a man to almost certain death in the baking heat of a mountain pass without learning his measure first. Without learning to trust what he says in a coin-spin instant, even if he is a fucking faggot. Egar got up and stared around.

"Right. We take the ferry."

"What?" Ringil frowned. "Don't these bumpkins lock up their oars?"

"Yeah, who gives a shit about *oars,* time like this. The Idrikarn flows hard this far out of the swamp, it'll carry us south faster than you can fucking run, mate."

The thing at Egar's feet stirred and moaned. The Majak looked down in surprise.

"Tough motherfucker, huh?" he said, almost admiring.

Then he reversed the ax in his hands, shifted stance, and chopped down with the bladed end. The swamp wraith's head rolled free in a messy burst of blood. He wiped some of it off his face, sniffed it curiously and shrugged. He cast about and found his dirk, gathered it up, and clapped Ringil on the shoulder.

"Come on, then," he said. "Arse in the saddle."

"Wait, give me his sword."

"What do you want his fucking sword for? What's wrong with the one on your back?"

Ringil stared at him as if he'd suddenly started gibbering like a Demlarashan mystic. Egar stopped in midturn, spread his bloodied hands.

"What?"

Ringil lifted his right hand as if it pained him, put it slowly and wonderingly up to his shoulder, and touched the pommel of his sword like, well, like he was caressing someone's prick, to be honest. Egar shifted uncomfortably, fiddled with his ax.

"You're a fucking weirdo, Gil. Same as it ever was. Come *on*."

Down to the darkened landing stage at a sprint, Sherin stumbling between them, and Ringil saw it was true, even at the bent edge of the river there was current running. Tiny leaves and other specks of river detritus drifted by at ambling pace. In the center of the stream, a taut swirl showed on the fitfully bandlit water. The ferry, a fat little demasted fishing skiff barely four yards long, wagged at the end of its moorings as if in a hurry to be off.

"Hoy! You!" They'd been spotted. "Wait, there—thieves—look. Hoy, stop them, that's my fucking *boat*—"

They leapt aboard. Egar hacked the ropes apart and gave the pilings a punt with one boot. Behind them, a spill of dark figures came pelting down toward the landing stage, yelling, gesticulating, brandishing weapons and fists. The skiff drifted away from the shore, agonizingly slow at first and then, as the current caught, swinging briskly out into flow. Balanced amidships, crouched over the collapsed and sobbing form of Sherin, Egar grinned at Ringil.

"Haven't done this in a while."

"You'd better get down," Ringil advised him. "They're going to start shooting in a minute."

"Nah. Too much else going on, they won't have a strung bow between them. They're not soldiers, Gil." But he bent and hand-braced himself to a seat on one of the skiff's cross-strut benches anyway. He craned sideways and peered. "That's just Radresh, pissed off 'cause we've nicked his ferry."

"You can see his point."

"Yeah, well. Never did like his fucking prices."

The two of them looked back in silence as the crowd on the landing stage boiled about in its own impotence. Something heavy splashed in their wake, but too far aft to be a cause for concern. No one was getting in the water, that was for sure. A couple of pursuers with some presence of mind ran along the bank, trying to keep pace. Ringil watched narrowly for a few seconds, saw them run into thickening undergrowth at the edge of the camp and clog to a halt. The pursuit died in curses and bawled abuse, growing ever fainter. He felt his heart starting to ease.

Until—

Up on the rise, flames burned merrily in the windows and opened door of the inn. It was hard to tell at the growing distance, but he thought a single tall, dark figure loomed in the doorway, unmoved by the fire at its back, staring after them with lightless eyes.

Run if you like, whispered a voice in his head. *I'll count to a hundred.*

He shivered.

The boat tugged onward, downriver on the water's dark swirl.

CHAPTER 30

I *had thought of Ennishmin, my lord.*

Archeth mimicked herself savagely as she stared out of the window. The Beksanara garrison tower was a stubby affair, barely two stories higher than the rest of the blockhouse, and the view from the top room was the same as everywhere else in this bloody country. Swamp and bleak trees, under a sky the color of spilled brains. You couldn't even see the river from this angle. You certainly couldn't see any trace of the morning sun.

She'd had the whole fucking Empire to choose from.

She could have been on a beach somewhere in the Hanliahg Scatter right now, bare feet in the sand and a pitcher of coconut beer for company, watching morning flood the sky across the bay with light. She could have been on the balcony of an Uplands Watch garrison lodge beyond the Dhashara pass, hot coffee and lung-spiking mountain air to wake her up, and the swoop-and-squabble courtship of snow eagles like a duel overhead.

But no, no, you had to follow your fucking hunch to this shit-hole end of the realm. You had to drag Elith back into her past and all the memories too painful to face that she'd left behind. Just couldn't resist it, could you? Archeth Indamaninarmal returns in triumph with the answer to the Empire's mysterious woes.

She'd found nothing. Two weeks of crisscrossing the settlements on the fringes of the Ennishmin marshes, of quizzing bored and resentful imperial officials already out of sorts with their miserable luck at being posted here. Two weeks of barely concealed sneers and sullen reticence under questioning from the artifact scavenger trash whose patriotic help she'd tried—and failed—to enlist. Two *fucking* weeks of old wives' tales and rumor, and trekking through swamp to look at a succession of curiously shaped boulders or rock outcrops with no significance what-soever. The big triumph so far was unearthing another glirsht marker to match the one Elith had hauled to Khangset. They dug it out of soggy mud, six miles into the swamp from Yeshtak where it had fallen on its face and lain, apparently for centuries, undisturbed. It was moss-grown and pitted with age, and one of its beckoning arms was broken off. Sweat-stained and mud-streaked, they let it lie where it was and plod-ded back to Yeshtak.

She saw the way Faileh Rakan and his men looked at her when they thought she wouldn't notice, and it was hard to blame them.

She was chasing phantoms, and it was turning out exactly as you'd expect.

And now this—sabotage or random viciousness, Idrashan fed some-thing in the stables that brought him mysteriously to his knees and forced them to stay overnight while they waited to see if he would live or die. There was no veterinarian worthy of the name in Beksanara, and not much in the way of law enforcement, either. Rakan bullied the village ad-ministrator into rounding up a few likely suspects, and the Throne Eter-nal men took turns knocking them around in the blockhouse cells. Outside of the exercise, they got nothing remotely useful from it. Blame cycled back and forth as it tended to in these situations, backstabbing and local family feuds, petty criminal misdemeanors brought to light and frankly implausible confessions, all seeded with the usual marsh mist crap: a mysterious plague on the air that afflicted horses when the wind blew from the northeast; bandits, the feral remnants of families driven out in the occupation, hiding in the swamp and slowly turning into something less than human; a tall figure in brimmed leather hat and cloak, sighted recently prowling the streets at night as if surveying the village for some evil purpose; shadowy child-sized figures seen skittering about in the gloom and making eerie, whinnying sounds. After six hours of it, Archeth made Rakan let everybody go.

They were still waiting to see if Idrashan would pull through.

Her mouth clamped. *By the Holy fucking Mother, if that horse dies . . .*

Boots on the stair.

She turned from the window, crossed the small square room, and went out onto the staircase. Faileh Rakan came around the turn below and looked up at her, eyes a little smudged with being up all night, tiny scrape on his temple where one of the tougher suspects had inadvisedly put up a fight. He stopped in midstep when he saw her standing there.

"Milady," he said, and inclined his head. It was an automatic deference but one, she thought, that was wearing rather thin.

"How's my horse?"

"It's, uhm—there's no change, milady. I'm very sorry. It's not that. There has been a fresh development."

"Ah. And what's that?"

"Well, the village administrator tells me his militia have arrested some boat thieves. They found them asleep and run aground on the meander below the village. The boat is without oars, so it's the usual thing."

Archeth shifted impatiently. The village administrator, name of Yanshith, was a miserable tub of guts, the depths of his incompetence matched only by the size of his belly and his self-importance.

"Yes? And this concerns us because?"

Rakan cleared his throat. "Well, it also seems that these boat thieves claim to have been fleeing from uhm, magical beings that live in the swamp. And one of them carries a Kiriath blade."

HORSESHIT.

She muttered it to herself a couple of times at least as they went down the stairs and out into the street, because there was an inexplicable pounding in her chest that she didn't want to be there, and she didn't know which scared her more—to be wrong and disappointed once again, or to be vindicated in her fears.

Horseshit, a fucking Kiriath blade. It's going to be some half length of scavenged scaffolding iron, ground to a ragged edge and wrapped around at one end with cord to make a grip. Seen it enough times before.

But it wasn't.

They reached the combined boathouse and storage shed at the other end of the village, where the thieves were apparently being held. On approach, she saw the confiscated weapons piled up between a pair of unkempt militiamen apparently detailed to keep the door. The thunder in her chest went up a notch at the sight: dirk, hand ax, a Majak staff lance and dragon-tooth ceremonial dagger, and there, dumped unceremoniously on top of everything else, the layered gleam of an An-Monal battle scabbard and the woven hilt of the broadsword it was clasped lovingly around.

She stopped dead and stared at the weapon. It gleamed back at her like an old and slightly smug friend, first meeting for years and suddenly made good beyond all expectation.

And then the drawling voice from within, faint through the door's wood but unmistakable. The soft over hard, slightly absent tone and the outrageous disrespect it accorded the tightly bound syllables of the Tethanne it spoke.

"You know, Sergeant, you really must have better things to do with the next few hours of your life than trying to stare me out. Like get a shave, for instance? Or just write your last will and testament. You can write, I take it?"

She almost took the door off its hinges going in. It banged back against the wall with a flat crack, bounced back again, and she had to catch it on her forearm, which hurt.

"Ringil?"

"Well, now." But behind the mannered monosyllables, she saw her shock mirrored back to her in his eyes. He leaned back a little on the upended rowing boat where he sat. Pause, recovery, all on the turn of a second. "Archeth Indamaninarmal. Enters dramatically, from center stage. The Powers really are getting their act together, it seems."

"Told you," grunted the man at Ringil's side, and then she recognized him as well. "Didn't want to believe me, did you?"

"Dragonbane? You here, too?"

"Hey, Archeth." The Majak grinned at her. "Why so formal? No one calls me that anymore."

"Well, now you know how I feel then," muttered Ringil.

There were four halberd-equipped militiamen in the room, weapons now drooping, faces gaping at this incomprehensible exchange between visiting Kiriath nobility and the three boat thieves they'd herded into the corner. Faileh Rakan said it for all of them.

"You *know* these people, milady?"

"Yes, I do. Well, this young woman, no, but—"

"Sherin Herlirig Mernas," supplied Ringil, with a courtly gesture, while the woman at his side stared in silence with hollow-eyed fatigue and wonder. "And *this* is Egar, son of Erkan, of the Majak clan Skaranak, known in your part of the world, perhaps rather grandiosely, as the Dragonbane."

Archeth watched Rakan's face change. In the whole Empire, there were perhaps twenty men honored with the title Dragonbane. Most had died earning it. The Throne Eternal captain took a short step forward, put fist to right shoulder, and bowed his head briefly at the Majak warrior.

"It is an honor," he said. "I am Faileh Rakan, commander first class, the Throne Eternal."

"Rakan." Egar frowned and scratched an ear. "You the Rakan who led that charge down the flank at Shenshenath fields back in '47, that time they had to dig Akal out of the ditchwork?"

"It was my honor to command the action, yes."

The Majak's face split in a grin. He shook his head. "Then you're a fucking madman, Faileh Rakan. That was the most insane thing I've ever seen. Not one soldier in a hundred I know would have run that risk."

Rakan's mouth twitched primly, but you could see he was pleased.

"Not one soldier in a thousand is chosen for the Emperor's guard," he stated, as if reciting it. "It was my duty, nothing more. The throne of Yhelteth is eternal, life in service to it must reflect that eternity in honor. Death is a price that must sometimes be paid, like any other honorable debt."

"Glad to hear that," said Ringil breezily. "Very uplifting. Hang on to that attitude, you're going to need it."

Rakan turned a frosty eye on him. "We have not had your name, sir."

"Oh, I?" Ringil raised one hand to mask a sudden, jaw-creaking yawn. "I'm Ringil of the Glades house of Eskiath in Trelayne. You may have heard of me as well."

Rakan's face changed once more. It became abruptly impassive.

"Yes, I have heard of you," he said shortly.

Ringil nodded. "Gallows Gap, no doubt."

But the Throne Eternal captain shook his head. "No. That name is not familiar to me. What I have heard is that Ringil Eskiath was a traitor to the imperial peace in the northern provinces, a corruptor of youth, and a faggot."

Egar bounced up off the curve of the upended boat back, face darkening. Archeth saw Ringil's hand fall on his arm, and felt a pang of relief. The distribution of weapons in the room did not invite brawling.

"*Fasc*inating, Eg," Ringil's tone was light and soft. Only someone who knew him well would have spotted the steel edge sheathed in it. "Don't you think? What they must be teaching in history books down south these days. I'll bet we find the Empire won the war against the Scaled Folk all by itself. And that the good people of Ennishmin and Naral were so grateful they spontaneously vacated their homes to allow imperial settlers to live in them."

Rakan lifted a finger. "I will not hear you—"

"That's enough, Rakan." Archeth stepped between the Throne Eternal captain and the others. "Gil, Egar, you told the militia you were running from dwenda, is that right?"

Ringil and Egar exchanged a glance. Ringil looked grim.

"Actually, I wasn't that specific," he said quietly. "What do you know about the dwenda, Archidi?"

The pounding in her chest seemed to be subsiding, settling to something colder and more patient that she recognized from the war years.

"I know they're here," she said. "In Ennishmin, in the swamps."

Ringil bent her a hard little smile.

"That's not the half of it. By tonight, they're going to be right here in Ibiksinri, walking the main street and knocking on doors."

THEY HELD THE COUNCIL OF WAR IN THE GARRISON HOUSE, AWAY FROM prying eyes. No point in alarming the locals, Faileh Rakan said. *No, Ringil agreed, they'd only gather up their children and flee for their lives. Can't have that, can we? Not in a border province.* The Throne Eternal captain fixed him with a baleful stare, but by this time Ringil had back the Ravensfriend and his dragon knife, had breakfasted heartily, and wore a faint, inviting smile on his face that Rakan knew well enough how to read.

Archeth put out the flames again, kept the two of them apart. They put Sherin with Elith in an unlocked cell downstairs, one of those the village administrator had been prevailed upon to equip with a few comforts when Archeth and her men were forced to stay the night before. They sent the administrator and his men away with some simple tasks to perform, told them there was nothing much to worry about, really, and locked themselves in the tower room. They got down to business, got up to date on the varied paths that had brought them to Ennishmin, which in itself was a lengthy business—and not without its awkward moments.

"Impossible! This is heresy." Halgan, one of the two Throne Eternal lieutenants Faileh Rakan had detailed to sit in, was not dealing very well with Egar's tale of his encounter with Takavach. "There is but One God and He has made himself known to us in the One True Revelation."

Ringil rolled his eyes. But Darash, the other lieutenant, was nodding agreement, and even Rakan's ordinarily impassive face was turned toward the Majak with a frown. Archeth couldn't be bothered; she let them get on with it. She stared out of the window and wondered why the mention of Takavach's leather hat and cloak seemed so familiar. Meanwhile, Egar grinned and poured himself more coffee. He was used to this sort of thing, had in fact always derived a rather childish satisfaction from scandalizing the imperials when he lived in Yhelteth. He lifted the callused blade of a hand at Halgan.

"Look, mate, I saw this Takavach take a crossbow bolt out of the air in midflight with his bare hand. Like that. He summoned an army of demons from the steppe grasses the way you'd call your children in from play, and he brought me the best part of seven hundred miles southwest to Ennishmin in the time it'd take you to snap your fucking fingers. Now—if that's not a god, then it's a pretty good imitation."

"Yes, an imitation." Darash insisted. "An evil spirit. A trick to steal your allegiance."

"Yeah, whatever." Egar slurped his coffee, put it down again and grinned. "Guys, you don't get it, do you? Takavach saved my arse out on the steppe. He butchered my enemies for me and then made me a gate out of air and darkness and hung it from a branch of my father's grave tree so I could escape. You know, for that—he's pretty much *got* my allegiance."

"But this is a *demon*, Dragonbane." Halgan was aghast, almost pleading. "You must see that. This is a devil, trying to steal your soul."

The Majak snorted. "My soul will walk the Sky Road *anyway*, whatever happens to me here on earth. It's not something you can steal like some lady's silk underwear. I killed a fucking *dragon*, man. My ancestors will have been polishing up my seat in the Sky Home ever since, grinning like idiots, probably. My father must be boring the Dwellers rigid with tales of my prowess."

"This is superstition," said Rakan dismissively. "This is not . . . truth."

"You calling me a liar?"

Ringil rubbed hands down his face. "Maybe, Rakan, it's your Revelation that's the superstition. Ever think of that? Maybe the Majak have gotten hold of the right end of the arbalest after all. Has the One True God shown up to save any of your skins recently? Has He appeared to any of you?"

"You know God does not manifest Himself," Halgan shouted. "That is also heresy. The Revelation is not corporeal. You know this. Why do you persist in this perverted speech?"

"I like perverted. Maybe you would, too, if you gave it a chance."

"Leave my men alone," Rakan said coldly. "Degenerate."

Ringil smooched a kiss at him. Rakan, out of nowhere, spat a curse and was halfway to his feet before Archeth snapped out of her daydream. She grabbed him by the arm and yanked him back into his seat.

"That's enough. You lot can sort out your religious differences some-day when there isn't anything more important to do. Right now, I want to know, *Ringil,* why you're so sure they'll come after you?"

Ringil exchanged a glance with Egar.

"You want to tell her?" he asked the Majak.

Egar shrugged. "We saw them on the bank. Twice during the night. Blue fire and a dark shape at its heart, watching us go past."

"Could that not be something else?" Halgan asked. He didn't want to believe in this any more than he had in Takavach. "Reflected light through mist around some scavenger taking a piss in the river? Or some effect from the marsh gases. The locals say—"

"The locals talk a load of shit, is what they do," Egar said flatly. "I've been working the swamp for the best part of a month now, and I've never seen anything like what I saw last night. And anyway, Archeth, it fits with what you told us about Khangset. Blue flickering light, shadow figures."

"It's how they come through from the gray places, the Aldrain marches." Ringil rubbed tiredly at an eye. Falling asleep in the drifting skiff had left him stiff and unrested. "As far as I can work out, there are places they don't need this aspect storm to do it, but there don't seem to be many of them. The heart of the swamp apparently, near where this Kiriath weapon is buried. Or maybe it's got something to do with these glirsht carvings you're talking about, I don't know. All I can tell you for sure is that Seethlaw turned up in Terip Hale's cellar as easily as if he'd just opened a door in the wall."

"That was at night, though."

"Yes. And I'd say the legends are right as far as that goes, too. The dwenda don't seem to like sunlight very much. Most of the time I was in the Aldrain marches, it was dark or dim, like twilight. One place we went, there was something like a sun in the sky, but it was almost burned out. Like a hollow shell of itself. If that's where the dwenda are from originally, it might explain why they can't tolerate bright light. And this pirate raid on Khangset you were talking about, I think I met one of the dwenda who went on it, name of Pelmarag. He told me they pulled out well before dawn because the sun was going to be too strong for comfort. *With* that *kind of sun coming up in a couple of hours' time,* he said."

"Ennishmin must suit them down to the fucking ground then," Egar grumbled. "I don't think I've seen the sun more than twice since I got here."

It provoked an unlooked-for burst of laughter from the imperials. The cranked tension around the table eased. A couple of despairing comments about rain and fog went back and forth. Darash grinned, made a loose vertical fist, and dropped it into his other hand a couple of times, Yhelteth symbol among the urbane for a good joke, a sense of humor well tickled. Egar made modest noises back.

"Can we stop them?" Archeth asked quietly, and the hilarity disappeared as fast as it had come. The gazes around the table tightened back to her. "At Khangset, they said they fired arrows that passed right through the blue fire and left the dwenda themselves unharmed."

Ringil nodded soberly. "Yeah. Eril told me the same thing happened to Girsh's crossbow bolt when he tried to stop Seethlaw. I think maybe when the aspect storm first comes through, it's like the dwenda's not completely there, like he's a ghost of some sort. But your guys at Khangset weren't as ineffective as they thought. Pelmarag said the expeditionary force he was in lost men. Six or seven of them on the beach alone. Now, that's got to be before any close-quarters fighting, we're talking about the moment the Khangset garrison realizes they've got company. So some of those arrows must have hit home. If I had to guess, I'd say this ghost aspect is short-lived. The dwenda has to let go at some point, has to become solid and grounded in this world. When they do." He smacked fist into palm. "You've got them. Pelmarag told me they lost another half a dozen warriors in the fight across town. Your marines did get to them, they were just too scared and demoralized to realize it. That's not a mistake we have to make. I crossed blades with Seethlaw, I felt the contact, even when the aspect storm was still around him. It can be done."

"Yeah, they kill easily enough," Egar rumbled. "I took two last night. Knife in the throat for one, fists and an ax haft for the other. They go down no different from a man."

"And the damage we saw at Khangset?" Archeth asked. "The Kiriath defenses were melted right through. It looked like the sort of thing dragonfire would do."

Ringil frowned and fumbled though memories already grown unreal and confused. He pressed his hands together, steepled the fingers, and pressed them to his mouth in thought. The small, carved figure in the swamp, the conversation with Pelmarag. *Tell you a funny story.*

"He said something about *the talons of the sun.* Something they unleashed through the aspect storm, before they went through themselves. Like an arrow flight before an advance or something."

"These were not arrow marks," said Rakan ironically.

"I don't think they have these talons of the sun here in the swamp." Ringil stared emptily off into dim recall. There was an odd ache in there with the memories, and he didn't like it. "They were different tactics. It was some dwenda commander who didn't agree with Seethlaw's approach. He wanted a frontal assault. That's not what Seethlaw's trying to achieve here."

"You know that for certain?" Archeth's tone was skeptical. "The dwenda are committed to a stealth campaign?"

"I don't . . ." Ringil sighed. "It isn't as simple as that, Archidi. This isn't like the Scaled Folk over again. It's not some massive migration across an ocean to escape a dying land, a whole race on the move, an invading people who have to either conquer or die. The dwenda aren't unified, they aren't anything *like* unified. There are factions, disagreements over strategy, constant individual disputes. There don't even seem to be that many of them at the moment, and even those, the handful I got to meet were squabbling with each other half the time."

"The Helmsmen say they are impulsive and disordered," Archeth said slowly. "Perhaps not even sane. Would that fit?"

Ringil thought again about the Aldrain marches. He shivered.

"Yes, it would," he said. "It would make a lot of sense. Seethlaw was . . ."

He stopped.

"Was what?" asked Rakan.

Ringil shook his head. "Skip it. Doesn't matter."

"Maybe not to you, degenerate," said Halgan angrily. "But to my men and I, it matters a great deal. You are asking us to stand and fight, maybe to die, on your word. Under the circumstances, I think you owe us the highest degree of clarity and confessed truthfulness."

"That's true," said Rakan. "Like an explanation for how exactly you came to be so closely taken into this creature's confidence in the first place. How it is that you traveled freely with him in these infernal realms, how it is that he allowed you to bring out your slave cousin."

Ringil smiled thinly. "You'd like that explained with the highest degree of clarity, would you?"

"Yes. We all would."

"Oh, well, it's easy enough." Ringil leaned across the table toward the Throne Eternal captain. "I was fucking him. In the arse, in the mouth. A lot."

Quiet slammed onto the table like a pallet of bricks dropped from above. The two Throne Eternal lieutenants looked at each other, and Halgan made a tiny but distinct spitting noise.

"You are an abomination, Eskiath," said Rakan softly.

"Well." Ringil gave the Throne Eternal captain another brittle little smile. "You know, the thing about fucking is, it's a lot less wear and tear than trying to kill each other with bits of steel. And it's the sort of thing that does tend to lead to confidences and favors if you play it right. Ask any woman, she'll tell you that. Unless of course your experiences in that direction are limited, as, come to think of it, yours probably are, to whores and rape."

This time it was Halgan who surged to his feet with an oath on his lips and a hand on the hilt of the sword he wore. Ringil sat back a little where he was, met the other man's gaze and held it.

"You clear that blade, and I'll kill you with it."

The moment held, seemed to creak.

"He means it," Archeth said quietly. "I'd sit down if I were you, Halgan."

Faileh Rakan made a short gesture, and his lieutenant sank back into his seat by inches. Archeth sighed and rubbed at her eyes.

"You're saying you insinuated yourself into this Seethlaw's affections in order to get your cousin back?"

"Yes, I am." The tiny, fading ache of memory, like a small, blunt knife turning inside his rib cage. He didn't know how much truth there was in the words. He couldn't remember anymore. "That's exactly what I'm saying."

"And you think Seethlaw's coming to get you because, what, he feels betrayed? Pissed off that you let him down?"

"No." Ringil drew a deep breath. "Seethlaw is coming to get me— and you, and *you*, Rakan, and *you two*, and everyone else in this fucking village—because he can't afford to have his plans brought to light. There's too much in play, too much he can't predict. You've got to understand, Archidi, you've got to see it from the dwenda's point of view. It's thousands of years since they had dealings with us. They're rusty, they don't know how to gauge us anymore. Seethlaw's had three years to learn contemporary politics in Trelayne, and that's it. Three miserable fucking years. He's hasn't done badly, he's built a covert power base, but by its very nature it's got to be limited. And elsewhere he's working nearly blind. He doesn't know the Empire at all, except through the lens of northern opinion, and he's smart enough to know you can't trust opinion any farther than a whore with your house keys. He has *no way* of knowing how Yhelteth will respond if it knows the attack on Ennishmin is a ploy. Worse than that, he probably can't tell what the parts of the Trelayne Chancellery he hasn't managed to corrupt will do, or any of the other cities in the League come to that. For all Seethlaw knows, the League and the Empire will unite the way they did against the Scaled Folk. He can't take the chance. Anybody human who knows about this, outside of his little cabal, has to die."

"He was going to let you live before," Darash pointed out. "He was going to let you go home. You sure this isn't just a lovers' tiff we're dealing with here? A falling-out between faggots, maybe?"

Ringil spared him a weary look. "Oh, you're a real fucking comedian, Darash. Yeah, Seethlaw was going to let me go home. He was going to let me go because he thought he could control me, and he thought I didn't give a shit about any of this, about the Empire or the League. And you know what, he was right, I *don't*." The violence jumped out in his voice, sudden and glad. "I think your beloved Jhiral Khimran is a jumped-up little turd masquerading as a leader of men, and I think his beloved father wasn't very much better. And I think the men who control Trelayne are carved from the very same richly stinking shit, they just haven't been as successful up north at feeding it to the rest of us, that's all."

"You'll answer for that, Eskiath." Rakan made no dramatic moves, but his face was a mask of cold intent. "No man, imperial citizen or not, speaks of my Emperor that way and lives. The sworn law of Yhelteth forbids it, and I'm sworn to uphold that same law."

"Oi, Rakan." Egar jerked his chin at the Throne Eternal captain. "You'll have to come through me first. Bear that in mind, won't you."

"He'll have to live through the night first, as well," said Ringil somberly. "None of us is going to have recourse to law, imperial or otherwise, unless we stop Seethlaw in his tracks."

"Or we fall back," said Archeth. "We take what we know and we run south. We can make Khartaghnal in three days if we push it. There's a levy garrison there, four hundred men under arms at least, and they have King's Reach messenger relay facilities on to the plains cities. We can get a message through to a heartland military governor inside another two days."

"Makes sense," agreed Halgan.

"No," said Ringil.

Archeth sighed. "It does make sense, Gil. Look—"

"I said no. We aren't going to do that." Ringil stared around the table, met their eyes one at a time the way he had the captains at Gallows Gap. "We are going to stop them here."

"Gil, I've got seventeen men, that's including these three sitting here now. With you two and me, that's twenty. The militia's going to run at the first sign of trouble, you know that."

"Like we're planning to, you mean?" Egar said, grinning.

Darash bristled. "This is a tactical withdrawal we're talking about, Dragonbane."

"Is it?" Egar shook his head. "Well, you know, there's a Skaranak saying for times like these: *Running away just makes your arse a bigger target.* If the dwenda can follow us downriver through the swamp the way they did last night, they can certainly track us across the uplands before we hit Khartaghnal. Three days means three nights, maybe four. You ready to stay awake that long, ready to fight worn out and maybe in motion on ground they'll choose to suit themselves? Sounds like a fucking stupid idea to me."

"Egar, it's like I said to Gil." Archeth spread her hands, gestured at the gathered company. "It's twenty of us, against something we can't quantify, something that scared my people four thousand years ago and still scares the Helmsmen now."

The Majak shrugged. "Ghost stories. Come the crunch, it can't be any scarier than a dragon, can it? Look, I killed two of these fucking dwenda things last night, and like I said they bleed and fall down just like men. And we all know how to kill men, don't we?"

"Everyone's afraid of what they don't understand," Ringil said quietly. "You want to remember that, Archidi. The dwenda are as uncertain of us as we are of them. They've got less reason, but they don't know that, and anyway it's not a rational thing. You know what Pelmarag said about your poor, scared shitless marine garrison at Khangset? *Fucking humans everywhere,* he said, *running around screaming and jabbering in the dark like the lost souls of apes, you know, cut one down and there's another right fucking behind him.* What does that sound like to you?"

The others looked at him in silence. No one offered an answer.

"And you, Archeth? Look at you, look at what you represent to them. They have legends about the Black Folk, the way we do about them. Horror stories about how you destroyed their cities and drove them out into the gray places. They talk about you as if you were demons, the same way we used to talk about the Scaled Folk until we understood them. The same way your fucking imperial history books probably *still* talk about them. Look, when Seethlaw and I arrived in the swamp, there was a minor panic on because one of the dwenda scouts had heard some artifact scavengers talking about a black-skinned warrior somewhere in the vicinity. Which I guess probably *was* you, now I come to think about it, but that's not the point. Even that, even the *rumor* of you, was enough to worry them."

He rested his arms on the table, and his gaze hooded for a moment. When he looked up again, Archeth caught his stare and a chill slithered between her shoulders and up her neck. It was, for just a moment, as if a stranger had climbed into Ringil Eskiath's skin and stolen his eyes.

"When I trained at the Academy," he said tonelessly, "they told me there is nothing in this world to fear more than a man who wants to kill you and knows how to do it. We make a stand here, and we can teach that truth to the dwenda. We can stop them, we can send them back to the gray places to think again about taking this world."

More silence.

The moment tipped, was falling away, when Rakan cleared his throat.

"Why do you care?" he asked. "Five minutes ago you're telling us how you don't give a shit about the Empire or the League. Now suddenly you want to take a stand, make a difference. What's that about?"

Ringil looked coldly at him.

"What's it about, Faileh Rakan? It's about the fucking war, that's what it's about. You're right, I don't give a shit about your Emperor and I care even less about the scum that run Trelayne and the League. But I won't watch them go to war again. I've been to war, you know, to save civilization from the reptile hordes. I bled for it, I saw friends and other men die for it. And then I watched men like you piss it away again, the civilization we'd saved, in squabbles over a few hundred square miles of territory and what language the people get to speak there, what color their skin and hair is and what kind of religious horseshit they get crammed down their throats. I saw men here, right fucking here in Ennishmin, who'd fought for the human alliance, some who'd lost limbs or eyes or their sanity, driven out of their homes with their families and herded onto the road to march or die, all to balance up some filthy fucking piece of political expedience Akal the so-called Great and his erstwhile allies could all save face on, shut your *fucking* mouth, Rakan, I'm not finished yet."

Ringil's eyes glittered as he stared the Throne Eternal captain down.

"I watched men who'd given everything come back home to Tre-layne and see their women and children sold into slavery to pay debts they didn't know they'd incurred because they'd been away fighting at the time. I saw those slaves shipped south to feed your fucking Empire's brothels and factories and noble homes, and I saw other men who'd given *nothing* in the war get rich off that trade and the sacrifice of those men and women and children. *And I will not watch it happen again.*"

Abruptly, he was on his feet. He drew a deep, shuddering breath. His voice grew low and grating, almost another man's altogether.

"Seethlaw doesn't know the Empire, but I do. If we run south, and if we make it, then Jhiral will send his massed levies, and Seethlaw will bring on the dwenda, and behind him will come whatever cobbled-together private armies this fuckwit cabal has managed to assemble in the north, and it will start *all over again.* And I will not fucking permit that, not again. We stop them here. It ends here, and if we die here, ending it, I for one won't be too fucking bothered. You will either stand with me, or all your talk of honor and duty and necessary death is a posturing courtier's lie. We stop them here, together. If I see anyone try to leave between now and tonight, I will hamstring their horse and break their fucking legs and *I will leave them out in the street for the dwenda.* There will *be* no more fucking discussion, there will be no more talk of tactical withdrawal. *We stop them here!*"

He drew another hard breath. He stared around at them all. His voice dropped, grew suddenly quiet again, and matter-of-fact.

"We stop them here."

He walked out. Slammed the door open, left it gaping on their silence. They heard his boots clatter down the stairs, sound fading.

Egar looked around the faces at the table and shrugged.

"I'm with the faggot," he said.

CHAPTER 31

The dwenda came, finally, with blue fire and terrible, unhuman force, in the small, cold hours before dawn.

AMONG THOSE WHO SURVIVED THE ENCOUNTER, THERE WOULD BE A lot of speculation over whether it was planned that way. Whether the dwenda knew enough about humans to understand that this was the best time to take their prey, the lowest ebb of the human spirit. Or whether perhaps they simply knew that a long, wakeful, but uneventful night of waiting would wear any enemy down.

Or perhaps they were waiting themselves. Gathering themselves for the assault in the safety of the gray places, or attending to some millennia-old ritual that must be observed there before battle was joined. Seethlaw certainly implied—according to Ringil's rather over-wrought and patchy testimony, anyway—that ritual was a matter of huge cultural significance among the Aldrain. Blood sacrifice was apparently required before the invasion of Ennishmin could be launched. Perhaps then, in this smaller matter also, there were solemn specifics to be honored before the slaughter could begin.

The speculation would go back and forth without end, turn and turn again, snapping at its own tail for lack of solid evidence one way or the other. Perhaps this, perhaps that. Humans, short-lived and locked out of the gray places for life, do not do well with uncertainty. If they cannot have what *might*, what *could*, what *should*, and perhaps most awful of all what *should have* been, then they will dream it up instead, imagine it into being in whatever twisted or beautiful form suits, and then drive their fellows to their knees in chains by the thousand and million to pretend in chorus that it *is so*. The Kiriath might have saved them from this, eventually, with time, had perhaps even tried to do so once or twice already, but they came too subtly, terribly damaged into this world to begin with, and in the end they were driven away again. And so men went on hammering with their bloodied foreheads at the limits of their certainties, like insane prisoners condemned to a lifetime in a cell whose door they have locked themselves.

You've got to laugh, Ringil would probably have said.

No, you've got to unlock the fucking door, Archeth might have replied. But of course, by then the key was long lost.

Perhaps, though—*look at it this way, makes a lot of sense if you think about it, man*—the dwenda were delayed by simple necessity. Perhaps navigation in the gray places was not the easy matter Seethlaw had made it appear. Perhaps, once in the Aldrain marches, the dwenda must cast about like wolves for spoor of Ringil and his sudden, murderous new friend from the steppes. Perhaps they must find the thin cool scent of the river with painstaking care, and sift it for the place where their prey disembarked. And perhaps even then, with their targets found, the dwenda storm-callers must struggle for position the way a swimmer struggles to hold station against a current.

Could be. Those who managed to live through the battle would nod and shrug, touch old wounds and shiver. *Who the fuck knows. Yeah, could be.*

Or could be—Ringil would have liked this one—it was politics that held them up, the disorderly individual dissent that he'd seen playing out among the dwenda. Perhaps it took Seethlaw awhile to convince his fellow Aldrain that this was something that needed to be done.

Or perhaps it was the other way around. Perhaps it was Seethlaw who had to be convinced, or at least to convince himself.

And so it went pointlessly on, the theorizing and head shaking and wonder among survivors of the dwenda encounter at Beksanara—or Ibiksinri, to give it the name those who built it would recognize, those who, for political convenience and a treaty not one in a hundred would have been educated well enough to read, were driven away in cold and hunger or simply butchered there in the street.

Ibiksinri, then. Site once again for blades unleashed and blood spilled and screaming across the murderous night. *Funny,* Ringil might have said, *how nothing ever fucking changes.*

The dwenda came in the small, cold hours before dawn.

But before that:

NOT LONG AFTER MIDDAY, THE SUN CAME OUT.

The villagers, who knew the value of such moments, got out and about in its warmth immediately. Bedclothes were brought out and hung up to air, lunch tables were set up in the street and in the small gardens of those homes that had them. Down at the river, while Rakan and some of his men watched in bemusement, the villagers stripped down to underwear and flung themselves into what was still very cold water, and splashed about like children. If the presence of the intensely black Kiriath woman and her soldiers put any kind of damper on the proceedings, it was hard to notice.

The imperials themselves weren't immune to the change. They muttered among themselves that it might be a good omen, and they took the opportunity to bask a little. But having come from the dusty heat of the capital only weeks before, they were neither overjoyed nor impressed, just faintly grateful.

Basking, and reflecting on omens—*my brother, my uncle, a friend of mine once saw* . . . and so forth—also seemed to help the time pass faster, which was something of a blessing, because there wasn't much else to do. Preparations for the battle were minimal, and largely symbolic. You can't build barricades against an enemy that pops into existence wherever it wills, and dwenda tactics were in any case a mystery yet to be revealed. Plans of a sort were laid, but of necessity they had to remain flexible; in the end they amounted to not much more than keeping the locals in their homes under curfew once night fell, and scheduling regular patrols around the village.

Archeth prevailed upon Ringil to give Rakan's men a brief lecture on what he knew about the dwenda, which he did with a surprisingly deft touch that made her blink. The mannered Glades aristo irony she knew so well peeled and flaked away like scabbing from a healed wound, leaving a dry warrior humor and easy, natural camaraderie in its place. She could see the men taking to him by the second as he spoke. He made none of the threats he'd used earlier, though his overall prognosis for the situation was no more optimistic, and he offered no better hopes for the outcome.

In the end, she realized, he had successfully invited them all to die simply by promising to do it with them.

It was all they would ask of any commander.

"Yeah, he was like that at Gallows Gap," Egar told her as they sprawled on the front steps of the garrison house in the sun, trying to avoid wondering how much longer they might have to live. "Similar situation, I guess. We all knew if we couldn't hold the pass, the lizards were going to sweep down and obliterate everything in their path, kill us whether we stood or ran. It took Gil to show them that was a strength we had, not a weakness. That it just made everything simple. The choice wasn't living or dying, running or fighting, it was facing death as an equal, or hearing it come up on you from behind like a hound, grab you by the scruff of the neck, and shake you apart." He grinned in his beard. "Pretty easy choice to make, right?"

"I guess."

She thought about the people and the things she still cared about—it wasn't a long list—and wondered how truthful she was being, how honest with herself, let alone with the Majak at her side. She missed her home, with an abrupt, almost painful pang, now that she thought she might never see it again. She missed the brutal sun and the hard blue skies over Yhelteth, the bustle and dust of the streets; the cool gray cobbles of her courtyard at first light, the first seep of cooking smells from the kitchen side; Kefanin's somber reliability and reserve, Angfal's drily erudite, half-sane ramblings in the cluttered study. The long, majestic sweep of the staircase, the spectacular cityscape views from the upper rooms. The big canopied bed and the sunlight that splashed across it in the morning, and maybe someday Ishgrim's supple, curving pale flanks under—*stop that, you slut.* Well, then, Idrashan's warm, powerful girth under her at the gallop. The gusty two-day ride out to An-Monal, and the melancholy emptiness of the deserted buildings there, the soft, comforting murmur of the tamed volcano through the surrounding stonework. Feeding Idrashan an apple from the tree under Grashgal's old study windows, murmuring to the warhorse as she clucked him homeward again.

It occurred to her suddenly that quite a lot of her reason for not opposing Ringil's stand might lie in an unwillingness to abandon Idrashan, who still lay on his side in the garrison stable and could not get up.

"I saw men die that afternoon with a grin on their faces." Egar shook his head, still lost in the memories of Gallows Gap. Sunlight gleamed on his face. "I saw men *laughing* as they went down. That was Gil, he made them like that. He was there at the heart of it, screaming abuse and bad jokes at the lizards, painted head-to-foot in their blood. I swear, Archeth, I think he was as happy then as any time I ever saw him, before or since."

"Great."

He looked around at her tone.

"We're doing the right thing, Archeth," he said gently. "Whatever happens here tonight, he called it right."

She sighed hard, pressed hands flat to the tops of her thighs and rocked a little on the step.

"Let's hope so, huh?"

Someone came out of the blockhouse door behind them. They both

twisted about and saw Ringil standing there. He'd bagged a cuirass—
from the militia store, by the slightly grubby look of it—along with a
pair of battered greaves and a few other assorted chunks of plate. None
of it matched, but it all seemed a reasonable fit. There was a Throne
Eternal shield slung casually on his shoulder. He stood and looked at
them in silence for a moment, and Archeth wondered if he'd heard what
Egar was saying about him. Looked at his face and thought yes, he
probably had.

"Shouldn't be long now," he said gruffly. "Listen, Archidi, I don't
suppose you're still doing krinzanz these days, are you?"

She faced front so she could dig in a tight inner pocket, pulled out a
cloth-wrapped slab she hadn't started on yet, and handed it back to him
over her shoulder. "All my old bad habits are intact, Gil. Disappoint
you?"

"Far from it. I'd hate to think you'd changed along with everything
else." He took the slab and weighed it in the palm of his hand with a
critical frown. "Like I told your men in there, these motherfuckers are
fast. And I was never faster than when I was riding a quarter ounce of
this stuff. You might want to check with Rakan, see if any of them want
a dab or two as well."

Archeth snorted. "No, I don't think I'll broach that one actually.
Read your Revelation. It's a first-order sin, pollution of the fleshly
temple and estrangement of mind from the spiritual self. These guys are
losing respect for me fast enough as it is. Trying to peddle them
unlawful substances steeped in sin is going to just about finish it."

"You want me to ask? Got to get a helmet from Rakan anyway, and I
think my faggot's reputation is in sufficient tatters by now it won't
matter one way or the other."

"Do what you like. It won't go down well, though, I'm telling you.
These are pious, clean-living men, worshipping at the temple of their
own bodies."

"Hmm. Sounds distinctly erotic."

"Pack that in, Gil." She squinted around in the sun to see if anyone
was listening to them. "You're going to spoil the good impression you
just made on the troops."

"Yeah, all right. Fair point." Ringil glanced at Egar. "What about you?"

The Majak skinned another grin. "Too late to make a good impression on me, Gil. I know you."

"The krin. I'm talking about the krin."

Egar shook his head. "Interferes with my breathing. I fucked up on that stuff back in the summer of '49, made myself really sick. Couple of friends of Imrana's had this high-quality supply through someone they knew at court, and I overdid the dose because I didn't realize. Fucking nightmare. Can't even stomach the taste anymore."

"Okay." Ringil turned to go back inside. "I'm still going to ask Rakan. Might save some lives if I can convince him."

Archeth squinted up at him again. "Nice shield he gave you."

"This? Yeah, it's his spare, apparently." The ghost of a smile touched Ringil's mouth. "I think he liked the speech as well. Seems maybe I'm not such a total degenerate dead loss after all."

"Well." She tried to think of something to say, to stave off thought. She was starting to feel slightly sick, even with the better weather. "It was a pretty good speech."

Egar grunted. "Yeah, not bad for a fucking faggot."

And they all laughed, long and hard in sunlight, while there was still time.

CHAPTER 32

The small cold hours before dawn.

Ringil was seated on a low wall down near the river, feeling the rush and scrape of the krin through the valves of his heart and barely aware of the outside world at all. He'd been waiting too long. The initial pounding anticipation in the first few hours of darkness had sagged and slumped sometime after midnight; for an experienced warrior, it wasn't something you could sustain for long. The tension, the itching preparedness to fight, even the fear itself grew dull after a while. He rode the krin looser, let himself detach from what it was doing to his physical body, topped himself up every couple of hours with another pinched fragment from the slab rubbed into his gums. Began to wonder if he hadn't made a mistake.

"Blue fire! Blue fire! They're coming!"

He snapped back to awareness, swiveled off the wall—more effort than expected, he'd forgotten he was wearing the armor—and snatched up his shield. He slung it on his shoulder, grabbed his helmet from beside him on the wall and crammed it on as he ran, up toward the main street. Unsheathed the Ravensfriend with a chime as the scabbard lip parted and grinned at the sound. The night breeze off the river seemed to hurry him along. The alarm had come from the boathouse end.

"Blue fire! Blue fi—"

It ended on a gurgled scream. He cursed and sprinted flat-out, went around the boathouse corner, and ran straight into the first dwenda. They bounced off each other, staggered and nearly fell. The Throne Eternal who'd yelled the warning was on his knees in the street, head bowed, bleeding out between futilely clutching fingers and a neck wound. His companion, the other half of the patrol, lay beyond in a broad pool of his own blood. Blue light shone off everything, made the imperials into melancholy silhouettes and the puddle of blood a solid, polished plate. The same glow clung about the big, black-clad form that had killed them like some enchanted armor.

The Ravensfriend leapt to block and Ringil saw the sweeping blue glitter of the Aldrain blade a second after. Lock, scrape. The impact shivered through him. He whipped his sword back, changed stance. The dwenda attacked again, up out of a low guard. He chopped it down, backed up, let the krin take his senses and smear them thin. The dwenda nodded its smoothly helmeted head and said something incomprehensible. He had a moment to wonder if it knew him.

"Come on then, you fuck. Let's see what you've *got*."

He leapt in behind the snarl, swung the Ravensfriend high, and kicked out sharp and low at the same moment. The blade deflected with a clang, no surprise, the lack of balance had made it a slow, graceless move. But his boot got through, hard into either shin or knee. The dwenda staggered. Ringil followed up, swinging his shield in and out as required, looking for a gap. They traded blows back and forth. Ringil saw his chance, looped the Ravensfriend under the other blade and swept both weapons aside. He got in close enough to belt the dwenda back with his shield and tried a Yhelteth technique to trip the creature. It didn't quite work; he was clumsy with the unaccustomed weight of the armor and the dwenda didn't go down. But it was clearly still off balance. Ringil screamed in its blank-visored face and launched a rapid flurry of attacks. The other sword blurred in response. He felt a blow get through and bounce off his helmet, another screeched and slid off the cuirass. He rode it all and drove the dwenda back. The krin gave him an edge he hadn't had with Seethlaw, and custom had robbed him of any fear the blue-glowing figure might once have inspired.

He killed the dwenda.

It came from nowhere, it was like a gift of dark powers. The black-clad form went almost back to the boards of the boathouse wall, then abruptly leapt out at him. Off the ground, not quite the floating grace Seethlaw had used to take him down in Terip Hale's cellar, not quite as high or as fast, or maybe it was just the krin again that made it easier to beat. Ringil flinched aside, hewed in with the Ravensfriend, and the dwenda gave up a muffled scream inside the helmet. The blade had sliced deep into a thigh, right through the black skinmail-looking garb. He felt it hit the bone and twisted instinctively, pulled back to free it. The dwenda fell out of the air and hit the ground hard, tried to stand on its damaged leg and fell again. Ringil stalked in and hacked down, into the right shoulder. Another muffled shriek, the Kiriath blade had gone deep again. The dwenda floundered, thrashed about, long-sword dropped somewhere. Ringil kicked it flat, stood on its chest, and stabbed the Ravensfriend through his opponent's throat. The dwenda shuddered like a pinned insect and made desperate choking sounds. Ringil kept his boot where it was, worked his blade back and forth to make sure, then yanked it back out. Blood spurted from under the lip of the strange smooth helmet and the dwenda shuddered once more and stopped moving.

Ringil threw back his head and howled.

Faintly, down at the other end of the street, he heard it answered, he did not know by whom or what.

EGAR MET HIS FIRST ATTACKER IN TORCHLIGHT ON THE STEPS OF THE blockhouse. The blue fire threw him for a pair of seconds, but he'd listened to Ringil's lecture just like everybody else. He stood firm, looked for the form at the center of the storm, and whipped the staff lance in at knee height. He hit something, but not with the solid chunking impact he was used to. It was more like swirling the lance through deep water. The dwenda moved at the heart of its radiance and seemed to chuckle.

A long, slim blade came leaping.

He blocked it, swung on the move, and shoved back hard with the lance. The dwenda retreated, seemed to wait for something.

Only the blue light from above warned him.

He caught it reflected in a puddle made in the angle of an unevenly laid flagstone at his feet, glimmering cold and separate from the glow of the blockhouse wall torches. He understood at some instantaneous, visceral level, and was swinging about as the second dwenda leapt from the roof of the blockhouse at him. He got the lance shaft up at chest height just in time, caught his attacker on it, and shunted him sideways onto the ground. The impact shocked him back a couple of steps, but he stayed on his feet, just. He saw the way the dwenda recovered, rolled upright again still indistinct in the blue glow of the storm, knew the other one was about to rush him from the left. Saw it happen out of the corner of his eye. No time for conscious thought—reflexively, he dropped his stance and slashed the lance back up to a braced horizontal. The right-hand end sent the second dwenda stumbling, maybe wounded, maybe not; the left was a brutal skewer pointed back past Egar's shoulder.

The first dwenda ran right onto it.

He felt the impact and knew without looking back. He grunted and twisted the shaft of the lance—the dwenda shrieked. Now he looked, saw the damage, grinned and jerked the lance blade free. The injured dwenda sagged backward, sword gone to the floor, both hands clutched over the wound the lance had made. Egar vented a berserker howl and swung back to where the second dwenda was squaring up to him with its sword in both hands. The last traces of the blue storm flickered around its limbs, inking out.

"Now you," Egar said grimly, and hurled himself forward.

Inside the blockhouse, screams.

ARCHETH FOUGHT IN A BLUR OF KNIFE BLADES AND KRIN.

Wraithslayer was gone from her hand, buried up to the hilt in a dwenda's back, and no time to withdraw it before she must move, dance on and duck and swing back in. Laughing Girl lay gleaming dully in a corner, thrown in error, wasted. She wielded Bandgleam and Falling Angel, right hand and left, and she still had Quarterless in the sheath at her back. There was blood on her face from a long-sword slash, a shrill Kiriath battle shriek in her throat, and bodies all around.

"*Indamaninarmal!*" The High Kir syllables poured from her mouth in venomous rolling torrent. "*My father's house! Indamaninarmal!*"

The dwenda had welled up inside the blockhouse like burning blue ghosts, exactly the way Ringil had warned they might. She was in the tower room when it happened, heard panicked yelling downstairs and went down the steps at a run. On the first turn, she met a dwenda coming up, all blue fire and vague, darker motion at the core. She cannoned into the thing, passed *through* it, distinctly felt the tugging it made, but came out the other side unharmed. *No time, no fucking time.* She tumbled down the remaining stairs barely on her feet and erupted into the main room of the blockhouse. Chaos flapped across her vision; two of the Throne Eternal already down, dead or dying on the flagstones, a third with his back to the wall, defending himself just barely with a long-hafted ax. No helmet, he must have taken it off earlier in the night—his face was bloodied and grim with knowledge of his chances. There were three dwenda in the room, driving him along the wall, spreading to bracket him. In another second, the angle would be too wide and he'd be dead. Archeth yelled and sprang. Two of the figures whipped around to face the new sound, black-garbed bodies and blank oval heads swathed in flickering blue light, long-swords raised toward her as if in admonishment. But she thought—*yeah, that's right, the Black Folk are here after all, motherfuckers*—they were taken aback.

She had Laughing Girl in her right hand.

She loosed the knife at the closest of the figures well ahead of conscious decision. The dwenda ducked and the knife spun off the gleaming curve of the helmet. She cursed, drew Wraithslayer on her way across the room, matched it with Falling Angel. A long-sword licked out, she was no longer there. *Almost* no longer there—she felt the heated wire of the stroke paint a line over one temple as she ducked. She let the shock drive her, whipped about behind the dwenda and drove Wraithslayer in hard at kidney height. The Kiriath steel went through whatever the dwenda was wearing; the creature shrilled and bucked, staggered away from her. She had to let go of the knife, leave it where it was. She filled her hand with Bandgleam.

The second dwenda rushed her, swinging his sword. She flinched aside, caught the weapon at its tip with Falling Angel's blade, and looped it away from her. Bandgleam flashed and probed, but the dwenda was quicker and swayed back out of the way. In the corner, the last remaining Throne Eternal was nearly done, wounded in one leg and fighting to stay on his feet. Blood poured down his thigh from the join in his armor. His attacker pressed in, gave him no space or respite. She dare not risk another throw; it wasn't clear the Kiriath blades would penetrate the dwenda's garb without a hand on the hilt to drive them in.

"Hold on," she screamed, and leapt back just in time to avoid another long-sword thrust from her opponent.

The move took her toward the door to the tower, and she knew it was an error as soon as she jumped. She knew—the krinzanz knew—the dwenda she'd met on the stairs was there, back down having found no one to slaughter up there, blade drawn and—

She dropped to the floor, heard the sword hiss past where she'd been, rolled desperately to get some space. A fallen chair blocked her, the dwenda from the tower came after her. Blank, smooth helmet inclined, long-sword held two-handed before him, poised and looking for the moment. It was like being stalked by something mechanical, as if there was nothing under the helm but air and a raw spirit of malice.

"*Dwenda!*"

It was almost a shout of joy.

It was Elith.

Up the stairs from the basement cells, half awake by the look of it, a tranced, wondering expression on her face, dressed only in a gray silk nightgown Archeth had given her. A few hours before, she'd been sleeping peacefully beneath a blanket beside Sherin, the two women huddled, perhaps unconsciously, together for warmth. Now she moved like a sleepwalker, and her voice had the tones of someone meeting her true love after years of absence.

"Dwenda!"

The armored form stopped. The featureless helmet lifted. Perhaps it expected sorcery; Elith was unarmed, but her hair was a wild, tangled halo of gray that seemed to catch the fading blue flickers from the dwenda, her face was a worn mask of age and suffering, and her arms were held up and out in mute echo of the glirsht markers. There was no fear on her face, her whole body denied the very concept that she could be afraid, and she moved forward as if she could not be harmed.

It was as good an impression of a witch as Archeth had ever seen.

"You come too late, dwenda," she declaimed. "They are all gone, the land is stolen, the sentinels thrown down, the memory faded. I am the last."

The dwenda shifted, made a decision any warrior could have read in its stance. Archeth opened her mouth to scream. Elith came on, arms outstretched. Smiling, it seemed.

"Take me ho——"

The dwenda chopped out. The sword sliced into Elith's unprotected side, cut deep into her midriff and pulled clear again. Archeth thought she heard a contemptuous grunt from within the smooth helmet, or maybe it was just relief. Blood drenched the nightgown. Elith made a noise that seemed more gusty joy than pain, and would not fall down. Archeth felt tears sting in her eyes. The dwenda moved in, chopping again, impatiently. The chair back Archeth had fetched up against blocked clear vision of what happened next, but Elith hit the ground three feet away, eyes staring at nothing.

The dwenda turned about and found Archeth on her feet, eight inches away, face bloodied and contorted into a snarl.

She shrilled and stabbed, both knives at once, Bandgleam in under the helmet lip, Falling Angel into the belly. She twisted the blades with every ounce of krin-fed rage she could summon. The dwenda screamed back at her, tried to batter her with the guard and pommel of the long-sword, but she was in far too close for it to be effective. She rode the blows and backed her opponent up on the knives, jerking upward, twisting savagely. The dwenda shrieked again, dropped its sword, and shoved her bodily away with both hands. She grunted, held on to the knives this time. She shook her head and grinned. The blades stayed where they were, the dwenda would have had to levitate eight inches off the floor to get unhooked. She knew it was insane, that the other two Aldrain would be finishing off the Throne Eternal soldier and turning to take her, but she could not let go.

"*Indamaninarmal!*" she snarled through gritted teeth. "*My father's house! Indamaninarmal!*"

It seemed to unlock something inside her. She put her shoulder into the dwenda's chest, shoved him away, and tugged the knives free. Came about to see the Throne Eternal down on the floor in the puddling crimson of his own blood, gasping and dying, ax fallen from his nerveless fingers, and the two remaining dwenda coming at her, kicking the tumbled furniture aside as they advanced, splattered with human blood but neither of them harmed as far as she could see.

She mustered a deep breath, squared herself, and lifted the knives.

"All right then," she said.

RINGIL RAN UP THE DARKENED, SCREAMING STREET.

He passed bodies here and there, villagers and Throne Eternal both. Doors in some of the houses were thrown open, and he saw a woman's corpse sprawled over the threshold of one. The dwenda had come, it seemed, into the homes and open spaces of Ibiksinri with random disregard, and were killing whatever they ran into. As he watched, another front door burst open and a young boy of about eight fled screaming toward him. Behind, in the interior gloom, he saw the blue flicker under the lintel and then the old familiar form, ducking to step through and out. The boy cannoned into him at hip height and he put out a hand, almost absently, to steady him.

"They, my mother, it—" the boy gabbled through streaming tears.

The dwenda came out into the street. It had a peculiar-looking ax in one hand and a short-sword in the other. Ringil tilted his head a little, heard his neck click.

"You'd better stand behind me," he said, and pushed the boy gently around his hip and backward. "There's no point in running from these things."

He let the dwenda come to him. He lifted one hand and pointed to his own face. He'd dipped fingers into the blood of the last dwenda he'd killed and liberally daubed his features until the bittersweet reek of the stuff was thick in his nostrils and throat. He didn't know if the dwenda had much of a sense of smell, especially from inside their smooth, blank helmets, but it was worth a try.

"See that?" he called out in slow, drawling Naomic. "That's from one of your friends. But it's drying up, I need fresh. *C'mere, you fuck.*"

He closed the last two yards of space himself, sprang in and swung the Ravensfriend like a scythe. He never knew if the blood ploy worked or not, the dwenda blocked him with the haft of the ax, danced out to the side, and stabbed in with the short-sword. Ringil took it on the shield, grunted with the impact, went to one knee to get his sword free of the ax lock and swung back again, savagely, at shin height. He hit something; the dwenda stumbled, but the blade didn't seem to have cut through.

Shit.

The ax whistled down. He flung himself inelegantly aside, tumbled on the street and rolled. Lost the Ravensfriend in the mud. The dwenda came at him, making some high-pitched barking sound he didn't like at all. At the last moment, he swung one booted leg up and unleashed a kick as his opponent rushed in. The dwenda yelped and staggered. The ax wavered, the sword drooped. Ringil got his feet under him, dropped his shield and launched himself, bellowing, crooked hands spread and grasping for the dwenda's weapons. He got a grip on the ax haft and the sword-hand wrist, and he thrust himself chest-to-chest with the creature and unleashed a savage head-butt full into the blank helmet.

It was pure krinzanz, the black, cackling will to do harm unleashed and squirming up out of the deepest recesses of his heart with no thought for consequence. He staggered back and sideways from the blow, helmet knocked aslant, head ringing, but his hand was locked around the ax haft and it came with him. The dwenda shook its head dizzily, seemed not to know where he was. He hefted the ax in both hands and swung, a deep, wide-stance blow the Dragonbane would have cheered. The ax bit deep into the dwenda's chest and it screamed. He tugged it loose, hewed again, as if into a tree. Aldrain blood flew in the dark, he caught the fresh scent of it. He brought the ax up over his head with a wild yell and slammed it down on the dwenda's head.

The helmet split, the ax jammed in the fissure, buried a handbreadth deep. Ringil let go and watched as the dwenda took three tottering sideways steps, lifted one hand to touch its head as if in wonder, and collapsed with a long, grinding moan. Ringil looked to see if it would move again, panting and swaying a little himself, then when it didn't, he cast about, found the Ravensfriend and his shield lying in the mud, and picked them up. His head was beginning to hurt as the initial numbness of the butt wore off. He tried to resettle the helmet a little more evenly on his head, found that the nose guard had slipped and gouged into the lower half of his cheek.

He saw the boy—he'd utterly forgotten him in the fight—watching him, frozen where he stood about ten feet away, wide-eyed with not much less terror than he'd had of the dwenda. Ringil shook his head and found himself laughing, an insane, dribbling little chuckle.

"Dragonbane's right," he said vaguely. "They fall down just like men."

The boy's eyes shifted, left over Ringil's shoulder, and he darted away like a spooked deer. Ringil swung about and found himself facing one of Rakan's soldiers. Relief stabbed through him.

"Ah. How you doing?"

The man made a noise. He was wounded all over, but none of it looked too bad. He still had his shield, but it was buckled and split, and he was down to a long knife for a weapon. Ringil turned and pointed, still breathing heavily.

"See that ax? If you can get it out of that motherfucker's head, it's yours. Then we'll go see what's going on at the blockhouse. Okay?"

The Throne Eternal stared at him. "They, they . . ." He gestured wildly over his shoulder. "They're fucking everywhere, man."

"I know. And they glow in the dark, too." Ringil clapped him on the shoulder. "Should make it easy, huh?"

EGAR CAME THROUGH THE BLOCKHOUSE DOOR WITH BITS OF DWENDA intestine on both blades of the staff lance, just in time to see Archeth stabbed to the floor. Fury detonated through him like an instant high fever. He yelled, berserker shrill and full, and leapt in on the two dwenda without thought. The first turned just in time to get the lance blade through the belly. The second stumbled back a step, as if from an actual blow, then came in swinging its sword. Remorseless, Egar drove the impaled dwenda back until it tripped over Archeth's body. He caught the swing of the other's blade on the lance shaft and kicked its legs summarily out from under it. He leaned hard on the embedded end of the lance, twisted the shaft back and forth, and the wounded dwenda screamed in his helmet and thrashed. Egar judged the damage well enough done, jerked the lance free, crouched and swung about to face the other dwenda just as it climbed back to its feet.

"You want to die, too? Come on then, *motherfucker*."

The dwenda was very fast. It whooped and leapt high over the lance thrust, cleared it entirely, lashed out with one foot and kicked Egar in the face. He staggered, didn't quite go down. Blood in his mouth, felt like a broken tooth, but—

The dwenda had landed only a couple of feet away, was twisting about to bring its long-sword to bear. Egar rushed it, slammed the lance shaft up and into the creature's chest, and bore it backward across the room until they both fell among the bodies and broken chairs. The dwenda dropped its sword. Egar rammed the lance shaft desperately up under the jut of the helmet. He got to his knees. The dwenda had a long slim knife from somewhere; it slashed at him but the lance shaft had its arms pinned and ineffectual. Egar got on his knees, rammed the shaft up again, and bore down with all his weight. The dwenda made an awful gurgling sound. The slim knife slashed again, gouged into his side, slid off a rib. Egar snarled and let go of the lance, grabbed the featureless helmet, and smashed it against the flagstone floor. The knife stabbed him again, felt like it got through this time. He gasped, struggled for purchase on the helmet's smooth sides, felt another fiery lash of pain along his ribs, stabbed out with a knee to hold the arm off. He gripped the helm's surface, squeezed and twisted with everything he had left. The dwenda thrashed and squawked. Egar bared his teeth in an awful grin, and kept on twisting. His voice grated from his throat.

"Yeah, yeah, I hear you. Nearly—done—just a—"

—the knife again, he barely noticed through the rising red mist, his voice came out small and tight with the effort—

"—little more—"

—the thing was screaming now, battering at him with the knife and a clenched fist, kicking, didn't matter, didn't matter, ignore that shit—

"—*little* more—"

Crack.

And the dwenda's head was suddenly loose and lolling in his hands. The creature's arms dropped to its sides. He heard the knife clink free on the stonework.

"That's it," he hissed. "Quiet down now."

He drew a hard, panting breath, yelped immediately at the flare of pain as his ribs moved. His eyes teared up. He blew breath through pursed lips as if he'd just swallowed something that was too hot.

"Ah *fuck,* that hurts."

"Tell me about it."

He turned about and there was Archeth, on her feet, limping toward him clutching one shoulder. But there was a bloodied knife in her hand on the injured side, and she seemed to be hanging on to it okay. He coughed a laugh, then wished he hadn't.

"Hey, you're alive."

"For the moment." She nodded behind her. "Finished your other pal for you."

He heaved himself up off the dwenda's body, looked under his left arm at the blood and grimaced.

"That was nice of you. I thought he was pretty much done. Saw his guts come out, that's for sure."

"Well." She shrugged and winced. "Aldrain magic, you know. Best to make sure. What's it like out there?"

Egar took a couple of careful, testing breaths. He ground his teeth and snarled in frustration. Bent to pick up his lance.

"Don't know, these motherfuckers are coming out of the dark everywhere you look. Saw at least five of your Throne Eternal boys down in the street, no idea if they took any bad guys with them. It's not good."

Archeth peered about on the floor for her other knives. She spotted Wraithslayer, crouched awkwardly, and picked it up.

"We'd better get out there, then," she said.

"Yeah, I was afraid you were going to say—"

And then they heard it, and at the sound the Majak's face lit up as if someone had magically wiped away all his pain.

Ringil's voice, bawling hoarse but crystal clear in Tethanne, out in the street.

"Stand! Stand your fucking ground! *They fall down just like men! Stand with me! STAND!*"

FAILEH RAKAN LAY DEAD IN THE STREET, HEAD SPLIT BY AN ALDRAIN AX. He'd accounted for a brace of dwenda—they lay about his feet—but the third was too fast. Ringil, jogging rapidly up the street toward the blockhouse with a mauled squad of survivors, saw it happen but got there too late to do anything about it.

The dwenda who'd finished Rakan spun about at the sound of his footfalls. Ringil rushed in. Shield up to block the ax, heave and shove it aside. The Ravensfriend chopped in for the thigh. He'd learned, in the past frantic quarter hour, that the Aldrain armor was strong below the knee, like some kind of incorporated greave under the material, rising to knee height. Above the knee, strength gave way to flexibility; the black leg garb was thinner. Human steel might not get through easily, but the Kiriath blade chewed it apart like rotten sailcloth. He hacked the width of a hand into the dwenda's leg, withdrew, and stepped back. Watched the creature fall to its knees and then skewered it under the helmet.

It was beginning to feel practiced.

He looked wildly about. What was left of Rakan's patrols had pulled back to the blockhouse as planned, but hard-pressed on every side by the encroaching dwenda. He counted four men—no three, there went another, spun about and down into the mud off a dwenda blade, spurting blood from a half-severed neck—and he had four more at his back, one of those in none-too-good shape.

And from all angles, still shedding tiny blue flickering flames as they moved, the rest of the dwenda came on. The krin hammered through his head, wrote the answer in fire behind his eyes.

He put a boot on the dead dwenda's helmet, tipped it back, and hacked down with the Ravensfriend. It took three desperate, brutal strokes, but the head came off. He bent—felt an odd, crooked smile slip onto his mouth—and plunged his left hand into the gory mess at the helmet's opening. Meat and pipes and there, the rough central gnarl of the severed spine. He grasped at the ragged bone end, picked up head and helmet, and strode to the blockhouse step.

Held it aloft in the light from the torches. Filled his lungs, and screamed.

"Stand! Stand your fucking ground! *They fall down just like men! Stand with me! STAND!*"

For a moment, everything seemed to stop. Even the dwenda appeared to pause in their onslaught. The torchlight gleamed hot yellow off the black curve of the Aldrain helmet. Blood ran down his hand and wrist.

Somewhere, someone human cheered long and low, and the others took it up.

It became a roar.

A dwenda came howling across the street at him, blade raised. Ringil swung the helmet and hurled it at his attacker, ran in behind.

Somehow, as he leapt in to meet the dwenda, he already knew it was Seethlaw.

The rest was a nightmare blur of blood and steel and speed. Seethlaw was fast, as fast as Ringil remembered from Terip Hale's courtyard, maybe faster, and now he was no longer constrained by whatever had stopped him from killing Ringil the first time around. He whirled and leapt, slashed in and out as if the long-sword were no weightier than some courtier's blade-for-show. He had no shield to slow him down, and he was clearly—Ringil could feel it coming off the black-clad figure in waves—raving with hate.

A dark lord will rise.

Ringil gave himself over to the krinzanz, and the memory of a young woman's living head, mounted on a tree stump, weeping silent, swamp-water tears.

It was really all he had left.

"Come on motherfucker," he heard himself screaming, almost continuously. "*Come on.*"

Seethlaw ripped open his face along the jaw, the gouging point of a thrust Ringil couldn't get his head away from fast enough. Seethlaw stabbed him through a gap in the ill-assorted pieces of plate on his right arm. Seethlaw slashed him across the top of one thigh. Scorched his neck where it emerged from the cuirass, smashed apart an already damaged section of armor on his right shoulder and ripped the flesh beneath. Seethlaw—

To Ringil, it felt like nothing. Like nothing at all.

He waded through the pain. He grinned.

And later, much later, one of the surviving Throne Eternal men would swear he saw a flickering blue light spark along Ringil's limbs in the dark.

Seethlaw struck down at his wavering shield. The blow ran a long split into the battered metal and the wooden backing, ruined it for the next blow.

But the blade stuck.

Ringil let go the straps. Seethlaw tried to withdraw, the weight of the shield dragged his sword down. Ringil leapt in, swung, yelled, hacked savagely down.

The Ravensfriend found the dwenda's shoulder, and bit deep.

Seethlaw howled. Still could not free his sword. Ringil sobbed, drew breath, hacked down again with both hands. The arm went dead, hung half severed. Seethlaw fell to his knees with the shock.

Once again, everything seemed to stop.

The dwenda reached up, let go his useless sword, and tugged at the helmet. Ringil, in sudden, numb suspension, let him do it. The helmet came off, gave him Seethlaw's beautiful dwenda face for the last time, contorted with pain and rage. He glared up at Ringil. His teeth gritted.

"What," he spat, in panting Naomic, "have you done? Gil, we—we had—"

Ringil stared bleakly down at him.

"I've had better than you drunk in a Yhelteth back alley," he said coldly, and chopped Seethlaw's head and face open with the Ravensfriend.

Withdrew the blade, brandished it high and screamed.

A dark lord will rise.

Yeah, right.

Then he set his boot on the dying dwenda's chest and shoved him aside. He took two suddenly shaky steps down into the street and what remained of the battle. The roar of the remaining men went on, the dwenda looked to be falling back. Ringil blinked to clear vision which had suddenly, unaccountably gone blurred. He stared around him.

"*Who's fucking next?*" he screamed.

And crumpled bleeding into the mud.

The road northwest out of Pranderghal rose into the hills on slow, looping hairpin turns, fading finally to a thin, pale gray line as it disappeared over the saddle between two peaks. On a day with clear weather—like today—you could see riders coming for a good two or three hours before they hit town.

Or you could watch a couple of them riding away.

Archeth and Egar sat out drinking tankards of ale in the garden of the Swamp Dog Inn, still slightly disbelieving that the warmth and good weather could hold up this long. There was a sporadic, ruffling breeze out of the north that robbed the sun of some of its comfort whenever it gusted, but it was tough to see how that would have justified complaint. Mostly, they were both just glad to be alive when so many others they knew were not. It was, Egar supposed, much the same feeling Marnak had talked about—*you start wondering why you made it to the end of the day, why you're still standing when the field is clogged with other men's blood and corpses. Why the Dwellers are keeping you alive, what purpose the Sky Home has laid out for you*—but mellowed into a slightly numb bliss beyond caring, beyond worrying much about the why.

"Swamp dog," said Archeth, tapping idly at the raised emblem on her tankard. It was a crude miniature copy of the painted sign that hung on the street side of the inn, and showed a monstrous-looking hound, up to its belly in swamp water with a dead snake in its jaws and a spiked collar around its neck. "Always wondered about that. First thing Elith said to me—*get between a swamp dog and its dinner,* I had no idea what she meant."

Egar snorted. "Seems pretty fucking obvious to me."

"Yeah, but you were out here working scavenger crews for months, working with swamp dogs day in, day out probably."

"Working *a* month before you showed up, a single month, and that was only because Takavach told me I had to. Not like I exactly took to the trade. Anyway." He spread his hands, gestured at her tankard. "Swamp. Dog. Got a sort of self-evident ring to it, don't you think?"

"Ah, fuck you then."

"Yeah, you keep promising, I keep waiting."

She kicked him under the trestle. But her grin smeared away almost immediately, and she grew serious again.

"This Takavach. You say he wore a leather cloak and a brimmed hat."

"Yeah. Always does, it's in all the stories. He's from, uhm." Egar frowned, groping for a decent translation from the Majak. " 'All the places the ocean will always be heard.' Something like that. Cavorts with mermaids in the surf and so forth. Cloak and hat's like a symbol for it; it's like a northern ship captain's rig." Egar propped himself up a little in his seat and peered at her. "Why?"

Archeth shook her head. "Forget it."

"C'mon. Why?"

She sighed. "I don't know. Just, the day Idrashan got better, got back on his feet again, one of the stable boys swore to me he'd walked in on some guy in a hat and cloak like that. Apparently, he was leaning over the rail of Idrashan's stall and talking to him in some weird foreign language. And I remember now, there was some talk of the same figure walking the streets at evening in Beksanara when we first arrived. Thought it was just the usual swamp horseshit at the time."

They looked at each other for a few moments in silence. For Archeth at least, it seemed that the breeze chose just that moment to chill the air, and a cloud wiped out the sun. But Egar only shrugged.

"Sure, could have been."

"Could have been what? Horseshit?"

"No, could have been that fucker Takavach."

Archeth blinked. "You believe that?"

Egar leaned forward a little. "Look, if he took the trouble to save my arse and magic me all the way down to Ennishmin, just so I could procure our old pal Angeleyes for the battle of Beksanara . . ." A shrug. "Well then, he's certainly not going to balk at feeding your horse a few rotten apples to keep you pinned there for the same reason, is he? Or are you going to tell me you don't believe in gods and demons and dwenda?"

"I don't know what I believe anymore," she muttered.

"Believe it, if it's cruel and unjust and brutal on the weak," said a somber voice behind her. "That way, you won't be far out."

They both turned to look at him, and it was still a struggle for Archeth not to catch her breath at the sight.

He stood in the knee-deep grass of the garden, clad mostly in black that made even his southern-blooded skin seem yellowish pale. His right arm was bound up in a gray cloth sling, the black cotton stitches were still in the wound along his jaw, and the other bruises and scrapes on his face had not yet faded fully away. But mostly, it was the eyes that told the story, that made her think Ringil Eskiath had not, after all, survived the dwenda encounter at Beksanara the way she and Egar had.

The pommel of the Ravensfriend jutted up over his shoulder like a spike driven into him.

"All set?" she asked, with a breeziness she didn't much feel.

"Yeah. Sherin's with the horses. Turns out, she's pretty good with them. Used to keep quite a stable apparently, back before Bilgrest pissed all their money away."

"You—" Archeth stopped herself. "She going to be okay?"

He shrugged. "I don't know."

"The doctor says she hadn't been harmed physically, at least not in the recent past. He's a good man, Gil, I know him. I asked for him specifically when we sent to Khartaghnal. If he says she's unharmed—"

"He's used to dealing with soldiers." There was a floating emptiness in Ringil's tone, as if none of this really mattered anymore. "With men grateful just because they can still walk out of his tent on two feet. Doesn't matter how good a man he is, his opinion's not going to be worth a harbor-end fuck. Sherin screams in her dreams, all the time. She flinches at the mention of Poppy Snarl's name, which I imagine means it was Snarl's company that bought her at the Chancellery clearinghouse. She's been a *slave*, Archeth. I know you imperials don't think that's any big deal, but—"

"Hoy!" She stood up to face him. "It's me you're talking to here, Gil."

The confrontation lasted a couple of moments longer than it should have. She felt a faint chill on her neck as she stared into her friend's eyes. Then he looked away, past her to the road and the hills it led into.

"Sorry," he said quietly. "You're right, of course. You're not like the rest of them."

But Ishgrim's lush pale form floated through her mind, and Archeth was suddenly terrified that Ringil could see into her head and know what she was thinking.

"Don't suppose the swamp time did her any favors, either," Egar rumbled with what was, for him, an oddly deft diplomacy. "Stuck out there with the dwenda and those ruins and all those fucking heads fencing her in night and day."

"That won't have helped," Ringil agreed quietly.

She heard the damage in his voice.

The heads were too much for most of them. The few Throne Eternal survivors of the Beksanara encounter, the war-hardened levy reinforcements from Khartaghnal or the Ennishmin scavenger toughs hired to guide them, even Egar, it made no real difference. Men stumbled away, sick-faced and shaking, after the few seconds it took to understand what they'd walked into. For quite a while, the stillness of the swamp was salted with the repeated sounds of Archeth's forces retching.

Ringil just stood immobile and looked on.

"Risgillen" was all he said.

It wasn't the ring of failed escapees beyond the fence that he'd described, not anymore. The dwenda had pulled out and whether for warning, ritual, or revenge, they had left nothing in their wake to be salvaged. The stable-type housing had been reduced by some process no one readily understood to a scattering of wet gray mulch, and out across the pools and soggy ground of the swamp, there were more than a hundred living heads, a more or less evenly sown crop, all carefully supplied with the depth of water that apparently served to keep them conscious.

While Archeth's men braced themselves against fallen trees or boulders, and trembled and cursed or wept as was their inclination, Ringil went quietly about, lifting each head from the water and placing it gently on raised ground, where the roots of the sorcerous trunks could not get sustenance. Behind the thick swatches of bandage masking his face, it was hard to know what his expression might have been. He grimaced occasionally, but that might have been the pain in his injured arm.

After a while, some of the other men regained enough self-possession to help.

When the heads were dry enough that life seemed to have left them, when the eyes had closed and the tears dried, and when they'd scoured the vicinity to be sure that there was not *one single fucking possibility* they'd missed any, Archeth drew axmen from the levy and had them split each skull apart.

That took quite awhile.

When it was done, they gathered what dry fuel they could find and built a pyre, then seeded it with some of the new oily wax cakes the levy carried for starting campfires. Archeth lit the pile and they all stood in silence for the time it took to catch. At Ringil's insistence, they pitched a camp down by the creek and waited for the pyre to burn down. Archeth found tasks to keep her men busy, but still the acrid smell drifted through the winter trees and found them, and men stopped what they were doing and swallowed hard or spat when they caught the scent.

Later that afternoon, Archeth missed Ringil and, following a not particularly inspired hunch, tracked him back to the pyre. By then, it had burned down to embers and bone fragments and ash. He stood in front of it in rigid silence, but when her foot cracked a rotten tree branch behind him, he whipped about with inhuman speed.

That was when she saw it for the first time—the thing in his eyes that still chilled her now.

"Always something worse," he'd murmured when she moved closer. "Perhaps they don't just fall down like men, perhaps they *are* men. Or they were once."

She stood beside him and watched the ashes smoke. She put a hand on his arm, and he turned to look at her, and for just a moment it was as if she was a total stranger touching him.

Then, abruptly, he smiled, and it was the Ringil she remembered.

"Do you think they'll be back?" she asked him.

He was quiet for a while, so quiet she thought he hadn't heard. She was about to ask again when he spoke.

"I don't know. Maybe we scared them away, yeah."

"*We can stop them,*" she quoted his own words back at him. "*We can send them back to the gray places to think again about taking this world.*"

The smile came back, faint and crooked. "Yeah. What idiot said that? Sounds kind of pompous, doesn't it?"

"Even idiots get it right sometimes."

"Yeah." But she could see that somewhere inside he didn't really believe it enough to dwell on. He turned instead and gestured at the great black buried spike of the Kiriath weapon. "Anyway, look at that fucking thing. It murdered an entire city, and turned what was left into swamp. If that won't scare you off, what will?"

"Scares me," she agreed.

It did, but not for the reasons she let him assume.

When they finally found the place—and even with the scavenger guides and Ringil's help, it took longer than you'd expect—most of the humans in the party could not see the black iron spike any better than the Aldrain bridge that led to it. She didn't know whether that was the dwenda's doing, some cloaking glamour to keep the scavengers away, or if it was something her own people had done when they built and unleashed the weapon in the first place. She saw it clearly enough, and so did Ringil. Some others could manage it for a few seconds at a time, if they stayed and stared and squinted for long enough, which most did not care to do. The majority claimed to see only an impenetrable mass of dead mangrove, a tangle of poisonous-colored vegetation, or simply an empty space that every instinct screamed at them not to approach.

"This is an evil place," she heard one grizzled levy corporal mutter.

That was one way to look at it, and another helpful corollary was that the evil came from the dwenda presence here, either the once-long-ago mythical city or the more recent incursion. But Archeth could not help, could not *stop* herself from wondering, if that sensation of evil came from the weapon itself; if there was not some smoldering remnant of its awful power still buried at the tip and if that was what came rising from the surrounding swamp like some ancient phantom in black rotting robes.

She had for so long been confident of Kiriath civilization, of a moral superiority that lifted her and her whole people above the brutal morass of the human world. Now she thought back to some of Grashgal's and her father's more brooding moments, their less intelligible meditations on the past and the essence of who they were, and she wondered if they had lived with this knowledge, of weapons to murder entire cities, and had hidden it from her, out of shame.

These fucking humans, Archidi, Grashgal had told her, and shuddered. *If we stay, they're going to drag us into every squalid fucking skirmish and border dispute their short-term greed and fear can invent. They're going to turn us into something we never used to be.*

But what if, Archidi, that wasn't the truth of the revulsion in his voice at all. What if the truth of Grashgal's fears was that *these fucking humans are going to turn us* back *into something we haven't been for a long, long time.*

She didn't want to think about it. She buried it in the day-to-day tasks of the clear-up, the creation of the new garrisons at Beksanara and Pranderghal and half a dozen other strategically placed villages around the swamp. If the dwenda were coming back, it was her job to ensure that the Empire was equipped to repel them with massive force. For the moment, nothing else need matter.

But for all that, the knowledge would not go away.

Even here and now, in the sun and the garden at Pranderghal, the great black iron spike stayed buried in the back of her mind just the way it was buried in the swamp, and she knew she'd never get rid of it. Knew, abruptly, looking at Ringil's slowly healing face and the stitched wound that would inevitably leave a scar, that he was not the only one the dwenda encounter had damaged for good.

He caught her watching him and gave her a grin, one of the old ones.

"Want to finish your beer?" he asked her. "Come out and wave good-bye?"

SO THEY ALL WENT OUT TO THE START OF THE ROAD TO SAY FAREWELL. Archeth had gifted Ringil and Sherin both with good Yhelteth levy mounts—and she thought she'd seen the faintest of sparks kindle in Sherin's eyes when the woman glimpsed her horse, and understood that it was hers to keep. It was a tiny increment, a trickling spring-melt droplet of good feeling inside Archeth, but she supposed it would have to do.

"What are you going to do when you get back?" she asked Ringil as they stood beside the horses.

He frowned. "Well, Ishil owes me some money. I guess that might be first port of call, once I've seen Sherin here safely home."

"And after that?"

"I don't know. I've done what was asked of me, there wasn't a plan after that. And to be honest, I doubt I'm very popular in Trelayne right now. I've dishonored myself and the Eskiath name by not showing up to a duel. I've crippled a member in good standing of the Etterkal slave traders' association, and killed most of his men. Fucked up the cabal's plans for a new war. I have a feeling it might be time to leave town again, soon as I'm paid."

Egar grinned and poked him in the chest. "Hey, there's always Yhelteth. They won't give a shit what you've done, long as you can swing a blade."

"There is always that," Ringil said gravely.

He took his arm out of the sling to get on his horse, winced a little as he swung up. In the saddle, he flexed the arm again a couple of times and grimaced, but he didn't put the sling back on.

"See you again, then," he said. "Someday."

"Someday," Archeth echoed. "Well, you know where I'll be."

"And me," the Majak said. "Don't leave it too long, though. We're not all semi-immortal half-breeds around here."

Laughter, again, in the warm sun. They made the clasp all around, and then Ringil nudged his horse into motion and Sherin, wan and quiet, fell in alongside. Archeth and Egar stood together and watched them ride away. Fifty yards out, Ringil raised a hand straight into the air for them, but that was all. He didn't look back.

Another five minutes and watching the tiny figures recede started to seem faintly ridiculous. Egar nudged her with an elbow.

"C'mon, I'll buy you another beer. We can watch them disappear over the hill from the garden."

Archeth stirred, as if from a doze. "What? Okay, sure. Yeah."

And then, as they wandered back toward the inn, "So, did I hear right? You're going to come back to Yhelteth with me?"

The Majak shrugged elaborately.

"Been thinking about it, yeah. Like Gil said, I'm not exactly popular back home right now. And I could use some sun. And from what you said about the Citadel, *you* could use some armed protection about the house."

"Nah." She shook her head. "I'm a fucking hero now. No way they can touch me after this."

"Yeah, not publicly, maybe."

"Okay, okay. You're invited. Stay as long as you want."

"Thanks." Egar hesitated, cleared his throat. "You uh, you ever run into Imrana these days?"

Archeth grinned. "Yeah, sure. Seen her around the court, on and off. Why?"

"Dunno, just wondered. I suppose she's married by now."

"A couple of times at least," Archeth agreed. "But I don't think she lets it get in the way of anything that matters to her."

"Really?"

"Really."

EPILOGUE

Grace-of-Heaven Milacar jolted awake.

For a moment, he couldn't remember where he was; he'd been dreaming of the past, the house on Replete Cargo Street, and now the room he woke to felt wrong. He blinked at the full-length balcony windows and their muslin drapes, the polished décor and space around him, and for that first waking moment, it all felt alien, as if it didn't belong to him or, worse, he didn't belong to it.

He reached out blindly in the bed beside him. "Gil?"

But the bed was empty.

And he remembered then where he was, remembered how he'd come to be there, the years it had taken, and last of all he remembered he was old.

He sagged back onto the bed. Stared up at the painted ceiling, the debauchery whose details it was too dark to make out.

"Ahhh, fuck it."

A sliver of the dream dropped abruptly back into his head, a piece that didn't fit with the nostalgia and the old house memories of the rest. He'd been standing out on the marsh, quite a long way from the city walls, and it was getting dark. The sunset showed amid ragged black and indigo cloud at the horizon, like a smashed egg in mud. There was salt on the breeze, and a few odd noises in the undergrowth that he could really have done without. There was a chill on the nape of his neck.

A young girl stood before him amid the marsh grass with a flagon of tea clutched in her hands. The wind plucked at the simple oatmeal-colored shift she wore. At first he thought she was going to offer the flagon to him, but as he put out his hands she shook her head and turned away without a word. She started walking away, into the gloom of the marsh, and he was seized with a sudden, unaccountable fear of her leaving.

He called out after her.

Where are you going?

I have other fish to fry, she said obscurely. *I don't need to watch this to the end.*

And then she turned back to look at him, and she was suddenly a red-tongued, white-fanged she-wolf, reared upright on its hind legs and grinning.

He fell back with a yell of horror—it was this, he guessed now, that had woken him—but she only turned her back again and walked off into the marsh grass, still balancing delicately upright.

He sat up again in the big bed. The dream had left him sweaty beneath the silk sheets, and he could feel the hairs on his legs pasted to his skin. He swallowed and looked around the room. He felt the sense of ownership, the sense of belonging settling back over him. He felt his skin cooling. He rubbed a hand down his face and sighed.

"Something keeping you from sleep, Grace?" asked the shadowed figure by the window.

This time, it was a full kick to the heart. He was awake, he *knew* he was awake now, and this was no fucking dream.

And outside of a dream there was no way anyone should be able to get in here if he hadn't invited them.

There was a cool breeze wandering through the room. He registered it for the first time, felt it on his skin. Saw the way the muslin drapes stirred by the open window.

He'd closed it before he went to sleep. He remembered.

The figure stepped out of the shadows at the casement edge. Bandlight crept in from the balcony and did its best to touch the face.

"See—" he began, and then clamped his mouth shut.

The figure shook its head. "No. Not Seethlaw. You won't be seeing him again."

"Gil?"

A grave inclination of the shadow-dappled head. Faintly now in the bandlight, he made out the features to go with the voice.

"Gil. How did you get in here?"

"Easily." A gesture back to the balcony. "You've really got to start picking your boys for competence, not looks, Grace. I walked right past three of them in the gardens. Could have been invisible for all the notice they took. Didn't have to kill them or anything. And then, well, ornate stonework's never a good bet if you don't want burglars scaling the walls. Like I said—easy."

Milacar swallowed. "We all thought you were . . . gone."

"I was gone, Grace. Into the gray places. You made sure of that."

Ringil moved again, closer to the bed. Now the bandlight caught him full, painted its pallid glow across his face. Milacar winced as he saw the scarring along the jawline.

"What are you talking—"

"Don't." There was a terrifying matter-of-factness in the single word. "Just don't, Grace. There's no point. I remember you in the garden. *I was just supposed to stay colorful for you here in the slums.* That's what you said. *Here* in the slums. Because that's where we were, wasn't it? The garden at the old place, across the river on Replete Cargo Street."

"Gil, listen to me—"

"No, you listen to me." There was a cold, hypnotic quality to Ringil's speech that Milacar didn't remember from before. "That's where I woke up the morning after Seethlaw. Replete Cargo Street. I thought at the time it seemed familiar, but I didn't make the connection. Stupid of me really—you even *told* me you'd hung on to your old address, that first night I came here to see you. It took me awhile to sort all this out in my head, Grace, try to put it all together, decide what was real, what wasn't. But you see, I've had awhile. I've had a long leisurely journey back here to think it all through. And you and the garden and the old place, that was real. It felt different from all the other stuff. I remember that now. Only thing I can't figure out is whether it was Seethlaw's idea, or whether you suggested it to him. Care to tell me?"

He met Grace's eye. Milacar sighed and slumped back on his propped elbows. He looked away.

"I don't . . ." He shook his head wearily. "Make . . . decisions where Seethlaw is concerned. He comes to me. He takes what he wants."

"Kind of exciting for you, huh?"

"I'm sorry, Gil. I didn't want you hurt, that's all."

Ringil's voice hardened. "No, that's not all. You didn't want me in Etterkal, just like everybody else. Or if I went—because you knew damn well they wouldn't be able to stop me—you wanted Seethlaw to know and have it covered. You sold me to him, Grace, you told him where to find me. Had to be you, no one else knew I'd gone to Hale's place."

Grace-of-Heaven said nothing.

"Back before I had to kill him, Seethlaw accused me of interfering with his affairs, and what he said was quite specific. *You brought your blade and your threats*, he said, *and your pride that no beauty or sorcery could stem your killing prowess.* He heard me say that to you, that first night here, out on the balcony. He was here, in your house, wasn't he? And then later he followed me home, along with a couple of your more inept machete boys. I scared them off easily enough, but Seethlaw stuck around to laugh at me. Can't blame him for that—you were both on me from the start. Cozy as fucking spoons in a drawer, and both laughing. Are you in the cabal, Grace?"

Milacar chuckled and shook his head again. There was more energy in it this time.

"Something amusing you?"

"Yeah. You don't get it, Gil. The cabal touches us all, you don't have to be *in* it for that to happen. The cabal is Findrich and Snarl and a few others in Etterkal, a handful in the Chancellery, a couple more up at the Academy. But that's just what's at the center. Beyond that, anybody and everybody with an ounce of power in this city has their feet in cabal mud. Just a question of how far up your legs you let it creep, how much you want, and how much you want to know. Me, Murmin Kaad, even your own fucking father. One way or another, we're all beholden. The cabal reaches out for what it needs."

Ringil nodded. "Needs a traitor in the Marsh Brotherhood, does it? You want to hear what happened to Girsh?"

"I know what happened to Girsh." A long sigh. "I'm in the middle here, Gil. I try not to get too deep in on any one side, try not to get too committed or locked in. It's politics. You get used to that."

"Seethlaw wasn't politics, though, was he?"

"Seethlaw." Grace-of-Heaven swallowed. "Seethlaw was—"

"Beautiful. Yeah, I know, you told me that. Of course, you also told me it was secondhand knowledge, but that was just the quick lie to cover your arse. Couldn't really admit to me you were fucking the fabulous dwenda in Etterkal, that would have ruined everything. I just wonder why you bothered mentioning him in the first place."

Milacar bowed his head. "I thought it might scare you off."

"Yeah? Or you thought I might be competition you could do without?"

"I just didn't want you *hurt*, Gil."

"So you keep saying. Look at my face, Grace. I got hurt."

"Yeah, well I'm *sorry*." Sudden, flaring anger. "If you'd fucking stayed out of it like I told you to, maybe you wouldn't have that ugly scar now."

"Maybe not."

Silence, like a shared flandrijn pipe between them. The shape of what was coming began to emerge in the quiet.

"He took you to the gray places," Milacar said finally, bitterly.

"Oh yeah." And though, just from looking at Grace-of-Heaven's eyes, he already knew the answer, Ringil asked the question anyway. "You?"

Milacar stared off across the room, into the dark corner Ringil had come from. "No. He talked about it, but . . . I don't know. Never the right time, I guess."

"Don't feel bad. You don't know how fucking lucky you got." Ringil leaned forward and tapped the scar along his jaw. "You think this is ugly? You should see what I'm carrying inside."

"You think I can't?" Milacar looked at him again, and now he was smiling sadly. "You need to take a look in a mirror sometime, Gil. How did you kill him, then? The gorgeous Seethlaw?"

"With the Ravensfriend. I carved his beautiful fucking face in half."

"Well." A shrug. "You did say it wouldn't stop you. That's you, Gil, all over. Start you up, you won't be stopped till it's done. Have you come to kill me, too?"

It took a moment to bring it to his lips. "Yeah."

"I'm really sorry, Gil."

"So am I." Ringil nodded at the bellpull on the far side of the bed. "You want to try calling your machete boys now?"

"Would it help?"

"No. Not unless you want company dying."

Grace-of-Heaven Milacar made a lordly gesture. If he was scared of what was coming, he masked it well.

"Then it seems rather wasteful, don't you think? All those young bodies? I think I'll just—"

And he came off the bed, very fast for his age, no weapon at all but his own weight and a lifetime of street-fighting prowess. Ringil let him come, it seemed only fair. He left his hands at his sides, made it look like there might be a chance. Then, as Milacar reached him, he dropped the dragon knife from his sleeve and whipped it up, into the side of Grace's neck. His other hand snapped out, caught the other side of the neck and pushed in against the knife blow.

He held Grace like that, eye-to-eye, as if to kiss him. Blood from the chopped artery flooded out, down the dragon's tooth and over his right hand. He heard it puddle into the carpet around their feet.

"Ohhh," Grace moaned. "Hoiran's . . . twisted . . . cock. That . . . *hurts*, Gil."

Ringil held him up while he died, looked steadily into the eyes until they dimmed. Then he jerked the knife out, let go convulsively of Grace's neck, and watched him hit the ground like a sack of meal.

Flicker of blue fire.

He spun, heart pounding.

Saw himself in the big mirror hung across from the bed.

He sighed, waited for the relief to hit, for the spike of fear to ease and his pulse to climb back down. He waited. But the moment passed, left him there waiting, and no relief came. The figure in the mirror stood and grinned at him. He saw the bloodstained hands, the gaunt, scarred face, and the eyes, the eyes glittering back from the dark glass. The jutting pommel of the Ravensfriend, the faithful killing steel on his back. The jagged curve of the dragon's tooth in his right hand.

You need to take a look in a mirror sometime, Gil.

He was looking now. Seethlaw's words in the swamp came back to him, desperate in their intensity. *I see what the akyia saw, Gil. I see what you could become, if you'd only let yourself.*

He remembered the beach, the creatures in the surf and the sounds they made.

They're talking about you.

And like a final hammerblow, like a blade going home, he remembered the fortune-teller at the eastern gate. The words he'd discounted at Ibiksinri when he fought the dwenda and took Seethlaw down in bloody ruin.

A fight is coming, a battle of powers you have not yet seen. A battle that will unmake you, that will tear you apart.

The cool night breeze came to find him from the opened window. It carried a faint note of salt.

A dark lord will rise, his coming is in the wind off the marsh.

He stared at himself.

A dark lord will rise.

"It's like that, is it?" he whispered.

The muslin drapes stirred; the breeze blew through the quiet room. He wiped his hands and the dragon knife on Grace-of-Heaven's silk sheets, and put the weapon away again in his sleeve. He settled the

Ravensfriend a little more comfortably on his back, shifted the pommel a fraction of an inch for a cleaner pull.

Then he faced himself in the mirror once more, and found he was no longer afraid of what he saw looking back at him.

He waited, patiently, for the flicker of blue fire to show itself again, and for whatever else might come with it.

ACKNOWLEDGMENTS

In case the influences worn so prominently on the sleeve of this novel should remain unclear, thanks are due to the following, for initial, momentous inspiration, way back when:

   To Michael Moorcock for Hawkmoon, Elric, and Corum.

   To the memory of Karl Edward Wagner for Kane.

   To the memory of Poul Anderson for *The Broken Sword* and *The Dancer from Atlantis.*

There are a lot of little anchoring glints of realism embedded in the fantasy of *The Steel Remains,* and for making some of these possible, I'm indebted to Robert Low, author of *The Whale Road,* and to Jon Weir. I'm also grateful to Alan Beatts for sowing a seed with his comments about sanity, and to Gillian Redfearn for hemming and hawing about the dimensions of staff lances.

For the rest, endless appreciation once again to my editors Simon Spanton and Chris Schluep, for—quite literally—buying into the idea in the first place, and then for putting up with the butchered and mutilated bodies of deadlines when things took longer than expected to whip into the shape I wanted. And thanks also to my agent Carolyn Whitaker for her continuing weather eye and all-around support.

And finally, and most of all, thanks to Virginia, for living day in, day out with the brooding excesses and antisocial abandon of Morgan the Barbarian, for the time it took to complete the work.

ABOUT THE AUTHOR

RICHARD K. MORGAN is the acclaimed author of *Thirteen*, which won the Arthur C. Clarke Award, *Woken Furies*, *Market Forces*, *Broken Angels*, and *Altered Carbon*, a *New York Times* Notable Book that also won the Philip K. Dick Award. Morgan sold the movie rights for *Altered Carbon* to Joel Silver and Warner Bros. His third book, *Market Forces*, has also been sold to Warner Bros. and was the winner of the John W. Campbell Award. He lives in Scotland.

ABOUT THE TYPE

This book was set in Minion, a 1990 Adobe Originals typeface by Robert Slimback. Minion is inspired by classical, old-style typefaces of the late Renaissance, a period of elegant, beautiful, and highly readable type designs. Created primarily for text setting, Minion combines the aesthetic and functional qualities that make text type highly readable with the versatility of digital technology.